TOKYO TRAFFIC

Awards and Reviews for The Last Train

Winner Shelf Unbound Best Independently Published Book (2018)
Solo Medalist Winner New Apple E-Book Awards for Mystery (2017)
Winner Beverly Hills Book Awards for Crime Fiction (2017)
Winner Best Mystery Book Excellence Awards for Mystery (2017)
Winner Independent Press Award for Mystery and for Thriller (2018)
Global Award Reader Views (2017-2018)
Gold Award Literary Titan Book Award (2017)
Silver Honoree IBPA Benjamin Franklin Digital Awards (2017)
Silver Award Feathered Quill Awards (2018)
Silver Award Independent Publisher Book Awards (2018)

"A flawless, dark, atmospheric mystery set in Tokyo. Our judges couldn't put this novel down."
Shelf Unbound Competition

"For anyone who loves crime and cop novels, or Japanophiles in general, this is a terrific thriller."
Blue Ink Review

"This exotic crime thriller is a lightning-fast chase to the finish line that'll leave hearts pounding and pages turning."
Best Thrillers

"A well-paced and absorbing mystery, with quick action and a look at urban life, an utterly page-turning adventure."
Foreword Reviews

"An absorbing investigation and memorable backdrop put this series launch on the right track."
Kirkus Reviews

"Gripping and suspenseful, this fast-paced thriller unfolds on the streets of Tokyo, where a clever and cold-blooded killer exacts revenge."
Booklife Prize

"Mystery readers will relish the progress of a detective torn between cultures, the reader of Japanese literature the depth of background."
Midwest Book Review

"Tokyo comes to vivid life in this taut thriller, an unrelenting portrayal of a strong female character and the heart-pounding search to find her."
Publishers Daily Reviews

"Nothing short of electrifying, a masterpiece that combines action with humor and suspense."
Readers' Favorite

"A fast-paced thriller that skillfully exposes readers to the seedy urban side of Japan and leaves readers waiting for the next in the series."
Feathered Quill

"Written from knowledge rather than research, he knows a lot more than he has any need to tell us brings the city gloriously to life."
The Bookbag

"A heartfelt, thoughtful ode to a strange and beautiful city, in the way that so many classic detective novels are. Lyrically written with plenty of suspense."
Indie Reader

"I would definitely recommend it to crime and murder mystery fans, especially those with an interest in Japanese culture."
Online Book Club

Awards and Reviews for The The Moving Blade

Named One of Kirkus Reviews Best Indie Mysteries and Thrillers (2018)
Grand Prize Winner Chanticleer International Book Awards
Global Thrillers (2018)
Winner Independent Press Award for Crime Fiction (2019)
Gold Award Literary Titan Book Award (2018)
Five Star Honoree B.R.A.G. Medallion (2018)
Gold Award Independent Publisher Awards for Mystery (2019)
Silver Medal Readers' Favorite for Thriller (2019)

"An elegant balance of Japanese customs with an American-style hard-boiled procedural. A tight, rock-solid installment in a series that's only getting better."
Kirkus Reviews

"A true page turner with main characters that come alive with intelligence, curiosity and imperfections."
Blue Ink Review

"An homage to Tokyo and a savagely entertaining mystery that will grip readers and keep them guessing until the violent, octane-fueled finish."
SPR Review

"One of the year's best thrillers. A string of grisly murders, high stakes geopolitics and the prose of a master craftsman elevate this crime thriller to rarefied air."
Best Thrillers

"Full of East Asian and international politics and plenty of sociological commentary. Fun and thrilling throughout—an exciting modern mystery."
Foreword Clarion Reviews

"This book made it to my favorites list before I even finished reading it. Suspense and intrigue from the very first chapter...and great writing."
Literary Titan

"Ripe with surprising plot twists that take the reader into the deep underbelly of Tokyo. An intriguing story of murder, mystery, and maleficence."

US Review of Books

"Detailed and compellingly plotted...for anyone with a fascination or even a curiosity about Japan, this is a great crime novel."

Crime Fiction Lover

"A powerfully written crime novel; often stark and unsettling, the characters spring off the page."

The Wishing Shelf

"A stellar novel with a unique storyline and setting, *The Moving Blade* is fresh and original."

BookLife Prize

"The second in the Detective Hiroshi series is another cracker: real tension and a scenario which is (unfortunately) only too believable."

The Bookbag

"More than most procedural crime novels...enriched by carefully drawn portraits of both political and cultural differences between Western and Eastern culture."

Chanticleer Book Reviews

"The action-packed plot is not just a dramatic whodunit piece, but a slice of life piece inspecting Japanese heart and minds."

Midwest Book Review

"Pronko brought this story to life so much that I found myself hoping that none of the negative aspects could possibly be true."

Reader Views

Tokyo Traffic
By Michael Pronko
First paperback edition, 2020
ISBN 978-1-942410-19-5

Typesetting by FormattingExperts.com
Cover Design © 2020 Marco Mancini, www.magnetjazz.net

* * *

For more about the Detective Hiroshi series and Pronko's other writing:
www.michaelpronko.com
Follow Michael on Twitter: @pronkomichael
Michael's Facebook page: www.facebook.com/pronkoauthor

And if you're interested in future releases and news and insights from Tokyo, sign up for my newsletter here:
www.michaelpronko.com/newsletter

ALSO AVAILABLE BY MICHAEL PRONKO:

Memoirs on Tokyo Life:
Beauty and Chaos: Slices and Morsels of Tokyo Life (2014)
Tokyo's Mystery Deepens: Essays on Tokyo (2014)
Motions and Moments: More Essays on Tokyo (2015)

The Detective Hiroshi Series:
The Last Train (2017)
The Moving Blade (2018)
Tokyo Traffic (2020)

TOKYO TRAFFIC

by Michael Pronko

Raked Gravel Press 2020

In the little world in which children have their existence, whosoever brings them up, there is nothing so finely perceived and so finely felt, as injustice.

—Charles Dickens

Real things in the darkness seem no realer than dreams. Ceaseless as the interminable voices of the bell-cricket, all night till dawn my tears flow.

—Murasaki Shikibu

Chapter 1

Crouching behind the plywood wall of the film set, Sukanya waited until silence echoed through the cavernous warehouse. Her skin was clammy and covered in goosebumps. Sweat sprang from every pore in her body. She hugged herself, shivering, listening, her heart pumping hard from the last injection of whatever it was.

When the silence and the cold became too much, she peered around the edge of the film set, shading her eyes from the white blaze of an upended light, and stepped out to survey the scene. Cold air floated down from the high, dark ceiling. Shadows loomed over the muted chaos below.

Chairs, tables, and cameras were strewn across the concrete floor. The legs of tripods, toppled in the struggle, poked up like spikes. The wall of the set was bashed and splintered.

Umbrella lights and soft boxes, open-faced halogens and LEDs threw light in crossed directions. One of the knocked-over key lights sizzled and popped, darkening a swath of the set. Another light winked off without a sound, deepening the dim expanse of the warehouse.

From the top of the sets to the high ceiling, the air barely moved. There was no longer anything to hide from.

Sukanya walked forward, careful of the broken glass strewn in front of the mock living room. The lingering smell was the usual—airless, sweaty, and coarse—though mixed with something different. From small, dark pools across the smooth concrete floor rose a metallic scent she remembered from the back of street stalls in Bangkok's markets.

She tried to catch herself, but doubled over and vomited. She hadn't eaten much the past three days in the warehouse, but she gagged and heaved, again and again, until she was all out. She spit and spit, tongued her teeth, spit again and started to breathe.

She forced herself to look at the bodies. Her insides jumped, but her legs stayed rooted in place. She stood there wishing she could take off and soar away, wishing she could scream.

She slipped her bare feet into a pair of plastic sandals at the edge of the set floor. They were a men's size, but she clenched her toes and shuffled them against the concrete, testing the traction. She could run in them.

From a gym bag on a bench beside the set wall, she dug out a towel. It smelled clean, so she wiped herself dry. She dug inside the bag and found a pair of running shorts, sizes too big, but she pulled them on and yanked the string tight around her thin waist. Her shoulders filled out a large blue soccer jersey that hung down to her thighs. She packed her long hair into a tight ponytail with a wristband.

Where was the other girl, Celeste? She was younger and called herself "Celeste," insisting that was what she would go by. She'd been more cranked by the shots. She sweated, twitched, and didn't eat after the assistant first injected them.

And where did that assistant go when things went berserk?

The third girl, Ratana, left hours before it started, with one of the men who'd driven them from the boat dock. Ratana had kept the three of them going on the boats, in the hotel, on the sets. She knew how to win concessions and dispute details, to resist and acquiesce, for better food and clothes, more sleep and showers.

Ratana might be back at any moment with one of the men, or Ratana might not be back at all.

To stop shivering, Sukanya pulled a leather jacket from the director's chair and slid inside it. Rolling up the sleeves, she surveyed the back braces and cheap plywood walls. The front door where they had come in a few days before had to be somewhere outside the maze of sets.

Peering down the path between the sets, she saw Celeste. Kneeling beside her, Sukanya checked for breathing and a pulse, but nothing moved under Celeste's smooth skin. Beside her, one of the tripods, folded tight, dripped gore.

Sukanya brushed the hair off Celeste's face. She went back for the towel and knelt down to wipe the blood off her face, neck, breasts, and arms. Sukanya had envied her dark eyelids, curved nose, and thick lips when they'd shared a bed on the boat and in the hotel, chatting and giggling until Ratana shushed them. After that, they were driven to the warehouse where they worked constantly, too tired to talk, too drugged to sleep.

Sukanya took a blanket from a mock bedroom. The cartoon-themed blanket had bright animals laughing big-mouthed and silly. She spread it over Celeste and pulled it over her thin, pretty face. She closed her eyes, placed her hands together and recited a prayer she'd learned from her brother long ago.

She blinked her eyes, dry from the drugs, and turned to an older man's body, careful not to step in the blood. She'd wondered at him taking photos the whole time, his fleshy face red from drinking. She leaned down to rifle his fancy, roomy suit. He had a lot of bills, but she didn't know what Japanese money was worth. She tucked them into the inner pocket of the leather jacket.

The director was bent in half, his glasses smashed to shards from the blows. She looked away as she rummaged through his pockets for his wallet and scooped out his cash. Beside him on the floor was the laptop where all the footage was saved. It was still recording from a toppled camera.

As she looked at the blank sideways screen, the big metal door on the first floor of the warehouse creaked. Footsteps on the metal stairs sent a hot whip of panic through her. She bent down, clicked off the laptop and shoved it into a shoulder bag. Under the fat man's round belly, an iPad poked out. She snatched it and popped it in beside the laptop and slung the bag over her shoulder.

She sprinted toward the front wall and crouched behind a cart stacked with chairs from where she could see the door. The same man who had stopped by the day before poked his head through the door and walked across the open expanse of warehouse. His white suit glowed in the gray emptiness. He walked slowly toward the off-kilter lights and pulled up short not far from the bodies.

He leaned forward, leaned back, rolled his head around, and fumbled for his cellphone. He put it to his ear and wrapped his hands, and his body, around it, as if trying to disappear inside.

When he appeared lost in the call, Sukanya padded softly to the door and slipped out to the stairs. She tiptoed down to the front door and nudged it open a crack. The murky light outside revealed a gravel parking area. Near the street was a car, but it was hard to see inside.

She ducked back and waited before easing the door open again for a better look. To the right, a gap between the warehouse and the next building looked just wide enough to slip through.

The door on the second floor above the stairs crashed open.

Sukanya put her head down and let the drugs propel her. She slipped out and started running. The gravel slid and shifted under her plastic sandals. At the end of the building, she squeezed through the gap and sped up. Her shin hit something and she flew forward, clawing the air until she landed on her knees.

It was a metal bucket, full of gravel. She twisted to see if anyone was following. Her wrists and knees were scraped, but she stood up, reset her feet in the sandals, and limped to the end of the buildings.

The long, narrow gap opened onto a wide sidewalk and a four-lane road. She rubbed her knees and elbows, and turned right. She wanted to keep running but managed to slow herself to a steady walk, turning at times to see if anyone was coming.

They weren't yet, but they would be soon. With her wrong-sized clothes and Thai features, her awkward foreignness, and not knowing where to go, they would find her even in the vast unknown of Tokyo.

Chapter 2

Kenta roared past the Lexus parked at the exit and slipped his dark orange Nissan GT-R into the extra-wide spot he'd set up for himself near the door. He was tired of cleaning up after everyone, especially in the middle of the night. Particularly when he had a rare night to spend with Mina. He let her sleep when he eased out of her apartment to drive halfway across the city.

Shibaura was right where he said he'd be, at the door to his warehouse studio. In the dim pre-dawn light, Shibaura looked like a specter, his shoulder-length gray hair and white suit framed against the dark gray of the huge roll-back door of Jack and Jill Studios.

Shibaura wouldn't be standing there at all if Kenta hadn't stepped in and saved his ass. For years, Shibaura had been running the studio into the ground. Kenta resuscitated the studio by renegotiating loans and bringing in new business, wondering all the while if Shibaura had actually been trying to go bankrupt.

He let his car rumble for a minute, just to badger Haruka, sitting behind the wheel of the Lexus. Shibaura's secretary, chauffeur, and partner, Haruka detested most men, but put up with them. Kenta never let himself react to the snooty way she tried—and failed—to keep him out of the business. But when either one of them needed something, they called Kenta.

On cue, Haruka slammed the door shut and started toward them. Kenta watched her in the rearview mirror as he set his alarm, immobilizer, and tracking device. She was busty and big-hipped, teetering on heels so high she could hardly walk over the gravel.

Kenta looked from Shibaura to Haruka and braced himself for another of their tiffs. Witnessing an older couple arguing was distasteful. Mina never argued with him. Why would she? He got out and beeped the locks.

One of Haruka's heels slipped into the gravel, tripping her, and she thrust out her hands for balance, her long white fingernails flashing in the dark. She righted herself and squared off with Shibaura.

Shibaura pulled his white suit over his shoulders and squinted at her. He looked shaken.

"Who was that girl?" Haruka asked him.

Kenta held up a preemptive hand. "Who was who?" he demanded, glaring at Shibaura. She was dressed for dinner in one of those sky-high restaurants with a view of Tokyo, not for a gravel lot between warehouses. Her perfume wafted on the night air.

Shibaura threw up his hands. "*What* girl?"

Haruka bounced on her hip. "The girl who ran out the door."

"What girl?" Shibaura glared at Haruka.

Kenta peered into the darkness of the gap.

"I've told you about young girls." Haruka advanced on him. "It's always trouble."

Kenta stepped between them, holding up his hands. "Look, what did you call *me* about?"

Haruka ignored Kenta and leaned toward Shibaura. "Right after you went in, a young girl ran out the front door and down there." She pointed at the gap between the buildings.

Shibaura lowered his voice. "Haruka, get back in the car, can you?"

Haruka stared at him, her shiny pantsuit shimmering even in the dark.

Kenta said, "Can we go inside so I can see whatever it is you have to show me?" Kenta rolled back the front door of the studio and started up the metal grate stairs to the second-floor maze of film sets.

Shibaura followed him in to the dark entryway and stopped at the bottom of the steps. "I don't want to see it again."

Kenta stared at Shibaura from a couple of steps up.

Shibaura pulled his jacket around him. "I need to get out of here."

Kenta nodded at the rack of surveillance cameras next to the door.

"Those have been busted for weeks," Shibaura said.

"And you didn't get them fixed?"

"It was on the list."

"And upstairs on the sets?"

"Those cameras run like you set them up, I guess."

Kenta started back upstairs. All filming was supposed to run through his laptop and automatically back up online.

"I'll meet you in the office," Shibaura shouted up to him, and he started down the first-floor passageway to the back.

Kenta pulled open the upstairs door into the massive warehouse of sets. Maybe getting involved with this whole Jack and Jill Studios was not the best idea. He hadn't bargained for Shibaura's anxiety medications and Haruka's complaints. And being woken in the middle of the night.

As he turned the corner to the open area in front of the set, he saw the director first. The top side of his head was red mush. What was his name? Noguchi maybe?

To the left was Takeo Suzuki, his body now as horizontal as those he liked to photograph. Kenta arranged entry to the shoots for Suzuki because a well-connected former government minister could always be of help. Now, he was going to be exactly the opposite.

Broken glass crunched underfoot as he walked toward the third body, under a bright-colored blanket between the sets. He used his handkerchief to pull back the blanket. He remembered her face, her body, her little groans. He let the blanket fall back.

He tried to remember how many people had been there when he stopped by the day before. The director, the assistant director, that plump assistant, the three girls, two or three actors, and Suzuki—he was going to have to track down all of them.

And where was his computer? Where was the iPad he lent to Suzuki? And the bag he let Suzuki use? Was the camera still running when things went south? He moved the small piles of broken equipment aside with his foot, but none of his stuff was there.

He pulled out his cellphone, but no new files had been uploaded in the past twenty-four hours. They must be on the missing computer, along with the other video files, his business contacts, accounts, and access to his online storage. He called Kirino, and then quickly hung up. Calling from there would be a bad idea.

Kenta walked between the sets to the stairs down to the back office, running an inventory of immediate tasks to keep his mind off the bodies.

Inside the office, Shibaura was setting out stacks of ten thousand yen bills on his U-shaped, leather-covered desk. Beside the Japanese bills were stacks of Thai baht, Philippine pesos, Vietnamese dong, and Chinese yuan. Kenta pushed him to use digital currency, had even set up accounts for the studio, but here was Shibaura packing stacks of cash into a plastic bag from some boutique Haruka shopped at.

"Here," Shibaura said, tossing six passports to Kenta, three Thai and three American. "Get these out of here."

"I don't want these, either," Kenta said. But maybe Kirino could use them when he arrived to clean this up. He'd wait to call him until he got onto an expressway and was calmed by the speed. He walked to the computer that channeled the studio's surveillance camera footage, but they were blank.

Kenta pointed at the fuzzy four-way screen. "You were supposed to upgrade this. I gave you money, called the company."

Shibaura kept packing his bag.

Kenta looked around the room. The curved sofa, top-shelf liquors, brand glassware, tube amp, and CDs were out of a period movie set.

"You'd better call this in," Kenta said.

"Are you crazy?"

"Have Haruka do it from a payphone."

"I'll need a head start."

"To where? California? Your place in Hawaii?"

Shibaura picked up the shopping bag.

"You're better off staying here and telling the police you rented the place. That's pretty much the truth. Kirino will take care of the rest."

"Once he gets here," Shibaura said. "It's a long way from Thailand."

"He'll be here tomorrow," Kenta said, unsure he would be.

"I'll have Haruka cancel everything for today. We'll lock the place up to get a head start." Shibaura looked around the office, clicked off the lights, and headed down the stairs to the passageway. Kenta followed him in the dark. At the front door, Shibaura started to lock up, but Kenta took his keys from him and left the doors open.

Shibaura headed to his Lexus without another word. He got in and Haruka drove off.

After they were gone, Kenta released his car alarm, immobilizer, and tracking device. He took a pocket knife and a roll of Gorilla tape out of the efficiency desk he placed in the passenger seat when Mina wasn't with him, and used it to pop out the cameras from the dashboard and back seat.

He walked to the middle of the lot and stood gauging angles. He walked to the wall of the warehouse building to the right and reached as high as he could, turning to eye the distance. He pulled off a couple of strips of the super-adhesive tape and positioned them on the wall.

He took one of the cameras and fixed it toward the entrance. He walked across the lot and did the same on the other side.

He walked back to his Nissan and turned on his laptop to make sure the cameras fed in. They did.

He clicked through his multiple tracking apps for computer, iPad, and bag, and waited patiently while the signal bounced around.

A green light popped up pulsing on the screen's map. The signal was for his bag. It was faint and moving slowly through the city. That was a start.

Chapter 3

Staring through the diamond frame of his upraised arms, Detective Hiroshi Shimizu felt for one still moment that a circuit connected, and his inner spirit took over. With a loud shout, he sprang forward and drove his sword onto the shoulder of his attacker, barely feeling the other sword strike his ribs.

Pivoting and facing off again, they reset for another still moment, shouted and drove at each other as if turning into pure human energy for an instant before reconvening into a solid state once more.

Across the kendo *dojo*, dozens of similar pairs squared off, reset, and attacked. Their blows thudded onto the tight-stitched padding and clinked off the lacquered chest protectors. If not for the armor, pads, and mask, the force of the blows would have broken bones.

Their eyes, hidden inside the silver gridded helmets, searched for the one small opening that would let them land a cruelly elegant blow. The shout-whacks, squeak of feet, and short screams formed a collective rhythm, like the buzzing attack of large, angry insects with hard shells and deadly stingers.

Learning to shout again had taken Hiroshi a long time. The years of not doing kendo had drained the spirit to yell. It took time to set his bare feet lightly, but evenly, on the wood floor. It took him even longer to put aside the overhead lights, airless room, and weight of the *bogu* armor, and relearn how to strike.

The first few hits of every practice session hurt his forearms but by the end of practice, he understood again that protection came from within, from how his reflexes moved him. The pain, which could linger for days from certain blows, started to feel like something to just set aside.

As practice drew to a close, it reached a crescendo as everyone set and struck faster and faster. At last, sensei called time and the pairs let themselves go slack. They stretched and walked off the exhaustion. As the partners pulled off their helmets and bowed to each other, and to the *dojo*, someone's cellphone started ringing in one of the bags at the side of the practice room. Everyone laughed at the timing except Hiroshi. He knew it was his.

Hiroshi's opponent pulled the helmet from her head and let her long hair cascade down over the dark-blue of her uniform. Hiroshi looked at Ayana's face, flushed and sweaty, as beautiful as when waking up, when smiling after a couple drinks.

Ayana bowed to Hiroshi with a smirk and was quickly swept up by her friends into a chatting, complaining, face-wiping, water-drinking circle.

Hiroshi ambled to his phone. He picked it up sheepishly, bowing an apology to no one in particular and everyone in general. He stepped into the hall to take the call, trying to hide from Ayana's irritation. His work intruding was not something she'd gotten used to.

"I'm supposed to be off tonight," Hiroshi insisted to his boss, Detective Sakaguchi, but he listened as he was told the details. Corpses couldn't wait.

Hiroshi watched Ayana gather her gear into the carrying bags as she chatted with friends. The women had drawn close, sharing a passion for the demanding practice and directed aggression of the kendo world.

Hiroshi walked back to their group, bowed to Ayana's friends, and started taking off his uniform piece by piece, wiping things down and placing them in his bag. Carrying the heavy protective gear was part of the training, Ayana told him when he brought home a pair of rolling carry bags as a moving-in-together present. But she accepted it, reluctantly, and after practice they wiped the bags together and set everything out to dry on the balcony of the apartment they shared.

After bowing deeply to the sensei and the *dojo*, and casually to her friends, Hiroshi and Ayana walked down the long slope that led away from the Kanda River toward Kagurazaka, Tokyo's old geisha quarters.

After moving into Ayana's apartment, Hiroshi let himself be mesmerized by the old sloping lanes, stonework paths lit by soft yellow lanterns, and reservations-only restaurants in the area. He'd become familiar with the chic bistros, smart cafes, and yeasty bakeries that subdivided the area into Little Paris in Tokyo.

As they got closer to home, Hiroshi said, "Let's eat out."

"Let's eat in. I'm sweaty," Ayana parried.

"OK. I'll stop by the deli. You go on home and shower."

"Why are you being so nice?" Ayana asked. "Ah, must be the phone call."

"I'm being nice because you had to work so hard practicing with me." Hiroshi would confess he'd be at a crime scene all night after he shopped. He'd negotiated a couple of hours' delay from Sakaguchi.

Ayana scoffed. "I needed an easy workout so I wouldn't be exhausted for the tournament."

Hiroshi knew she was right. She was better at kendo than he was, and worked harder.

Ayana handed him one of the lightweight shopping bags she kept tucked everywhere. He turned toward the shops along Waseda-dori, but turned back to watch Ayana just as he'd always done after he walked her to the station when they were at college.

They had been in the same seminar and were on the kendo team together. And once on the beach at Kamakura after a kendo tournament, they'd been lovers. After watching the sun set, they huddled under their kendo gear on the fine sand and spent the night in each other's arms. In the morning, they stumbled to a public bath and ate breakfast together.

But Hiroshi's uncle had pressed him to study accounting in America, and too confused and heartbroken to explain, he left without even saying goodbye to her. They did not see or hear from each other until they met again during a case the year before. They had both made their mistakes by then and their feelings picked up where they'd been on the beach that night.

Hiroshi hesitated moving in to her place because the apartment was part of Ayana's divorce settlement, and his last attempt at living together ended with his girlfriend, Linda, moving back to Boston. After making up for lost time, moving in together seemed the obvious thing to do. They hardly even discussed it. His lease was up. She cleared out her closets to give him room.

At the deli counter, Hiroshi ordered a kilo of Ayana's favorite ravioli, a little carb-loading before her tournament. He picked out a deli-made white sauce and a bucket of salad with beans, olives, and pickled peppers tossed with greens he couldn't remember the names of. Next door, he picked up two bottles of French wine, but he knew he shouldn't drink. When he didn't, Ayana would know he was going back to work.

Ayana was out of the shower when Hiroshi got back and began setting the table by the balcony. Trying to decide when to tell her, he set everything on the table and kissed her. She shrank away in mock horror after sniffing at him and shoved him toward the shower. He came out to find the ravioli boiled, the sauce warmed, wine opened, and salad in her favorite bowl.

He started to explain, but she cut him off with a wave of her hand and a slug of wine. "I can guess." She looked out the sliding glass doors of the balcony.

"I put them off for a while. So we could eat."

"That's progress," she said, swirling her wine. She set down her glass and went to the kitchen area. She brought back bottled water for Hiroshi and poured it into the wine glass she'd set out for him.

"Recently, you're getting more phone calls than ever. *Keitai interruptus.*"

"I've been getting home earlier, haven't I?"

"But you never turn the *keitai* off."

"You said I should take the promotion."

"If I'd known you were going to abandon me tonight, I would have hit you even harder."

"You hit hard enough." Hiroshi touched his ribs where she'd done damage.

"Wait until next time," Ayana said, laughing in the way she often did before sinking into silent brooding.

"Can we do dinner tomorrow instead?" Hiroshi said cheerily.

Ayana swirled her wine. "Sure, unless there's a midnight call from Interpol, an accounting scam in Panama, a cryptocurrency fraud, or..." Ayana paused and looked at him.

Hiroshi looked at her until she pointed at the food. He had to get to the crime scene, but he knew better than to go before she let the wine turn to steam. He poured himself a glass of wine anyway and they ate in silence.

13

His promotion arrived soon after he moved in. It was more for the benefit of the homicide department than for him. Nothing had changed: workload, salary, office. He was an accountant before, "senior" accountant now, and still the *only* accountant. Hiroshi's forensic accounting skill was helpful with most homicides, since money could be found at the root of most cases.

His English ability helped with international crimes, of which there were more than ever. After his years in America, he was the only one in the department to cover the English side of things—contacting Interpol, translating documents, liaising with foreign police networks. Some days, all he did was translate.

He wasn't a detective like Sakaguchi, head of homicide, or Takamatsu, his mentor, who had both worked their way up through the police force. So, most of the time he followed their lead.

Ayana looked at him, her wine glass pressed against her cheek, and sighed. "I'm sorry. The tournament is coming up, so I'm thinking of that. Tomorrow will be the last chance to go out before then."

Hiroshi got up and kissed her on the forehead and then fell on her, smooching all the ear, neck, cheek, and chest he could land his lips onto until she pushed him away.

"All right, all right. Apology accepted. I'm going to spill my wine."

"So, spill it," Hiroshi said, leaning down to tickle her until she did.

Chapter 4

LED balloon lights whitened everything from the ceiling to the backs of the three-walled sets. Specialists in lab coats moved gingerly—the floor was a hopscotch maze of blood pools, chalk marks, and taped-off zones. Small numbered markers rose up beside cameras, chairs, props, and lights scattered across the floor.

Hiroshi let his mind follow the numbers on the markers, fifty-six pieces of evidence in view. It kept his mind off the body outlines chalked on the concrete floor. Hiroshi was glad he missed the bodies. Unlike the other detectives, the only thing he got from examining a corpse was nausea.

Sakaguchi's huge sumo wrestler bulk was lit from behind at the corner of one of the sets. Sakaguchi turned and nodded as he signed a form from one of the young detectives.

Hiroshi sniffed the air. "Did someone vomit? One of the young detectives?"

"No, that was here when we got here," Sakaguchi said.

"What is this, a film studio?" Hiroshi asked.

"Porn film studio," Sakaguchi answered.

Hiroshi surveyed the scene. Taking photos and gathering evidence would take twice the usual time in the sprawling warehouse space. Each of the dozen film sets potentially held a clue.

"I'd have thought Takamatsu would take lead on anything salacious like this."

"He's sorting out the shooting of some gang member. Confiscated a lot of guns. Paperwork on that takes forever. He'll be here soon." Sakaguchi signed another form from a technician in white mask and white gloves stained by blood.

Hiroshi looked away and crooked his head up at the ceiling. "So, who were the dead bodies?"

Sakaguchi walked Hiroshi over to one set of chalk marks. The head was only partially drawn, as a pool of blood made it impossible to chalk the concrete. "He was a director. Mid-twenties. From a rich family, good school. Ryota Noguchi, not a famous name. He'd done several features, then turned to soft porn, then harder stuff. Trying to find who to contact."

They stepped over to a larger, half-chalked outline. "Whoever did this didn't think of stripping away the ID. Bureaucrat in the Ministry of Finance. Chief's already called about him."

Sakaguchi walked around the side of the set and paused at a thinner outline with less blood. "This was a young girl, not Japanese. Southeast Asian maybe. I guess she was the... um..."

"Central character?"

"Central victim."

"How young?"

"Teenager, judging by the size of her wrist." Sakaguchi growled deep in his chest.

Hiroshi looked away at the numbers on the evidence markers, adding the numbers, and subtracting them, to keep his eyes from the chalk outlines, which looked like ghosts waiting to haunt him.

"Can you go take a look at the files? Half are in English. Office is around back." Sakaguchi pointed the way.

Hiroshi walked carefully past the three-sided walls of the sets—a convenience store, a high school locker room, an elevator, a massage room, a hospital, a train car—each perfect in itself. The single-room sets pointed in random directions, as if tossed away from a troubled dollhouse. Were those the most common scenes, the most commercial fantasies? Behind the rooms, the set walls were made of cheap plywood with angled braces held down by bags of dribbling sand.

Shibaura's office was crowded. Detective Ueno's tall, fit body and Osaki's ex-rugby forward's weight seemed to fill the room. They stood looking at what two young detectives handed them from the U-shaped, leather-covered desk, deciding what to bag and how. Sugamo, who was almost the size of Sakaguchi, was turning over everything on the shelves with prim white gloves.

16

"You're here," Ueno said. The two young detectives bowed and got out of the way.

Hiroshi had written to the National Police Agency training center to demand they include English in their coursework and training. And even though money trails extended like spokes from every murder, few of the detectives could grasp financial statements, bank records, or spreadsheets. They couldn't speak the world's two most common languages—English and numbers.

Hiroshi sat down at the desk to translate both. After looking through them for a few minutes, Hiroshi turned to one of the young detectives waiting to the side. "There will be a second set of books someplace. Operations like this always have different internal and external records."

"Where would those be?" the young detective asked.

"There's no safe?" Hiroshi nodded at the wall with glass shelves of liquor and a rack of video equipment.

The young detective nodded, perplexed, but started checking the walls, floor, and ceiling.

Hiroshi pulled open a folder of receipts, everything labeled and ordered impeccably. It was strange that the accounting for a porn studio would be organized with such care, but in terms of numbers, it was a business like any other. In terms of product, it was like no other.

"Someone can start gathering computers, laptops, tablets, cellphones, whatever electronic devices you can find," Hiroshi said. "Photograph them, fingerprint them, bag them. I'll start on those once they break them open at headquarters."

Ueno said, "Any ideas?" Osaki stood beside him.

Hiroshi stood up and shook his head. "Porn's a business that's very, um, connected."

"Too connected," Sugamo said from the back wall.

Hiroshi looked around the office. "Maybe we can find that one special file that explains all the others. There's always one that's the key."

Hiroshi left them to it and went back out to talk with Sakaguchi. Hiroshi found him staring at the chalk mark where the girl died. Her outline glowed under the LED lights.

"Find any files?" Sakaguchi asked.

"The only meaningful thing the chief ever said to me was that money and murder go together."

"That's why I called you."

"You sound like Takamatsu."

"And there he is."

Takamatsu was looking at one of the sets, a high school classroom, talking with one of the crime scene specialists. He walked over, straightening his yellow tie over a yellow shirt and popping the cuffs with a snap. "My first kiss was in the back of a classroom," Takamatsu said.

"I don't think there's much kissing in these films," Hiroshi said.

"*Au contraire*," Takamatsu said, in badly accented French.

Hiroshi wondered where he picked that phrase up. Some French-speaking hostess in Roppongi, no doubt.

"Kissing is its own fetish, always at the beginning, sometimes in the middle, and always at the end, depending," Takamatsu said.

"It's good we have a specialist here," Hiroshi said.

Takamatsu laughed, lit a cigarette, and twirled his cigarette lighter before slipping it back inside his tight-fitting jacket.

Sakaguchi interrupted. "As a connoisseur, do you have any thoughts on what went on here?"

"The guys outside told me blunt trauma for the two men. Hand wounds and head wounds. They didn't find anything on the girl." Takamatsu smiled. "So, maybe amphetamines. They load them up, I've heard."

"An S&M scene that got out of hand?" Hiroshi wondered out loud.

"There was blood on everything, and pieces of scalp on the tripod," Sakaguchi said.

"Robbery," Takamatsu said. "They probably run the business on cash."

"You're thinking nineteen-sixties. They'll have a lot of electronic files," Hiroshi said.

"See. That's why we hired you. To keep us up to date." Takamatsu smiled, blowing smoke up toward the high ceiling.

"Was there any video?" Hiroshi asked. "Maybe the film was rolling when—"

"If there was, someone took it," Sakaguchi said.

Takamatsu said, "They record straight to computer these days, don't they?"

"There were computers in the office," Hiroshi said.

Takamatsu put out his cigarette in his pocket ashtray. "Guess who's here?"

Hiroshi groaned, knowing it would be the chief. It was. His Borsalino fedora and gray worsted wool suit caught the white lights. Making an appearance seemed his main job.

The chief strode over with his coat draped over his shoulders, careful to not step on anything. He sniffed the air and frowned. "Some newbie lost it?"

Sakaguchi shook his head no. "It was here when we got here. It's evidence now."

"Who called this in?" the chief asked.

Sakaguchi shrugged. "We're tracking the call. Anonymous, but enough details to send the local cops. Front door was open."

"Why didn't anyone find this earlier? This has been sitting here all day?"

Sakaguchi sighed.

"A person's conscience works on its own schedule," Takamatsu said.

The chief ignored him and pointed at Hiroshi's chest. "Hiroshi, you're on the financials here, right?"

Hiroshi nodded.

"Good, good. And Sakaguchi, you're on the bureaucrat. I've already got calls to keep things quiet. The Ministry of Finance doesn't like scandals, even though some of our detectives do." The chief looked at Takamatsu.

Takamatsu lit another cigarette, against crime scene rules.

"He was important in the ministries," the chief said, smug about his inside knowledge of bureaucrats. "If this guy was caught up in this, then the ministries will be. And our work will be a lot harder."

"However high he was in the hierarchy, his hobby of taking photos at porn shoots wasn't so elevated," Takamatsu said.

"And no pushing buttons to get a result." The chief stared at Takamatsu, who stared at the cigarette smoke dissipating into the expanse above. "And Takamatsu—"

19

Hiroshi cut him off. "I'll keep an eye on him, even though *he's* taught *me* everything."

"You'll have to unlearn most of that. No mistakes with this one." The chief resettled his overcoat on his shoulders. "Well, things are well underway here," the chief said, giving the scene a satisfied once-over before picking a path through the evidence to the door.

Hiroshi said, "Is this studio well known?"

Takamatsu smiled. "Jack and Jill Studios. Very famous."

"You watch that kind of stuff?"

Takamatsu shrugged. "No, I read most nights. Can't get to sleep otherwise."

Hiroshi couldn't tell if he was joking or not.

The two young detectives who had been searching the office navigated toward the three main detectives. The first held out a laptop in a plastic evidence bag. "We found the safe. The safecracker's working on it."

Hiroshi sighed. "I'll wait around to see what's inside."

"We also found these," said a young female detective who had just joined homicide. She held out an accordion folder filled with passports.

Hiroshi looked through them. Philippines, Taiwan, Vietnam, Thailand, Indonesia. "All women?"

The detective nodded.

"The embassies open in a few hours," Sakaguchi said, nodding at Hiroshi.

"And one more thing." She held up several plastic bags filled with women's clothes.

"What's this?" Hiroshi asked.

"Women's clothes. Expensive. All different sizes." She hesitated, then went ahead. "They couldn't be for the same girl."

Hiroshi asked, "So, two girls?"

"Three, I'd say," the young detective said.

Takamatsu said, "No killer would be going for a bureaucrat, a film director, and foreign girls at the same time. So, who was the target and who was the collateral damage?"

Chapter 5

Sukanya had walked through Tokyo for a long time in a daze, replaying the scenes in her mind. The drugs kept propelling her forward and made it hard to focus. It had gotten light, then dark. She sat on a bench outside a coffee shop for a long time, and in a park for a while, and then it got light again. She had no idea where she was. Tokyo never ended.

Her legs and insides hurt, but the drugs kept pushing her forward, making her sweat. Tokyo's clean, empty streets had no early morning noodle stalls, but the city had a lot of vending machines. She stopped in front of a tall, thin red one, and decided on what looked like tea. She slid in a bill and the bottle clunked down, along with the change, coin by coin. The tea was warm, almost hot, and very sweet, just what she needed after so much walking. She gulped it down, and felt a wave of fatigue.

She realized she would never find Ratana again. Even if Ratana had made it back to the warehouse studio with their new passports, after zigzagging through the city for so long, Sukanya knew she'd never find the place again. She was on her own. She had to keep going.

As she walked, the buildings became bigger and the streets lined by shops, the goods so many they spilled out on racks and bins in front. Shopkeepers splashed water outside, scrubbing already clean sidewalks and wiping down windows. Everything gleamed, and she wondered if she'd wandered into Disneyland.

A few signs said, "hotel," but she didn't feel like sleeping yet and they might ask for ID. She couldn't walk forever, though Tokyo people seemed like they could. No one had noticed her yet, but eventually someone would, and that would be trouble. She knew what happened to girls who didn't do what they were told. She learned that her first day in Bangkok. She saw what happened over the years. And what happened to Celeste.

She walked across a huge intersection and followed some young girls about her age. They had school uniforms on and Sukanya followed them into a round multistory building with a giant sign that read, "109." The shop clerks bowed as she entered. The store's circular floors looked like they would sell everything she needed, but first she needed to pee. The sweet tea went right through her.

Inside the toilet, two girls in tights were chatting and changing their skirts. Sukanya went inside one of the stalls and sat down, but then stood back up. She took a big breath and eased herself lower. It hurt to sit, and hurt to pee, and there was blood in her urine. She'd have to figure that out, but she needed clothes first, food second, pads next. She folded over the toilet paper and set it inside the shorts.

The girls were putting on makeup when Sukanya came out. They tried to talk with her, but Sukanya hurried out to the elevator and took it to a floor that specialized in accessories. It was better not to talk to anyone unless she had to.

A saleswoman with teased-out hair and a dark tan came over to help her find a pair of sunglasses. When Sukanya tried to pay with the whole roll of cash, the saleswoman gasped and took it from her. She rolled it into a tight bundle, slipped a rubber band around it and reached across the counter to tuck it deep inside Sukanya's inner pocket. She took one bill to pay for the sunglasses and tucked the change in Sukanya's outside pocket, patting the bills and coins in place. Sukanya put on the sunglasses, and felt comfortably hidden.

The next shop sold bags shaped like animals. She selected a large elephant with a trunk, floppy ears, and dangling tail. She paid, being careful to pull out only the small fold of cash.

On the next floor down, she found tennis shoes. She felt embarrassed at her sandals, but the saleswoman wiped her feet with a scented towel. She tried on several pairs in borrowed socks. The shoes were cushiony soft, a relief after the sandals. She added two three-packs of thick socks.

She found comfortable sweat pants and long, loose T-shirts in pastel colors that the salesgirl said were "easy wash and dry." The saleswoman took a big, soft, springy hair tie from a rack on the counter and handed it to Sukanya. "*Sabisu*," she told Sukanya.

"Free?" Sukanya asked.

"Yes, free. Present. For you."

Sukanya took the hair tie and smoothed her long hair together and slipped it on in front of a mirror. "Gorgeous," the girl said in English. "You so pretty!"

The money was worth a lot more than she imagined. She took another bill from the roll and bought two bras and a half-dozen underwear. She went into a toilet and used her teeth to tear open the plastic and bite off the tags. She changed into her new clothes and folded the rest into her elephant backpack along with the iPad and computer.

She shoved the men's clothes into the leather computer bag and dropped it in a trash can.

Outside the 109 building, she sat gently down on the steps, and watched people walking fast in all directions. The morning air was burning away. With the smells wafting out from the shops with each automatic open-close of their doors, she felt hungry, then not hungry, then hungry. She craved a bowl of *khao tom*, but she knew she should eat whatever she could find.

She stopped in front of a crepe store and looked in the brightly colored window at the array of fruits and toppings in silver bowls. The girl working inside, in a white apron and pink hat, shouted "*Irasshaimase*" through the window and waved her inside. The crepes looked magical.

The counter girl spread the crepe batter onto the heated griddle, smoothed it into a circle, and let it crisp to a golden brown. Sukanya pointed at chocolate stars, banana slices, and rainbow sprinkles. The girl loaded them on, drizzled on red syrup, flopped whipped cream on top and tucked it all inside a paper holder.

Sukanya folded her two hands together into a "*wai*" and the shop girl replied, "*mai pen rai ka*." Sukanya took a minute to realize she spoke in Thai, then started asking her a million questions.

The girl shook her head and said in English, "Thailand, vacation only. You vacation here? Tokyo vacation?"

Sukanya said, "Yes. Vacation." She tried to smile.

Sukanya took a stool by the window, sitting gently down to give

23

her attention over to the gooey, creamy, fruity crepe. The sugar flooded through her and eased the ache.

The shop girl made a phone call and looked over as she talked, then smiled and went back to work.

Sukanya ate and watched the people passing, wondering who the girl called. Could she smile while talking to the police, or to someone worse? Sukanya didn't want to be caught. She had heard stories in Bangkok of girls taken into police stations. Tokyo would be no different.

Sukanya scanned the sidewalk outside the shop and stood up. She threw her elephant backpack over her shoulder, tossed away the rest of the crepe and ran out the door. The girl called after her, but Sukanya kept going.

She walked fast uphill and over to a street that led downhill, checking behind her each time she turned.

She stopped in front of a pachinko parlor and stared inside, checking in both directions. She stood riveted by the hypnotic clunk of balls on pins, ringing bells, and synthetic melodies, like a hundred alarm clocks going off at once. The repetitive noise reminded her of the factory where she worked before she went to Bangkok.

* * *

The factory was dirty and noisy, with wide, high ceilings. Machines punched out metal pieces at a ceaseless pace. The press she stood at just missed the tips of her fingers a thousand times a day, clunk, clunk, clunk.

Her father and his younger brother were smugglers in the north of Thailand, though she thought of them as traveling salesmen. When they were home, her father worked at the factory and her uncle trained elephants.

One summer, the army clamped down on the cross-border trade and in the ensuing uprising, her father was shot and killed. Her two older sisters were already promised in marriage, so Sukanya dropped out of school to take his place at the factory, a cherished position secured by a bribe.

But because of the troubles, the factory closed and the owner moved to a bigger, safer town farther from the border. Sukanya was old enough for the owner to arrange a household job for her in

Bangkok. The day she took the bus, her uncle took her for a ride on one of the elephants he trained. He gave her money and saw her off at the long-distance bus station.

The man who picked her up at the Bangkok bus station never took her to any house, but to an apartment with other girls from other villages. There, they were trained to put up with everything. They were beaten when they resisted or cried, and even when they didn't.

She wasn't even sure where her village was, though she knew it was in the north because the Bangkok girls teased her about her accent. But there was no going back.

Before she left, her brother had become a monk—she remembered him shaving his head—but there were hundreds of monasteries and he could be at any one of them, or he could have gone back to work.

Years later, Oskar tried to help her find them, and helped her get letters written. He would do that at least, in between all his other demands, but she never received a letter back.

* * *

Except for the factory, her memories flowed in silence. She stared along the row of seats where the players hovered over their machines, keeping the silver pachinko balls leaping and bouncing in incessant motion. The machines' screens spun a flashing, cackling carousel of anime characters—buxom girls in bikinis, grinning spiky-haired boys, and big-eyed monsters. The balls seemed to bounce randomly, despite the focus of the players and their tight grip on the lever.

Maybe the money in her pocket was enough for a ticket to America, but without a passport or a visa, it didn't mean much. Maybe she should try to call Oskar. He was back in Germany, but he could tell her how to get from Tokyo to America. Maybe she could get into the computer and call him that way if she could find Wi-Fi. She remembered, sort of, how to do that. When they lived together in Bangkok, she watched him do it every day.

She wasn't sure which way to go, but thinking of Celeste dead in the studio warehouse, every direction felt forward.

Chapter 6

At the wheel of his Nissan GT-R Nismo, Kenta ordered the voice app to start the trackers for his computer, iPad, and leather bag. The computer or iPad had to be turned on for it to track, but the bag, an expensive one he got in the Honolulu airport, was supposed to give a constant signal, though it didn't. He drummed his fist on the steering wheel, waiting for the pulse of the little dot.

As he pulled out of his apartment parking lot into the morning traffic, he hoped that the computer and iPad were with the bag. Once he found those, things would be fine.

His computer would have a month of video backups, along with outtakes, behind-the-scenes, and close-up shots—normally the kind of unedited footage he sold to the highest-bidding porn site. He'd have to delete all that, but video evidence was not something to let bounce around the internet, even on 2channel or whatever imageboard they shared the stuff.

More worrisome was someone snooping around inside his iPad. If they knew how, they could probably get through his encrypted passwords into his contacts, emails, messages—his whole business.

Finding all three would mean he was done with his part of the clean-up and could let Yoshitaka Kirino do the rest. Kirino was not the kind of businessperson to lose control of assets without compensation. He'd hold someone responsible for the girl on the studio floor, and for the other two girls, wherever they were. That was just how he did business. Kirino would be sure no trail led back to his enterprises.

Thinking of that, Kenta realized that he himself would be the route back. He handled everything for Kirino on the ground in Tokyo. It wouldn't get to that stage, though, if he could find his devices.

Kenta stopped at a traffic light and glared at the pulsing dot on his cellphone screen. As traffic started up again, it pinged. "Game on," he growled.

The GT-R, which he received as payback on a loan to a high-stakes poker player, could top out on the expressways, where reflective blockers and a laser jammer stymied the speed cameras, but until this blew over, he'd keep to the limit.

Kenta pulled in to a gasoline station at the top of the hill above Shibuya. He handed a five thousand yen note to the attendant, told him there'd be another one in twenty minutes if he let him park there. It was nerve-wracking to leave the car without the two spy cams he set up on the studio door, but he didn't want to get stuck in an underground parking lot with surveillance cameras.

Kenta followed the flashing dot on his cellphone downhill. He waited for the light to change and hurried across the wide street, cellphone in hand, like everyone else.

Past the station, he stopped in the middle of the sidewalk. The pulse came from the Shibuya 109 building, the mecca of teenage girl fashion. The GPS had no altitude marker, so whoever had the bag could be on any of the ten floors, each a circular tangle of small boutiques. He had been in there only once, the only guy in the place, when he took Mina shopping during one of her cute outfit phases.

He stopped at the entrance. It would be best to go to the top and work his way down. He got into the elevator with a gaggle of schoolgirls in sailor uniforms and already felt like a pervert. Seeing a man in their territory, the girls on the elevator got out on the next floor. Their chirpy giggles lingered as they skittered away.

The signal weakened for a second, so he got off on the top floor. The whole place smelled like cheap perfume. Mannequins sported short skirts and skimpy tops. Display racks offered face creams, lipstick, bracelets, and necklaces dangling anime characters, good luck *kanji*, and cutesy ornaments.

Kenta breezed by the stores and stopped near the stairs. He saw two salesgirls nod at each other and head off, no doubt to call security. Men snuck in to the store to take secret photos, and surveillance was tight. He would have to hurry. Kenta followed the beeping GPS to the toilet in the stairwell. He looked at the door and waited.

Kenta knocked on the door and whispered, "Anyone in there?"

From inside, a girl's voice said, "*Hai.*"

"Is there a girl from Thailand in there?" Kenta whispered a bit louder. "She's my girlfriend."

"No," one of the girls said, laughing.

"Are you sure?"

"Come in and see for yourself." They giggled.

Kenta slid into the women's room. The girls dropped their eyelash curlers, backed away, and screamed.

"Sh-sh-sh," he cooed, holding a finger to his lips, smiling reassuringly.

The two girls backed against the wall.

There was nothing in there except the two high school girls, their bags, and a trash can.

Kenta ripped the top off the trash can and dug inside. There was his leather computer bag. Kenta pulled out a pair of men's shorts, a blue soccer jersey, a wristband, and a pair of sandals, but no iPad or laptop. He slung everything but the bag into the trash can. He checked his phone, but this was the origin of the pulse.

Before he could turn around, one of the girls pulled out a long safety pin she kept for *chikan* train perverts who groped her on the crowded morning train. Kenta didn't notice her preparing to follow the advice of her favorite girl's lifestyle website. She opened the pin, bent it out and jabbed it deep into Kenta's butt.

Kenta howled and grabbed the girl by her arm so tightly she dropped the long, sharp pin. He coiled his arm to slap her a good one, but two security guards in uniforms pushed open the toilet door, their walkie-talkies squawking.

"What are you doing in here?" the first guard shouted.

"These girls stole my bag," Kenta said, holding up his leather bag with one hand and rubbing his butt cheek with the other. She must have hit a nerve, or bone.

The girls screamed denial and started whining. Kenta stepped toward the door, waiting for the opening that would let him squeeze past the plump middle-aged man.

But the man stood his ground.

Kenta shrugged and delivered a sharp punch to his solar plexus. The man dropped to the floor, coughing for breath, his cap and walkie-talkie tumbling onto the floor.

Kenta stepped over him.

In the hallway, the second guard held his walkie-talkie in front of him and set himself in a defensive posture, one leg back. Kenta didn't want to hurt the old guy, but he didn't want to be detained, either. He swung a hard kick just above his knees that toppled the guard sideways. Kenta kicked the walkie-talkie down the stairs in front of him.

His butt hurt so much from the little bitch who drove a pin into his ass that each step was like another jab. He wiped the sweat from his forehead and hurried down the stairs.

He stopped at the stairwell on the first floor, looking for the local police. Shibuya was so crowded there were police boxes all over. They could get almost anywhere in a few minutes.

It was a straight shot out the door. He kept his head low, away from the store cameras, and strode out.

On the street, he hurried into the crowd. He slipped a hand down the back of his pants and pulled it up to see blood. Back in the day, he picked up girls like those two from the streets of Shibuya and kept a cameraman on call so he could polish off a couple of "authentic amateur" videos, sometimes two a day. Now, here he was hobbling up the street bleeding from his butt cheek.

Those days, he had done anything to make money. He lived freely, sleeping late, playing pachinko, working when funds ran low, partying when he had cash. Now, every morning was account balances and email, loan contracts and bank forms, online transfers and cryptocurrency wallets.

He made it to the gasoline stand, limping slightly, and handed the attendant another five thousand yen. Before he eased himself into the car seat, he pulled a small towel from the glove compartment to protect the Alcantara upholstery. He spun the car sharp left onto Omotesando Avenue.

Now, at least he knew it was one of the women. It wouldn't be that makeup girl, so it had to be one of the Thai girls. He'd have to wait until it was turned on, though, and that could be a long time. It was best to outsource this.

He would call in a few favors from street-level guys in Shibuya who Yoshitaka Kirino knew.

Following their directions, he pulled around the crowded part of

29

Shibuya to a wide street where three young guys were waiting. They were Shibuya lifers, even if they did keep an office in the upscale area up the hill. They were paying for the address, thinking that mattered. Maybe Kirino got them the office.

The tallest of the three guys wore a sweatshirt under a leather jacket. He pushed his hair back with sunglasses and swaggered over. Kenta had talked with him before when Yoshitaka Kirino was in town. He'd come to Jack and Jill Studios, too, but didn't seem interested in watching the action. Kenta wondered if his ponytail, a short bob pulled tight and oiled, was some attempt to copy Yoshitaka Kirino's ponytail or was his own bad taste.

Close behind him was a stocky guy who turned his face, battered as a boxer's, back and forth. He was either the lookout or had a nervous tic. He was trying to look tough, but he'd have been chewed up the first day in the prison ward Kenta had been sent to.

The third punk was bald, with a bomber jacket and a thick chain necklace that flowed over the fat of his neck. He was broad in every direction and not much older than a teenager. Only someone that young would try to look so hard.

The tall gangly guy with the ponytail took off his sunglasses and leaned down to Kenta's window.

Kenta handed him the key.

"Parked in the same place?"

Kenta nodded. "Same floor. Dark-blue Subaru with a spoiler in back."

"I remember."

Kenta held up his cellphone with the photo and the tracking app name and password so the kid could take a photo of the information.

"Is Kirino in on this?" he asked. He took a photo of the information with his cellphone camera.

"Not yet. Let's keep it that way. Watch the app and bring her to me. You know how it works?"

"Yeah, we know how it works."

30

Chapter 7

Hiroshi took a taxi back to the Kagurazaka apartment after spending a few hours looking through the contents of the safe. When he came in, Ayana was still sleeping. He tried not to wake her as he slipped into bed. She murmured something unintelligible and snuggled up to him, sleep-warm.

Hiroshi turned toward her, then away, then rolled onto his back, but couldn't relax. The chalk outlines of the bodies in the cold warehouse felt projected on the inside of his eyelids. They floated over the studio account books he'd skimmed through before having them packed up to send back to his office.

He rolled out of bed without waking her, got dressed and snuck out to the nearby bakery for her favorite *pain au chocolat* and artisanal yogurt. The fruit and vegetable stand had *nashi* pears—Ayana preferred the crunchy varieties—and he picked out some squarish orange *kaki* persimmons. The old lady who ran the shop wrapped them in a paper sack and dropped in two large strawberries.

He smelled the coffee brewing when he stepped in the door.

"Where did you go?" Ayana asked. She poured out two cups and set them on the table.

"Where do you think?" Hiroshi set everything on the kitchen island counter. Ayana looked delicious in the morning, swollen-eyed and puffy-cheeked, hair unbrushed. She scratched and stretched and flopped around, her clothes wrinkled and loose.

"You went all the way to the bakery?" Ayana yawned. "I thought you left for work."

"Why aren't you at work?"

"I told them I was coming in late today."

31

"Perfect then."

Hiroshi washed the fruit and cut the *nashi* and *kaki* into quarters. Ayana set out the yogurt, honey, and spoons. The sun peeked over the apartment building that blocked the very first of the morning light.

"Did I wake you?" Hiroshi asked.

"My sore muscles woke me."

"Even when I can't sleep one night, I sleep better the next."

Ayana smiled. "It's your work that takes most of your energy."

"Is that a criticism or a request?"

"Both."

"Both noted."

Ayana chomped into the *nashi* and chewed loudly. As graceful as she was through most of the day, in the morning, she ate as sloppily and unselfconsciously as a child.

"Will you make kendo practice today?" Ayana crunched her *nashi*.

"This new case..."

"Always a new case."

Hiroshi kissed her on the forehead and held her head against his chest as she crunched her *nashi*.

* * *

At his office, he did a triage of cases to make room for the porn studio finances. Before moving in with Ayana, he'd spent most nights in the office, working all night and dropping off to sleep about the time his assistant Akiko arrived.

The windowless room off a stairwell in the annex to police headquarters was ideal for work or sleep. Having a quiet, private space was a rarity for anyone at his pay grade.

Akiko's transfer from the main office was a relief. She'd worked there for several years, but was ready for a new challenge, she said. Because she spoke English, she'd moved over to work with Hiroshi on international cases. Though she never studied forensic accounting, Akiko was quick to pick up the details of financial scams, embezzlements, tax evasion, and mortgage fraud. She never forgot a detail, date, number, or fact once it crossed her desktop.

"You're here before me again!" Akiko laughed and hung up her coat on the rack by the door.

Hiroshi got up to make an espresso for her and another for himself. The aroma from numerous cups over the last year had helped, cup by cup, to win the battle against the cleaning supply smell, leftover when his office was converted from a janitorial supply closet.

After the espresso gurgled out, Hiroshi said, "You remember that scandal last fall? Everyone wanting to get rich investing in film companies. Do you remember the names?"

"Of the companies or the ministry officials?" Akiko asked, clicking on the computer.

"Both." Hiroshi set her double espresso in front of her. Hiroshi had a "cat's tongue"—he couldn't drink or eat anything hot—but Akiko sipped hers without waiting for it to cool.

"The Ministry of Finance officials weren't too helpful, were they?" Akiko said in a sing-song sarcastic voice.

"But that doesn't mean we can't ask them again."

Akiko set her cup down and searched for the files.

"And find out everything you can about the porn industry." Hiroshi sat down at his desk.

"Um, what?" Akiko leaned back in her chair.

"I mean, about how the banking and finances work. We need to find out how the industry moves its money."

"The legitimate businesses or the associated businesses?"

"Not sure we can tell them apart. And what was that initiative about child porn?"

"The nonprofit organizations forced some legal changes. And something about contracts for women workers," Akiko said, trying to remember.

"Let's find the NPOs that deal with human trafficking. I'll stop by in person."

Hiroshi and Akiko worked all morning, ordering ramen delivered for lunch, *kotteri* with extra *chashu* pork slices, flavored egg for Akiko and *asari* for Hiroshi. They set the bowls outside the door on the delivery tray to be picked up later.

As the drowsiness of post-lunch work came on, Akiko leaned forward to read from her screen. "I found the NPOs...and this article. It says Japan only ratified human trafficking protocols a couple years ago."

"It wasn't a crime before then?"

"Apparently not. But after being pressured by the NPOs, the

government finally said it wanted to crack down, to reassure the world that Japan was not a hub of sex trafficking."

"Even if it is," Hiroshi said. "Shame is the only thing that works with them. And maybe transparency—"

"They want to open the country but control it at the same time." Akiko tut-tutted the screen, and they both got back to work.

* * *

Halfway through the afternoon, Sakaguchi knocked on the doorjamb as he swung his huge sumo wrestler body through the door.

Akiko stood up and bowed. "Thank you for those sumo tickets!" Sakaguchi hummed deep in his throat.

"The last match was amazing. Everyone threw their cushions. I was so impressed!" Akiko gushed.

"On TV, it was all *tsuki-oshi* pushing until the last match. The *mawashi* belt work is so rare. Maybe these foreign wrestlers will help change back to the old styles."

"Let me go get you some tea," Akiko said, and she rushed off to the vending machines down the hall, ignoring Sakaguchi's protests.

"I thought you didn't like the foreign wrestlers," Hiroshi said.

"They're here for good now," Sakaguchi said.

Sakaguchi was head of homicide, but he wasn't much of a talker. Even by Japanese standards, his silence-to-speech ratio was high. Hiroshi had come to appreciate Sakaguchi's quiet, often silent, manner. It was only a matter of time, though, before Takamatsu took over again as head of homicide. He had seniority, after all.

Takamatsu and Akiko came in together, chatting amiably. Akiko had a can of green tea for Sakaguchi.

"Make me one of those Italian thingies." Takamatsu waved his hand in a circle at Hiroshi. "Goes with my Italian jacket."

"That'll be a big help if we ever get a designer clothing case," Hiroshi said.

"Don't say things like that. It makes them happen," Takamatsu said.

Takamatsu was just the opposite to Sakaguchi, babbling constantly, sarcastically, irritatingly. Even after being suspended and reinstated at lower rank, Takamatsu talked as much as before. It took Hiroshi a year to realize he didn't need to listen to everything

34

Takamatsu said. He talked to loosen people up, while listening and observing them closely.

"Where are we on this thing?" Takamatsu asked.

Sakaguchi paused so Takamatsu kept talking.

"Let me tell you what I've got. The Ministry of Finance guy, Takeo Suzuki, was retired after a long career, but he returned as a consultant."

"What did he oversee? Cryptocurrency exchanges?" Hiroshi asked.

Takamatsu looked at him as he held up the small espresso cup Hiroshi handed him. "That was a good guess."

"Not a guess," Hiroshi said.

"Well, his portfolio included, what do you call it, cryptocurrency?" He stumbled over the English word at the end of his sentence.

Hiroshi said, "Those porn businesses run on untraceable cash. Maybe the bureaucrat was helping them. The account books will point us in the right direction."

Takamatsu shook his head. "You think money is the root of all evil."

"No, but it finances it," Hiroshi said.

"You think he wanted to be in with the cryptocurrency exchanges for his own benefit?" Akiko said.

"We can see if he had some accounts set up, but they're all encrypted," Hiroshi said.

Takamatsu said, "Getting in with new companies before they move their finances to digital currency would make for quite a nice *amakudari*, 'descent from heaven.'"

Hiroshi said, "If he could retire as a consultant to the cryptocurrency exchanges, it would be a very smooth landing. He'd be able to connect the exchanges with the right government offices."

"And to his own account." Takamatsu smiled.

"More like an ascent *to* heaven," Akiko said.

"Too bad he was addicted to porn," Sakaguchi said.

Everyone turned to him.

"He had quite a collection at home, the detectives told me. They're still looking through it. Never married. Lived alone," Sakaguchi said.

Takamatsu set his cup down. "What was he, about seventy?"

Sakaguchi nodded. "And if, as Hiroshi said, the porn world runs on cryptocurrency, we have to wonder if our finance minister was helping them out, too."

35

Takamatsu said, "And vice versa."

"And what about the film director?" Hiroshi asked.

Takamatsu said, "That's why I stopped by. I've got an appointment for us."

"Us?" Hiroshi asked.

"They live near Roppongi, big apartment building, looks like. He's the scion of an aristocratic family that long supported the arts."

"Maybe not his kind of arts," Sakaguchi said.

"Or maybe they did, secretly," Hiroshi said.

"We can ask," Takamatsu said, humming.

"What about the girl?" Akiko asked.

Sakaguchi shook his head. "Seems like the girl had a heart attack from an overdose of amphetamines. There was blunt force to her head, too. Not as much damage as the finance minister."

"How old was she?" Hiroshi asked.

Sakaguchi's thick eyelids folded shut and he cleared his throat. "Their initial estimate is fourteen. Based on a wrist scan and dental X-ray."

Akiko started fiddling with her computer, shaking her head.

Sakaguchi squared his shoulders and stretched.

Even Takamatsu, for once, was quiet.

"Fourteen. That's another kind of crime altogether," Akiko said in a low, angry voice.

Chapter 8

Sukanya worried that the more she walked, the easier it would be for something to happen, for someone to stop her. She had to get off the street someplace safe, to sleep. The drugs were easing, but she didn't feel tired. Her body felt heavy, as if she were carrying someone on her back. She went into a convenience store and bought rice crackers, coconut Pocky's, and another hot tea.

Outside the store, she squatted down, uncomfortably, on a landing two steps up from the street. Nearby, schoolgirls in uniforms chatted in quick, cut-short phrases, checking their hair in little mirrors and fondling their cellphones.

Sukanya leaned back against the glass of the convenience store. The rice crackers had no spiciness, but she had to eat something. The little chocolate Pocky sticks at least had coconut flavor.

One girl offered her some chips. She took one and offered the girl rice crackers.

"Where from?" the Japanese girl asked.

"Bangkok," Sukanya said.

"Thailand?" the girl said, and let out a long *"Ehhh? Ii na."* Two other girls skipped over and huddled close, squatting on their over-stuffed blue school bags with their skirts riding high on their thighs. They seemed to be discussing Sukanya in friendly voices.

"So pretty," one girl said in English, touching her ponytail and offering a bag of crispy orange cone somethings. Sukanya took one, but it had no taste. She smiled thanks anyway.

"Where going?" the first girl asked.

Sukanya swallowed. "Just visit. Vacation."

"Vacation. *Ii na.*" The other girls joined in the chorus. "School vacation time?"

Sukanya smiled.

One girl pawed Sukanya's elephant bag and said, "*Kawaii!* Where buy?"

"Down there." Sukanya couldn't remember where the store was or what it was called.

The girl asked, "How Tokyo?"

Sukanya drank some tea. "Very clean."

"*Berry kureen,*" she repeated to the amusement of everyone.

"Some place Tokyo *kureen.* Shibuya *wa, ne.*" She laughed.

Sukanya smiled at the high school girls, wondering what they studied. Not English apparently.

One girl pulled her cellphone around to take a selfie with Sukanya. "Let's selfie."

Sukanya dropped her snacks and stood up rigid. "No photo." She reacted more angrily than she wanted.

The girl backed away. "OK, sorry, sorry, no photo." They all stood up, confused and concerned, showering Sukanya with what English words they could muster. "Love Thai. Sorry. Oh my God. Sorry."

Sukanya resisted the urge to punch the girl.

Never waste a punch was one thing the coach emphasized when Oskar took her to a Muay Thai gym. She'd suited up and learned the kickboxing basics while he took photos, thousands of them, of her and the professional girl fighters working out. He got photos and she got kickboxing lessons.

Sukanya took a big breath, apologized, and folded her hands into a *wai.* The drugs still made her jumpy, but she could feel them releasing their grip and no longer pushing her forward.

The girls shouted, "*Ja, ne,* bye bye," as they danced off into the Shibuya streets.

Sukanya gathered up her stuff, put her bag over her shoulder and turned down a gently curving slope lined by stores with handmade signs. Most of the signs were written in English, but even then she couldn't make out what the meaning was. Her new shoes felt good on her feet and she kept walking.

She came to a coffee shop with a chalkboard that said, "Free Wi-Fi." She went in, pointed at orange juice and a piece of chocolate cake, paid, and sat at the only empty table. The six tables were close together and several other people worked alone on their computers.

She turned the computer on, hoping it didn't need a password. The guest user function came on, and she clicked it, saying a little prayer. The screen turned black. After a pause, it blinked on. She wanted to clap.

She had memorized Oskar's WhatsApp info and used it several times before to send a message to him in Germany. He hadn't answered the last message she sent when she was leaving Bangkok. After that, they'd taken her cellphone and tossed it over the side of the boat.

She clicked on the browser for a map of Tokyo. She could see she was near Shibuya Station, but there were many other train and subway stations nearby. She sent a message to Oskar, hoping he might answer right away.

She drank her juice and finished the cake and looked outside. She didn't feel like walking anymore. She would have to find a hotel, and she clicked on the computer to search for one. If the hotel asked for ID, she had nothing but money. She could search for the studio, but she had no idea what it was called or where it was.

She searched for Ratana online, but she didn't know her full name. After scrolling through pages and pages of Ratana images, she gave up. Ratana might have been given their passports, or got a hold of the money, but she was gone now.

A guy at the next table kept looking over and Sukanya felt like he was going to talk to her. He wasn't bad-looking, and could be a place to stay for the night, but everything hurt, so she turned off the computer, tucked it into the bag and stood up. He spoke to her in Japanese, but she took her plate and glass to the return shelf and left quickly.

She started back the way she came. When she stopped at a light, three young guys came up beside her. She thought they looked familiar, but that was impossible. She knew no one in Tokyo.

One of the guys stepped in front of her. He had a beat-up face and rocked back and forth on his feet, blocking her way. "Speak English?" he asked, pointing with his fingers like a hip-hop video.

Sukanya stepped around him. "Not interest."

"Hey, hold up, hold up," the guy said. "Just being friend-er-y." He kept looking at the other two guys, who chuckled from behind.

Sukanya stopped in the middle of the crosswalk. "I say, not interest. So, go." She pointed at a far distance.

The other two guys circled in close. One was short and fat with folds of fat around his neck. He smiled and said in badly accented English, "We buy you dinner. Nice day Shibuya. Nice night."

The third guy, tall with a small ponytail, came up on the other side and raised his sunglasses. "Where from?"

Sukanya pushed between them and hurried away.

The three of them laughed and followed. One of them caught up and put his hand on her elbow.

Sukanya raised her elbow and stared at him. "Do not touch," she said as she ripped her elbow down.

The three guys chuckled, and the fat, bald one reached for her elbow from behind. As soon as he touched it, Sukanya set her hips, spun and landed a back kick that hit his thigh. He bent over to rub it and she lifted herself up and swung a roundhouse kick to his ribs. He doubled over clutching his side.

The other two laughed hysterically.

Sukanya gripped her elephant backpack and took off running. She looked for a shop to hide in, threading her way through the crowd, but she was too tall, her hair too glossy, and she moved too differently from the Japanese to lose them.

She turned into the huge open entrance to Mega Don Quijote, the most densely packed shop she could find. She rushed past two huge tropical fish tanks and head-high displays of snacks, and dodged down the first aisle past boxes of discount wine, party decorations, and barbecue utensils. She took the back stairs two at a time to the third floor without looking back.

She hurried past displays of summer swimsuits, sandals, and beach balls, turned down an aisle of discount canned food and stopped underneath a display of cute furry hats. She turned and looked back. Now that she was here, how would she get out? They could wait outside forever.

She pretended to shop, but not for long. One of the punks, the one with the ponytail and sunglasses, came slinking along the aisle toward her.

Sukanya sprang to the next aisle, but another of the guys was coming down that one. She moved to the next aisle, a long straight one, and started to run. Halfway down the aisle, the fat, bald guy stepped out and she was trapped.

Sukanya let her bag dangle and looked both ways at them closing in on her. She tried to remember what the coach at the kickboxing gym told her about timing and balance.

This time all three guys stopped steps away.

The tall, gangly leader smiled at her as he tucked his sunglasses into his shirt pocket.

Sukanya picked her bag back up and nodded an obedient OK. She walked down the aisle with her head hung for a moment before she reached up and yanked down a stack of shoeboxes, and then another. She turned on the fat guy, lifted her right knee and landed the ball of her foot square in his stomach. He dropped to his hands and knees and she jumped over him, pulling down everything she could from the shelves behind her.

At the end of the aisle was an employees-only door. She bumped it open with her shoulder and entered the cool, dark storage area. She pulled a rack of dresses in front of the swinging doors. She was more tired than she realized, and felt dizzy. She looked around wildly for an escape route.

In the dim light, she looked into the startled face of a girl about her age in a red and white Don Quijote uniform holding a clipboard.

The doors hit the racks and Sukanya ran over to a stack of large boxes. They were light enough to push aside and duck behind. She looked back once into the girl's eyes before climbing into a large box filled with sweatshirts. She let the lid fall back and pulled some of the sweatshirts over herself, and curled up to wait.

She could hear arguing and the doors opening and shutting again and again, the dress racks being wheeled around and crashing over. She heard scuffling and more voices, raised, guy's voices, and women's voices, and then the sound of men's voices deep and commanding. Everything was muffled from her spot inside the box.

She stayed there for a long time, until it quieted down. She felt her body loosen and fatigue pull her down. Her breathing slowed and deepened and her eyes blinked closed. The last thing she heard before falling asleep was the sound of the doors swinging open and shut.

41

Chapter 9

With his hands on the steering wheel of hand-sewn leather and every button anyone would ever need, Kenta felt better already. He tested the tight turn of the wheel as he pulled onto the Shuto Expressway south. His ass cheek still hurt, but less than before he got some sleep.

A long drive over Tokyo Bay Aqua-Line highway would help him focus. Whipping over the bridge, water on both sides, sky above, engine humming, chassis lifting with the crosswind, felt like flying. The bridge was the best place to think clearly.

It was also the best place to get a blowjob. He flipped through his cellphone contacts, looking back and forth from the screen to the cars. A lot of women owed him money, but not all of them woke up early. He scrolled through the list. The kanji of women's names read like terse poems of elegant virtues, moral qualities, exotic trees, delicate flowers. Daughters' names held the family's hopes and ambitions, expectations and dreams.

Too bad so many of them couldn't manage their personal finances. Online shopping and easy credit set up his business and the economic downturn established it. It was too early for most of them. They slept late and were crabby in the morning. He would call Mina. She relaxed him as much with her conversation, before and after, as with her lack of hang-ups. She was usually busy, but could sometimes take off a couple of hours for a drive.

First, he needed to check on the cameras monitoring the studio. He pulled off to a family restaurant and parked half over a line at the back to take two spots and ensure no one could park close. The parking area was on the ground floor and the restaurant on stilts above.

He took a seat near the window, ordered the breakfast set with unlimited refills on coffee. With the strong Wi-Fi and table dividers, he could get right into the surveillance videos. The quick scan function would let him get through hours of footage before he finished eating. The family restaurant food, bland as it was, seemed to keep him full, especially on days when he didn't have time to eat right.

He sipped his iced coffee and watched the police go in and out. It took them hours to work over the place. They carted out three bodies and tons of files.

All Shibaura needed to do was to go in to the police and explain it was rented out to people he didn't know. Kenta would write out a script for them to follow. Drugs and depression had made Shibaura slow and pliable, so he sometimes lost the thread. But he could handle this, with Haruka's help. That was the best option.

In between bites, he took stills to hand over to Kirino. Kirino liked to see who and what he was up against. Kirino often seemed to be several steps ahead, as if Kenta was just reconfirmation, but this was something only Kenta could provide.

Kenta realized he was the link between Kirino, Shibaura, the studio, the finance minister, and the murders. If things got worse, he'd be trapped in the middle of it all, and Kirino would toss him over the side as easily as he did everything else that got in his way.

Shibaura and Haruka needed to either go all-in or get out. If they screwed this up, Kirino would step in.

He called Shibaura. It went to voice mail—the guy slept half the day. Kenta said, "Shibaura. Haruka. We need to talk. Now. I mean like right now. Pick up. I know you're there."

Haruka answered. "Shibaura's sleeping."

"Wake him up."

"He took a sleeping pill."

"When does he not? I'll be there in fifteen minutes." He would have to give up on Mina and the relaxing drive he'd had in mind.

* * *

Shibaura's place was in Shirokane, an upscale neighborhood whose apartments were bought with old money and new. The buildings were tall and modest from the outside with good parking and good security. Other than that, Kenta didn't like the atmosphere of the area. It was too cold and quiet. Or maybe it was the residents, well-connected and wealthy.

He pulled into the guest spot in Shibaura's building, plugged in his second cellphone to recharge and checked the tracking app. It wasn't pinging yet, or he'd missed it if it had. Those guys in Shibuya would catch it when it did. The three guys had his back-up car, and he had a tracking app on that, too. It looked like they'd parked in Shibuya.

He double-locked the doors, set the sensor alarm, and hurried to the entrance. The apartment was on the ninth floor.

Haruka let him in and he followed her to the living room. He didn't much like the upper floor, picture window view of the city, or of Haruka. She was the old ideal of a Japanese porn actress—fleshy mounds of juicy desire. She was pretty, yes, but even soft focus couldn't hide her boxy jaw. At forty-something, she dressed like she was twenty, with clingy shirts and skinny-leg jeans, and rows of necklaces that rode her breasts like gold piping on a pillow.

"Where is he?" Kenta asked.

"He's out cold. I told you." Haruka walked toward the bar by the picture window. She let her hands drop onto the top-shelf liquors on the drinks trolley and looked out the sliding windows at Tokyo Tower. The Eiffel Tower knockoff offered the only color—orange—in the Tokyo skyline of endlessly unfurling gray.

"Tell him he needs to go talk to the police," Kenta said.

"He doesn't want to do that. He wants to leave."

"Convince him."

"Not my job. Plus, I agree. We should get—"

"You don't know what happened, do you? In the studio?"

Haruka looked at him.

Kenta couldn't believe it. She didn't have a clue. She was an actress, but not that good an actress.

"Shibaura's in serious trouble, which means you might be, too."

"And that means *you* might be, too."

Kenta wanted to smack her.

Haruka looked out the window. "You don't want me to touch the accounts, and now you want me to help you?"

"I'm going to tell you the best way to handle this."

Haruka shrugged. She turned from the window to Kenta. "So, what happened? Shibaura hasn't said a word."

Kenta shook his head. "There were three dead bodies in there." That should get her attention.

Haruka looked shaken. She stared at him and then stared out the window. She might act like an airhead, but that was on the surface. She wasn't stupid. "Who were they?"

"You don't need to know. I'll take care of the mess, or my associate—"

"Who? Kirino?"

"You should not even mention his name. He'll dump anyone he has to."

Haruka stared at him, then looked away out at Tokyo below.

"For now, I need the account books. The real ones, not the ones for the tax agency. So, where are they?"

Haruka looked out the window. "The accounts are all on the shared folder you set up."

"I want the paper copy."

"That's not my problem."

"No, it's *our* problem," Kenta said. "You don't want Shibaura to lose the studio and go to jail, do you? Or worse?"

Haruka kept her gaze outside.

It might have been easier not to tell her, but shaking her up was the only way to get action. "You called it in, right?"

"Called in what?"

"You were supposed to call the police."

"I didn't call anybody. We picked up groceries and came home. Shibaura wanted to sleep. That's about all he does these days."

"Maybe he called when..."

"I've been with him the whole time. I cradled his head until he fell asleep and then made myself some breakfast."

"Then who called in the murders?"

"How would I know? I didn't even know what happened." Haruka walked up to Kenta then stepped around him and headed toward the bedrooms down the hallway, calling back, "I'll wake him."

Kenta went to the liquor bottles and looked through them. Shibaura didn't drink since he started on the medication and Haruka once told him she'd drunk enough on the sets to last a lifetime.

Haruka came back. "Look, he's really out. He's usually like that for twelve hours before he struggles back to the waking world."

45

"Don't be stupid. The computer is missing. You can understand the importance of that, can't you? Just go in to the police and tell them what you know, which isn't much, after all."

"It's a lot more now that I know what happened," Haruka said.

Framed in the picture window with Tokyo in the background, Haruka looked smaller than usual, like a little girl dressed up in her mother's clothes.

"I'll show myself out," Kenta said.

* * *

Haruka stood there until she heard the front door click shut. She sat down on the edge of the sofa and considered her options.

She could go to Shibaura's place in Hawaii or Los Angeles, with or without him, and wait it out, but the last thing she wanted was to have Kirino or his people looking for her.

Or she could take Shibaura in to the police and try to bluff their way through. This was supposed to be her retirement years, spending money, running the business, enjoying life, but all she did was do the books or wait around in one of the apartments, nursing Shibaura.

She flopped back onto the sofa. The cushions sighed and curled, and from between the two cushions, a small black lacquer case bounced out. It was Shibaura's *hanko*. It must have slipped out when he sat down to take his sleeping pills.

After she prepared contracts, payments, invoices, and other documents for him, Shibaura would reach inside his pocket, pull out the *hanko* personal seal, tap it in the red ink blotter, and gently place the seal in the right blank to finalize the document. Each time, he put it carefully back in his pocket, the one thing he was scrupulous about.

That was the everyday *hanko* that kept the business running. *This* was the real one, the *jitsuin inkan* that he used only for the savings account, loan contracts, and business ownership.

She had never seen the elegant, finger-sized lacquer case outside his hand, and even then, rarely. She opened the small clip case and took out the slim cylinder of ivory and held it up, looking it over.

After a few minutes, she slipped the *hanko* back in its case and slid it between her breasts down to the bottom of her bra where the underwires curved together.

46

Chapter 10

"Aren't you glad you came?" Takamatsu said, laughing.

Hiroshi leaned back to look up at the forty-four stories of luxury apartments ensconced in an office-condominium complex carved out of Akasaka's high-priced real estate. The corners were rounded by mirrored glass and the rest of the outside was lined with deep-set balconies up to the penthouses on the top floors. It was the kind of luxury apartment building he'd only imagined from numbers on spreadsheets. It was hard to believe such places actually existed.

"No one this rich would ever need to kill anyone. They could just buy them off," Takamatsu said.

"What's a porn director doing living here?" Hiroshi asked.

"His family lives here. We still haven't found his address," Takamatsu said.

They stepped into the curved entryway and walked past designer chairs and artsy sofas to a reception desk at the end of the atrium. Their footsteps on the black marble floor echoed between the sweeping, grained wood wall and floor-to-ceiling windows that looked out on a wide, gently flowing pool of water.

"Is that a moat?" Hiroshi whispered.

"A symbolic one. We could fit the entire police headquarters in here," Takamatsu whispered back.

The receptionist called to the director's family and led them to an elevator, where a security guard bowed and held the door open for them. When they got in, he turned the key in the panel, bowed again, and in the slow, silent motion of the elevator, said, "I used to be a cop in the Azabu district."

Takamatsu smiled. "You must find this a little quieter."

47

"Considerably. And it pays about the same."

"You retired?" Hiroshi asked.

"I had enough of the streets. Life's too short."

"Can't buy more, either," Takamatsu said.

Hiroshi pulled out his cellphone and showed the guard a photo. "Did you ever see him coming here?"

The security guard leaned over. "Yes, he stopped by from time to time. He's the son of the family, but they never gave him his own key."

"He won't be stopping by anymore," Takamatsu said. "He died."

"Oh, I'm sorry. He always chatted with me." He bowed as Hiroshi and Takamatsu stepped into an entryway with another floor-to-ceiling window and a massive fresh flower arrangement in a huge brown vase.

The door opened and a maid with dark skin and a Japanese apron dress invited them in. They took off their shoes and put on slippers before following her through a hallway into a spacious living room.

The windows curved around the corner of the building and light poured in and reflected off a set of soft white leather-covered furniture. Hiroshi followed the curve of the windows for a wide-angle view of Tokyo. It was a clear, crisp winter day, and they could see the city stretching out to the horizon.

"Nice. It looks out on Aoyama Cemetery," Takamatsu said.

A prim older woman came out and stopped at the door. She wore a shiny brown dress with orange accents that didn't match her thick outdoorsy slippers. She showed no trace of sorrow in her face or manner, nor did she bow. She walked right over to the sofa and gestured for them to sit.

"We're very sorry for your loss," Hiroshi said. "We don't want to bother you at this difficult time, but we have a few questions."

"I'm Ryota's mother," she said, and gestured again for them to sit. "I imagine you have a lot of questions, but I can't answer the main one, what led to this."

"We just need to confirm a few things," Hiroshi said. "Was he living with you?"

She shook her head, no. "My husband forbade him from visiting. I still gave him money. A lot, actually. But after my husband died, he came more often and asked for more. He talked, but he never told me much."

"Was he in debt, do you know?"

"He was not a good businessman. He hired the best editors, bought the best equipment, paid the actresses well, but he never made it back. His films were pirated and distributors took a huge chunk." She pulled a pack of cigarettes from a lacquer box on the table and offered them to Hiroshi, who declined. Takamatsu pulled out one of his own, getting up to light her cigarette before his own.

"Your husband, Ryota's father, was also a film director."

"Yes, that's right. He made *pinku eiga* films in the sixties to get his start. That's what pays for this place, not his later serious work." She gestured with her cigarette hand. "At least that old porn had plots and irony, and social criticism. Ryota told me he wanted to make films like that again, but it wouldn't sell."

"You're sure he was losing money? Some of these films make a lot."

"He had a large alimony payment. He married a Thai actress, a beautiful woman, but she divorced him and took the kids. There was some doubt as to their paternity, but Ryota paid anyway. I don't know what else he might have been throwing money away on."

"Where was he living?"

She shrugged and inhaled, then blew a huge cloud of smoke toward the windows. "Someplace out there. Families can hide from each other as well as anyone else."

"Did he ever mention Takeo Suzuki, a former Ministry of Finance official?"

She shook her head no, and looked out the windows.

"What about Jack and Jill Studios?"

"I just don't know the details of his life or of his work. I wish I could help you." She pushed the cigarette into a white ashtray and stood up. "He's a mystery to me. Just like his father was."

"Thank you for your time," Hiroshi said.

Takamatsu leaned over to put out his cigarette in the ashtray and bowed politely.

As they walked to the car where Sugamo waited, Takamatsu said, "Start with the Thai embassy. Let Sugamo take you. I'd better check the director's movies. See if there's anything there that might help us."

"Better you than me," Hiroshi said.

49

Sangrawee Vipakavit, the foreign officer at the Embassy of Thailand leaned across a wide table of finely carved teak. It was covered with file folders, hundreds of them. Looking on from both corners of the room were two large wood elephants, taller than the teak desk, with carved tusks of what looked like real ivory.

After introductions and an exchange of *meishi*, she smiled and said, "We don't have any information that connects with any of these passports. Did you really expect us to?"

Hiroshi offered her a consoling sigh. "These files you have…"

"None of these files is complete," Sangrawee continued, her long, thin fingers gesturing across the table. "Some are police reports. Others are inquiries from families. Others are employers chasing them." She shook her head.

"How many are…?"

"…reported? We don't have time to count. A volunteer non-profit organization comes in to compile semiannual figures. But the final numbers are uncertain at best. The corruption runs so deep. It's been around so long."

"Can you trace them back to…"

"The girls come from places where they don't keep good records, often from the north, Chiang Rai, Nong Khai, Phayao. You've never even heard of those places, have you?"

"I had a case of bank fraud in Chiang Rai once." Hiroshi sipped his jasmine tea.

"That's money. These are people. They turn people into money." Sangrawee shifted in the high-backed teak chair. "Each of these files contains a life, but most of these lives are over." She moved a few of the files around, looked at one and shut it.

"New personal information is devised when they move to Bangkok?"

"Move? They're *sold*. Trafficked."

"I'm sorry. That's what I meant."

"They bring them to Japan with visas, or without, and they end up going back, or going on, or…we don't even know. Even when one comes here to the embassy or calls our hotline, and we can protect them, the girls don't even know their parents' full names. They've hardly finished basic schooling." She picked up a file, shaking her head. "And most of *these* files are for people with legit, or semi-legit jobs. The real problem is when they have no file at all."

"So, these files are not all that came to Japan?"

"If they come to Japan first, it's easier for traffickers to move them on to the Middle East, America, Europe. They're cracking down in other places, but Japan is still a springboard. The women and girls work off some of their debt here and get trafficked elsewhere. The men are taken to a fishing boat or a construction site. Could be anywhere."

Hiroshi had spent so much time tracking bank accounts, untangling contracts, finding the routing of offshore accounts, he'd never thought about the international flow of human beings.

"We need anything you can give us," Hiroshi said. "This is an ongoing investigation."

"So were these." Sangrawee looked at Hiroshi directly, her large brown eyes not glancing away like most Japanese women. "If the traffickers suspect a problem, they take care of it quickly."

"Take care of it?"

Sangrawee leaned forward. "You're an accountant. It's simple cost accounting. Line up the costs, risks, profit, then make a decision. Some investments are a loss. Better to liquidate right away. That's how they think."

"If she wanted to get help inside Japan, where would she go?"

"She'd need a new passport." Sangrawee shook her head. "They sometimes come here."

"If anyone comes in, can you contact me right away?"

"Of course," Sangrawee said. "From time to time we repatriate one, save her. But if we followed up on all these files, we'd have no time for the rest of our work."

"Doesn't Thailand file formal complaints with the Japanese government about this?"

"There are plans to increase the number of guest workers allowed in from Thailand, so we've been told to not complain," Sangrawee said.

"I've taken up too much of your time," Hiroshi said, standing up. "You've been very helpful."

"If she's still in Japan, the other place she might go is Morning Light," Sangrawee said, waving to one of the interns to start packing up the files and putting them back.

"What's 'Morning Light'? A club?"

"It's the NPO that comes here to compile data. The woman who runs Morning Light shelters the girls, finds them a lawyer, and conducts research and lobbying. Not that anything changes."

"Where's her office?"

"Let me get the number for you." She called to the office staff in Thai. A young woman came in with the number and address written on a piece of paper.

Hiroshi folded it into his pocket.

"You're the first person to come from the police in years," Sangrawee said, bowing with her hands in a *wai*. "Someone Japanese must also have been killed."

Chapter 11

Hiroshi found the Morning Light NPO office after a long walk from the station. The rundown building was crammed between a university training hospital and an old apartment complex. Far from the station, it was the old Shibuya of backstreet boutiques, friendly restaurants, and funky music clubs.

Closer to the station, that older Shibuya had already been transformed into an MBA's dream—retail, office, exhibition, and entertainment space plunked into brand-new thirty-story skyscrapers. There, Shibuya had started to *look* digital, but that faded farther from the station.

The building that housed Morning Light looked like small apartments converted to small offices. Hiroshi had to turn sideways when someone exited the elevator in the cramped entrance hall. He wedged himself in and pressed the fifth floor. It took a minute to realize the elevator was actually moving.

At the office, Hiroshi knocked on the open door and stepped in.

"*Sumimasen,*" Hiroshi called out. Light came in from windows along the rear wall of the room over the top of a row of filing cabinets. Five desks, pushed together, took up the center of the room. Unlike in the detectives' office, everything was orderly, with colored folders and potted plants. Posters in Japanese and English, and, Hiroshi guessed, Thai, Indonesian, Vietnamese, and Tagalog covered the walls. To the left was a small kitchenette, and to the right was a chalkboard with the chalk mostly erased.

Hiroshi leaned in further and tried again, "*Gomen kudasai.*"

The front door was pulled open from behind him. "Oh, sorry. You must be the detective?" A woman in a sweater and long cotton skirt held the door open.

Hiroshi stumbled forward into the room. "I'm Hiroshi Shimizu, from the homicide department."

"I'm Junko. I should have been here, but I got stuck at the hospital next door."

"Are you OK?"

"Better than the woman I took in."

Hiroshi waited for her to explain.

"Badly bruised. Usually, they speak a little English or Japanese, but not this time. I'm waiting on a Vietnamese translator. I need to go back when the translator arrives."

"Yes, of course. You must be busy."

She opened her arms wide toward the small, neat room. "Welcome to Morning Light nonprofit organization. Though as you can see, we don't have much light, and not much organization, either."

Hiroshi was about to comment on how cozy it was, but a young woman in jeans and a black T-shirt came in. She bowed, but didn't introduce herself, and hurried to make coffee.

Junko turned to Hiroshi, brushing back her long hair and straightening her loose, baggy sweater. She had a pale face with a scattering of moles, and a direct way of looking into his eyes. Hiroshi guessed she spent a lot of time overseas.

Hiroshi gave her his *meishi* and bowed.

Junko took it and went to her desk to get hers. Her eyes were curious and vibrant, but her face serious. "I left two of our staff with her in the hospital. We need to find a place for her to go."

Two young women came in. "Did someone come?" Junko asked them.

"The hospital put a security guard on the floor," one of them said. These two looked even younger than the first, but maybe all were college students. They talked to Junko in low voices, Junko nodding and OK'ing everything.

"It's broken," shouted the first woman.

Junko asked one of the other students to run out for coffee, but Hiroshi said, "I don't need anything. Really."

"We have water."

"I'm fine," Hiroshi said.

They gave up on being polite and Junko pointed at the center table, gesturing for him to take the seat closest the door.

The other three women sat down and pulled out notepads. As soon as they were all seated, Hiroshi passed the other three women his card. They quickly jumped out of their chairs and scrambled for their own *meishi*. They sat back down, introduced themselves and picked their pens up, ready. Hiroshi looked again at the chalkboard. The half-erased chalk reminded him of the outlines of the victims on the floor of the warehouse studio. He shuddered and refocused.

"These are our interns. They're still at university, Rin is at Sophia, Yuna is at ICU and Nozomi is at Waseda, my alma mater," said Junko.

"All very good schools," Hiroshi said. "Are you studying international issues?"

"They started university circles to highlight trafficking issues, joined forces with each other, and then with us. They're writing their graduation theses on trafficking. I hope we'll be able to get funding to hire them after they graduate, but we just lost a big donor. That's why our coffee machine is on the blink. Anyway, that's the nonprofit side of things."

"Sangrawee Vipakavit at the Thai embassy said you might be able to help." He placed a photo of the dead girl from the studio on the table. "I'm sorry, it's a bit grisly."

Junko took the photo. "This is nothing. She died peacefully compared to some of the others." She handed it to the interns, who passed it around.

"I heard that sometimes girls come here for help," Hiroshi said.

"I wish more did," Junko said. "We put up notices and post online." She pointed at the posters in various languages lining the wall. Each one of them had the phone number and website address of Morning Light.

"They've learned not to trust anyone," Rin said. Like the others, she had an impatient stare.

Hiroshi said, "So, you get them to a hospital, file a police report, and find a safe place to stay?"

"Morning Light was set up for research. The first year or two, we tracked numbers of people trafficked to Japan and lobbied to change the laws, but then we became hands on." Junko rearranged her baggy sweater.

"How many—"

"It's numbers you want? OK. The last time we compiled our data, we found that thousands of victims of sex trafficking come through Japan every year."

Hiroshi leaned back. "Thousands?"

"As a detective, you have more access than we do. Let us know if our data is wrong."

Yuna spoke up, looking down at her notepad, the top page still blank. "The National Police Agency only started specifying trafficking as a separate category a couple years ago."

Nozomi said, "We're still not using the word 'slavery' as some NPOs abroad do."

Hiroshi nodded and made a mental note to see what Akiko could find on all this. He felt too embarrassed to write anything down.

Rin spoke up. "One woman a week gets placed somewhere safe. They tell us about others who don't come in. The women are the best source of information, but they won't talk to the police."

Junko said, "We write down what they tell us, pack it into reports, and send it to Diet committees, Cabinet secretaries, the Police Agency, the media." Junko spoke in measured tones, neither angry nor tired. "There are conferences, lectures, and research groups at universities."

"We'll try to change that with this case," Hiroshi said.

Junko nodded at him politely and, Hiroshi felt, condescendingly.

Rin said, "After each case, though, Japan remains a hub for trafficking."

"Hubs can be changed. Spoke by spoke." Hiroshi cleared his throat. He felt like he was the only unprepared student in a university seminar.

The four women stared at him, quiet, patient, their blank notepads in front of them on the table.

"This girl was killed, but another one, maybe two, may have escaped. From a porn film shoot," Hiroshi said.

"But you're not sure?" Junko asked.

"We're not sure yet."

Junko said, "What they usually do is bring the girls over for as many films as they can. An assembly line. The industry here makes twenty thousand porn films a year, many with foreign girls and women. That's worth hundreds of billions of yen. High profit makes it worth the risk. And in Japan, there's hardly any risk. They rent the girls out on the side."

"After the films are made—"

"The girls are sent to other brokers, here or in other countries. They film them and then send them along. The young-looking ones bring in a lot, apparently."

"How do—"

"Listen, aren't you supposed to know all this?" Junko asked, and the three university students stared at him with impatient eyes.

"I'm not in that division. I'm in homicide. Actually, I'm an accountant."

The women looked at him quizzically.

Junko said, "We understand you're here to listen."

Nozomi and Yuna put their pens down on their notepads, disappointed to have nothing to write.

Rin spoke up. "Some Diet members push for keeping track of the data, but until they enact a law with teeth, we won't really know."

Hiroshi cleared his throat. "I'm interested. Was there a Jack and Jill Studios on any list you remember?"

Junko nodded for one of them to check on her computer. "We need better computers, too. They're using their own."

Yuna clicked, scrolled, and printed out several sheets, which she gave to Hiroshi.

Junko said, "Japanese girls work there, too. The film companies claim compliance with age restrictions, but Jack and Jill has been taken to court repeatedly for exploitative contracts. We can't get a case into the courts without a police report, and those can be hard to come by. Harder for non-Japanese."

"So, there's no assistance for you with any of this?" Hiroshi reached for his notepad again, but then left it in his pocket as the interns continued to eyeball him, their youthful impatience barely contained.

Junko smiled at Hiroshi. "A Diet committee is investigating. Supportive words from the Cabinet, that kind of thing. But possession of child pornography was only criminalized two years ago. And companies like Jack and Jill are still hard to prosecute. Most prosecutors choose to resolve things quietly."

Yuna said, "In my thesis, I'm working on the money angle. The industry relies on cryptocurrency."

Nozomi spoke up. "I'm working on how the Ministry of Foreign Affairs streamlines some of the visas."

Hiroshi frowned. "I thought some come in without going through immigration?"

"They do, but many have visas, which come from somewhere in that ministry," Nozomi answered.

"Anything else?" Hiroshi asked.

They stared at him with what Hiroshi felt was tolerance.

He tried not to look at the chalkboard as he bowed and stood up to leave, but he couldn't help looking.

Junko, Rin, Yuna, and Nozomi stood up and bowed as Hiroshi left.

In the cramped elevator, he took out his notepad and jotted down "cryptocurrency" and "foreign ministry," feeling like he'd just gotten out of class.

Chapter 12

Sukanya woke up and looked around at the sweatshirts she'd been sleeping on. Above her leaning over the large box, was the girl with the clipboard, looking concerned. The girl spoke in Japanese, but Sukanya shook her head, trying to wake up.

"Do you speak English?"

Sukanya nodded yes. "Little."

"I let you sleep until the end of my shift," the girl said.

"What time is?" Sukanya asked.

"It's evening."

Sukanya nodded yes and stood up. "Night?"

"You slept for a long time. What's your name?"

"Sukanya."

"Where are you from?"

"Thailand."

"Who were those guys?"

Sukanya shrugged.

"Are you in trouble?"

Sukanya looked away and nodded yes.

The girl looked back at the storage area. "I'm Chiho."

"If they gone, I go, too," Sukanya said, dusting herself off. Sukanya pulled her bag on her shoulder and climbed out of the box.

"The police are just across the street. I'll go with you."

Sukanya grabbed Chiho's arm. "No police. Please."

Chiho took her hand. "OK. No police. But you can't sleep here."

"I go now. Thank you."

Chiho put her hands on her hips. "If those guys are not out there, someone else will be. Come with me."

The storage area was quiet with no other employees around. Chiho led Sukanya through a narrow back way that ran the entire length of the store. Sukanya followed, holding tight to her bag. They rounded the corner into a loading area. Chiho pressed the button for the freight elevator.

Sukanya looked back at the boxes in the low-lit storage area before Chiho pulled open the scissoring door to get on. They rode down to a rear service entrance. Chiho took off her name tag and uniform smock and stuffed it in a locker. She pushed open the outside door with her butt and peered both ways, then waved Sukanya out.

The employees' door clunked shut leaving them in a narrow alley with exits at either end onto lively shopping streets.

Chiho looked at Sukanya. "You really should go to the police."

Sukanya said, "No. I go from here. Thank you very much."

"Do you even know where you are?"

"Shibuya."

"Where will you stay?"

Sukanya looked in both directions.

Chiho took Sukanya's arm and headed to the right.

At the end of the alley, Chiho hesitated, looking both ways.

Sukanya looked where Chiho looked, but the wide street was a blur of couples and friends strolling together, eating and talking loudly, single people weaving through the crowd, cellphones at their ears. Every building held stores on all floors and light spilled from all of them.

Chiho pulled Sukanya through the surge and scramble of people. They turned from street to street, and then headed up a steep slope. Chiho stopped at the top and turned to look downhill.

In a few seconds, a young man in baggy jeans and a loose, gray sweatshirt turned onto the sloping street and came toward them. When he saw Chiho and Sukanya standing at the top looking back at him, he pulled up short. He pressed the call button on his phone and leaned against the window of a ramen shop staring straight ahead.

Chiho pulled Sukanya around the corner and they took off running uphill through small streets. Sukanya's legs started to feel wobbly and her head throbbed. At the top of the hill, the ground leveled out and Chiho started running faster.

Sukanya kept up for a few turns, then lagged as Chiho turned and turned again, and headed back down a smoother slope.

Sukanya felt dizzy and tried to steady herself, but she felt like throwing up. She tried to hold it in, gulping, but she leaned over and spilled her stomach into the gutter.

Chiho ran back to her and Sukanya said, "I'm sorry."

Chiho patted her back and handed her some tissues.

Some rock fans began coming out of a concert, everyone wearing T-shirts with the same band design. Chiho pushed the two of them into the nearest building, which housed small bars, two or three on each floor, all the way to the top. Small, neat signs for each bar were pasted on the wall.

Sukanya said, "I can't run more."

"OK," Chiho said. She put her head around the door and looked down the street. The rock fans filled the street, talking excitedly.

They got in the elevator at the back of the entry hallway. It was barely big enough for the two of them. Signs and notices were taped on the walls, and the carpet was skewed from the floor. They stood quietly as it rattled upwards.

The elevator doors creaked open on the sixth floor. They stepped into a narrow hallway and Chiho pushed open a door to a stairwell that ran up the outside of the building. They sat down on the stairs, catching their breath. The elevator headed back to the first floor.

The cool night air made Sukanya feel better. The drugs were gone but the fatigue felt like a weight on each of her limbs.

Sukanya heard the elevator start up from the bottom floor, the voices of the guys shouting back and forth.

Chiho cocked her head to listen. "Let's go," Chiho whispered, taking Sukanya's hand.

Sukanya shouldered her bag and followed Chiho up the landing of the outdoor stairwell to the next floor.

The next building over was another tall, thin jumble of bars with a parallel landing for its outdoor stairway. Chiho and Sukanya looked down the long narrow shaft between the buildings, a straight drop to the cruddy, trash-filled bottom below. It was wide enough to plummet down, but close enough to crawl across.

Chiho hoisted herself up on the low wall, swung her leg over, and leaned over to grab the rail on the wall of the other building. She stretched her upper body then flipped her leg and arm over the rail. She wiggled to shift her weight. In a quick motion, she pushed and pulled herself over to safety on the other landing.

She put her hands out for Sukanya's bag, which she set on the landing behind her. Then she reached for Sukanya, who started breathing heavily.

"Don't look down," Chiho said. "Look at me."

"I can't."

"Hand me your coat."

Sukanya stripped off the leather jacket and tossed it across. She was taller and leaner than Chiho, but when she put her hands on the wall, she instinctively stepped back. She heard the guys pounding on doors on the floor below.

Chiho waved her forward with both hands. Sukanya leaned out over the edge and slung one leg over the tiled wall. She winced at the pain from her groin but balanced herself. She leaned over and the two of them clasped wrists.

"When I count to three, I pull and you push," Chiho said.

Sukanya nodded and set her foot against the wall. They looked in each other's eyes.

"One, two, three!" Chiho said.

Sukanya's foot slipped down the side of the tiled wall, but Chiho tugged back with all her strength and Sukanya's stomach landed on the railing, her legs dangling. Chiho dug in and pulled and Sukanya summoned the last of her energy to flip a leg over the rail. Another tug and she was over.

The sound of male voices echoed up from the other building. Chiho pushed Sukanya down against the wall, out of view of the landing they'd just escaped.

They could hear the guys stomping around checking the building. One of them went to the next floor, and one spit down the gap between the buildings.

Chiho and Sukanya huddled against the low wall, waiting.

When the men's voices sounded distant, Sukanya picked up her bag and followed Chiho through the fire door into the building. They rode the elevator down to the basement. A passageway connected that building to the basements of other buildings. Small signs noted the bars and clubs above. Sukanya wondered if the entire of Tokyo was somehow connected underground.

Chiho stopped at a stairway and walked up one flight into the first-floor lobby of another building. "Can you still walk?" Chiho asked.

"Yes, a little more, I can," Sukanya said.

They rode the elevator to the top floor. There was only one door, covered with a thick string of beads and "Agra" stitched into a soft cotton wall hanging. Sukanya followed Chiho into the dark restaurant and felt comforted by the thick sandalwood incense. A bar extended along one wall, and people lounged on huge cushions that lined the other wall. The blue glow of their cellphones illuminated their faces like ghosts.

Chiho sat Sukanya down on one of the cushions. Sukanya toed off her tennis shoes, pulled her legs up and rubbed her feet, longing for sleep. As she sat down, the smell of Indian spices made her hungry again. She watched Chiho go to the bar and talk with the bartender. He wrote down an order on a pad and passed it into the small kitchen.

Chiho carried two beers back.

Sukanya sat up and took a sip.

"What kind of trouble are you in?" Chiho asked. "Those guys said you were their girlfriend."

"Just opposite." Sukanya took another sip of beer and shifted her sore legs underneath herself, trying to figure out how to explain, or whether it was worth explaining.

Chiho said, "This place, the owner is my friend. I knew him in India, in Goa. He helped me there. He set up this restaurant when he came back."

Sukanya nodded, listening.

"I was stuck there once. My passport gone, money gone, boyfriend gone, too."

"What happen?" Sukanya asked.

"Everything happened. I lost him there. And when I got back to Japan, I'd lost someone here." She sipped her beer and looked at the Indian lamps on the wall.

Sukanya stared at her, thinking Chiho was different from what a Japanese girl should be. She had seen many Japanese tourists in Bangkok. The women always looked nice and friendly, plump at the edges of their faces and figures. They always looked so happy, springy and smart, strolling the shopping malls and riding in *tuk-tuks*, snapping endless photos, balancing their shopping bags on their arms. Chiho was not like them.

The bartender waved Chiho over. Sukanya finished the rest of her beer and watched Chiho talking with her friend, the owner. She had eaten in Indian restaurants in Bangkok. Oskar liked them especially. It was similar to Thai flavor in strength and spiciness, though not in subtlety.

She set her beer back on the tray and leaned on a pillow, her eyelids batting closed. She let them shut and listened to the soft sitar music in the background.

* * *

When Chiho carried the tray back with two more beers, deep-fried beans, and popadam, she found Sukanya exhaling a light snore. One of her legs was tucked beneath her and the other dangled to the side. Her hands flopped over her stomach. Her long hair, half out of the hair tie, fell over her wide shoulders, long neck, and graceful face.

She slept just like Chiho's younger sister used to on the futon they'd shared. Chiho always balled herself up tight, but her sister slept like she'd been spun around and tossed on the futon. They'd slept side by side all through their childhood, until Chiho ran away to Tokyo.

Chiho pulled the leather jacket over Sukanya's legs and feet. She sipped her beer and nibbled the popadam, wondering what had just happened and puzzling out what to do next.

Chapter 13

A light fog hung over the water of Tokyo Bay as a cold morning wind swept along the long, quiet dockyards of Shinagawa. Out in the bay, reefer cargo boats moved so slowly they seemed to be anchored. Their decks were stacked tight with shipping containers. Even at a distance, it seemed like a large wave and a small tilt would spill them into the water.

As if mocking the large, slow boats, a sleek black speedboat skipped over the waves, zigzagging toward shore.

Looking out the front windshield, Yoshitaka Kirino surveyed the long stretch of dock, peering at the storage warehouses that lined the concrete coastline. His tall, thin figure, sheathed in black clothes and a black leather jacket, looked out of place on the boat, as if resisting the first of the morning sun. His ponytail was long and tied neatly, and his body, thin and hard, leaned forward, scanning the docks for the car he was supposed to meet.

Arriving days earlier than planned was troublesome. It was a long way from Thailand, but he had to oversee the cleanup of what could grow into a much larger mess. Containment was a lot of what he did, but never the profitable part. It was the protective part.

When he saw the car, he pointed it out to the captain at the wheel beside him. The captain turned to steer them toward the car parked along the vast, empty stretch of pavement between the water and the storehouses. The boat churned up a long spray and a thick wake as it sped toward the drop-off point.

In the distance, a ship-to-shore gantry crane dangled containers and a few forklifts zipped along the smooth concrete, but they were too far away even to see the people operating them. It was too early in the morning for much work to be underway.

Straight ahead, on shore, three men waited by a low-roofed blue Subaru, watching their approach.

The speedboat captain slowed as they got closer. The tide was low, so they would have to pull up to one of the stairways that led up to the dock. One of the crew came out from below deck and tossed a rope to the nearest bollard. The boat rocked in its own wake, and Kirino timed his step-off from the back of the boat to the concrete landing to avoid getting his black boots wet. The landing was barely above the water level of Tokyo Bay. Kirino turned on the steps to look at the captain and motioned for him to wait before he climbed to dock level.

The three men were a mismatch, standing on different sides of the sports car. One was tall and neatly groomed with a short, oiled ponytail, the next rough as a street fighter, and the third was bald and indifferently dressed, with a fat neck.

The three were not connected to any syndicate that Kirino knew of. They seemed pleased to spend their youth running errands and spend their earnings on simple pleasures. He doubted they were armed. They never had been before, even when they should have been. He could bring them each something next time, promote them, in a sense.

They'd earned it more than Kenta had. Kenta had been in prison, but he'd never really been on the streets. His college-boy smarts were helpful, to a point, but he'd balk at what had to be done. Some messes didn't clean up easily.

"Is that Kenta's car?" Kirino asked.

The three of them turned and nodded yes, and shrugged.

The gangly, natty leader pulled his sunglasses off and tucked them in his shirt pocket. He bounced on his heels as Kirino looked the car over.

"I know someone who'd be interested in it, for a good price." Kirino walked to the front and looked at the car from where the leader of the three stood.

"Talk to Kenta. He loaned it to us," he said. "We're supposed to give it back."

"I will talk to him," Kirino said. He looked around the area. "So?"

The fat bald guy pulled open the passenger side door and reached inside. He pulled on the arm of a young Thai woman, who wobbled out of the car. He held her up and she swayed unsteadily, putting her feet out to stop herself from falling. Her hair hung over her face. She wore skinny jeans in a dark blue color, a tube top, and rainbow-colored tennis shoes with reflector patches. She had no jacket and hugged herself in the cold.

"Which one is this?"

"Says her name is Ratana. But she wasn't there. Someone took her out before it happened."

"That's where you picked her up from?"

"A hotel. We had to untie her. Took forever."

"And...?"

"We left the guy there. That seemed easiest."

"He—"

"Once he gets untied himself, I doubt he'll talk." The three of them chuckled. "We took plenty of photos and found his workplace."

"She knows the others?" Kirino stared at her.

The tall leader moved his sunglasses to the top of his head and brushed back his hair with an indifferent, affirmative nod.

"And she knows where the studio is?"

"I doubt she remembers. She doesn't know Tokyo."

Kirino said, "You'd be surprised what people remember."

The fat guy pushed the girl toward Kirino. She let herself be pushed and raised her face and blinked at the sky. Her long black hair fell around her shoulders in knots and tangles. She leaned against the car and hugged herself against the cold.

"So, where's the other one?" Kirino asked.

The quiet guy, with the beat-up boxer's face, pulled his cellphone out. "We're tracking her."

"Is the tracking something Kenta set up?"

"Something wrong with that?" He looked confused, turning to the other two for support.

"If it works, it works," Kirino said, observing the girl. "And if it doesn't?"

The three looked at each other, and then back at Kirino.

"We'll talk to Kenta."

Kirino looked at each one of them in turn. "Just a little advice. You guys are young, and you do good work. But listen, you need to use parallel approaches. Same time, same goal, different route. If one doesn't work, the other will." He paused to let that sink in to their thick, young heads. He looked up at the eastern sky, lightening in the dawn.

Kirino nodded at the storage warehouse behind them. They all turned to look. "And is this the space you rented?"

"It has everything you asked for. That's why I said we should meet here."

"What's inside?" Kirino stared at the warehouse, looked up and down the dock, recording the place.

"I thought we'd look it over together. To be sure it's right."

Kirino looked at him. "Where's the key?"

The boxer-faced guy took the key off his keyring and walked over to Kirino.

Kirino put it on his keyring. "And you have a copy, right? We might not arrive at the same time."

"We have a copy, so we'll come back whenever you say. The owners went bankrupt and sold the whole thing, along with whatever they left inside. You want us to clear it out or leave—"

"I don't want it cleared out. There's no time. We'll need it soon as things fall into place. I just want to know what's in there. I don't like surprises."

"It's just packing equipment for breaking down loads and reshipping them. We'll go in tomorrow and send you photos."

Kirino stared at him. "You Japanese are addicted to your cellphones."

The ponytailed leader said, "Well, you're half-Japanese, and you couldn't do business without yours."

Kirino glared at him and looked back at the boat crew. Maybe the insolence was a good sign. The three of them couldn't stay kids forever. "You're going to get in trouble using the phones too much. They're not secure."

They turned when the fat bald guy shouted, "Hey!"

The girl had started running, and he chased after her across the empty expanse of concrete.

Kirino squinted into the distance along the dock and then back at the road. It would be a long run in either direction. The nearest road was around the storehouses, across a large open area, and the nearest dockside activity was the far-off gantry crane. She'd have to

68

scale a fence and run a kilometer, and it didn't seem like she could even walk.

"Did she try that before?" Kirino asked the tall leader.

"Run?" He looked amused. "She didn't have a chance. We kept her pretty busy."

The fat guy caught up with her and she tried to slap and hit him, but he just laughed and held her at arm's distance as he dragged her back. She stumbled on the uneven pavement and he half yanked her up and forward by one arm.

The other guy with the boxer's face stepped over and took the girl's other arm. They carried her to the top of the steps.

Kirino said to the tall leader, "Be sure this place doesn't have any cameras. You need to go over it carefully. You know how to do that?" Then he turned to where they held the girl and continued. "And let Kenta follow you, so we can follow him."

The leader frowned, not understanding, but agreeing.

"He'll have put a tracking device on the car."

The leader looked surprised.

"But don't worry, we can use that."

"Use that?"

Kirino looked at all three of them closely one by one as if they were stupid. "And find the other girl." Kirino reached inside his black jacket and pulled out an envelope. He handed it over and said, "There's a lot more waiting, so be sure to answer your phone."

"Where are you going?"

"I'll be in touch."

"Are you taking her back to Thailand?"

Without answering, Kirino turned and walked to where the other two were holding the girl. He took the girl's arm and walked her down the steps to the boat.

Chapter 14

Sukanya woke up with a start. She pulled herself up on one elbow and her head bumped the underside of a desk. She wiggled out from under it and sat up.

Beside the desk, two sets of headphones hung from the wall. Sukanya leaned back and her head hit a guitar hanging on the wall behind her. It clanged a random discord. The rest of the wall was entirely covered with clothing on hangers slung over small hooks, neat but near collapse. Sukanya pulled the blanket onto her lap and tried to wake up.

She was sitting on a black mattress that extended to the walls on three sides. Two pillows and a neat stack of blankets were piled under the desk. Her leather jacket was hung on the opposite wall and her elephant bag beside it. A narrow shelf above the desk was packed with shoe boxes and small plastic storage cases. The desk had two computer monitors, one draped with bras.

She scratched her head as she remembered a plump, scraggly guy helping her out of a taxi. She remembered being carried on someone's back, his maybe, and set down on the cushions, with a blanket on top of her. She remembered the chase in Shibuya and the cushions at the Indian bar. Once in the night, she rolled over and felt Chiho beside her, but fell right back to sleep.

Looking around, she felt wobbly, nauseous, and her eyes hurt, like someone was stabbing them from inside. Her body ached, her legs felt tight, and she had to pee, badly.

By the door, her tennis shoes were in a step-down area next to Chiho's. But there was no sign of her other than that.

She walked on her knees to the light switch and turned it brighter.

Fluorescent light spilled through the small space. She walked on her knees to the door, slipped her shoes on, opened the door, and peered down the silent corridor, the walls black in both directions. She pulled on a bathrobe that hung on the back of the door.

The corridor had a row of doors on each side. A small white sign at the end pointed toward the toilet/shower area. Sukanya looked back and counted the number of doors to remember which door she'd come out of. They all looked the same.

It hurt to sit down on the toilet and there was a lot of blood. It had soaked into the sweatpants she was wearing. Whose were they? Chiho's? She rolled up a fistful of toilet paper and pushed it into the pocket of the bathrobe for later. She would have to find something more soon, but she wanted a shower first.

She took a couple of towels from the stack by the door and hung her dry clothes on a hook outside the door of one of the shower stalls. She fiddled with the shower handles, freezing herself, then burning herself, then getting it balanced.

She shampooed her hair twice, rinsing and rinsing before turning the water cooler and letting it roll over her as if it would never run out. She pumped soap into her hand from the plastic dispenser and scrubbed herself hard to get off the outer layer, everything that wasn't her.

After she dried herself, she put on the T-shirt, wrapped her hair in a towel and slipped the bathrobe back on. She went to the toilet and finally found some sanitary pads. She threw out the toilet paper and put the pad in place. She peeked out of the door down the corridor, worried someone would see her, but the place seemed deserted. She squinted in the low light as she tiptoed back.

She could hear the clicking of keys on computer keyboards inside one or two cubicles, but nothing more. The clicking reminded her of Oskar, always typing on his computer while she snoozed or watched TV. She could never type as fast as he did, but she practiced when he was gone.

She pushed back into the room, feeling more awake. The hangers with layers and layers of shirts and pants and T-shirts cramped the space. She pulled open her bag and got out a shirt and underwear and a pair of pants. She dried her hair with the towel.

Around the computer, the desktop was covered with plastic bags from a convenience store, inside which was a bottle of tea and small buns. Seeing the food, she felt immensely hungry and stuffed the buns in her mouth, washing them down with tea.

After eating, she leaned back on the pillows and folded blankets. The food, as little as it was, made her feel bloated and exhausted again. The only thing she wanted was to curl up and give in to sleep, but sleep would bring back the images of Celeste's body and those of the dead men, the Tokyo streets, the guys that chased her, and the feeling of how lost she felt.

The door opened. Sukanya sat up.

"How are you?" Chiho asked, toeing off her shoes and climbing onto the mat. "You slept a long time!"

Sukanya sat up. "Thank you everything."

"You found the food?"

Sukanya touched her stomach. Sukanya took a couple of big breaths and tried to smile. Her entire body felt swollen.

"You found the shower." Chiho pulled a small table from under the computer desk and folded it out on short legs. Chiho dropped down a big bottle of water and a convenience store bag. She took out two cartons of yogurt, two sandwiches, and two bananas for them both. Sukanya took hers with a bow. She was still hungry.

"You should drink some water," Chiho told her. "The air in here dries you out." She was dressed in khaki pants and a dark blue blouse. Her hair was pulled behind her, and she was wearing only two earrings, one on each side, with several holes empty. She pulled off her pants and blouse and hung them carefully on hangers as Sukanya ate and watched her.

Chiho slipped on a pair of sweatpants and a T-shirt with "The Slits" and a photo of the band members.

"What is shirt?"

"It's a punk band. All girls." Chiho flopped down and took one of the small cartons of yogurt for herself.

"And this one?" She pointed at the shirt she'd woken up in.

"The Clash. All men. But good."

"Where you go?" Sukanya asked.

"Work. I took a vacation for the next few days."

Sukanya said, "I feel better after sleep. I guess drug is gone. I sleep deeply."

Chiho frowned. "What drug?"

"They give me."

"Who gave you?" Chiho asked, startled.

Sukanya finished her sandwich and put the wrappers into the plastic bag. "I must go. You nice. Thank you. But I go."

"Go? Where will you go?"

Sukanya looked at the hangers along the wall, filled with clothes. "Do you have your passport?"

Sukanya shook her head no, looking down. "That's where I go first."

"You're from Thailand?"

"Yes, but new passport is America."

"Where is it?"

"They take."

"Who?"

Sukanya thought how to answer. "Another girl, Ratana, my friend, has."

"Where is she?"

Sukanya shook her head. She didn't know.

"Is that your computer in your bag?"

"Not mine."

"You stole it?"

"Not stole, borrow." Sukanya looked down, breathing deeply, remembering.

"You have a lot of money. Did you borrow that, too?"

"I earn that. Not borrow."

They sat quietly for a while.

"What is this place?" Sukanya asked. "You living here?"

"It's an internet cafe. The cheapest place to live in Tokyo. I've been here a few months."

Sukanya thought about that, looking around the small cubicle room.

Chiho said, "You can stay here until you get your passport back."

Sukanya nodded.

"You're going to need my help."

Sukanya wrapped her arms around her legs and put her chin on her knees. "My passport maybe is where we working."

"What about your old passport?"

"They took."

"Who?"

73

"We come here to work. Few weeks. Then, new passport, America, is promise."

"Where did you work?"

Sukanya looked down. "Big place, how you call that, ware..."

"A warehouse? You worked in a warehouse? What was the name, do you remember?" Chiho took out her cellphone to look.

"Something. I don't notice. I..."

"Would it be on the computer?"

"I can't open. Only as guest it open."

"Daisuke can help."

"Who is Daisuke?"

"The guy who runs this internet manga cafe. He's a computer whiz."

"He carry me? I remember."

"Yes, that was him."

Chiho got up and went out. Sukanya heard her padding down the hallway. When she returned, an oversized Japanese guy stuck his head in the door. She remembered the shaggy hair around his plump face from when he carried her in.

"This is Daisuke," Chiho said.

Daisuke's smile lit up his face. His long hair, baggy eyes, pale skin, and Metallica T-shirt fit his role as manager of a net cafe, but the smile came from someplace deeper.

"You open this?" Sukanya handed him the computer. "And this?" She handed him the iPad.

Chiho said, "He went to Tokyo University."

"He go university but working here?"

Daisuke blushed. "Just for now," he said in English.

"He's speaking English, too?" Sukanya asked Chiho.

"He lived overseas when he was young," Chiho said.

Sukanya handed the laptop and cellphone to Daisuke. "But no look, OK? I am looking. Not you. OK?"

"What's on there?" Chiho asked.

"He is not looking, OK?" Sukanya said to Chiho, getting up on her knees. "Many things on there." Sukanya wasn't sure what, but the way the men crowded around the laptop, the way they handled the iPad, made it clear it was very important.

"OK. OK," Chiho said. "But listen, with some ID, we can just go to the Thai embassy—"

"I am not going there," Sukanya said.

"I'll go with you," Chiho said, standing up.

"I need to find other girl, Ratana. That girl have passport."

"Where is she? Do you know—?"

"Maybe she leave things in warehouse. We go back and look." Sukanya raised herself up on her knees and started to stand up, but she felt dizzy and sat back down.

"I have a friend who can get you an ID," Chiho said.

Daisuke looked at Chiho and they switched to Japanese. Sukanya listened while they talked for a long time, arguing sometimes, agreeing sometimes, she could tell.

At the end, Chiho said, "We'll ask my old friend. Is that OK?"

"More easy to go back and look first."

"Let's do both," Chiho said. "Daisuke will get this open."

"Not everything opens," Daisuke said, cradling the computer and iPad in his arms.

Chapter 15

Hiroshi hurried in to his office and Akiko started talking before he even hung up his coat. "How was the embassy and the nonprofit place?"

"Educational."

"That's good, right?"

"Maybe. We've got two hours to get this report in order."

"I pulled the information on cryptocurrency transactions." Akiko nodded from her desk toward Hiroshi's computer. "Up at the top of the shared files there."

Hiroshi clicked open the file and started reading.

Akiko continued, "I called Interpol about passport forgeries and trafficking convictions. The tax office will send tax returns for Jack and Jill Studios tomorrow. I've got a list of companies affiliated with Jack and Jill and a list of video distributors."

Hiroshi stared at his screen. "There were four hundred thousand money laundering cases last year?"

"Yes, but cryptocurrency crimes were identified as a separate category last year for the first time. That narrows it to seven thousand."

"That's not so narrow. I see that you cross-referenced those with traffickers. Forty cases last year, no convictions. Amazing." Hiroshi shook his head.

"Most of them fled the country."

"Easy to do if you can access your money from anywhere."

"As for underage girls filmed in Japan, that's in another folder. You see it?"

"I see it, but it'll take forever to get the girls to talk, if we can even find them again. Plus, this girl was not Japanese." Hiroshi hummed.

"Cryptocurrency exchanges seem to be the weak link. If the chief bounces this to the ministries, and we worry them about Suzuki leaking out, they can get the exchanges to cooperate. I think that's the way to tackle this."

"Peer-to-peer exchange, high-speed networks, blockchains, it's all a bit confusing."

"It's clear enough to get past the chief in today's meeting."

"You think he'll do something?" Akiko stopped and looked at Hiroshi. "The chief is pretty old school. Does he even know what cryptocurrency is?"

"He has contacts in the ministries," Hiroshi said. "If we can get into the cryptocurrency exchanges, we'll find who it was right away. How much time do you need to print five copies?"

"Five?" Akiko said. "The chief called to say there'd be fifteen at the meeting."

"Fifteen? Who's coming?"

"He didn't say, but he did say to keep the report short."

Hiroshi frowned as he got to work editing, re-ordering, and formatting the information they had, which wasn't much.

* * *

Akiko helped carry the fifteen copies of the 120-page report to the main building. Twenty-two places were laid out, so Akiko hurried off to make more copies as Hiroshi set the report around the rectangular layout of tables in the bland, indifferent meeting room.

Sakaguchi and Takamatsu arrived with stony faces and sat down, Sakaguchi near the chief, Takamatsu at the back next to Hiroshi. The chief came in with vice-chief Saito, followed by more detectives who dropped into their seats sullenly. The chief and Saito stood at the front of the room.

When only five seats remained empty, in walked five men in identical navy blue suits, with one young man following. The chief and Saito bowed to them, and they nodded back. Everyone in the room stood up and bowed. The young man set down voice recorders on the front tables, turned them on, and stood back against the wall.

Akiko arrived with the copies and set them out as the chief made small talk with a distinguished-looking man, the oldest of the five.

The chief turned to the room. "The Ministry of Finance is here today to learn how much progress we've made."

So that was it, Hiroshi thought. This would be one of those meetings where he was supposed to just listen, maybe answer a question as vaguely as possible. That's why Takamatsu had already sealed his lips.

The bureaucrats sat down in order of hierarchy. The oldest official spoke first. "We're from the Ministry of Finance, but we'll be meeting with the Ministry of Foreign Affairs and the Cabinet secretaries later today. We already spoke with the Ministry of Justice. We're very concerned about resolving the case with Takeo Suzuki for both professional and personal reasons. He was a personal friend of many who still work in the ministries."

The chief and Saito both bowed to him. That seemed to be all Saito did these days, follow the chief around and bow to higher-ups.

The chief looked down the row of detectives and turned to Sakaguchi.

Sakaguchi set his huge arms on the table and leaned forward, making the table appear to shrink. "We're where we normally are in an investigation of this type—making steady progress. We are looking into the production company and owner of the warehouse. We also will get into the finances to see where the money goes."

It was the longest speech Hiroshi had ever heard Sakaguchi make, but the bureaucrats frowned at its concision. The bureaucratic contingent blinked their eyes and the young man stepped forward to check the voice recorders.

The chief looked impatient as he asked questions down the line of detectives.

When it should have been Takamatsu's turn, the chief skipped him and said, "Hiroshi, I suppose you have something at least?"

Hiroshi wondered if he should turn to let Takamatsu speak first, since he probably did have something important to say, but Takamatsu leaned back in his chair with a disgusted snort and folded his arms in resignation.

Hiroshi made eye contact with the older man from Finance, whose name he still did not know, and said in his most elevated, polite Japanese, "In the report in front of you, there are several important issues that have a great bearing on this case."

The ministry representative, the chief and Saito started flipping through the pages and frowning. Everyone else pretended to look at a couple of pages.

Hiroshi said, "Our primary aim is to go after the cryptocurrency exchanges, which is how the trafficking industry moves its profits." As he started his summary of the report, one of the bureaucrats leaned to another and whispered something out of range of the voice recorders.

Hiroshi continued. "We need some way into the cryptocurrency exchanges—"

"Hiroshi, can you make this brief?" the chief interjected.

"Yes, of course. But I've barely started."

"You're not going over the entire hundred and twenty pages, are you?" the chief asked, setting the report down.

"No, but I do want to be sure that the ministry officials here today understand that promoting cryptocurrency helps illegal industries like drugs, trafficking and stolen vehicles, as well as borderline businesses like pornography that are known to exploit minors."

The chief cast an awkward glance at the officials. "I think everyone in the Ministry of Finance is aware of all this. Tell us what you've found so far."

Hiroshi started again. "On page twenty-five, you can see that we have identified part of the way the industry, including Jack and Jill Studios, work. They control the money flow carefully. At certain points, though, they can't avoid sending and receiving payments for products and services, which is run through I2P and Tor networks. That's detailed on page forty-two. This system—"

"Hiroshi. Get to the point." The chief turned to the officials. "Hiroshi is our resident accountant, returned from the States, where he learned to overexplain."

Hiroshi looked at Sakaguchi, but he was staring blankly at the corner of the room, his eyelids a patient dash. The other detectives stared at other parts of the room.

Hiroshi cleared his throat. "I'm sure that the Ministry of Finance is well aware of these issues, so let me get to the point. The porn industry and the even more vicious trafficking industry—and it is an industry—run on cryptocurrency. If we can get in there, we can not only solve this case but contain the rest of the criminal networks. If you turn to page—"

"If this is all in your *extensive* report here, perhaps we can move on?" The chief turned to the officials and asked them if they had questions. They didn't.

The chief asked if the ministry officials had any information to pass on, and with that, one of the blue-suited officials opened his folder and spoke for the next forty-five minutes. Hiroshi hardly listened to the pronouncements on policy measures against trafficking and crimes related to the porn industry and cryptocurrency.

At the end of his briefing, the official shut his folder and looked around the table at the detectives, who sat up at the promise of the end of the meeting. He didn't ask for questions.

The chief stood up, with Saito following. Everyone else filed out of the room as quickly as they could, leaving the ministry officials talking with the chief and Saito.

* * *

Halfway back to his office in the underground corridor from the main building to the annex, Hiroshi felt Takamatsu's hand on his shoulder.

Takamatsu chuckled. "I had a case once where the final report ran to eighty pages. I think that's still the record, even after computerization, but now your hundred-and-twenty page report *in the middle of* an investigation will stand as a record for the ages."

Hiroshi ignored him and kept walking.

Takamatsu said, "I've found exactly nothing on the director's videos so far. It seemed like a lead. Now, it seems like nothing. But that's how it goes."

Hiroshi kept walking.

Takamatsu said, "What you need to do is go to the currency offices. You can't do everything from your computer."

"You can do more sometimes."

Takamatsu scoffed. "You will tell yourself anything to save legwork."

Hiroshi turned to Takamatsu. "You told me about a couple of big busts of porn distributors you worked on before."

"Almost killed my sex drive."

"And you caught them how?"

"Through bank information." Takamatsu nodded. "I get your point, but I was out pushing buttons on both of those cases, not pecking a keyboard in my office."

They turned into Hiroshi's office.

Akiko said, "How did the report go? Were they interested?"

Takamatsu laughed. "Wrong question."

"Oops." Akiko looked back and forth at them.

Hiroshi leaned toward Takamatsu. "So, imagine there's no bank. Only a trail of numbers."

"OK, OK," Takamatsu said. "I get it. We need to get in there. The chief will OK it or better yet, we'll work around him. At least we can scratch the director off the list. Anyone into him would just keep milking him."

"The girls are innocent, too," Akiko said.

"They're innocent, but their commodity value expires quickly," Takamatsu said. "We need to get out there, not write reports. We need to get into the real world where crimes occur."

"I was just there." Hiroshi stared at his computer screen.

Takamatsu made a face at Akiko. "No, you weren't. That was a meeting. It wasn't real. It was just words."

Chapter 16

Hiroshi didn't make it to the *dojo* until the final round of practice. Everyone was in full sweat, leaping at each other with practice swords, the hall reverberating with whacks and shouts and the squeak of bare feet finding footing. Unlike the meeting with the Ministry of Finance, you could hear and see the hits here.

Hiroshi found a spot at the edge of the auditorium and took off his work clothes down to his underclothes, pulled on the thick, indigo-blue *keigoki* top and *hakama* bottom, and tied everything in place. The sensei waved him over.

Hiroshi bowed to the sensei and to his new opponent. Hiroshi remembered him as someone whose small size belied the force and speed of his blows. Hiroshi's power came from being taller, but the best *kendoka* drew on inner force more than size.

Hiroshi stopped thinking when the first whack landed on his shoulder. He and his partner worked through warm-up *kata* strikes and a set of *kirikaeshi* moves, then got right into the elegant, violent flow. The movement of his opponent made him self-conscious. He was smoother, stronger, and faster than Hiroshi.

His own strikes kept landing out of place and thoughts of work floated up—the ghost outlines of the bodies, the women as objects for profit, the money hidden from view.

A sharp whack on his shoulder brought him back. Did he need new shoulder pads? They felt thin.

Hiroshi stepped back to breathe and reset. His opponent waited ready until Hiroshi let the pain go and planted his feet on the wood floor. They reset and struck again, and again, until his mind stilled and focused and he hit where he intended. He focused on breathing, as the back and forth intensified with each leap and lull, each turn, pause and drive, until it sank down into his being.

And then practice was over.

Hiroshi searched for Ayana as everyone peeled off their helmets. She was on the opposite side of the circle as the sensei spoke to the group. He called out the names of the *kendoka* who would represent their *dojo* at the tournament. Ayana's name was called, as he knew it would be, but his was not, as he knew it would not be.

He looked at her listening to sensei's speech and felt a flush of desire for her sweaty hair and flushed face. He pictured her body hidden deep inside the thick cotton and armor and tried to pay attention to what sensei was saying.

When he finished, everyone turned facing discreetly toward the wall, no one looking at the others as they changed back to casual clothes, women on one side and men on the other. Hiroshi folded his practice uniform and stowed it in the rolling *bogu* bags.

Everyone drifted toward the door. He hoped Ayana had not made plans to go with the other women tonight. He wanted to be with her, take her to one of their favorite *izakaya* on the way home.

He walked out ahead of her and waited on the sidewalk, bowing as people left, until she came out. Maybe her excitement over the tournament would keep her mind off his faults. Her friends thankfully drifted away.

When he finally got next to her, Hiroshi said, "What about Kimura's?"

"Just what I was thinking," Ayana answered.

"Shower first?"

"Eat first."

"Drink first."

They walked the two hills that separated their neighborhood from the kendo *dojo*. Kagurazaka was darker than most areas of Tokyo, illumined by light filtering out from boutique shops and small restaurants. Large signs and bright lights weren't prohibited in the neighborhood, they just weren't anything anyone wanted.

Ayana took his elbow. "I didn't even notice you arrive to practice."

"You were too busy."

Hiroshi pulled his gear bag to the side for a woman pushing a stroller with a dog in it. "I'm proud you're going to be in the tournament."

"You could be going, too, if you practiced more seriously."

"I get by on my height. That's not enough."

"Height doesn't help or hurt either way."

They climbed the last slope to Kagurazaka's main street. It was more brightly lit than the side streets, and busier with people from the neighborhood, running errands, buying groceries, picking up dry cleaning. Other people came to savor Kagurazaka's cobblestone steps and tiered lanes, a rarity in the as-new-and-tall-as-possible aesthetic that drove the rest of Tokyo.

They pulled their bags down a lane lined with potted bamboo in rock-filled planters. The lane had only three doors, one of which was Kimura's.

"*Irrasshaimase!*" Kimura boomed out from his spot behind the grill. He was a tall man with a scarf tied over his head and a short Japanese chef coat tied across his broad body. He pointed them past the long counter in front of the U-shaped kitchen toward the smaller booths in the back.

Around the upper wall, a narrow shelf held a sweeping line of *tengu* masks, ink brush paintings, ceramic sake bottles, dried shafts of rice, and aprons from the *sake* breweries Kimura visited all across Japan.

A waitress came over with *oshibori* steaming hot towels and a small dish of green vegetables with a gleaming slice of white fish. They wiped their faces with the hot towels. When their beer mugs came, Hiroshi held his up and toasted Ayana on her kendo tournament. "The Budokan! *Omedeto! Kanpai!*"

"I'll never win," she said, slugging down a big gulp of beer.

"Being in it is what matters." Hiroshi finished half his mug in one go, the cold beer sloshing down his gullet.

Ayana smiled and looked down at the handwritten list of specials. When she looked up, Hiroshi waved his hand for her to order whatever she wanted and took another slug of beer, almost to the bottom.

The waitress made a mental note of the dishes Ayana ordered and Hiroshi ordered sake, whatever the *master* recommended. He missed drinking with Sakaguchi and Takamatsu, but being with Ayana was better. It was not work.

"Is it going well, the case?"

"No, it isn't."

"That's what your body has been telling me."

84

"This beer seems to help. The sake will, too."

"Drink it away, OK." Ayana looked back at the menu.

"No, it's just that...I don't—"

"You think my work is stress-free?"

"No. I know the archives can be demanding. But you're suited to it. And trained for it." Hiroshi leaned back, trying to quiet himself. He looked around. "Books and documents are what lasts. I work with what doesn't last—stolen funds, dead bodies."

Hiroshi leaned back when the waitress brought two small sake glasses set in a square, lacquer *masu* box. She turned the large sake bottle over once, her finger on the plastic top before she flipped it upright. She poured the sake out and it flowed over the glass lip down the sides and up to the brim of the box, stopping just when the surface of the sake held quivering in place, exactly at the brim. She did the same for Hiroshi.

"Surface tension," Hiroshi said in English.

"What?"

"Holds the sake in place." He leaned down to eye the liquid surface arching delicately up from the rim.

"You really must have had a bad day at work."

Hiroshi jiggled the *masu* box slightly, but the surface held and didn't spill.

"Do you prefer looking at it or drinking it?" Ayana asked, taking the final gulp of her beer.

He bent over to take a sip from the glass and then plucked it up. "Both."

Ayana bent to sip, then put her glass up to clink a toast.

Hiroshi said, "Same with you. I like both looking at you *and* I like drinking you up both."

Ayana faked a frown and set her sake glass into the overflow.

"You should take a sip from the *masu* first, or pour a little out into the glass."

"I know how to drink sake."

"I know you know, but you shouldn't spill."

"I won't." She took another sip without spilling and set her glass down. "I'm just used to regularity. In the archives, the books are in order. I get off work the same time every day. And I'm in a good mood when I leave."

"That's the problem. I never leave." Hiroshi looked down at his glass. "As an accountant, I wade through what should be in order, but isn't. That I can handle. It's the homicides."

"I'd just like to know you won't get called away at odd hours forever."

"I moved what overseas calls I could to the daytime and pushed the others to email."

"I meant called away to dangerous situations. I can't stand imagining where you're going. I can't sleep. I worry."

Hiroshi sighed. The sake was starting to soak in and take hold. "Takamatsu and Sakaguchi are used to it, but I never will be."

"Why don't you consider—"

"Quitting? I consider it every day."

"Then why don't you—"

"I don't know why. Obligation. Stubbornness. There's things that have to be, I don't know, righted."

"Righted?"

"Witnessed. Recorded. Reset."

"But can't someone else do that? I thought when we started living together..."

"...in your apartment."

Ayana leaned back. "We can move if you want."

"I love that place. Don't get angry."

"I'm not." Ayana looked down. "I'm sorry. My first marriage really screwed me up."

"My relationships did that, too."

"We never even talked about moving in together."

"I thought that was the best part." Hiroshi looked at her until tears came to Ayana's eyes and she looked away.

Snuffling, Ayana said, "That's what throws me off. It's been so good. I keep thinking the bad part will arrive."

"There's no bad part coming. Just more good."

The waitress brought over a dark-blue plate filled with golden tempura, *kabocha* squash, bell pepper, lotus root, and *shiso* leaves—two of each—arranged in a jumble intended to make them easy to pluck out with chopsticks. A finger squeeze of grated daikon and a small spoon of salt waited on the side. The waitress came back with bowls of light-brown sauce.

86

They both reached for the *kabocha* at the same time, their chopsticks on the same piece. Hiroshi laughed and let her take it, and Ayana put the other one on his plate. He dipped his in salt and Ayana dipped hers in the dipping sauce.

Hiroshi put down his chopsticks. "I'll quit if you want me to."

"The money is always connected, you said, so I guess they need you."

"The money is what—" Hiroshi's cellphone buzzed.

They both groaned and set their chopsticks down.

Chapter 17

Sukanya took the narrow stairwell sideways with one hand on Chiho and one on the handrail. The stairs were as steep as a ladder and each step made her wince inside. The black walls held a slapdash collage of concert flyers and band stickers. Heavy rock music blew up the stairway, fast and angry. A wooden sign with "The Lost Melody," the name of the club, hung on the wall.

The bouncer on the bottom landing, in a worn black leather jacket with pyramid studs, was a door in himself. He put out a hand to stop Chiho, but she spoke to him in a loud voice.

The bouncer looked at the people coming down the stairs and he poked a finger at Sukanya, who instinctively backed off. "How old?" he asked in English.

"What are you talking about?" Chiho stepped close enough to his pyramid studs to bite one off. They stared at each other until the bouncer turned his attention to the cashbox on the tall stool beside him and they slipped into the club.

Chiho shouted, "Do not get separated from me, OK?"

Guitar overdrive and screamed vocals electrified a small sea of dancers in front of the stage. Strobes and swirling lights multiplied the motion of their long hair, loose clothes, and antic dancing. It was the loudest music Sukanya had ever heard.

Sukanya followed Chiho through the crowd past a long bar with genderless bartenders in black clothes and black eyeliner. Sukanya took in the parade of club-goers without a word. Their T-shirts, with underground bands and ironic lyrics, swirled past them.

Sukanya followed Chiho to a hallway that led past a calmer back room where young people posed in ripped jeans and tight tops, red raccoon circles around their eyes, their arms draped over each other.

To Sukanya, they all looked like Instagram posts.

A girl leapt up off the couch and came running over to Chiho. Sukanya stepped back, afraid for a moment, but Chiho hugged the girl and held her as they talked in excited tones. They brushed each other's hair, talking and chuckling, their arms lingering on each other, until Chiho pulled away.

Chiho explained, "We were in a band together."

"Is nice, old friends," Sukanya said.

Chiho took Sukanya's arm and led her to the end of the hall. She shoved open the fire door and took a flight of concrete steps down to a dark hall past changing rooms and equipment storage. At the end of the hallway, Chiho stopped.

"This is Yotaro's office," Chiho whispered, and slowly pushed open the door.

Sukanya didn't know what she was expecting, but the room held two massive aquariums that rose to the ceiling. Bright-colored tropical fish swam gently, calmly through miniature pagodas, science fiction skyscrapers, craggy coral shapes, and unreal flora. Here and there, plastic figurines jigged around on the upward stream of bubbles.

Sukanya thought of when Oskar took her scuba-diving. Krabi, in southern Thailand, was a place so different from Bangkok it felt like another country. At the end of their diving tour, she begged Oskar to stay another day, to let them snorkel back out again, the only thing she'd ever asked him, and he let her. He was too tired to go diving again, so he stayed on the boat drinking beer with the pilot, who was about his age. A young guide, even younger than her, swam alongside her pointing out fish and coral. She'd loved the feeling of being just another swimming creature in the warm, salty water.

The other walls held shelves packed floor to ceiling with DVDs and CDs. T-shirts spilled out of boxes and a large flatscreen TV showed the band on stage, muted. Surveillance camera monitors showed the interiors of all the rooms. Behind a large desk with two large computer monitors, a tall leather chair sat empty.

On the way out the front door, the bouncer spoke to Chiho. She stopped on the first step without turning around and nodded OK before pulling Sukanya upstairs.

At the top, Chiho took Sukanya's arm and said, "Did you ever have *okonomiyaki?*"

Sukanya shook her head, no. "But we come back? I need ID for passport and..."

"All we can do is wait for Yotaro to come back. So, let's eat something."

"Also, I need, um, for monthly." Sukanya pointed at her stomach.

Chiho headed them into a big, bright orange-colored drugstore at the end of a small pedestrian lane. Sukanya followed Chiho down long aisles divided anatomically into sections for eyes, ears, feet, face, hair, armpits, and facial hair.

At the women's section, Sukanya looked back and forth with big eyes. "All is for that?"

"Japanese women." Chiho shook her head and starting looking. "Is it heavy?"

"Yes, very. And hurts."

Chiho explained the choices of tampons and pads, and then read the backs of the bottles of pain relievers, finally choosing two. Chiho tried to pay but Sukanya demanded to use the money she kept in the pocket of the leather coat.

Outside, the Shimokitazawa streets curved and criss-crossed past galleries, boutiques, coffee shops, and clubs in a vibrant tangle. Even at night, clothes racks jutted into the narrow streets, and vintage clothes—no two alike—were displayed with nonchalant appeal.

They walked around the corner to a wood-front restaurant with a single yellow light and a simple, handwritten menu. Chiho rolled the door open and they stepped onto a rough concrete floor. The interior was divided by wooden slats into small booths. The old woman who ran the place waved them toward a back booth with oil-dappled *zabuton* cushions on either side of a flat grill rimmed with wood.

Sukanya went to the toilet with the pads. When she squatted down, it hurt worse than the day before. She took out the pad she'd been using. It was covered in blood, much more than she'd ever had before. It made her want to scream, but she felt relieved to have better pads, lots of them, and the medicine. She washed her hands and went back out and eased herself down on the doubled *zabuton*.

"Is it bad? Take these." Chiho tapped out several pills, read the instructions, and said, "Better double the dose."

Sukanya swallowed the pills dry.

The old woman who ran the restaurant waddled over with two large silver cups. Inside was thick batter filled with shrimp, scallops, egg, shallots, cabbage, and bean sprouts. The other cup had slices of pork and bacon swimming in batter. She turned on the flat grill from below and said, "*Go-yukkuri.*"

Chiho swirled the small cotton brush and painted the grill top in oil. It smoked and spread, and she started mixing the ingredients.

"This is my favorite," Chiho said.

Sukanya poured water from a pitcher into small glasses. The grill started to warm up the booth and made her feel sleepy.

Chiho checked the temperature before pouring the contents onto the grill and working them into two round pancakes with the small spatulas. She neatened up the runny edges as the batter hardened and held its shape.

"Can I try?"

Chiho handed her the spatulas. "You like to cook?"

Sukanya flipped the pancakes over to crisp and brown on the other side. "I love cook. Always I try to make my mother's food, what remember. But, usually is eat out. So many good food Bangkok."

The old woman brought over two large mugs with lemons floating in clear, bubbly liquid.

"What is?" Sukanya asked.

"Lemon sour. It's *shochu* with lemon and soda. You'll feel better. *Kanpai!*"

Sukanya drank half in one go.

"Slow down, girl." Chiho finished the same amount. "Or no, go ahead. I'll keep up."

Sukanya listened politely as Chiho explained her personal technique for making *okonomiyaki.* She nodded and kept the pancake plumped and grilling, the spatulas clacking on the grill top.

"Your guitar and the club owner guy, Yotaro, is connect?" Sukanya asked.

"Yotaro was my manager. I was in a band. A really good band. All girls. A huge following. Lots of pervy guys, but—"

"What means 'pervy'?"

"Sexually, um, perverted, interested, too much, in us girls. Our bodies."

"All guys are like that," Sukanya said.

91

"Except Daisuke." Sukanya moved the *okonomiyaki* around to keep it from burning.

Chiho smiled. "Critics and writers liked us. We played all over Japan. Went to America to a festival. But I had this boyfriend. From Switzerland."

"You learn English from him?"

"Yes. Where did you learn?"

Sukanya handed the spatulas back to Chiho. "Many place. Work. I live with man in Bangkok, Oskar. Is from Stuttgart, near Swiss. I learn English him. When he go home, I think come Japan. What about your guy?"

"The other girls in the band didn't trust him. I thought they were just jealous, because he looked like Johnny Depp."

Sukanya sat forward. "Oh, nice. Like young Johnny or little older one?"

"Young with a thinner face. He took over managing us. They were right, though. We kept selling out clubs, but never made a profit."

"He take money?"

Chiho checked underneath the pancakes. "The band was falling apart, so I took some, um, different work, which paid a lot. But my boyfriend, it turned out, took that money, too. The band broke up, so he and I went to India. Thailand first—"

"Where you go?"

"Beaches in the south."

"You like?"

"Very much."

"I went Krabi. Snorkel."

"We went the other side. Ko Phangan. Lots of raves. I wish we'd stayed there. But we went on to India."

"What India like?"

Chiho looked up and reached under the table to turn off the grill. With a brush, she slathered brown sauce over the two pancakes, ribboned mayonnaise in thin rows, and sprinkled a big pinch of dark green seaweed and another pinch of dried bonito flakes on top. Sukanya watched the light-brown bonito flakes dancing and wriggling, and laughed out loud.

Chiho cut the pancakes into neat, narrow triangles with the spatula and handed Sukanya a plate and chopsticks.

"He leave you?" Sukanya asked. "Men all same maybe."

"Goa was cheap living with lots of parties and lots of drugs. We lived on the beach. It was fun at first. He sold our passports for money, said we'd get new ones and sell those, too." Chiho looked at the cut *okonomiyaki.* "One morning, he didn't wake up. He was taking a lot more than I thought."

Sukanya put down her chopsticks.

Chiho picked up her lemon sour in two hands and Sukanya leaned toward her and wrapped both hands around Chiho's with the cold, empty mug inside.

Chapter 18

On the way back to the club, Sukanya looked with admiration and envy at the young people milling around. They seemed happy taking selfies and chatting idly.

Halfway back, Daisuke called. Sukanya listened as Chiho talked to him. When she hung up, Chiho said, "He didn't get the computer open, but he found the name of the studio. Does Jack and Jill Studios sound right?"

Sukanya tried to remember, but she had been in such a hurry to get away. "Yes, maybe. I think. But I ran so fast."

"What were you running from?" Chiho said.

"Everything." Sukanya walked ahead for a block, looking at the busy, lively streets of Shimokitazawa. "He like you."

"Who?"

"Daisuke. Love you maybe." Sukanya smiled.

"Don't be silly." Chiho guided them through the lattice of small streets.

"I must go there. That studio. The other girl, Ratana, leave passport there, and other thing, a wallet, she say, or code something."

"In the studio?"

Sukanya stopped. "She maybe leave in one place I remember now. I go back there."

"What happened in the studio?" Chiho asked.

Sukanya walked several steps ahead without answering, and then they were already at the stairwell to the club.

The bouncer didn't give them a glance this time. There was a line of people down the stairs waiting to get in. He was taking the admission fee and wrapping a re-entry bracelet around their wrists. Chiho and Sukanya stepped around him without paying and entered the club.

The crowd was wilder than before. The band had long hair, no shirts, and tattoos. They jumped and leapt and posed on stage. Sukanya had never heard a band howl and thrash like that.

The hallway and back areas were packed with a lot of girls dressed in short, tight skirts and T-shirts with torn sections showing off colored bras. Their stripped-thin hair was dyed in rich colors. The guys dressed in baggy jeans, long T-shirts, and caps with slogans. Sukanya hung close to Chiho.

The door to the office was closed. Chiho knocked, waited a second, and then knocked again as she opened the door. Inside, Sukanya peered around Chiho to see a bald man with a thick goatee seated behind the desk in a high-backed chair. His face was soft blue from the aquarium with a dash of white from the monitors. He looked at Chiho, switched his glasses and leaned back in his chair.

Chiho took a step toward his desk and pulled Sukanya in after her.

He looked amused, cleared his throat and said, "You brought a friend."

"This is Sukanya."

Chiho turned and said, "Sukanya, this is Yotaro Uramura. An old friend."

"Old friend?"

"I need a favor."

Yotaro's laugh came out quick, harsh, and forced. He was handsome in a traditional Japanese way, with a strong jaw, sharp black eyes, and strong forearms. As he stood up and worked his way around the large desk, his right leg dragged behind and he kept one hand on the desk to balance his heavy-set frame. When he got to the front, he moved his leg with both hands and set it in place in front of him, then leaned back on his desk and folded his arms.

Sukanya stared at his leg and put her hand on Chiho's arm.

Chiho stared, too. "What happened?"

"Loan collectors like to be paid back on time," Yotaro said, pulling on his goatee.

Chiho turned to Sukanya and eased her over to the aquarium, whispering, "I need to talk with him in Japanese, OK?"

Sukanya moved toward the underwater fish world, taken in by the undulating flashes of tropical orange, red, and yellow against the blue and green backdrop. Even the little bands of gray and black on the fins and thin bodies glowed intensely.

Chiho let her go and stepped toward Yotaro, covering her mouth with her hand and glancing at Yotaro's leg.

"I was in traction in the hospital for a couple months, but they'll collect anywhere. Too bad you and your boyfriend weren't here. You could have brought flowers, meals, sympathy."

"I had no idea," Chiho said.

"I know you didn't." Yotaro laughed again. "Well, lesson learned. Be careful who you borrow from. And who you borrow *for*."

"He died. Overdosed in India."

"If he hadn't run off with you and the money, he could have gotten thrown off the balcony with me. Or instead of me. I landed on some bushes, though they aimed me at the parking lot. Lucky, right?"

"Yes, very lucky. I, I'm sorry." She took a step toward Yotaro, but stopped, and reached back for Sukanya.

"The great Japanese answer for everything. Sorry this, sorry that. But I don't see you getting down on your knees, cutting off a little finger, handing me an envelope stuffed with cash. All I hear is words. How sorry is that?"

"I should have called or—"

"Or paid back the loan. You could have got it from his family. They owned a bank, or didn't you know?"

Chiho frowned.

Yotaro laughed again. "You didn't know? Really?" He chuckled and refolded his arms.

"I didn't even know he took the money until we were in India. I just figured you were..."

"OK with it all?" Yotaro nodded, his face wide-eyed and comic, as if telling a joke. "You didn't have to know until then. That's how he was. Your bandmates knew it. I knew it. You pretended not to."

"Did you get it paid off?" Chiho asked.

"Would I be here if I hadn't?" He shifted his foot. It flopped as if unstrung, before he set it and leaned back on the desk. "Club's packed every night. I can't stand most of the music. All that overdrive, distortion, and compressors, it all sounds the same. I liked your band. You and the others, you had the thing." He hobbled over to the CDs lining the shelves, pulled one out and Frisbee'd it to her.

Chiho caught it and looked at the cover. On it, four women with spiked mohawks and bandannas over their faces stared at a wall spray-painted with Banksy-like images of themselves in schoolgirl outfits. Slogans about punk's demise circled around the band's name, Grapple.

Before she could say anything, Yotaro edged around his desk, his loose leg stopping Chiho from talking.

"So, you have a favor to ask me. Maybe you'd like an advance? Because you're going to start a new band? Or go out solo? Or, maybe you want to get back into film? The ones you made still sell well. There've been royalties, of course, but I borrowed on them to pay for my rehabilitation."

"That was his idea, not mine."

"You want to pay your debt. Do another film. Your girlfriend is a beauty. Marketing's easier these days on the internet. You two can do it together. Sell even more."

"That was a one-time thing."

"So was this." Yotaro pointed down at his leg with an elaborate stage gesture, and then burst into a hard, forced laugh that gave Sukanya a chill.

Chiho shook her head. "I need your help."

"To get back into the scene? The Shibuya scene is gone. Real estate developers bought up all the land, tore down the buildings, kicked us out. It's all skyscrapers with chain stores and office space now. The last things Japan needs more of."

"I will talk about that with you later."

"Later? Where did I hear that before...wait...oh, yes, a great phrase from your druggie boyfriend."

Chiho lowered her head. Then she raised it up. "I need an ID. For her." Chiho pointed at Sukanya, who forced a smile on cue.

Yotaro looked at her. Sukanya let him look.

"She needs a passport."

Yotaro laughed. "Well, what about an apartment in Azabu, a monthly stipend, maybe a car? Tinted windows? Shouldn't be too hard with her looks."

Chiho glanced at Sukanya and squirmed. "I have something. Something you can sell."

"Sell?"

"For a lot of money."

"What is it?"

97

"Unedited footage. Lots of it."

"Oh, one of those blackmail things. I do the muscle work and you get the profit. Not interested."

Chiho put her foot down. "You think things were fair before?"

"Things are never fair." Yotaro limped around to his chair. "They're indifferent."

"This is not blackmail. It's product to be sold. It's on a computer."

"What kind of thing?"

"I haven't seen it."

Yotaro looked too tired to laugh again. "You don't know what it is, but you know it will sell? You are something."

Chiho pleaded with her eyes until Yotaro looked away. "It has other stuff on there, too. Important stuff. Information."

Yotaro shrugged and gestured at his monitors.

"I'm sure you can sell it."

"You're sure?" Yotaro laughed.

"She really needs some kind of ID."

"Where's her passport? How did she get into the country?"

"She was promised a new passport."

"She came in with traffickers? They are not to be—"

"Do you know Jack and Jill Studios?"

Yotaro looked surprised and eased himself into his chair. "Unfortunately, I do. I know the guy who rents it out."

"You do?" Chiho looked surprised.

He pointed at his leg. "I can't get around like I used to. So, I have to work with a lot of different kinds of people." Yotaro laughed again, hard and dry.

"If you can't get a passport, at least an ID, so she can get a new passport herself."

"She'll need more than one ID these days." Yotaro shrugged. "Lucky for you the video you made before you and your druggie boyfriend ran off was a huge hit. Without that, I'd never have dug myself out."

"Which video?"

"You know the one."

"I thought you were talking about the band's music video." Chiho looked disgusted.

"You really trusted that guy, didn't you?" Yotaro leaned forward in his chair. "Who do you think was taking all the money? His Japanese

98

was very good, I have to say."

"He didn't mean to."

"He didn't *mean* to?" Yotaro shook his head. "He was a drug addict. More drugs is the only thing he *meant* to do."

Chiho stared at Yotaro, and then she walked out of the office without another word.

Sukanya gave Yotaro a last, insistent plea with her eyes before catching up with Chiho and following through the club and up the stairs.

The pumping beat of hard, angry music from the club became quieter and quieter behind them. In the cold night air outside, Chiho squatted against a wall with her arms around her knees. Sukanya stroked her hair, waiting for her to cry.

She wasn't sure what they'd said, but she could feel the turmoil. Sukanya rubbed Chiho's shoulder and stared into the dark. They'd have to try something else.

Chapter 19

When Hiroshi arrived at the coffee shop in Asagaya, Takamatsu was outside smoking.

"What are you doing out here?" Hiroshi asked.

Takamatsu waved his cigarette, irritated. "They don't have a smoking area. The whole city is becoming intolerant."

"Becoming healthier."

Takamatsu held up his cigarette. "I need this. I've been watching porn videos all afternoon."

"I thought you said to get out of the office?"

"I should have followed my own advice."

"Find anything?"

"I found it's slightly better on fast forward, but not much," said Takamatsu. "I had to stop when it got to latex bondage and plastic wrap. Seems that was a favorite of our director."

"Plastic wrap?"

"They run plastic wrap around and around until they can't move. Then they get after it. Only, with all the plastic, there's not much you can do—or see. It's like watching plastic wiggle around."

Sakaguchi came out of the coffee shop.

"What did you bring me here for?" Hiroshi asked. "I was having dinner—"

"The acting agency told us two of the actors working with the director that day live around the corner from here."

"What do you need me for?"

"Takamatsu said you'd want to come," Sakaguchi said.

"He said *what*?" Hiroshi looked at Takamatsu, and threw his arms wide in exasperation.

Sakaguchi walked off and Takamatsu stubbed out his cigarette and followed without looking at Hiroshi.

The apartment building looked like the kind of building that would become kindling in an earthquake, a dozen two-room apartments divided by particle board. Exhaust fans emptied onto the narrow walkway and each unit's washing machine was lined up outside, attached to faucets. Plastic storage containers were stacked up to the windows and cheap umbrellas hung from the railings.

Sakaguchi said, "It's on the second floor."

Takamatsu moved his friction lock baton to the front pocket of his European jacket. "Those guys work out."

"We're just talking," Sakaguchi said.

"The acting I've seen, I'm not sure they know how to talk," Takamatsu said.

Sakaguchi waved Takamatsu to the far stairs while he took the other side. Hiroshi waited on the ground floor. Takamatsu put his hand on the rail and pulled it back covered in rust. He wiped it off with a handkerchief.

Sakaguchi's weight on the rickety exterior stairway rocked the entire building. Takamatsu waited a few steps from the door. Hiroshi watched below.

Sakaguchi knocked and after a long silence, the chain was pulled back and the latch opened. Takamatsu put a hand on the door to keep it open.

"Yuichi Sato?" Sakaguchi asked.

A handsome, tanned man in his twenties, dressed in tight, clean exercise clothes nodded that he was.

"I'm Detective Sakaguchi and this is Detective Takamatsu." When he flashed his badge, Sato flinched. Takamatsu pulled the door open the rest of the way.

"Can we come in?" Sakaguchi asked.

Sato looked at both detectives and down at Hiroshi, before backing inside. Hiroshi hurried up the stairs and along the narrow walkway. He pulled the door open, took off his shoes, and stepped into the small kitchen. It was just big enough for a table, a two-burner grill, and a chest-high refrigerator. There was hardly room to walk.

In the other back room, exercise shorts, shirts, towels, and headbands hung from plastic racks hooked over the cornice along the wall. The clothes were the only color in the place.

Sato knelt on the worn tatami by a fold-up floor table. Sakaguchi ducked under the wall divider but didn't sit down. Takamatsu stood at the edge of the kitchen, fingering the baton in his jacket pocket. Hiroshi stood by the door.

"We already know you were at Jack and Jill Studios. We need to know what you saw," Sakaguchi said.

Sato plucked his workout shirt from the contours of his buffed body. His shoulders and stomach looked sculpted by hard workouts and his legs were bike-training thick.

Sakaguchi, twice his size, stared at Sato as the circular fluorescent light buzzed overhead.

Sato said, "I came back from a break. I saw blood. I thought it was a new scene. They never tell us anything about what's coming up."

"You mean, you thought it was just part of the film? The bodies?"

"But I could tell it wasn't. I'd never seen anything like that, even in the movies. I took off."

"You left your workout bag?"

"I left everything and ran."

"Before you ran, what did you see?" Sakaguchi asked.

"The director, some guy taking movies, and one of the girls. On the floor."

"Where was the girl?"

"She…" He shook his head. "Around the side of one of the sets."

"And the director?"

Sato looked pale. "His head…"

"And the guy taking movies, who was he?"

"I don't know, but the director knew him, and so did everyone else."

"You'd worked with the director before?"

Sato nodded, yes. "He was a good guy, treated us right, paid better than average."

"You went on a break with Naoki Takamura? He lives here, too, right?"

Yuichi Sato looked surprised. "We share this place. We're saving up."

Takamatsu said, "And where is he?"

"He's working out. He'll be back soon."

"Pretty late to work out," Takamatsu said.

"The gym's open twenty-four hours. Naoki does two-a-days, morning and night."

"So, your roommate, Naoki, came in with you from a break?"

"No, he'd already left. He had another gig. I told him about this when I came home."

"What kind of gig?"

"I don't know."

"Who else was there?" Takamatsu asked.

"Before that, just the assistant."

"Who was she?"

"Yoko, is all I know. She did everything for the director and ran the set."

Hiroshi said, "Did she pay you?"

Sato looked back toward the kitchen. "Yes, she had us sign for it."

"Do you have the receipt?"

Sato dug in a drawer and pulled out a receipt.

Hiroshi took a photo of it and sent it to headquarters to have them run the address for Yoko Kawase, the assistant. "And you got paid in cash or by cryptocurrency?"

"By digital currency, yes. They said that was like an investment. It could be worth more," Sato said.

"Why didn't you call the police?" Sakaguchi asked.

Sato looked at the drying clothes as if looking at something far away. "I was too scared."

"You must have known there were records through the agency and that we'd find you."

"I thought about that later."

"So, you've been waiting for us?" Takamatsu asked.

Sato slumped sideways and leaned on the laminated fold-up table. "I thought of going in, but Naoki said to wait and see." Sato looked up at Sakaguchi. "I didn't see anything until it was over. You have to believe me."

Sakaguchi looked over at Takamatsu. Takamatsu's sideways glance told him he believed Sato's story.

Sato looked up, remembering. "The other girl was there, too. I heard something behind one of the sets."

"What other girl?" Sakaguchi asked.

"The other girl in the film. She was a real beauty. Great figure, long black hair. She was..." Sato looked back out the window.

"She was what?" Sakaguchi asked.

"Tough."

"The girls were under eighteen," Takamatsu said.

Sato looked unsurprised. "We're not paid to know. We're paid to keep going."

"She was a child," Sakaguchi said.

"With the costumes and make-up..."

Sakaguchi took another step toward Sato.

Sato kept looking out the window. "She was experienced, the pretty one."

"The one who hid behind the set?"

"The other two kept at her."

"Other two?" Takamatsu asked.

"That was the day before. Two other actors. I don't know their names, never saw them before."

"And..."

"She had that something, the director said. He kept yelling at us to pull her hair back so the camera could zoom in on her face."

"Where did she go?"

"I don't know. She was hiding. In shock, I guess, like me."

"So, with younger girls, they pay you more?"

"Look, I used to work construction, but I got injured. I took all this on temporarily," Sato explained. "Naoki kept saying we'd make more money."

The front door opened, and all three of them turned to see a handsome young man with brown-dyed hair in jogging clothes. He shouted, "*Tadaima*. I'm home." Then, before toeing off his running shoes, he saw Hiroshi, Sakaguchi, and Takamatsu.

He paused for a second, dropped the plastic bag of groceries, and ran.

Hiroshi just missed grabbing him. He jammed his feet into his shoes and took off after him.

On the landing outside, Naoki pushed a washing machine over and knocked umbrellas off the railing in his path. Hiroshi leapt over everything and raced down the stairs after him.

Hiroshi flew past small two-story buildings with signs and potted plants jutting out, down a narrow side street that ran parallel to the Chuo Line tracks. He came to a T-intersection, but saw nothing in either direction.

Hiroshi backtracked and saw Takamatsu slowing down across the street. Takamatsu pointed toward the next lane over and Hiroshi cut through a small pathway toward the square in front of Asagaya Station.

Hiroshi could see no one running in the wide, open bus and taxi circle, but then he caught a glimpse of Naoki's head at a four-way crossing under the overhead tracks.

Dodging people, Hiroshi zipped under the tracks to a small lane of bars and restaurants. On the other side, in both directions, he could see nothing of Naoki. Maybe he went in one of the places.

Hiroshi stood there deciding which one to try, and Takamatsu, winded, caught up with him.

Hiroshi pushed ahead and opened the door to the first bar. It was a dark, bottle-lined western-style bar, with only the bartender behind the counter. "Anyone come in here?"

The bartender looked confused.

Hiroshi went in and pulled open the toilet door, and the bartender looked even more surprised. Hiroshi held up his badge as he walked out.

Takamatsu was working the other side, where the restaurants had open windows.

Hiroshi pulled open the white door to the plush purple interior of a karaoke snack bar. "Anyone come in here?"

The mama-san smiled and waved a plump hand at Hiroshi to come inside. "Nothing gets going until evening. Want to stay?"

He didn't bother with the badge.

Up ahead, Takamatsu leaned over with his hands on his knees.

Hiroshi caught up with him, looking at the line of bars and restaurants stretching as far as he could see in both directions under the overhead tracks. "You should quit smoking," Hiroshi said to Takamatsu.

Walking in a small circle trying to catch his breath, Takamatsu was breathing too hard to disagree.

Hiroshi's cellphone buzzed. It was Sakaguchi.

"He was too fast," Hiroshi huffed.

Sakaguchi said, "Sato said he's training for the Tokyo Marathon. So, you might as well come on back. Sato's a real talker. He'll tell us what we need for now."

Chapter 20

"You're sure you want to get out here?" the taxi driver asked Chiho. Shuttered warehouses and storage companies lined the streets. Here and there, delivery trucks—empty, it seemed—were parked silently waiting for sunrise to start their deliveries.

Chiho paid without answering.

The driver turned around to look at Sukanya and Chiho. "Do you work near here?"

The driver took the money from her with a frown and started to say something more, but Chiho pushed Sukanya out along the seat and walked her in the opposite direction from the studio. The driver closed the door and drove off.

When the taxi was gone, Chiho stopped. "Are you sure you want to do this?"

"I'm sure," Sukanya said. "Ratana find something like money. I remember she hide and want come back. But she not come back."

"If we get caught..."

"I remember maybe where she put."

Chiho nodded and checked her cellphone. They turned around and headed toward Jack and Jill Studios.

Sukanya tucked in her long hair and pulled the hood over the knit hat they'd picked up, along with gloves, at a convenience store. At Daisuke's instruction by phone, they'd also bought a plastic bottle of tea and small scissors when they switched taxis halfway to the studio, another precaution he advised. As they rode, they finished the tea and cut out a section from the plastic bottle.

They walked by the lot, which was marked off with yellow tape, but kept going past it.

"Is that the place?" Chiho asked when they stopped at the corner.

"Yes." Sukanya started breathing heavily. She didn't want to go in, but if the passport was where she thought it was, she had to. Celeste's body was so crumpled and the sounds were so loud. The blood was everywhere and she felt nauseous. Sukanya stared up at the sky and took a deep breath.

Chiho said, "There's no guard in the parking lot, but that means there might be one inside, and cameras, too." Chiho pulled her hood down and tightened the string of the sweatshirt Sukanya wore under the leather coat.

"Are you ready?" Chiho asked.

"No, but try." Sukanya took Chiho's hand and led her to the narrow passage she'd fled through. She didn't think there would be cameras there. They stopped where it opened into the gravel parking lot.

They ducked under the yellow tape that encircled the warehouse and headed for a small door along its side. Chiho stepped up to examine the door handle. It seemed like the simple type of lock Daisuke had shown her in a video he forwarded to her cellphone. Above the handle, she worked in the cutout section from the plastic tea bottle.

She made sure it was all the way in before pushing down. Nothing happened.

"Watch the front," she told Sukanya as she reset the plastic to try again. After sliding it in at a sharper angle, she pushed down quick and hard with the side of her hand. The plastic nudged the latch bolt and auxiliary latch, before sliding in and springing the door. They pulled back the door and peered into the dark.

The light from Chiho's cellphone glowed enough to let them see. The pale light zigged around as their eyes adjusted. They were in a corridor jammed with lumber, props, costume racks, and backdrops.

Sukanya pulled Chiho toward the front stairs. They walked up the metal grate stairs, treading lightly. Daisuke's warnings about the guards and cameras made them cautious and they peered into the shadows around them. If there was a guard inside, they were ready to follow Daisuke's other advice—run like hell.

At the top of the stairs, Sukanya led Chiho up to the door into the massive space that held the sets, trying to remember how she got out. At the top of the stairs, Sukanya rolled back the door along its track, cringing at its rattle.

It was dark inside the huge space holding the sets. The silence amplified the whisper of their breathing. Their footsteps echoed faintly as they crept forward into the massive hall.

In the dim light, Sukanya could see the chalk marks outlining irregular shapes and the glistening stains on the concrete floor. A slew of triangular plastic markers stood in a cryptic pattern, the numbers barely visible. Throughout the cavernous hall, the three-sided sets made of flimsy walls held darker shadows inside.

Sukanya tried to remember where they had left their things. Ratana might have taken the passports and information with her when they came for her, but that didn't seem likely. She would have hidden them. Did she come back to get them? Did she escape on her own? Maybe the police got her?

The men who brought them from the boat had treated Ratana as their leader, and so had Sukanya and Celeste. She spoke better English than Sukanya and had been to Hawaii for modeling and acting. She knew how things worked.

Sukanya tried to remember where they dressed, but the place was big and there were many sets. She headed for the last set they'd used, a big fluffy bed with calico sheets, lace pillowcases, mirrors and dolls. Chiho kept watch while Sukanya looked around with the cellphone light, pulling open drawers and searching under the bed.

Sukanya walked to the next set, a fake school classroom, Chiho following and keeping watch. Sukanya stepped onto the set and went to a cabinet along the wall below the blackboard. She looked in each door of the cabinet and then opened each of the school desks.

In the next set, a hospital room, Sukanya opened the white cabinet doors one by one. They had left some of their clothes in there, but they had been cleaned out, maybe by the police. Sukanya remembered that Ratana put her bag in one of the cabinets but it was gone. Were the passports in that bag? She had seen the small, colored folded paper Ratana stole, but never the passports.

Sukanya came back to where Chiho waited at the edge of the set and clicked off the cellphone light. Chiho pulled Sukanya's hat down.

Sukanya walked to the next set of fake brick walls around a black-floored room with a wooden stockade, sling chair, bondage bench, and cage. BDSM gear was scattered around. There was no hiding place on that set.

Sukanya kicked the sling chair and then kicked it again.

Chiho hurried over and wrapped her arms around her. "You've got to be quiet."

"Is not here," Sukanya said.

"You're sure the passports were here?"

"Not sure, but must be."

"Maybe the police found them?"

"Ratana clever. Too clever. She hide well. Too well. We were here couple days."

"A couple days?" Chiho blinked and looked at Sukanya.

"The drugs stop sleeping. So, maybe more."

Chiho put her arm around Sukanya's shoulders.

Sukanya said, "Ratana must take with her, passport and everything." Sukanya stood thinking.

Sukanya worked through the sets again, getting more frustrated with each yanked-open drawer, pulled-up cushion, pushed-aside bed.

Chiho followed with the cellphone light, which reflected off the mirrors, leather upholstery, and chrome fixtures.

"Police must come, but Ratana had one small thing easy hide."

"What was it?"

"She said it was like money."

Then, the creaking of the wide front door sounded from the entrance of the studio warehouse. In an instant, heavy footfalls resounded from the metal grate stairs at the other end of the warehouse.

Sukanya pulled Chiho out of the office back to the spiral stairs. They could hear heavy footsteps echoing in the large open space. Sukanya's first step caused the staircase to rattle. Chiho pulled her back. Sukanya stepped to the edge with a hand on the curved rail, and the rattling stopped.

Sukanya got to the bottom and looked down the corridor toward the side door where they'd come in. When Chiho stepped off the staircase, it bounced upward and clanged.

They dashed for the side door, sidestepping props. They heard the same clang from the circular staircase and quick steps descending.

They scrambled outside, and shoved the door shut. Sukanya tugged a metal barrel under the handle and Chiho dragged a cinder block behind that. The wall at the back of the building was too high to climb, so they ran to the front.

A fancy, low-roofed car was parked with its headlights on and another car was angled in blocking the exit. Sukanya headed to the right, along the front of the building, aiming for the same gap they'd snuck in. Sukanya ran as fast as she could, but inside the gap she slowed to make sure Chiho saw the bucket of gravel she'd tripped over before.

When they got to the large street on the other side, they ran as fast as they could down the sidewalk until they could run no more. Chiho pulled Sukanya against the wall and they looked back as they caught their breath. The cars would come around the corner any second.

They ran across the street to a maze of smaller streets winding away from the studio. Chiho wasn't sure where they were, but Sukanya kept them moving forward with each turn. Chiho finally stopped and pulled out her cellphone to check the GPS as Sukanya kept watch. They heard the sound of cars, but in the maze of narrow lanes, it was impossible to know from which direction.

Chiho pointed down one long, narrow street that led to a wide avenue. They ran to the corner and peered carefully in both directions. A taxi was coming. The off-duty light was on, but Chiho stepped into the street waving her hands. The driver slowed, looked at them, and stopped.

Chiho pushed Sukanya inside and thanked the driver. They kept looking behind them so much that the driver noticed. But he only switched the meter on and drove in silence.

After a few blocks, Chiho turned away to look out the side window. She rubbed her face with both hands and kept her hood down over her head.

Sukanya stared out the window, furious she couldn't remember where it was, and terrified that she had remembered, but found nothing there.

Hearing a few snuffles, Sukanya realized Chiho was crying. She scooted over to put her arms around her, pulling back her hood and wiping her tears with her sleeve.

Chiho started crying harder, and in a wet voice, mumbled, "I'm so sorry. I'm so sorry."

Chapter 21

Sugamo picked up Sakaguchi, Takamatsu, and Hiroshi at the circle in front of Asagaya Station and they climbed in the car.

Hiroshi said, "You sure it's OK to leave him? We better send someone to watch him at least."

"Sato's not a runner," Sakaguchi said.

Hiroshi said, "You're leaving him there as bait."

Takamatsu said, "That's not a nice way to say it."

Hiroshi said, "Why don't we talk to the assistant in the morning?"

Takamatsu said, "Some people talk more if you catch them sleeping."

Sakaguchi said, "She's central to this."

Hiroshi leaned back for a snooze. Takamatsu cracked a window to smoke as they shot through the expressways heading west from the center of Tokyo.

* * *

After exiting in Hachioji, Sugamo slowed down amid the grid of apartment blocks, *gyudon* shops, manga cafes, and family restaurants. Sugamo pulled into the brightly lit parking lot of a convenience store across from the apartment where Yoko Kawase, the assistant to the dead director, lived.

The apartment building was ten stories of anonymous living space, a bus ride to the station, walking distance to chain stores. Takamatsu lit a cigarette, and in a few minutes, a couple walked out the front door, and Takamatsu shuffled in, with Sakaguchi and Hiroshi behind.

Takamatsu knocked on her door softly enough for the neighbors not to hear. He repeated the knocks until they heard a sleepy voice ask, "Who is it?"

"We need to talk with you about Jack and Jill Studios. This is the police. I don't want to wake your neighbors."

They heard the chain slipping off the thick metal door and the creak as it was pulled back. Inside, a young woman stood in a pink and white Minnie Mouse sweatshirt and matching sweatpants. She stared at them for a few seconds before turning and plodding to the kitchen along a hall adorned with neatly framed movie posters from films by Kurosawa, Mizoguchi, Ozu, Imamura, and Seijun Suzuki.

The kitchen's appliances, refrigerator, and oversized trash can looked unused, as if she was never home other than to sleep. She leaned on the counter for a moment and then collapsed to the floor.

Takamatsu sighed as Sakaguchi pulled out a chair from the table and Hiroshi picked her up and set her on it.

She bent over with her face staring down at the floor, her arms wrapped tight around herself.

"It's OK," Hiroshi said. He motioned for Takamatsu to get her a glass of water.

Hiroshi put the glass into her hands and helped ease it up for her to take a sip. "Just take a drink of water and relax."

She looked up at him with a sweaty, red face, scared or confused, Hiroshi couldn't tell. She looked like she'd been crying already.

Takamatsu pulled a chair over for Hiroshi and stood by the door. Sakaguchi stood by the refrigerator.

She wiped her face with the sleeve of her Disney sweatshirt and turned the glass in her hands. She nodded, reassuring herself, and pushed her hair back. "I knew you would find me eventually."

"We need your help." Hiroshi leaned forward and spoke in a soft voice.

Hiroshi pulled out his cellphone, balanced it on his knee and pressed record. "Can you start with your name?"

"I'm Yoko Kawase. I was the assistant director to Ryota Noguchi. I saw the scene...I mean...I came back...and I..." She looked up at Hiroshi. "I can't do this."

"Yes, you can."

Yoko breathed in, turning the glass in her hands. "I saw director Noguchi, the fat man and one of the girls. Dead. On the floor."

"One? How many girls were there?"

"Three, but one was taken away earlier in the day."

"And the other one?"

"She'd been the center of attention. I don't know where she went." Yoko started to cry. Sakaguchi handed her some tissues from the kitchen counter. She set the glass down and took the tissues. She wiped her eyes and nose and balled up the tissues.

Takamatsu walked softly out of the kitchen, turning toward the living room and bedroom down the hall.

"Do you know where the girls came from?" Hiroshi asked.

"I just knew that...well, they didn't have work permits."

"You handled the payments for the actors?"

"But not for those girls. They came, worked, and were gone."

"How did you pay the actors?"

"We started to use digital currency, through an exchange."

"What's the name of the exchange?"

"Aracoin. Everyone who rented at Jack and Jill used it."

"So, you paid everything through this exchange? To keep things secret?"

"It was easier than sending it from the ATM at the bank, which is what I did for years."

"You handled all of Noguchi's payments?"

"What there were of them in recent years."

"You worked with him a long time?"

Yoko took a big breath. "About five years. I did everything except editing. I wanted to be a director."

"For this kind of film?" Takamatsu asked.

"No, but I had to start somewhere, Noguchi was the only director who would take me on. I had to get experience," Yoko said. "At first, it was shocking, of course, but I learned about making films, and it paid better than the film company where I started. Or it did at first." Yoko kept her eyes down.

"What happened then?"

"The money started to run out. For a few films, I didn't get any payment at all. He was from a rich family, but I..." She twisted the wet tissues in her hand until they crumbled and dribbled to the floor.

Hiroshi waited.

"And then director Noguchi started to become distant, and the films became rougher."

"You mean, he filmed rougher kinds of sex?"

"Yes. Rape scenes. Humiliation scenes. Younger girls."

"But it was all acting." Hiroshi waited for her to respond.

"Not always. Some of the girls...well, they didn't understand their contracts. Noguchi wanted to capture them surprised."

"Surprised?"

"He started to use girls who really looked like high school girls."

"Were they underage?"

"Some were, I guess. I was the only woman on the set, and the girls trusted me."

"Why didn't you go to the police?"

"I wanted to be a director. Inside the studio, it all seemed..."

"Normal?"

"It wasn't, no. But...I don't know...it was just gradual." Yoko shook her head.

"And then?"

"Then they started to bring in girls from other countries, Thailand, the Philippines, Indonesia." She paused. "When I started, we had stories, sex inside a drama. Not the other way around."

"This was Noguchi's decision?"

"Not completely. Another guy came in to advise."

"Who was that?"

"A guy named Kenta. Kenta Nakamura. He's the one who set us up with Aracoin."

"He's a businessman?"

"He's a money lender who wants to be a businessman."

"Was he there on that day, too?"

"He stopped by the set almost every day."

"Was he the one who brought the drugs?"

Yoko looked surprised. Then she shook her head. "It used to be. But this time, it was a guy with a short, tight ponytail. A couple street guys came with him, one tough, one fat. They'd borrow the girls, too."

"Borrow?"

Yoko looked away.

Hiroshi looked at Sakaguchi. He could hear Takamatsu in the other room.

"What about the older man? You know who he was, right?"

Yoko nodded. "Some bureaucrat. He had a thing for behind-the-scenes photos. Kenta brought him there, but Noguchi just ignored

114

him." Yoko looked away and started crying again. She wiped her face with her sleeve and looked away.

"Did any of the girls complain?"

"Some did, but Kenta used the videos to threaten the girls, saying he would tell their parents, classmates, or teachers about it, post the video online with their real names. I didn't know that until one of the girls told me. He tried to do the same with me."

"With you?"

"Yesterday, Kenta emailed me, threatening me with a video."

"What video?"

Yoko took her cellphone, scrolled down, and handed it to Hiroshi. Sakaguchi leaned forward to look at the small screen of her smartphone video.

Hiroshi leaned over, frowning as he watched.

Sakaguchi cleared his throat.

Hiroshi knew anything could happen during an interrogation, fights, revelations, breakdowns, but this was the first time to be shown a video of a woman masturbating. It took Hiroshi a minute to realize the woman in the video was the woman in front of them—Yoko Kawase.

Hiroshi cleared his throat. "This is you, right?"

Yoko shook her head, yes.

Hiroshi muted the sound.

"Kenta sent me this video telling me to stay quiet or he'd release it and send it everywhere."

"When did you film this?"

"A year ago. I'd seen so many by then, it didn't seem strange. This was my casting video. Keep watching," Yoko said, looking away and plucking at her hair.

Hiroshi looked back at the small screen. In a minute, a young man with an erection came onto the screen. Onscreen, a very made-up and sexily dressed Yoko got down on her knees from the sofa and stared up with big eyes. His face came onto the screen for a grinning selfie.

"That's him," Yoko said. "That's Kenta Nakamura."

Hiroshi said, "We'd like a copy of that."

"Nobody will see it except the police, will they?"

"No. We need it as evidence."

Yoko looked relieved that the worst was over. Hiroshi gave her his email address and Yoko sent a copy of the video then quickly tucked her cellphone back in her pocket.

They sat quietly for a few minutes.

"Was there anyone else there on the sets?"

Yoko thought quietly, and then frowned. "Once or twice a strange man with a long ponytail came. I hated him."

"What did he look like?"

"Tall, thin, pale face with a long ponytail. He dressed in all black. I thought he was an actor at first. For a horror film."

Takamatsu came back from the other room and nodded he was ready to leave.

"Do you have somewhere to go? I mean, someplace safe?" Hiroshi asked.

"I can go back home. To Kobe. Is that far enough?"

"Go pack a bag. We'll give you a ride to Tokyo Station and put you on the Shinkansen. It took a lot of courage from you to say all this."

Yoko stood up and looked at him. "It wasn't courage. It was anger."

Chapter 22

At breakfast at his favorite family restaurant, Kenta read the newspapers, several in Japanese, and a couple of articles in English. Reading newspapers over a big meal was the best start to the day.

In prison, he'd been allowed to read the newspapers, which had opened his eyes to how society really worked. At university, before his arrest, he'd only learned how the world was *supposed to* work, which wasn't very useful.

Kenta lined up his cellphones and tablet beside his plate of eggs, bacon, hash browns, and toast, making sure not to drop crumbs on the devices, but the caffeine from multiple coffees was not taking hold.

His drive with Mina had been interrupted by the pinging of the motion sensor on the cameras at the studio. He had to drop Mina off, after she furiously finished him off, and race to the studio.

Now, at least, he had footage of the girls. Their faces were covered up, but it would make it easier to find them and bring them to Yoshitaka Kirino.

Still, it wasn't the girls in the video footage who killed Suzuki, the director, and the girl. So, who was it? And why? There was no connection between those three that he could think of, other than being in the wrong place at the wrong time.

Yoshitaka Kirino took care of business that way, he suspected, though he was careful never to ask. Girls came and went, people helped him for a while, and then Kenta never saw them around anymore.

He flipped through the calendar in his tablet and made notes on what loans needed collection. He'd have to curtail the small ones until he sorted out the studio mess. Business was a constant triage of what to do and what to let go. His business schedule was getting upended by this mess.

Everything he used to keep track of his finances, of the loans to Shibaura, of the loans to everyone else was on the computer and iPad, all in code and password-protected files, but that wouldn't be enough if Kirino got a hold of it, much less the police. If anything, the police finding it would be better. If Kirino got it, Kenta would be lucky to have a chance to explain.

He turned on the tracking apps, but there was nothing, not even a blink. The car he loaned the three guys was parked somewhere near their office. They probably slept there.

So, he could wait for a ping or he could stir things up. He looked through the list of actors and called their agency. Claiming to be a director, he got their CVs with a photo in an instant. He called the home number and found where one of them would be. He packed up, headed for the register, and paid.

In the parking lot below, he checked his car for dings or finger-prints before hopping in and setting his GPS for a gym near Asagaya Station. It was a thirty-minute drive along Kannana-dori, the oldest ring road in Tokyo.

* * *

The sports fitness club was getting crowded when Kenta arrived. Elderly people in mismatched sportswear streamed in the front door, which Kenta held open for them with a cheery smile. The front desk people were decked out with prim sportswear and trained dialogues about membership.

"I'm thinking of joining," Kenta told the front desk crew.

A girl in a purple workout outfit handed him a form on a clipboard with an enthusiastic wiggle. "Were you recommended by one of our members?" she asked.

"Yes. My friend, Naoki Takamura. Is he here now by the way? I'd like to say hello."

"I can check," she said, clicking on the computer. "He's in the building. We can look for him as I show you around." After he filled in the form, she handed him a visitor's card on a lanyard and a map of the facilities. "Let's start on the first floor," she enthused.

"I've got this map," Kenta said, smiling. "I can poke around on my own."

"There's a few things I can explain," she said, stepping around the counter.

118

"OK, then. Thank you for taking the time," Kenta said. "What's your name?"

"Sayaka." She turned back to him every other step. She had an athlete's body and a springy step, her hair pulled back in a ponytail.

"Have you worked here a long time?"

"Two years. I graduated from the Japan Institute of Sports Science, but I wasn't much on science. I like working with people more."

"I can see that. That's a famous school."

"Do you know it?" Sayaka looked pleased as she held the door open to the machine room.

"Everyone knows it," Kenta assured her.

Sayaka blushed as she stopped in the middle of the room, clipboard in both hands. "There is always a trained coach ready to assist. Free weights are over there."

"Cage machines and free weights. That's my workout!" Kenta started talking enthusiastically as he scanned the room for Naoki Takamura. A few elderly people worked on some of the machines, but no one even in the same age bracket.

Kenta followed Sayaka, who kept outlining workout regimes. "The running machines, bikes, and ellipticals are in the next room. Do you use those, too?"

"Yes, of course." He saw someone who had to be the guy. He was buffed and tanned with long hair, a small nose, and a big angled jaw. His face wasn't going to be on any of the films anyway.

He was working on an incline bench with cables, pulling his body up and down the sliding bench. With all these people around, not to mention Sayaka and the rest of the staff, he couldn't go too far. But Kenta needed to know, and needed to make a point.

"Do you want to see the swimming pool?" Sayaka said, safe in her routine.

Kenta said, "Uh, yes, but you know, that's my friend there on the incline bench. Give me a minute to say hello?"

"Of course," Sayaka said. "Take your time."

Kenta walked over to the bench and leaned over Naoki Takamura, who was on his back. "Aren't you that actor?"

Naoki sat up and wiped his face with a towel. "You must be mistaken."

"No, I'm sure. You're Naoki, right?"

119

He wiped his face again and looked up at Kenta, then started to sit up, but Kenta pushed him back down.

"What are you doing?" He held his arms up. "Do I know you?"

"Yes, you do. From Jack and Jill Studios. We need to talk."

Naoki sat up and wrapped a white towel around his fist.

"Unwrap that. We're just talking."

Naoki swung from where he was seated, but Kenta parried, twisted his wrist, and bent it double until Naoki screamed and dropped to his knees. Kenta pulled Naoki's wrist behind his back until he was bent over the bench with his arm behind him. Kenta reached for one of the weight cables and strung it under Naoki's arm. Naoki winced but couldn't move.

Kenta looked over at Sayaka, who was silent with shock. Beside her, two elderly people had stepped off their machines. He'd better make this quick.

Sayaka ran off to the front desk.

Kenta leaned his knee onto Naoki's backbone, pressing him onto the bench, and whipped off his lanyard and lassoed Naoki's neck, yanking his head back.

Kenta whispered into Naoki's ear. "Did you see everything?"

"See what?"

"You know." He yanked on the lanyard.

Naoki coughed and tried to move his head to ease the pain around his throat. "Yuichi and I left."

"Then why were your clothes still there? And your bag? You saw what happened." Kenta tugged on the lanyard, cutting off Naoki's air.

Naoki coughed.

Kenta eased off.

"We were done...and gone. That bag was from the day before. I don't know whose it was."

"You're lying."

Naoki stretched his free arm down to the floor to push back, but Kenta cranked the lanyard tighter and pressed him harder onto the bench.

"Who was there the day before?"

"I don't know." Naoki coughed and squirmed.

"What time did you leave?"

"I don't remember. We didn't even get paid."

Kenta yanked tight. "Doesn't look like you will."

"What...are you...?"

"I ask the questions. Who was there?"

"When?"

"For the filming."

"Just the girls, three of them..."

"Three?"

"Yes, three. The two of us guys. A director and some girl assistant."

"Now I know you're lying." Kenta yanked the lanyard, then loosened it.

"And some old geezer who kept taking photos. Irritating as hell."

"And who else?"

"No one. That's all."

"No one else left or came in?"

"Someone came to take one of the girls..."

"What did he look like?"

"It was three guys."

"What did they look like?"

"Like three guys."

Kenta let the lanyard go for a second. Was it...? It couldn't have been. Did Yoshitaka Kirino call them? "And where was Kirino?"

"Who?"

"Yoshitaka Kirino? The guy who hired you."

"We were sent by the agency."

Kirino wasn't supposed to be in Tokyo for days. So, who was there when it happened? Someone did the killing. Someone took his stuff. Kenta heard a commotion at the door of the weight room.

"If you talk to anyone about that day, I will do much worse than this. Are you clear?"

Naoki nodded OK.

"Say it."

"I understand."

"Say it again."

"I'm clear. I get it. I don't have anything to tell anyone."

Sayaka came back with three of the male staff, all dressed in the same prim sportswear. They were bulked up, but not fighters, Kenta could see.

The elderly people in sweaty outfits stood by the mirrored wall at the other end of the room.

Kenta straightened his clothes. He hated getting other people's sweat on himself, including most women, except for Mina. He took one of the towels from the machine and wiped his hands and forearms.

On his way out the door, he handed the lanyard and visitor tag to Sayaka.

"This place isn't quite my workout style," he told her, and continued out the front door.

Chapter 23

"Easiest case we've ever had. They're coming to us." Takamatsu told Hiroshi in the hallway outside the interrogation rooms.

The smell of perfume lingered in the hallway. Probably Ayana had not even noticed he had come home, showered, and slipped in bed beside her before Sakaguchi called him and he slipped back out before she woke.

"They came in voluntarily," Sakaguchi said. "Just as I got to sleep in the bunks."

Takamatsu peered into one of the interview rooms. "I better take the porn actress."

Hiroshi raised his hand. "Unless you can follow a spreadsheet, it's better if I talk to her. It's probably her that signed the tax forms."

"She doesn't look like an accountant," Takamatsu mused.

Sakaguchi said, "Their coming in doesn't quite make sense. I thought they'd flee overseas, wait us out."

"Let's make sense of it," Takamatsu said, and walked in to the room where Shibaura was waiting.

Hiroshi watched from the observation room. Through the one-way glass, Shibaura's chiseled features and wide shoulders would have put him in front of the camera as a younger man, but hunched over with the overhead light on his stubbled face, he looked disheveled and creaky.

"Is that the camera up there?" Shibaura asked.

Takamatsu nodded, yes.

"Everything is cinema these days," Shibaura said. He pulled out a cigarette and Takamatsu leaned over to light it for him.

Shibaura said, "So, you're the good cop?"

Takamatsu said, "No, I'm the one who tells the detectives to turn off the video so I can punch you in the face when you piss me off."

Shibaura blew the smoke out of the side of his mouth. "Oh, you're that one."

Sakaguchi said, "You're Jo Shibaura, the owner of Jack and Jill Studios."

Shibaura nodded, yes, and sucked deeply on the cigarette.

"What time were you filming on the day of the murders?"

"I wasn't."

"Who was?"

"I don't know." Shibaura squirmed. "My secretary—"

"Your secretary was there?" Takamatsu asked.

"No, she was with me." Shibaura looked toward the door. "I don't know why you need to put us in separate rooms."

Takamatsu said, "So we can talk more freely. Where was she?"

Shibaura said, "She was with me, and the information was, is, with her."

Sakaguchi said, "Tell us what happened that day."

Shibaura looked for a place to tap his cigarette.

Sakaguchi got an ashtray from the table by the door and set it in front of him.

Shibaura tapped off his ash. "I rent the studio out. But I don't always know how they're going to use it. No one follows contract stipulations anymore."

"So, who did you rent the studio out to? Not to the little girl," Sakaguchi asked. "She died."

"To the director. He died, too."

"You know everything that happened, then?"

"I do now." Shibaura shrugged.

"Who handles the renting?"

Shibaura smoothed his gray hair back. "Haruka takes care of all that."

"She's right next door answering the same questions. The problem here, though, is whether your answers will be the same. I'm inclined to believe hers."

Shibaura nodded. "She's the one who convinced me to come in. If we didn't have the same information, why would we do that?"

Takamatsu stood up.

Shibaura crushed out his cigarette. "Look, you should talk to whoever set up the shoot, Kenta or whoever."

"Kenta. A name, finally." Takamatsu put out his cigarette and leaned forward.

"Kenta Nakamura." Shibaura smoothed his long gray hair. "He contracts the studio all the time. He's there more often than I am."

"Where do we find him?"

"Haruka keeps track of all that."

"Who did he bring in that day?"

Shibaura shook his head, indicating he didn't know, and pulled out another cigarette.

Sakaguchi stood up and leaned on the desk.

Shibaura cleared his throat. "Some people pay cash. And don't sign anything. Haruka handles all that. Haruka from the inside. Kenta from the outside."

Sakaguchi rubbed his face. "Kenta brings in the business and Haruka handles the money?"

"Yes, that's it, basically."

"Basically? What's the non-basic part."

"Kenta makes extra money by bringing in, well, an audience. There's plenty of old guys who like to watch. I really don't know who they are, government officials, retired businessmen, old guys past it."

"Any regulars."

"Why don't you look at the surveillance camera footage?"

Sakaguchi said, "That's the problem. You didn't have any. Any idea where it might have gone?"

"Kenta handled security for the studio."

Takamatsu smiled. "Kenta again? Tell me again what do *you* do around the place?"

Shibaura looked at Takamatsu for a moment.

Sakaguchi said, "The dead girl was underage."

Shibaura shook his head. "We make sure in the contract..."

"Where are those contracts?"

"Haruka knows where they are. If they did that, it's on them."

"If it's in your studio, it's on you."

Shibaura pushed back his hair. "There was another man, tall, silent. He handled the girls."

"Foreign girls?"

"Japanese, too."

"Where did the foreign girls come from?"

125

"Thailand, Philippines, Cambodia, I don't know."

"We found quite a few passports from different countries. And different currencies."

"You opened my safe?" Shibaura looked stricken.

"You're really *not* a detail man," Takamatsu agreed.

"Look, I told you everything," Shibaura said, rubbing his neck.

"We're going to keep you here a few days," Takamatsu said. "Maybe not the full twenty-three, but long enough."

Shibaura got up halfway out of his chair. "What? Why? I've got—"

"You're safer here," Sakaguchi said.

* * *

Hiroshi left the observation room and walked to the other interview room. Inside, Haruka's perfume filled the room with the smell of cherry blossoms and a hint of fresh-cut wood. The perfume was so strong he felt it in his eyes. He set a can of hot green tea in front of Haruka and tried not to stare.

Hiroshi said, "You look like more of an espresso drinker, but my machine is in the annex building, a long walk from here."

"I'll make do with this." Haruka popped open the tea can with a quick pull and took a sip, looking up at him with big eyes.

"I'm Detective Hiroshi Shimizu, and if you can answer a few questions, it will help us a lot."

"That's what we came in here for." Haruka was "voluptuous," a word he remembered from long ago in Boston. She was not just a full female figure in a country of slender shapes, she had big eyes, round cheeks, and full lips. Hiroshi tried to keep his eyes on her eyes, otherwise his inner camera would keep zooming in.

Takamatsu had looked her up and found she was awarded Bests in several categories of the Japanese Adult Broadcasting Awards. Those videos were now classified as "vintage." Sitting across from her in the interrogation room, there was nothing vintage about her layered haircut, white knit top, and indigo-blue jacket.

"Coming in here was your idea or his?" Hiroshi asked.

"Mine. I told him detectives appreciate honesty."

"From what I've seen in the records, you do all the accounting."

"Even the tax office doesn't believe it. Must be the way I dress."

"But it's all your work?"

"I was an accountant before I was an actress. I passed the exam, again, and now I'm an accountant, again."

"What is your relationship with Shibaura?"

"Let's say...colleague," Haruka said.

Hiroshi waited.

Haruka smiled. "We *were* something more. For a few years. But all he wants to do these days is sit around a pool in Hawaii, or LA. I mean, that's *really* all he wants to do."

"So, you handle the contracts and run the business?"

"He hasn't set up a film project as director, or producer, for years. Now, we just rent out the place."

"You rent directly?"

Haruka tapped the tea can with a long, square-cut, peach-colored fingernail. "There are contractors and subcontractors. We can't know exactly who's going to be there. If we had known there was anything illegal..."

"You would have charged them more."

Haruka leaned back and frowned at him.

"Maybe you should sue them for a contract violation?"

Haruka looked away. "We came in here to help. We were shocked, too. Shibaura more than me. We won't be able to rent the space for a long time, and even after that, some people will never rent the place again. There's no insurance to cover stupid."

"Whose stupidity was it?"

Haruka looked into Hiroshi's eyes and said, "You should find the trafficker. He's the one who's caused all this trouble, and Kenta, who thinks he's a big entrepreneur."

Sakaguchi came into the room.

Hiroshi said, "This is Detective Sakaguchi."

"He's a big one," Haruka said, tapping the tea can with her fingernails.

Sakaguchi sniffed the air. Hiroshi had started to get used to her too-strong perfume. "Shibaura said you handled all the contracts, so you must have known there were films with underage girls."

Haruka leaned back in her chair. "In this business, people will say anything, sign anything. The contracts are a layer on the outside that makes it all seem legit."

"But it's not."

"It's not all the time, no. What is? Detectives follow the rules all the time?"

"Who wasn't following the rules of this contract?"

Haruka laughed. "You haven't been around traffickers. They don't have rules."

"What do you mean?"

"Shibaura doesn't much care as long as the money's in hand." Haruka sighed. "All I have is that little piece of paper. Shibaura should have stuck with the people he and I know. I told him to run the business through close connections, but he wanted more."

"More what?"

"More money, time, empty days, prescriptions, another apartment he doesn't use."

"And he got all that?"

Haruka smiled. "Yes, he did. But once he got it, he started drifting."

"Drifting?"

"Mentally. He can't focus. That makes him want more money, strangely. The people who pay more are the ones who don't follow rules."

"Shibaura doesn't listen to you?"

"Men *look* at me. They don't *listen* to me," Haruka said. "Look, porn is an industry that can be run any number of ways. I told him a million times. I wrote business plans for him. I found better directors and production teams..."

Hiroshi leaned over the table. "So, accountant to accountant, Shibaura used the studio as his personal bank."

"How would that make it different from most private businesses?" Haruka raised her eyebrows.

Hiroshi cocked his head, thinking. "It doesn't quite make sense to risk trafficked girls, no matter what it pays."

"Go next door and explain that to Shibaura," Haruka said, snorting.

Sakaguchi said, "If you can let us know who arranged all this, you'll be a lot safer."

Haruka nodded, thinking, deciding, finally saying, "Kenta Nakamura is his name. Shibaura believes anything that kid says."

"Where do we find him?" Hiroshi asked.

Haruka shrugged. "And there was another one, tall, pale, dresses in black."

"He's the trafficker?"

"I don't know. I never dealt with him."

"You don't want to know."

Haruka twisted in her seat. "That's right. I don't. But now I know anyway."

Chapter 24

Sukanya and Chiho had walked—and run—for hours from the film studio. Before dawn arrived, they ducked into a 24-hour family restaurant with an all-you-can-drink service, and fell asleep on the booths.

When they woke, they refilled their drinks, used the toilet, and went out to find a taxi. The sun was out and felt good after being up most of the night.

Sukanya stared out the window of the taxi, dulled by the lack of sleep and the need to accept that the passport and papers Ratana had were not there, and were never going to be.

Chiho said, "We should get something for breakfast, and for Daisuke. He stays holed up lost on the internet for days. But he loves to eat. There's a bakery on the way."

"Bakery?"

"Donuts and pastry."

"Bangkok has donuts place. What is pastry?"

"Sweet bread, like donuts or dessert."

"Dessert for breakfast. In Tokyo is common thing?"

"Not common, but we need energy."

"And sleep."

"They have bread, too."

"I need passport."

"Yotaro will help," Chiho said. "We'll go back. I shouldn't have walked out."

Sukanya smiled and nodded OK at the only choice she had left.

Chiho told the driver how to get to the bakery on a backstreet off Omotesando Avenue.

Young businesspeople in clingy casual suits strode the wide sidewalks, leaning into the day. Workers from the fashion industry and IT companies waited at takeaway coffee windows.

Sukanya paid for the taxi. "Is close to where those guys—"

"The police took those guys away. They'll hold them for three weeks, the limit. We don't need to worry," Chiho said, and took Sukanya by the arm into the neat, white store.

Sukanya stopped at the entrance, stunned by the aroma of yeast, butter, and baked sugar, the mixed zing of chocolate, *matcha*, and cinnamon filling the air. A row of baskets brimming with breads, buns, and soft-shaped loaves stretched to the back of the shop.

The belly-high shelves in the center of the room were topped with deep-fried donuts, fresh-baked croissants, and multicolored bagels. Under a glass counter in front of the large ovens, rows of sliced cakes, nut-topped cookies, and macaroons waited in neat silver trays.

Sukanya couldn't move. She stood motionless, wallowing in the excess of the place.

Chiho, her tray already half loaded, circled back to rescue Sukanya, handing her a tray and tongs.

Sukanya walked the perimeter in a daze.

"Let's get for Daisuke first." Sukanya pointed with her tongs. "What he like?"

"I'll get Daisuke's favorites, small bagels and chocolate donuts. Just get for yourself, OK? Enough for a couple days."

Sukanya started to load her tray, thinking how sick she would get if she ate all she wanted, but thinking, too, that would be OK. She took fruit-covered cakes, *matcha* cookies, and melon bread. She put in a small loaf of dark rye bread, the kind Oskar liked, that she'd come to like herself. She'd take a photo and send it to him.

Sukanya caught up with Chiho near the register. They surveyed their trays with girlish delight and Chiho said, "Let's eat a couple here before we go back."

"OK. I am paying for all," Sukanya said.

Counter girls in starched white uniforms and neat brown caps wrapped their choices one by one, leaving on top the ones they'd eat in the store. They sat down at small marble-topped tables in the back and Chiho got them iced lattes.

Sukanya took a huge bite of melon bread.

131

Chiho sipped her latte and checked her cellphone messages. "Good news. Yotaro will come through with an ID for you."

"Really? That easy? I'm..." Sukanya choked back a flood of feelings and held her melon bread in front of her.

Chiho smiled. "You know, you look like my little sister."

Sukanya said, "I feel like. Where she now? Back in hometown?"

Chiho stopped chewing and stared at the wall mirror. "Yes, in my hometown," she said and bent down to check her cellphone.

"What Daisuke say?"

"No word from him. He usually texts me every hour."

"I think you and he..."

"It's not what you're thinking." Chiho put her phone away and refocused on food.

"He text you every hour."

Chiho looked back at her cellphone.

Sukanya pulled a chocolate donut out from her paper bag and held it up in the wrapping paper for a moment, before chomping into the sugary relief.

Outside the bakery, they walked to the boulevard with their bags. Chiho waved a taxi down, and when they got in, the taxi driver sniffed the aroma filling his cab and hummed.

"You want?" Sukanya said, reaching for one to hand him.

The driver said something that made Chiho laugh, and Chiho waved Sukanya's hand back. Chiho chatted with him as Sukanya watched the city roll by.

After the sugary breakfast, she felt sleepy. It would be wonderful to take a shower and sink into the mattress of the net cafe for a long, deep sleep.

Outside the internet cafe, Sukanya paid the driver. She was excited as they rode the elevator up to their floor, peeking inside the bags. She wanted to see Daisuke's face when he saw everything they bought.

When they got off the elevator, the absence of the usual click of keyboards and the leaking babble of video games and movies felt odd.

Chiho called out to Daisuke through the curtain behind the counter where he stayed.

She set down her bag, twisted around the counter, and pulled back the curtain.

Sukanya set down her bag and stepped over.

They looked down on a tangle on the floor. Daisuke's thick curly hair was wet with blood. One arm was sprawled at an odd angle.

Chiho cried out and dropped to her knees, whimpering and waving her hands.

Sukanya dropped to her knees beside his head and put her ear to his mouth to make sure he was breathing. He was—in short, jagged gasps. She stood up and looked down the aisle. All the doors were shut.

She ran down to the shower area and yanked an armful of clean towels from the shelves. She soaked a couple in cold water and hurried back, listening for any sound from any of the dozen doors.

Chiho was cradling Daisuke's head in her lap and pushing the blood-soaked hair from his head. Sukanya stooped down with a wet towel for Chiho to wipe his face. She pulled a blanket from the roll-out bed where Daisuke slept and placed it over him.

"Is for shock," Sukanya explained. "Too cold, he worse. Keep little warm."

Chiho cleaned his face.

Sukanya looked around the previously tidy office. His two computer screens were spiderwebs of cracks. Wires ripped from connections lay in tangles. DVDs, books, papers, and clothes spilled every which way.

Chiho pressed one towel to the side of his head where it was dripping blood. His earring had been ripped out. His body seemed to sag with the effort of each breath and he had pissed his pants.

Sukanya helped wipe the blood off his arm and shivered at the sight of it how contorted it was.

"Let's call ambulance, go hospital," Sukanya said, rinsing the towels. "Hurry." Sukanya stepped back to the counter to see if anyone was there. She saw and heard no one, and dropped back to her knees by Daisuke.

His eyes fluttered open and Chiho pulled his face toward hers.

"Daisuke?" Chiho said, staring into his glazed eyes. "What—"

His breathing came under control and he swallowed. Sukanya got up and ran to get water from the vending machine.

"Daisuke, tell me what happened," Chiho demanded.

"I cracked them," he whispered. "A geek friend helped."

"The computer, the iPad?" Chiho asked.

"There was a GPS tracer," Daisuke said. "It's the only way."

"A GPS what?"

"Three guys came, after I opened them." He resettled himself and his face flooded with pain.

Chiho shivered and held him.

Sukanya's face froze and she backed several steps down the darkened corridor. "They not at police?"

"They must have let them go," Chiho said.

"They..." His eyes fluttered shut.

"Daisuke, we have to get you to a hospital."

He shook his head. "No," he groaned. He tried to raise himself up.

"They came here because of the computer?"

Daisuke nodded again, yes.

"Did they take it?"

Daisuke shook his head yes.

"And the iPad?"

Daisuke shook his head, no.

"Where's the iPad?"

Daisuke motioned toward the storage area for the blankets and pillows. "I hid it under the blankets." He coughed and swallowed.

Sukanya got a chair to reach up to get the iPad from a high shelf.

"Do *not* turn it on," Daisuke said, his voice cracking.

Chiho said, "The iPad will be enough. Put it in your bag."

Sukanya took the iPad and slipped it into her elephant bag.

"We have to call the police," Chiho said.

"No."

"We're calling an ambulance."

"No. Go pack your bags. Both of you. Just necessities," Daisuke said.

"Where's all the customers?" Chiho said, helping him to sit up.

"I don't know. They must have fled," Daisuke said, pushing himself up. "Go. Hurry."

They stared at him.

"Now," he tried to yell, but his voice cracked and he coughed.

Sukanya and Chiho went to get their things. Chiho said nothing as she tucked whatever she could grab into a backpack and a big shopping bag.

Sukanya could fit almost everything of hers into her bag.

They shut the door to the small room and locked it, peering down the silent, empty hallway before hurrying back to Daisuke.

134

He sat up and checked that his wallet and cellphone were in his jeans. "Fold that towel and tie it around my neck and under my arm."

Chiho stared at him, too overcome to listen.

Sukanya set down her bag, folded the towel, tied it around his neck and made sure it was snug. Looking down the aisle at each of the doors, Sukanya wondered if they'd be waiting outside again.

Chiho said, "We have to go."

Sukanya stood there for a moment and then came over to help get Daisuke up. She positioned herself under Daisuke's arm and Chiho grabbed his belt, being careful not to touch his broken arm. They yanked him up, joint by joint. Once he got balanced, he could walk.

Sukanya threw the blanket over his shoulders and picked up her bag before slipping Daisuke's arm over her shoulders again. Chiho balanced him from the other side, both hands on his belt, her bag over her elbow.

They hobbled to the elevator. Chiho leaned forward and pressed the call button.

The doors opened to an empty elevator.

They walked Daisuke on and turned around. As the doors closed, Sukanya stared back at the two tall bags filled with sugary delights they'd dropped on the floor and would have to leave behind.

Sukanya watched the floor numbers on the display drop from seven to one.

Chapter 25

Kenta pulled his Nissan GT-R Nismo up to the gate of his apartment's parking lot and buzzed himself in. The security gate rolled up, and he waited for it to roll down, watching in the rearview mirror.

He pulled slowly through the parking lot. None of the other cars were as expensive as his. He had been thinking of upgrading again, since business was good—or had been good. It would take time and effort to restore the previous serenity of mind and stability of income.

There wasn't much to do but wait for the trackers to ping. Maybe those three punks would help with that, but he was losing faith in them. And threatening people, even done right, wouldn't make up for getting his computer and iPad back.

He parked in his spot and set the new cameras, alarm and immobilizer. He stared at the cinderblock wall in front of his car. He'd have to tell the building manager to get it painted. Maybe Mina could come over. No, he needed sleep.

He got out and locked the door—and jumped.

Standing in the shadow of the wide pillar beside his car was Yoshitaka Kirino.

"Let's go for a drive," Kirino said, his voice like tires on gravel. "See what this baby can do." He ran his fingers over the finish and tapped the warm hood.

"How—" Kenta looked at Kirino's blanched face, the skin pulled taut by diet or design, drugs maybe, his hair in a sleek ponytail. He was rake-thin and hard, as if strung together by tendons. It was hard to look at him for long.

"Parking lot security is never what you think." Yoshitaka Kirino slid the small black door opener over the hood of the car.

Kenta snatched it, angry it might scratch the finish.

Kirino said, "You don't have one of these? Take that one. I have another. Helps us export cars to Russia, China, and wherever else."

"Now watch this." Kirino slid his hand into his pocket and Kenta's door lock popped open. "See what I mean? Technology is amazing, isn't it? Why I love traveling through Asia. Souvenirs like these." He slid the second universal opener across the hood. "For you."

Kenta snatched it with even greater irritation.

They got in and Kenta put the two openers in the center console, undid the alarms and immobilizer, hit the gate opener—his own—and pulled out onto the street.

"Let's get up on the highway. I want to see how fast this goes," Kirino said.

Kenta headed the car toward the closest entrance ramp a few blocks away and rolled up on the Shuto Expressway heading west. Kenta punched the accelerator. From both sides of the two lanes, sound-dampening walls turned the car noise into a steady hum. Overhead, another level of the expressway zoomed in the other direction.

"Come on. Let's see what this does," Kirino said, smoothing his ponytail with one hand, then the other. "I had a request for one of these from a client in Tajikistan. I want to let him know how it feels before he decides. I don't think he'd want this dark orange color, though."

"It's a rare color. Most cars in Tokyo are white or black." Kenta had gotten this one as part of a loan payback. "The guy I got this one from probably has others."

"What's his name?"

"I'll set it up for you."

"Where's he keep them?"

"I'll arrange it." Kenta sped up a bit more, dodging through traffic.

"OK, set it up for me." Kirino looked straight ahead. Each passing blink of car and street light caught his thin face and sallow neck before disappearing in the black sheath of his clothes.

Kenta asked, "Is that why you broke into my parking lot? To ask me that?"

"No, I wanted to ask you in person if everything's on track."

"All I need is to lock into the GPS on the computer with the tracking app. Problem solved."

"Don't worry about that now."

Kenta looked over at him, unsure what he meant. "That's all I've been worrying about." His whole operation was on the iPad. The video files, both surveillance and porn, were all on the computer.

Kirino looked straight ahead. "There was another girl there. She got away, right?"

Kenta nodded, yes.

"What did she see? Did she take anything?"

Kenta pulled around a couple of big trucks. "Just the computer as far as I know." He didn't want to mention his iPad, but he was starting to feel that Kirino somehow knew about that, too.

"And the actors? Where did they get to? There was no assistant?"

Kenta didn't want to tell him about the assistant. She was too scared to do anything. The one actor he'd talked to in the gym hadn't see anything, he was sure. Kirino didn't need to know everything. "I thought you hired the actors."

Yoshitaka Kirino smiled. "That's true. I did. So, I'll sort that out." He patted the dashboard. "Is this the fastest this car will go?"

Kenta zipped past a line of cars, cutting into the right lane and then back into the left. He went out for a highway drive to clear his mind every day, but this drive was muddling him.

"The police seem to be taking this one seriously," Kirino said.

"How do you know?"

Kirino said, "A friend with friends in the police."

"Friends. Well, the police aren't going to figure out what happened."

"The police figure out a lot of things you wouldn't expect."

"Look, the girl will be tracked down. Problem solved."

"You just said that." Kirino spoke in a louder voice. "Are you going to show me what this can do or not? Go around."

Kenta said, "The expressway doesn't widen into more lanes for another twenty minutes. There's no shoulder here." He sped up anyway.

"A young man like you should be able to handle two lanes and no shoulder."

"Every kilometer there's an overhead camera." Kenta realized he forgot to turn on his laser jammer. He pressed a black button on his steering wheel to click it on.

"Speaking of which, did you get the cameras from the studio?"

"They were broken."

"So, nothing was recorded?" Kirino turned toward Kenta.

"I just need to get the computer back to be sure."

"You said that before, too."

"I've got it under control."

"And that ex-ministry bureaucrat? Police get sticky about things like that."

"Not if it's going to embarrass them."

"You have something on him?"

"He liked a lot of things. I can send it on."

"I think he was not helping us as much as he pretended to be."

"What do you mean?" Kenta braked for a delivery van. They were all driven by retired guys these days. He hit the horn, slowed, and pulled up behind the truck until it got out of the way.

"I mean, he helped us with the cryptocurrency exchange, but helped himself, too."

"What?"

Kirino smiled. "Look, in Thailand, you can trust bureaucrats. They get paid and they do what they say they're going to do. But in Japan, they feel they can make their own decisions."

"That's true, but Suzuki helped us with the currency and the visas." Kenta braked hard. Both lanes were blocked by delivery trucks.

"What about Shibaura?" Kirino asked. "How much did he see? He probably saw everything. What if he starts to talk?"

"I doubt he will. As long as he has his medicine. When he gets out, he'll probably take off for Hawaii or California. He has places there."

"I hope he does. And his woman, the porn actress?"

"She's an accountant now. I talked to her already. Shibaura might have seen something, but he didn't tell her."

"What's her name?"

"Haruka."

"Maybe we should keep her on as an accountant after Shibaura is gone. Let her restart the business. We can lose money for a while, but not forever."

Kenta drummed the steering wheel with his thumbs.

"Maybe this is a sign to change things around? Internationalize a bit more." Kirino looked at Kenta. "Cars from Tokyo sell for more overseas. Japanese girls earn more in Saudi than they do here. Thai girls we bring here are solid earners. That's globalization."

"That's multiple revenue streams," Kenta said in English.

"What?"

"That's what they call it in business. 'Diversified' might be the better term. Revenue streams."

Kirino hummed deep in his throat. "Call it what you like, but we need to make sure Jack and Jill Studios keeps performing its accounting services."

"I've got that set up. I told you. Once it gets into the cryptocurrency exchange, there's no tracing it. And no need for clever accounting." Kenta nodded. "It'll be cleaned up."

"You need to clean faster. We're going to need new accounts. The old ones are not working so well."

"What old ones?" Kenta felt confused.

"I was using other cryptocurrency accounts, before we teamed up."

"I didn't know that." Kenta realized he wasn't going *to be* cut out of the loop, he always *had been*.

"But now we need new ones. The old ones have become, well, tainted."

They drove in silence as the traffic opened up, weaving back and forth in the lanes with only a tap on the brakes from time to time to slow down enough to pass.

Kirino said, "I was thinking you might want to take over things in Bangkok."

Kenta looked over at Kirino. His pale face and sunken cheeks lit up under each passing light, then flitted back to shadow. That was the last thing he wanted to do. If he went there, Kirino would really have him under his thumb.

"We need someone like you in Bangkok, a fresh perspective. You've got the currency thing going. And you'll want to get out of town for a while."

"OK," Kenta said. He didn't want to insist again, as he had in the past, that Jack and Jill would become his baby.

"If you want to keep working with me, you need to take care of the loose ends."

"There aren't that many."

"All it takes is one. I do my part. You do yours. That's how things work."

Kenta's cellphone buzzed. He ignored it.

"I've got a lot to do and I'm only in Tokyo for a short time. So, if there's something else, it's good to tell me now."

"Nothing else."

"Good. Drop me at Yokohama Station," Kirino said, smoothing his ponytail. "I might tell that guy in Tajikistan he should get a different car. This one isn't that fast."

Kenta kept his eyes straight ahead and pulled off the Tomei Expressway and headed southeast on Route 16 back toward Yokohama. He was getting very, very tired of Yoshitaka Kirino telling him what to do.

Chapter 26

"*Tadaima*," Hiroshi called out as he came in the front door. He took off his shoes at the *genkan*, waiting for Ayana to shout back, "*O-kaeri nasai.*"

Not hearing it, Hiroshi braced himself with a clear explanation about why he had been home for only a couple hours before he got called away again. He'd worked all day, except for a nap while Akiko took a long lunch. He'd pulled out his futon bed in his office and it felt like old times, before he moved in with Ayana, when he'd slept in his office most nights.

He had not found much on the case all day. Every direction ended with nothing. The cryptocurrency accounts disappeared, Jack and Jill's finances seemed aboveboard, and missing foreign women were all long-since cold cases. Even the cases of child pornography didn't trace back to Jack and Jill, but led in other directions. At six, he packed it in and headed home.

He was proud to be home at a reasonable hour and wanted Ayana to notice how hard he was trying to not overwork like a typical *salaryman*. Whether she noticed or not, being home on time for a meal with her felt like a slice of heaven. Knowing the apartment and Ayana were there calmed him in a way he'd never felt before. And excited him, too.

As a librarian at the National Archives, Ayana came home without being jangled, disgusted, or drained by the chronic futility he felt every day. Hiroshi knew his calm was a mask he put on at the front door, while hers ran deep. It was why she was going to the Budokan for the kendo competition and he wasn't. She could do things outside work, while all he did was recover.

"We should get a cat," Ayana said when Hiroshi got to the kitchen. "Didn't you hear me come in?"

"I'm cooking." She went up to kiss him, first on the lips and then on the side of his neck.

His parents had led separate lives together in the same home. He couldn't remember ever seeing them touch. He only remembered his father touching him for the first time at his mother's funeral, a heavy hand on his shoulder at the crematorium. After that, setting aside sports, it wasn't until Ayana, making love on the beach in Kamakura after a college kendo competition, that he remembered any loving touch at all. Now, he had it all the time.

Hiroshi said, "What about a dog?"

Ayana hummed her approval. "A dog? They have bigger tongues." She licked him with the flat of her tongue and watched his reaction, her face bubbling with energy.

Hiroshi said, "Whatever pet you want, you shall have."

"We could start making cute pet videos."

Hiroshi groaned, thinking of the videos on the case.

Ayana sashayed back to the kitchen area. Hiroshi watched the roll of her hips and took a deep breath, planning his initial move after dinner. Maybe just carry her into the bedroom. The couch would be fine, too.

"What brought on this pet urge?" Hiroshi set down the wine he'd picked up from the nearby deli and washed his hands.

"Did you sleep? I had a dream you were beside me."

"It wasn't just a dream. I came home and got a couple hours beside you before I was called away again."

"Was there another—"

"Just back to the station. But that was after running through Asagaya and driving out to Hachioji."

"Sounds like a strange dream for you."

"It was. And frustrating. What are you making?"

"Cheesecake."

"We're having cheesecake for dinner?"

"And a little something else."

Hiroshi wondered how she could do that and kendo both. "I've got to get a shower. What else are you cooking?"

"A little French dish."

"French? We're surrounded by French bistros in Kagurazaka and—"

"Every time I walk by one, it makes me want to cook. Why not put your feet up after the shower."

"I worry I won't be able to get back up again."

Hiroshi showered and dropped onto the bed. When he woke and stumbled out to the kitchen, the whole place smelled like sausage, chicken, and herbs. Ayana was drinking red wine and held up her glass. "Wine?"

"How long did I sleep?"

"As long as it takes to make dinner."

Hiroshi poured himself a glass and wiggled the bottle. "More wine for you?"

"Trying to cut back for the kendo competition." Ayana swirled her glass and took a tiny sip.

"Do you think master swordsmen stayed sober before battle?"

"They stayed sober even when they drank. I just get drunk." Ayana leaned over to open the oven and a whoosh of baked heat gushed out followed by a meaty, deep-herb aroma that filled the room.

Hiroshi sipped his wine and watched Ayana. Every time she cooked, she seemed to have the right bowls, tools, and cutlery, the right cookbook, technique, and timing. It was all a mystery. He had never cooked anything, and none of his previous girlfriends had either. Until he moved in with Ayana, he'd assumed eating out was normal. His office had more kitchenware than his old apartment.

"Voila!" Ayana shouted, pulling off the top. "Cassoulet. The simplest, and yet most challenging, dish in the world."

"Jesus!" Hiroshi shouted, in English. "That's amazing? How did you...? What is in...? This looks fantastic."

"I took a cooking class when my ex and I went to Paris. While he was going to meetings and screwing other women. As it turns out, I got the better end of the deal."

"No, I did," Hiroshi said, wrapping his arms around her from behind and staring into the rich mixture of meats, beans, tomato, and herbs. Hiroshi let her go, put on some music, and set out the plates and cutlery. For the cassoulet baking dish, he got the cast-iron trivet, one of the few things, along with a paulownia cutting board, and jazz music, that he contributed to the kitchen.

The Kagurazaka apartment was part of the settlement of Ayana's divorce. Hiroshi gave up looking for traces of her former husband a couple weeks after moving in. Ayana and her husband had bought it right before he was suddenly posted to America, so they'd never moved in. During the divorce, she decided it was worth keeping, and after returning to Tokyo, she moved in alone after the tenants left. It was all hers, financially and emotionally.

"What made you want to make cassoulet?"

"I saw a photo of it at that French bookstore down the street and remembered how delicious it was."

"It smells amazing," Hiroshi said, bringing the wine bottle and glasses to the table as Ayana carried in the cassoulet dish.

In the morning, they ate looking out the glass doors to the balcony over the tops of the buildings to the horizon. But at night, with the balcony lights off, the glass reflected the interior, mirroring their soft, secret drama, doubling its intensity, and impeding any thought of the outside world. Hiroshi looked at their images in the glass, blurry and indistinct, as if floating underwater. He wrapped his arms around her and rocked her back and forth.

"What is it?" Ayana said, holding him tight.

"Nothing," Hiroshi said.

"Aren't you hungry?"

"I'm ravenous. It's the best meal I've ever smelled."

"Well, we better eat it before you get a phone call," Ayana said.

"Just another minute like this," Hiroshi said, not letting her go.

Ayana nuzzled him, ran her hands up and down his back. Then, suddenly, she tilted her head down and started to weep, quietly at first, then louder.

"What? Why are you crying?"

"I'm just tired."

"Tell me what it is."

In a wet voice against his chest, she said, "I don't want a dog, or a cat. That would be too perfect."

"Too perfect?"

"Then something would happen."

"What would happen? What kind of thinking is that?" Hiroshi tried to see her face, but she buried her face in his chest.

"Something could happen when you go out. Something bad."

"Nothing's going to happen."

"It could."

145

"I'm an accountant. I only go out sometimes. And I get busy at work, so I can't always get home at regular hours."

Ayana tried to stifle her crying, but it came out harder. "I'm jealous. Of everything. Even your work. It's childish. I can't help it. My ex-husband, all he did was work. My father, all he did was work. They both cheated and lied the whole time."

"You don't have to be jealous of anything. My hours are not regular, that's all."

Ayana wept into his shirt, until it was soaked down the front. Ayana dabbed at it and rubbed it with her hands. "Why do people think tears are so beautiful, but nose snot is repulsive?"

"I like your snot. It looks good on my shirt."

Ayana laughed. Hiroshi leaned over to get her a tissue from the table.

As soon as she blew her nose, Hiroshi's cellphone rang from where he'd left it on the counter of the kitchen island.

"See? I told you it was too good to last." Ayana laughed. She battered her fists against his chest and arms and then tried to wipe his shirt with the wet tissues, which fell apart and got all over. "You better get it."

"Whatever it is, I'm going to finish dinner with you first."

Ayana nodded OK and brushed bits of tissue from his shirt before he walked to his cellphone and listened without responding or even nodding.

Chapter 27

Every car was in use or already gone, so Hiroshi had to take a taxi to the scene. The driver kept heading down long, straight roads lined by chain-link fences and stacks of shipping containers. Kudzu, dead for the winter, curled up in long brown swirls over the tall fences and empty roadside tracts.

Hiroshi rolled down his window. The salt smell of the ocean was mixed with oil and metal and seaweed. He leaned over the seat to talk to the driver. "Can you see where that light is coming from?"

"That's over by the restaurant area."

"That looks like police lights to me."

"Maybe," the driver said, and headed away from the industrial area toward a development project of chic offices and spacious restaurants, the new face of Shinagawa. A policeman stood at the corner redirecting traffic. Hiroshi paid the driver and followed the policeman's directions.

He'd been down to the area before to a huge canal-side beer place, but he didn't remember the foot bridge which was lined with gawkers trying to see the crime scene. A young detective was stringing up a higher tarp to block it from the glassed-in patio of a restaurant with a wide view of the water. The only authentic thing in the area *was* the water, which slid into the canals from the bay.

Hiroshi headed to the entrance, showed his badge to the duty cop and ducked inside.

Sakaguchi, whom he always noticed first, stood talking with several younger detectives. He waved Hiroshi toward the body, the last place he wanted to go. Police photographers were taking shots from all angles and a medical examiner kneeled by the body. Hiroshi slipped on white shoe covers and gloves and walked to where Takamatsu was standing on the blocked-off sidewalk smoking a cigarette, away from the water.

"Did you see her?"

"I'll wait until they pull her out of the water," Takamatsu said.

"I thought you always went at it first?" Hiroshi looked at Takamatsu, confused, but he was in no hurry himself. Before Hiroshi left home, he told Ayana that seeing dead bodies didn't bother him, but he was lying.

Hiroshi left Takamatsu on the sidewalk and walked toward the body. The lawn down to the canal bank was more rocks and gravel than grass. The girl's head rested out of the water, her long hair draped over the contours of a smooth rock. The rest of her floated in the canal, gently rocking with the lapping water. Her arms were wrapped in plastic, which wound around her, pinning her arms in place and immobilizing her thighs. Below her knees poked skinny jeans and rainbow-colored tennis shoes.

The crew started working a thick plastic sheet under her, but one of the crew's feet slipped into the canal and he almost fell in. He caught himself and cursed as the others laughed and offered him a hand. He shook his soaked leg and got his feet set on sturdy rocks before grasping a corner of the tarp. They slid the sheet under her from the other side. After setting themselves, the crew shouted, "*sei no*" and tugged her up in unison.

Water spilled back toward the rocks and two of the crew picked up their side to drain the rest of the water from around her body. Water flowed out from inside her along with watery beige vomit. The wet brown skin and black hair on either side of the plastic cocoon gleamed under the lights.

Ayana had asked him what the bodies looked like. Hiroshi couldn't describe them, and didn't want to try. The images were seared into his mind's eye and stayed there like a photo he couldn't delete. The image of this woman's body bound in plastic, her dead eyes staring up at the night sky would be in the album in his mind forever.

At the edge of the white plastic sheet, Hiroshi, Takamatsu, and Sakaguchi put their hands together and bowed their heads in prayer. Everyone stopped their work for a few quiet moments.

When they finished, the crime scene crew slid sharp scissors up the plastic and laid it out on either side of her. They started going through her pockets, pulling out a wallet, a cellphone, and a zippered case with several passports. The crew set these out on a separate plastic sheet and the photographers started recording them, turning them with gloved hands.

Takamatsu came over and said, "There was another woman wrapped in plastic two years ago. She was found in a park where the Arawaka River spills into the bay. It washed up on a golf course they built on reclaimed land. Scared the golfers half to death."

"Plastic wrap?"

"It's a fetish thing. I forgot that until the video the other day."

"Was the case—"

"Never solved. Even though we found the source of the plastic." Takamatsu stooped down next to the medical examiner. "What kind of plastic is it?"

The examiner, a stolid woman in a white coat and a pleasant voice, stared at him. "We'll analyze it later."

"Industrial plastic, right? Like you'd wrap a palette of boxes for delivery."

The examiner nodded, maybe. "The contusions in her stomach look like the main problem at this point. She was beaten pretty badly. She doesn't have travel abrasions, so maybe she fell in close by here. Maybe from a boat. None of her muscles are too stiff yet." The examiner tested the lividity of her arm.

"She couldn't begin to swim with all that plastic around her."

The examiner smiled at Takamatsu. "With this much plastic around her, she couldn't have moved at all."

"More efficient than rope. But you can't get a big sheet of it like this except on one of those industrial wrappers. They have handheld ones, too, portable but not as wide. That old case..." Takamatsu shook his head.

The examiner pulled up one of her hands. "Looks like she fought back. I'll see what we find under her fingernails. The back of her head took a blow."

"Couldn't that be from the rocks?"

"If the waves were strong here, it might be. But this is a canal. I'm still not sure how the currents brought her in."

"You have any idea about those shoes?"

"You look at what's on the bodies. I look inside. Remember?" The

149

examiner smiled at Takamatsu. "Let me get the poor girl into the lab first. She had a brutal last day or two."

"Probably a brutal life." Takamatsu nodded tersely and let it go.

Sakaguchi came over and said, "Want to take a boat out and look?"

"Thanks for the offer, but no, thank you." Takamatsu scoffed. "They might have tossed her from shore."

"Look at this," Hiroshi called out. He was peering at the contents of her wallet. He read out, in English, "Jack shall have Jill/Nought shall go ill."

"What's that mean?" Sakaguchi asked.

"I think it's Shakespeare. But whatever it means, it's on a *meishi* for Jack and Jill Studios." Hiroshi turned the card over. "And here's the address."

"She's got plenty of passports," Sakaguchi said. "Three Thai and three American."

"Same photos in each?" Hiroshi asked.

One of the crime scene crew opened the first passport with tweezers, but the photo was waterlogged. The American passports had no photos at all.

"Maybe they didn't have time to switch the photos? Or maybe that's where she was going?" Takamatsu said. "But three of each, and three girls in the studio adds up pretty neatly."

"So, is this the one who left and didn't return, or was this the one who saw everything and left after?" Hiroshi took a deep breath.

"Won't know until we find the other one," Takamatsu said. "If one of these was her passport, she can't go far. The photos don't look too American, though, do they?"

"Everybody *can* look American," Hiroshi said.

"Is that why everyone wants to go there?" He pulled out his cigarettes, tapped them, and put them away. "So, these girls have been trafficked in, worked, given new passports?"

"Those old-style American passports are not going to work these days," Takamatsu said. "Wherever they got them, they were cheated."

"Old-style?"

"They're a good copy."

"Maybe they're just wet."

"There's no computer code. You should notice things like that, Hiroshi."

The examiner held up a piece of paper with a QR code and a run of thirty-some digits, surrounded by two shiny strips of multicolored tape. Some of the color was water damaged. She held it up with tweezers.

"Well, that's a new one," Takamatsu said. "Where did that come from?"

"It was tucked into her shoes," the examiner said.

Sakaguchi came over, the white shoe covers already torn from his too-big feet. "What is that?"

"It's a paper wallet," Hiroshi said. "For cryptocurrency."

"Speak Japanese," Takamatsu demanded.

"They call them 'cryptocurrency wallets.' It was the old way of storing access to Bitcoin or other online currencies."

Takamatsu and Sakaguchi looked at him and then at the frail, wet piece of paper. The examiner kept turning it back and forth.

"Does it still work?" Takamatsu asked.

"Those wallets are as out of date as the passports, but they probably still work. Maybe our girl took something she shouldn't have," Hiroshi said.

"Or felt it was her payment. How much would that be worth?"

"You have to get online to know."

"Looks like you have another thing to track down tomorrow," Sakaguchi said to Hiroshi.

Takamatsu said, "I'll look into the shoes and the plastic. How many shops selling rainbow-colored shoes can there be?"

"More than selling plastic stretch wrap machines."

"Hard to say," Takamatsu said.

"The money trail might connect things," Hiroshi mused.

"That's what you always say, but connections are made by getting out and finding them," Takamatsu said. "Have they surveyed the whole area around here? I don't like this kind of crime scene."

Sakaguchi nodded. "You ready to get out of here?"

Takamatsu dragged out his cigarettes, lit one, and walked off.

Hiroshi looked back and forth at them.

Sakaguchi said, "He doesn't like being near water."

"What difference does that make?" Hiroshi asked.

Sakaguchi smiled. "He can't swim."

"Who?" Hiroshi asked.

Sakaguchi nodded at Takamatsu.

"Really?" Hiroshi said. "I thought he could do everything."

"Not that." Sakaguchi looked out at the canal. "Why would they dump her here and not out in the middle of the bay? No surveillance cameras out there."

Hiroshi looked over at her small body lying in the middle of the tarp like a child sleeping on a great big bed. "I guess so she would wash up and share her torment."

Sakaguchi nodded for the medical examiner to go ahead and take her away to the autopsy lab, where the body of the girl who died in the studio still lay unclaimed in the morgue. Takamatsu had taken Hiroshi there once, and Hiroshi swore to never get near the place again.

After they lifted her on the gurney and covered her up, the detectives and crime scene crew all put their hands together and bowed their heads in prayer.

As they pushed the gurney over the rocky, unkempt lawn towards the waiting ambulance, her arm fell out to the side from under the cover, dangling free for a moment, before one of the crew hurried over to tuck it back in and roll her away.

Chapter 28

When the elevator doors opened on the bottom floor, Chiho and Sukanya looked long and hard into the hallway. The door started to close before they got the nerve to move. Daisuke waited patiently between them. When it started to shut, Sukanya put her foot out to block the door bumper and keep it open.

The hall was empty.

Sukanya set Daisuke's arm over her shoulders and Chiho grabbed his belt buckle from behind to walk him down the hall one step at a time. At the outside door, they paused, saying nothing and thinking everything.

Chiho said, "I'll get a taxi. You hold him here." She leaned outside and looked both ways down the sidewalk.

When a taxi came, Chiho sprinted across the sidewalk to wave it down. Daisuke said nothing as they helped him in to the back seat, but he hardly had the strength to slide in. Sukanya sat in front and Chiho dropped in the back next to Daisuke.

The driver twisted to look at Daisuke. "Is he—?" Daisuke cut him off by giving him an address in a dry voice.

Sukanya sat in front so Daisuke could stretch out in back. Chiho pulled the blanket over him. Daisuke said nothing more during the entire drive.

Sukanya turned around in her seat to watch behind the taxi, but she was not even sure what she should be looking for. She didn't know one car from another.

It was her fault the three guys had found Daisuke instead of finding her. He had taken her punishment. She had turned Chiho's life upside down. She thought she'd be on a flight to America by now, but she was still on the run, messing up their lives, and getting further into danger.

If only she had an idea where Ratana was, she could get the passport and be on her way. As the taxi rolled through Tokyo's streets, she stopped herself from hoping and focused on deciding. She'd have to leave them, but when?

* * *

The taxi stopped in front of a traditional Japanese style gate of thick wood that hung between two anchoring tree trunk posts. Plaster walls extended in both directions. Daisuke pushed himself up and told the driver to pull up close so he could speak into the intercom. Chiho had to lean out to press the call button for him.

"What this? Temple?" Sukanya whispered.

Chiho shook her head. "It's not a hospital. Maybe a hotel?"

Daisuke spoke into the intercom and the gate opened onto a driveway of flat stones that curved through a tidy garden of small shrubs and sculpted trees. Lights clicked on from inside a Japanese building of arched wood and a tiled room. The taxi pulled to a stop.

Sukanya leaned forward to pay and then hurried around to help Daisuke. Chiho stood by the door as they eased him up and out. Daisuke put his arm around Chiho and hobbled across the stepping stones toward the front door.

Sukanya hurried around to get the bags. She lugged them to a bamboo bench by a stone lantern, and ran over to help Daisuke up the old, wooden steps to the entrance.

The door rattled opened and an elderly woman with a tight bun of thick gray hair hurried out. She wore a white *kappogi* over a dark brown *kimono*. She hurried down the steps and shouted, "*Ara!* Daisuke-*chan!*" Then she called back into the house and bustled down to help Daisuke up the last few steps.

At the top, Sukanya let Chiho and the woman get Daisuke inside and went back for the bags. She set them inside the *genkan* and stared in wonder. The entry space was huge, a room in itself. A waist-high vase filled with tall orange flowers rested to the side, and a cabinet of lattice wood filled one wall. An ornate rock rested in a precisely carved base. Maybe it was a museum.

The old woman tutted as she pulled open the door to a room to the left of the entryway. The room was dark with lacquered wood walls and a tatami floor. She pulled *zabuton* cushions from a stack to tuck underneath Daisuke.

Sukanya stood helplessly as Chiho spoke in a rushed voice to the woman. Sukanya couldn't imagine who she was or what she thought about the mess they brought with them.

Daisuke settled himself on the *zabuton* floor cushions and winced at every movement. Chiho kneeled down to set more cushions around him.

A spry man in an indigo *samue* jacket hurried in. He was so tall he had to stoop under the door. He had long gray hair and a thick, square jaw. He eyed Chiho and Sukanya before kneeling down next to Daisuke, interrogating him with frowns and growls and questions.

Daisuke mumbled replies.

The man stood up and removed a wool throw blanket from a *tansu* drawer to drape over Daisuke. He looked from Daisuke, who had closed his eyes, to Chiho and Sukanya, and back to Daisuke. The man sighed and went back down the hall.

Sukanya watched him carry her gray elephant bag and Chiho's backpack and overstuffed bag down the long wing away from the front door. The bags looked small in his hands as he stooped under the overhead cross beams. At the end of the hallway he slid open a door and disappeared inside.

In a few minutes, the sound of a car brought the old woman shuffling back to the *genkan*. Chiho and Sukanya stood helplessly to the side as a middle-aged man came up the stairs. He was dressed in a black coat, which the old woman took from him along with a maroon scarf and a wool fedora.

Without introduction, he asked the woman questions as he listened to Chiho's answers. When he was done, he grunted and Chiho bowed deeply. Sukanya put her hands together in a *wai*. The man looked at them, hummed deep in his throat, set his bag on the tatami and slid the door shut.

The old woman came back and said, "Please, come this way," in English.

"We should stay here," Chiho said.

She stared at Chiho. "That's the doctor."

Chiho and Sukanya followed the old woman down the hallway, which seemed to stretch all the way around the house. Sliding glass doors looked out on the garden.

At the end of the hallway, the old woman pulled back the door into a large tatami room with a wooden ceiling, floor screens, and a display of purple flowers in a large white vase. Sukanya looked around. You could fit dozens of the net cafe rooms inside this one massive tatami-floored area.

The old woman knelt down at a brown-red lacquer table. She placed a hot water pot next to a small teapot, turned teacups upright and opened the tea caddy. After she made tea, she opened a lacquer box and set out small, green *matcha* cakes and little brown *manju* bean cakes.

"Welcome to our home," the old woman said in halting, scratchy English, and she bowed toward them on the tatami.

Sukanya and Chiho bowed with deep thanks and deeper confusion.

The old woman said, "The bath is out that door, and there are *yukata* there." She pointed to a lacquer tray with soft cotton *yukata*.

"And Daisuke?" Chiho asked.

"The doctor will let us know whether he needs to go to the hospital."

"Excuse me, but where are we?" Chiho spoke in polite *keigo*.

The old woman looked at Chiho with a blank face for a minute until one eyebrow raised and she stood up. "Didn't Daisuke tell you? He'll never grow up. Daisuke's grandmother will explain later. Take a bath. I will call you. *Go-yukkuri.*" She shuffled to the door and bowed as she left.

Sukanya kneeled on the tatami and looked at Chiho, with no idea what to do or say. Chiho looked at her and then around the room. Sukanya took one of the little cakes and popped it in her mouth, thinking of the bags of pastries they had left behind. Chiho ate one of the bean cakes. They sipped their tea in silence.

Finally, Chiho said, "We might as well take a bath. There's nothing we can do about Daisuke for now."

Chiho pulled out the *yukata* and Sukanya looked around before taking off her clothes. Chiho frowned at the blood on Sukanya's underthings. "Are you OK?"

Sukanya looked down. "Yes, OK, but heavy. More than usual."

"Do you want to talk with the doctor?"

"No, no. No."

"We can rinse them out in the sink. Let's take a change of clothes."

Sukanya followed Chiho toward the bath. She kept losing her

slippers as they walked and had to step back and slip them on again.

In the changing room, the scent of cedar and minerals flowed out with the steamy air from the bath. They put their clothes in a basket and took small towels into the bath area separated from the changing room by a frosted glass door.

The bath walls were made of black stone tiles. Three low showers lined one wall, with wooden stools and wooden buckets tipped to dry.

The cedar wood bath was big enough for several people at once. It was wrapped with long copper bands that held the curved planks tight. It was sunk into the floor and circled by a narrow catchment space filled with smooth black stones.

"Wow!" Sukanya said.

"This whole place is *wow!*" Chiho said.

Sukanya followed Chiho. They soaped and rinsed and soaped and rinsed again. Then, they pumped long dollops of shampoo over their hair and worked it into a wet mop of suds. Soap splattered the mirrors and nozzles and floor.

Chiho stood up to help rinse out the shampoo from Sukanya's hair, and then Sukanya did the same for her. Chiho pushed Sukanya back onto her stool and slipped her hand under the strap of a bath brush. She loaded on soap and started scrubbing Sukanya's back.

Sukanya squirmed and wiggled.

"Too hard?"

"No, feel good."

"My mother used to scrub my sister and me so hard."

Sukanya let her back ease and loosen, bending forward and squirming as Chiho worked the brush in circles. Sukanya rinsed off and made Chiho turn around to get her back scrubbed.

Chiho groaned as Sukanya worked the brush over her skin and into her muscles.

They rinsed off and tiptoed to the cedar tub. They eased their legs over the lip of the tub, screaming, "Hot, hot, ouch, ow, ah," until they got used to the heat and sank down into the trouble-melting comfort of the bath.

Sukanya said, "Better already."

Chiho said, "I wish they had one of these in the net cafe."

They both sloshed water over their heads and shoulders with the bath towels, letting the heat sink in bone-deep.

Sukanya said, "Will Daisuke be OK?"

Chiho hid her face under the bath towel and mumbled, "He'll be fine."

When Sukanya let her eyes shut, she thought she heard sniffling, but Chiho wiped her face and rested her head back on the rim. Maybe it was just the water trickling over the edge of the bath. It was getting harder to leave, but Sukanya knew she had to.

Chapter 29

Kenta took pride in whiskey having saved him, not ruined him like in some old blues song. He parked on a side street of Shimokitazawa, intent on a drink of top-shelf stuff at Whiskey Creek, the whiskey and cigar bar he owned half of. He needed to rid himself of the presence of Yoshitaka Kirino. He'd left the windows open on the drive back, but whiskey would work even better.

He pulled open the door to the cigar-smoke, sour-mash interior and headed to a seat at the counter. Shun was tending bar as always, dressed immaculately in a tux with a sharp new haircut, buzzed around the neck with long strands curling down. He had been a model before he inherited the bar from an uncle. What he didn't inherit was good sense with money.

Kenta worked there for a year, after prison, learning and lending Shun money until the day when he owned half the place. He liked Shun and didn't want to squeeze him all the way out. It was better he ran the place and Kenta handled finances.

Whiskey Creek was the ladder that let him climb from post-prison revenge to entrepreneur. He had worked, borrowed, lent, until his anger was gone and he had a decent loan business that focused on bars, clubs, and small restaurants. They always needed loans to tide them over, and Kenta was there.

But with all his information in limbo and Kirino pressuring him, his years of work were in peril. Kirino didn't let things go. He followed where things led, which for him was always in one of two directions—a profitable up or a violent down.

Shun wiped a spot on the bar top for Kenta. "*Hisashiburi*," Shun said.

Kenta settled onto a stool. "You got the cigars?"

"People spend as much on cigars as on whiskey."

Kenta smiled. "What did I tell you?"

"You were right. Can I get you something?"

"A small sip. I'm driving."

Shun pushed back his permed hair and reached to the top shelf. The wall used to have a mirror in the middle when Kenta worked there, but it had been covered over with bottles in all shapes and sizes, all expensive brands.

Shun poured out the whiskey without letting Kenta see the label.

Kenta picked it up, eyes closed, and took a sip. He let it swish and burn before he growled and said, "Yamazaki?"

Shun nodded yes.

"Single malt?"

Shun shrugged, as if that would be obvious.

"I'll say vintage, but..."

"Twelve years old, but they've got the vintage taste," Shun smiled at his half-victory in testing Kenta. "Smoked oysters and risotto?"

Kenta said, "Yes, but I'm in a hurry."

Shun said, "I got a new girl in the kitchen. She goes to cooking school."

"What was that last girl's name? Yuka?"

"That was three girls ago."

"High turnover."

"The men harass them. That's why I let this one stay in back cooking."

"She a looker?"

Shun raised his eyebrows and called back to the small kitchen under the *noren* curtain. He ducked under the bar and went out the front door.

Kenta walked back to his stool, and the chef, her long hair wrapped with a blue head towel, set out a steaming hot *oshibori* towel and silverware. He settled in on the stool and sent a text message to Mina, seeing if she'd be free later. The oysters and risotto would be just enough to hold him over.

Mina answered with a huge open OK finger emoji, a very large "O." Kenta sent her a thumbs up emoji with a suggestively large thumb, and a photo of his whiskey.

The chef brought out a half-dozen small, smoked oysters on a ceramic plate. She came back in a minute with a shallow bowl filled with risotto topped with sautéed mushroom and flakes of black *nori*.

"Are you going to cooking school or something?" Kenta said.

She smiled and said, "How did you know?" And headed back into the kitchen without another word. Kenta followed her with his eyes as he took a bite of risotto.

How did Yoshitaka Kirino get all his information? When he'd asked, all he could pry from him was: "Pay for it." Reasonable enough, but he'd had enough of Yoshitaka Kirino. They had different business models. This was what he should be doing, more whiskey bars.

Shun came back in the front door and checked on the two other customers smoking cigars in a brick-lined, cushioned booth. Their talk was drowned out by the jazz playing in the background. Kenta had taken the sound system as payment on a loan and installed it with Shun's help.

Shun ducked under the bar and reached inside his tuxedo vest. He pulled out a thick envelope and placed it next to Kenta's whiskey. Kenta put the envelope in his pocket.

* * *

When he got out of prison, Kenta followed them for weeks with a knife in his pocket. The other five students who ran the Super Open Club were rich kids from connected families, and he wanted to make them pay, see them suffer. He had no money for the kind of lawyers who got them suspended sentences. He did serious time, while they got slaps on the wrist.

The Super Open Club ran huge parties at DJ dance venues, bringing students from all the best schools in Tokyo. The profit was huge. Students would pay almost anything to get in. For Kenta it was easy to run the money side of things. The others were too rich to have ever thought of budgets.

Handling money, setting up accounts, and watching the cash was what he'd learned helping his mother with her lunch place in a small town in Shimane, until she got too sick to work. He passed the entrance exam on his own, without any expensive cram school. Once he got to Tokyo, he gave up his local accent, and started to talk, and act, like Tokyo people.

He'd handled all the money, he admitted at his trial, but it was the rich kids who drugged the girls and filmed them in the back rooms.

The worst of the guys, who always went first, tried to blame Kenta for everything. They got off and Kenta did a few years.

So, once his sentence was served, Kenta set out to even the score. The plan was simple—stab them with the knife and film them crawling around in pain, just like they'd done to those drunk freshman girls.

But after two months of planning, he decided that his vengeful anger was not making him any money, and he was tired of living hand to mouth. He started as a bartender at Whiskey Creek and started saving, investing, and thinking bigger.

* * *

Now, he was in the same fix again. He sipped his whiskey, but didn't ask for another. He was going to have to find Kirino, but more likely, Kirino would find him. He wasn't going to take the rap—or worse—for someone else a second time.

He finished his oysters and risotto, and washed the whiskey down with a glass of water. Shun smiled and bowed when Kenta left, but they had no need for words. They were partners.

The streets of Shimokitazawa were humming. Young people walked in all directions. The low lights of small places softly lit up the streets. Kenta walked toward the music club a couple of blocks away, but stopped at the window of a new restaurant, a small bistro, to look at the menu. A waitress came out and said, "*Irrasshaimase.*"

Kenta smiled. "Just opened?"

"Last week." She was a college student, bouncy and smiley, maybe her first part-time job.

"Always as busy as this?" There was no one inside.

"It's not busy yet. But the chef studied in France, so I think we will be."

"I'll be back," Kenta said, thinking this was just the kind of place Mina liked, intimate, stylish, and overpriced.

His news notice alert pinged, and there it was, another murder in Shinagawa, a foreign girl. Was that Kirino's work? There was no photo, so he couldn't be sure. He scrolled past the article and put his cellphone away.

It pinged again.

His computer tracker was now moving quickly along the Shuto Expressway from Roppongi toward Shinagawa. Someone in a fast

162

car had his computer now. Why did they turn it on? Did they know he was tracking it? Were they luring him into following? Or had they made a mistake, or maybe didn't care either way?

He hurried around the corner to The Lost Melody and stared down the stairs at the bouncer, a bald bruiser in a leather jacket. Kenta gestured to him he'd wait upstairs. The bouncer went inside the club and another bouncer came out to take his place, a tall guy with spiky hair and a torn T-shirt. It was between sets so there was no one in line.

In a few minutes, the first bouncer hiked up the steep staircase with two envelopes. One, filled with cash, Kenta tucked in his inside pocket. The other envelope held a note. Kenta wondered why the owner didn't just send a text message like everyone else, but folding the note out and reading it, he understood. Yotaro, agreed to help.

He had to do something about Yoshitaka Kirino and it had to be rock-solid believable. Kirino was not an easy person to fool, so Kenta's plan had to be lined up perfectly and executed precisely. With Yotaro's help, it could be.

Chapter 30

Hiroshi saw Akiko standing alone at a table at the back of the long, narrow *tachinomi* standing bar. She looked small beside Sugamo, Ueno, and Osaki. Salarymen and office workers clustered around cuts of plywood plunked on plastic beer crates, hoisting drinks, clacking chopsticks and talking in loud, unrestrained voices. Hiroshi headed to where they were with Takamatsu following and Sakaguchi turning sideways to squeeze through the circles of standing, drinking customers.

"The chief called five times," Akiko said. "He's upset."

Takamatsu took off his jacket, brushed out a few wrinkles and hung it carefully on a hook on the wall. "Getting upset is his job."

Sakaguchi threw his huge coat over a stack of beer crates, took the steaming hot *oshibori* towel from the waiter and buried his face in it. The waiter cleared more space for them to stand by pushing another table out of the way. They took up the entire back section of the bar.

Takamatsu ordered beer for everyone, and the waiter came back quickly with mugs in hand. He took out a pad to write down the food orders Takamatsu reeled off.

It was not a cheerful *kanpai* toast. They sipped their beers in silence. Everyone else in the place was red-faced and loose-limbed. The time to catch the last train was approaching, but the detectives were just starting.

Akiko pulled out her notepad and started to read. "So, Kenta Nakamura never graduated from university."

"That punk who was in the video the assistant showed us?" Sakaguchi asked.

"Yes, do you want to hear?"

The waiter brought a large bowl piled with shiny red *maguro* slices ringed with grated *wasabi* and shredded *daikon*. Hiroshi set out small dishes for everyone, waving with his finger for Akiko to keep reading from her notes.

Akiko said, "Turns out he was involved in the Super Open Club scandal."

"Why does that sound familiar?" Hiroshi said.

Akiko nodded. "It was a group of university students who organized events where they got first-year college girls drunk, raped them, and filmed it."

"A huge scandal at the time," Sakaguchi said.

"That was when I was in the States," Hiroshi said.

"One of the most elite universities in Japan." Akiko hoisted her glass and dug her chopsticks into the fresh *maguro*. "They set up a pyramid scheme."

Hiroshi took a plate of golden-fried vegetable *tempura* from the waiter and set it inside the ring of beer mugs.

Akiko said, "They forced their *kohais*, first year students, to sell tickets to the events. Those students sold them, had others sell them, or covered the cost themselves. So, the leaders of the club made money that way, but apparently wanted more, so they started selling the rape videos."

"That's how they got caught," Takamatsu said.

Akiko took a big slug of beer. "Apparently, our friend Kenta wasn't the ringleader. He was the accountant."

"How did you find all this out? Police database?" Takamatsu looked amused.

Akiko shook her head. "I have a classmate who works in the Educational Affairs Office at his old university. I took her to lunch."

"Did you find an address for him?"

"I found all his prison records."

"Long?"

"Three years. The others got a few months or suspended sentences."

"For rape?"

"Only one of the victims pressed charges. The others settled out of court."

"Too bad they didn't catch them after they changed the law."

"They changed the law *because* of them," Akiko said. "First change

165

to sex crime statues since the end of Meiji Era. They can prosecute rape without anyone pressing charges now."

The waiter brought a bowl of deep-fried chicken *karaage* slathered in diced shallots and red pepper sauce and another bowl with the house specialty, a tower of shaved beef over mashed potatoes.

"Decent food here," Sakaguchi said, digging in to the tower.

"I ate at home," Hiroshi said.

"Let's get some *shochu*," Takamatsu said. "I need something stronger, to burn things out a bit."

The back wall above the prep area was lined with a hundred or so *shochu* bottles each in its own perfectly sized cubby hole. A row of glasses sat under the two rows of bottles. The waiter noticed them looking and came over.

"*Imo* sweet potato," Sakaguchi said.

"*Mugi* barley," Takamatsu told the waiter.

"I'm going with the Okinawan *awamori*," Akiko said, before knocking back the rest of her beer.

Hiroshi said, "I'll take that Kyushu one, *shiro?*"

Ueno and Sugamo declined, since they were driving. Osaki ordered a traditional rice-based *shochu*.

Sakaguchi heard his cellphone ring, chugged the last of his beer and dug through the pockets of his coat. He listened to the call, nodding his head, and then put his cellphone back in his pocket and bellied back up to the table just as the glasses of iced *shochu* arrived.

"*Kanpai!*" They clinked glasses and sipped the harsh, flavorful white liquor.

Akiko shivered and Hiroshi had to take a deep breath.

Takamatsu held up his glass. "Traditional things are traditional for a reason. They work."

"Who was the call from?" Hiroshi asked.

"The medical examiner. The girl was still alive when they threw her in. Swallowed a lot of salt water."

Hiroshi said, "She wouldn't have even been able to swim."

Akiko shook her head and set down her *shochu*.

Sakaguchi continued, "Her stomach was beaten so badly, it was mainly the plastic that held things in place."

Hiroshi eyed the bowl of fresh *maguro* and looked away at the bottles on the shelves.

166

Sakaguchi said, "That studio should have been shut down years ago. There were repeated violations, contracts, underage girls—"

"Do you think they can go after every porn studio in Tokyo?" Takamatsu shook his head. "They'd be doing nothing else. We have a connection now, from the second dead girl to the studio."

Sugamo said, "How are we going to find the third girl?"

Takamatsu said, "Maybe she'll come to us."

Osaki sipped his *shochu* and said, "And what if she doesn't?"

Hiroshi said, "Then we follow the cryptocurrencies. They'll lead to the Ministry of Finance official. It's got to be him that drew the killers."

Sakaguchi looked at Hiroshi. "Tell me what cryptocurrency will tell us."

"The porn studios run on well-hidden transfers. But there will be a record of transaction IDs. I'm pretty sure some of them were irregular. I won't know that until I talk with the security people at Aracoin, the currency exchange Yoko Kawase told us about."

Takamatsu smiled. "But we still need to get into the actual offices, right?"

Hiroshi nodded. "That would help. But if someone was sending money in the wrong direction, we need to find where it went. And if we find out who facilitated Aracoin's establishment, that gives us another, more likely suspect."

Akiko said, "For digital currency, I read that Japan is already behind other countries, like Singapore and Korea, not to mention China and the US."

"Japan's behind? That's what they always say." Takamatsu swirled his drink. "You start in on the ministries and you won't do anything else."

Sakaguchi said, "We know Takeo Suzuki, the dead guy who liked to make his own photos, was in the Ministry of Finance. So, Hiroshi, follow up with the digital currency wallet on the dead girl. We can see if it moves up the ladder or not."

Akiko dug into her cellphone. "The chief's main reason for calling five times was to give us the phone number for the secretary of Takeo Suzuki. The chief kept telling me how his extensive contacts would help break this case."

Takamatsu threw down a big gulp of *shochu*. "If he'd ever worked on a serious case, he'd know that all he gave us was a potential lead, and not a very good one."

Hiroshi said, "Just the same, Akiko, set up an appointment with him for tomorrow morning. I'll go. And I'll talk again with Junko Ayase at the NPO. And the cryptocurrency exchange Aracoin."

Akiko wrote everything down. "The chief said he thought Takeo Suzuki was just in the wrong place at the wrong time."

"Innocent bystander?" Takamatsu looked astonished. "Those bureaucrats and business leaders think they have immunity from university to business to government to whatever they do in their off time. The chief's the same."

"Relax. The chief's not breaking any laws," Sakaguchi said.

Takamatsu said, "By the way, I've got a line on Kenta Nakamura."

Sakaguchi looked at him. "Why didn't you say so?"

Takamatsu shrugged. "I'm not like the chief, bragging about what I do."

Sakaguchi looked at him. "What about just keeping us informed?"

"I got lucky on the surveillance footage near the studio. I told the interns to find a fancy sports car." Takamatsu looked pleased at his good luck.

Sakaguchi said, "Take Ueno, Osaki, and Sugamo. They can tail him."

Sakaguchi waved for another round for everyone and then began to speak, "You know, this case has been bugging me."

"It's a grim one," Hiroshi said.

"It's not just that. When I was young, one of my cousins disappeared. She was older than me and quite pretty, but a little wild." Sakaguchi took a big breath, and his thick, round face became serious. "She was the first one in our family to take the entrance exam for college. After she passed the exam, she started working to save money for tuition. One day, she didn't come home. For a week, my family searched all over Osaka. I went with my uncle and older cousins to talk to the owner of the bar where she worked part-time."

Sakaguchi looked at the bottles along the back of the bar. "The bar owner was scared, so he sent us to a film studio. We went there, not sure of what it was, but as soon as we stepped inside, we knew. They were tough guys there, the toughest Osaka streets ever made. But we beat them until they pissed themselves and couldn't move. That was the first time I ever hit someone except at sumo practice. I was fourteen."

Another round of *shochu* arrived. Takamatsu put out his cigarette and all three of them looked down, listening.

Sakaguchi continued. "We trashed the rooms where they made their auditions, and found a photo of my cousin in their files. But they denied everything. We went back to the snack bar and beat that guy unconscious, smashed his liquor bottles, broke his karaoke machine. His friends came. We left them sprawled on the floor, too."

Sakaguchi took a big swallow of *shochu* and set his glass down empty on the plywood tabletop. "We searched for my cousin for years. We even hired a private investigator. He finally found a photo that looked like her from a morgue up in Hokkaido. My aunt wouldn't accept it was her, and never put up a *butsudan* altar at home. Until the day my aunt died, she was still waiting for my cousin to come home."

Takamatsu, Hiroshi, and Akiko looked at their untouched *shochu*. Sugamo, Ueno, and Osaki stood silent.

Sakaguchi looked at them and took a breath. "That's why I can't watch porn. She used to walk me to school."

Chapter 31

"Are these for us?" Sukanya asked, dropping to her knees on the *tatami* in the room beside two large lacquer trays. A long mirror and floor-level dressing table had been pulled into the middle of the room.

"Must be," Chiho said.

Sukanya picked up a swirl of silk as big as a sheet. Bright rectangles of purple, black, dark pink, and white jutted and angled in all directions, layered over with swirling flowers of marine blue and deep red. She spun around with it in her hands. The tray was filled with sashes and pleated front skirts with long ties, all brightly colored.

Chiho picked up hers, held it in her hands and turned it around, a white and pink background layered with red and black rectangles. A folded maroon skirt was embroidered with sprigs of silk flowers around which darted little black birds with long wings.

They laughed at the sheer beauty of the clothes, doing a dance in front of the mirror, holding them over themselves.

"Which do you want?" Chiho asked.

"I don't know. You choose," Sukanya said.

"You have the one that you picked first. The bright colors fit you best."

Sukanya nodded OK and slipped off the bath *yukata*. Chiho helped her put on the white under skirt, but she stopped and looked at the tray.

"I don't remember how to do this. I only wore one once, on a photo shoot." Chiho put down one and picked up the next. "Let me remember, this goes on first, then this, but I can't remember how to fold them...hmmm." Chiho pulled the outer layer off as Sukanya spun around.

"It's OK," Sukanya said. "Maybe not for us."

The door opened and the older woman who had led them in bustled over.

"Help us!" Chiho cooed.

The older woman clucked at Chiho and took all the clothing from her. She set Sukanya in front of the mirror, deftly adding layer on layer, tucking in the edges, tying the sashes around with crisp knots, light colors inside and deep on the outer layer. Sukanya's waist was so narrow, she had to wind the sash one extra time. Sukanya kneeled down as the older woman twisted her hair into a simple braid from both sides, pinned with a black barrette.

Looking in the mirror, Sukanya giggled. "I'm Japanese."

Sukanya watched as the older woman stood Chiho in place and arranged her layers, from the inside out, until she was wrapped in vibrant, fluid colors that seemed to move on their own. Chiho's hair, she did in loose braids with a thick bun in back.

"It's so nice to have women in the house. Look how beautiful you are," the old woman said, positioning them both in front of the mirror. "Well, we ordered something to eat. We thought you might be hungry, and Daisuke always is," the old woman announced. "Daisuke's grandmother is looking forward to talking with you."

She led them to the other side of the home through wood and glass walkways to a room with a long floor table, the far end of it set with placemats. One wall was a long line of sliding glass doors, beyond which lights shone on the garden.

Sukanya followed Chiho's every movement. Moving in the tight layers was not easy, but she watched Chiho kneel on the tatami and tried to do the same.

In a few minutes, the door slid open and a solid, round woman walked in. She was dressed in a deep green kimono patterned with dark gray dots, and a broad *obi* of greens and blues. Her thick hair, swept in a clutch of barrettes, drew Sukanya's eyes, as she knelt down and bowed.

"I'm Daisuke's grandmother," she said in English. "And you must be Chiho and Sukanya."

"I'm so sorry to cause trouble for you by our arrival," Chiho said, her head bowed.

When Chiho bowed, Sukanya followed.

"I knew Daisuke would be back sooner or later. But I didn't except him to come back quite so beaten up. Nor did I expect he would be accompanied by two such beautiful women," she said.

171

"Is he OK?" Chiho asked.

"The doctor took him for X-rays and a CAT scan. Broken arm, bruised ribs, a broken finger. He was always getting hurt as a boy, too."

Chiho bowed her head. "Daisuke did nothing wrong. He saved us."

Daisuke's grandmother hummed. Sukanya liked how she met her eyes directly, more like Thai people.

Chiho said in Japanese, "Sukanya also needs to see a doctor. I'm sorry to be so rude to ask."

Daisuke's grandmother nodded. "About what?"

"She's been bleeding heavily. From down there."

Daisuke's grandmother turned to Sukanya and spoke in Thai, surprising the two women so much they gasped. Sukanya leaned forward, tears starting at the sound of her own language.

"Do you need to go now or can we go to my doctor tomorrow when her clinic opens?" she asked.

"Tomorrow is OK." Sukanya looked down but didn't feel shy. "I'm OK."

"I'll take you tomorrow morning after breakfast to my women's clinic, or maybe she can come here." Daisuke's grandmother asked Sukanya about Thailand, where she came from and why she was in Tokyo, and how she met Chiho and her grandson.

Sukanya rattled off the answers as honestly as she could. Chiho looked back and forth in amazement, shut out of the conversation.

Sukanya covered her mouth and twisted to Chiho. "She so smart. Speak perfect Thai language. Better than me!"

Daisuke's grandmother switched to English. "My husband was posted in Thailand for several years. I don't like shopping, so I learned the language. Thailand has the kindest people in the world. And I know. I lived many places," she said.

"Like where?" Chiho asked.

"Paris, London, New York. Casablanca, and Cairo for the longest time. My husband was in the foreign service."

"I thought Daisuke was just a heavy metal fan from the suburbs."

Daisuke's grandmother laughed. "I came back to take care of him when his parents died."

Frowning, Sukanya asked, "They died?"

"When he was thirteen. In a plane crash. I came back to raise him. This is my husband's family's house."

"He grew up *here*?" Chiho asked.

The old woman who had tied their kimonos brought in small dishes, cups, a ceramic flask, and two large round lacquer bowls covered with a taut layer of plastic wrap. Two dozen different kinds of sushi lined up inside like a miniature fish market.

"Daisuke's favorite," she said. "I hope our local sushi delivery will be sufficient."

"Wonderful," Sukanya said, putting her hands together in a *wai*.

Daisuke's grandmother said, "I hope this will be the last of his adventures. But it's better he gets it out of his system when he's young." She took her chopsticks and put the first sushi on Sukanya's plate and another on Chiho's. She poured soy sauce out into small dipping plates, and poured sake from the flask into the tiny cups.

"*Kanpai*," she said, holding up her cup and smiling. "Daisuke will join us in a while, but let's get started."

They chatted, switching back and forth between Japanese and Thai and English, Daisuke's grandmother humming interest, listening to everything. Chiho and Sukanya asked about Daisuke. His grandmother asked about Bangkok and Chiho's band.

After nearly half the sushi was gone, the door slid open and Daisuke came in. He wore a *hakama* with brown squares at the top that edged into pure black at the bottom. Sukanya was surprised he looked as comfortable in traditional clothes as he was in jeans and a heavy metal T-shirt. His arm was tucked inside a black nylon sling and his long hair was combed back.

Chiho and Sukanya got up on their knees. "Are you OK?"

"It could have been worse." He limped over and lowered himself down in the chair across from Chiho with a series of grimaces, being careful with his left leg.

Daisuke's grandmother spoke in sharp, quick Japanese to Daisuke, scolding him, Sukanya assumed. Chiho looked down at the table, but Daisuke only listened without replying until she was done.

"I need some sake," he said, reaching for the bottle.

He poured for Sukanya, but Chiho took the flask and poured for Daisuke's grandmother and then for Daisuke and finally for herself.

"A toast," Daisuke said.

Sukanya savored the cold, lovely sake. She sniffed and tasted the sake slowly and carefully.

Chiho filled Daisuke's up again, and then Sukanya's.

"So, this is your home? Where you grew up?" Chiho asked. "You never told me you went to university."

"You never asked." Daisuke shrugged and made a face. Even shrugging seemed to hurt him.

"He didn't like any school he ever went to. He's been to the University of London, the Sorbonne for summer school, and now Waseda," his grandmother said.

"Such famous schools," Chiho said.

Sukanya said, "What is you study?"

"Now? Sociology."

"Why you work at net cafe place when you go famous school?" Sukanya felt confused.

"I wanted to see another way of life."

"You've seen it now, I guess," Chiho said. "Satisfied?"

Daisuke sighed.

Daisuke's grandmother said, "I thought you were doing research? I'm still paying tuition."

Daisuke looked away and took a large sip of sake.

"What kind of research?" Chiho asked.

Daisuke's grandmother said, "Into the sociological complexities— how did you put it?—of internet cafe culture."

Daisuke pulled back. "Not exactly. I talked with all the men who'd lost their jobs and were kicked out of their apartments. I interview them when they're willing." Daisuke took another gulp of sake.

This time, Chiho did not fill up his glass.

Daisuke's grandmother said, "I'm going to let you young people stay up and talk. This is too late for an old woman like me, though I did love staying up all hours when I was young."

Chiho got on her knees on the *tatami* to thank her in the politest language. Sukanya said thank you in Thai, English, and Japanese.

They fell quiet after she left. Sukanya smiled, lost in her own thoughts.

Chiho loosened her waist sash and turned to look at Daisuke. "So, you were researching everyone in the net cafe? You were researching *me*?"

"That's not how it was."

"You lied to me."

"I never lied to you. I just...well...you didn't seem interested."

"After you finished researching me, what were you going to do? Move back here?"

"I didn't think that far ahead," Daisuke said.

Chiho leaned back. "What happened to Sukanya's computer?"

"The guys who beat me up took it." Daisuke turned to Sukanya. "What was on there?"

Sukanya looked at the outside garden. "It too embarrass to say."

"It's OK," Chiho said. "You don't have to say."

Sukanya smiled at her. "Embarrass is one part. I want erase that part. But other part is about business, information and numbers. To get money."

"Money? What money?" Daisuke asked.

Sukanya shrugged. "She didn't explain."

"Who didn't explain?" Chiho asked.

Sukanya stared out at the garden. "Ratana, girl who leave and not come back. She said, we deserve more. It was on computer, maybe on iPad, too. I don't know."

Chiho said, "We need to find out."

Chapter 32

Yoshifumi Arai, the dead minister's former secretary, lived a long walk from Denenchofu Station close to the Tama River, longer than Hiroshi expected from the map. Near the station, sidewalks lined the wide, curving roads with old trees planted at regular intervals in front of well-appointed homes two or three stories high.

But as Hiroshi got nearer the river, the streets narrowed, the lots got smaller, the houses closer to the street. Urban planning evaporated into the usual Tokyo muddle of designs, from minimalist Japanese to European chic to industrial concrete. The latter was where the minister's secretary lived. Hiroshi rang the bell, which gave out a faint clonk from inside.

He walked to the side of the house. On tiptoes, he could just peek over a thick concrete wall. The bottom floor of the house was another flight down and large windows rose up all three floors. A prim, triangular courtyard gave the illusion of open space. Hiroshi walked back to the front and stood looking around.

He was about to leave when a tall, lean man came walking toward him at a brisk pace. He was wearing bright orange tennis shoes, an unzipped sweatshirt, and formal wool pants.

Hiroshi bowed and waited for him.

The man said, "You must be Detective Shimizu. Sorry I wasn't home. I had to mail some things. I'm Arai." He waved Hiroshi into the house, but didn't say anything more as he took off his shoes and sweatshirt in the large *genkan* entryway. The main floor was down a flight of concrete stairs with a simple wood rail.

The industrial chic hanging lights and Scandinavian furniture looked more appropriate for a thirty-something software designer than a retired bureaucrat.

Arai noticed Hiroshi's puzzled face. "My daughter's an architect. She designed this place but then got transferred to London. I sold our house when my wife died, so I'm here keeping the spiders out until she returns."

Arai started boiling water at the burners of the open kitchen.

Hiroshi said, "Thank you for seeing me. I wanted to ask you a few questions."

"I think I might have your answers." The water boiled quickly. Arai set out teacups on a tall table in the center of the room, filled the pot with leaves, swirled it vigorously, and poured out aromatic black tea.

Arai waved Hiroshi to a stool at the tall table. Large sliding glass doors looked out on the triangular garden, where a spindly apricot tree and three hydrangeas fronted the concrete walls. The hydrangeas were trimmed short and bare for the winter, more unfinished basket than flowering shrub. Smooth white stones covered the ground but ran sparse in places, exposing a gray crush of dust below.

"I promised my daughter that I'd work on the garden but haven't made much progress," Arai sighed.

"It's good to have a project," Hiroshi suggested.

"That's retirement—one time-killing project after the next."

Hiroshi waited for the tea to cool a little before sipping. The tea was strong and bracing. "Delicious," Hiroshi said.

"It's from Assam. My daughter did a project there. This is the last of what she sent. I gave up drinking and smoking once I retired, but I needed something. It's amazing what I missed out on over the years. This tea has a subtle smokiness, doesn't it?"

"Is that yours?" Hiroshi nodded toward the framed calligraphy hanging on the concrete wall.

"That's another project. One I like better than gardening."

"I can't quite grasp the meaning."

"It's a Chinese saying. In Chinese, *nande hutu* means 'it's difficult to be confused.' And of course, the opposite follows, that it's all too easy to be clear."

"As a detective, it's usually all a muddle until you write the report."

"Same with ministry reports. It all looks good in the final draft, even when it isn't."

"They conceal as much as they record."

"Exactly. Well, I guess you're here not to talk about tea or calligraphy, but about Takeo Suzuki? I figured someone would be by eventually."

"Did he have a history of going to such things?"

Arai looked out at the unfinished garden, cradling his tea. "He had a history of many things. He was good at what he did, as a bureaucrat. The top in many regards. But that meant there was never anyone above him to steer him toward his better instincts. I did the best I could."

"How long did you work under him?"

"Thirty years. Though we both moved around a bit."

"All in the Ministry of Finance?"

"The Ministry of Foreign affairs for a few years."

"Who knew what he did—"

"In the evenings? Rumors get around, but who *knew*? Everyone who needed to, probably."

"You did?"

"Yes." Arai drank his tea and looked out at the garden. "He always got his work done, regardless of what he did at night."

"When did you know Suzuki—"

"It was an addiction like any other. I told him there were other...um...options. But he was not a man to listen to others when he had it in his head to do something."

"What did he do at work that was so—"

"Special? Japan has a lot of bureaucrats, but most of them just take up desk space. He helped Japan open its banking and currency systems. That ushered Japan into the world economy. You couldn't imagine the system before he and a few others started to push for reform. It was a century out of date. Before he got there, most reports and budgets were written by hand."

"Did his reforms include digital currency exchanges?"

"He was the lead on DCEs. He kept saying cryptocurrency was Japan's solution to its moribund banking system. If banks and businesses used digital currencies, then Japan's economy could globalize. Many others disagreed and wanted to keep Japan insulated. I felt he was rushing things, not getting enough consensus, but that was also one of his strengths, pushing ahead. He was trying to make Japan a home for cryptocurrency."

"Is that possible?"

"It happened in Singapore and Korea."

"But what about criminals using the system? It provides them secret cover to do whatever they like."

"Criminals already find cover. But many different kinds of businesses want to conduct transactions more freely than Japan's banks allow. Suzuki-san believed it was the best solution to Japan's long economic slump."

"Sounds like a long shot."

"The only kind left."

"What about your time at the Ministry of Foreign Affairs? He did the same there?"

"He shepherded Japan toward a more open labor market. That was uphill work. He encouraged visiting worker programs, revised the visa process, reformed residency requirements. With Japan's shrinking population, there wasn't any other choice, but he was the first to take concrete steps."

"Many people must have argued against him about that, too?"

"He was in constant battles. But he got things done."

"Would someone want revenge?"

"Wasn't it a heart attack?"

"His head was caved in with a blunt instrument."

Arai turned his teacup in his hands. "Murder's not how revenge plays out in the bureaucracy. It's usually *amakudari*, forced retirement with a cushy landing. He could have moved to the Keidanren, the Japanese Business Federation, but he didn't want to go. That would have been too easy. Not his style."

"What about outside the ministry? Someone must have introduced him to the film shoots."

Arai looked out the window, as if he could see past the dried plants and concrete walls. "He knew people of all kinds, charmed them, enjoyed them. It was part of how he got so much done."

"Did he have loans, or do favors or—"

"If someone wanted revenge, they could have just exposed his obsession. He was a strange, complex man. He wanted the best for the country and the worst for himself. He told me he had cirrhosis."

"When was that?"

"The last time I talked with him. About six months ago."

"You retired before him?"

"Yes, three years ago."

Hiroshi looked out at the garden.

Arai sipped his tea and looked out the windows. "It was bad luck he died so shamefully. It's disappointing that would be his legacy. And mine by association."

"So, you don't think someone was out to get him?"

"No, I don't." Arai looked out at the garden and then at Hiroshi. He got up from his stool. "I'll be right back."

Hiroshi watched him walk to the back of the open room and climb the circular stairs to an open second-floor area. The stairs continued to a third floor.

In a few minutes, he came back with an envelope that held a thick sheaf of papers. It was made of *washi* paper more fit for a wedding invitation than for government documents and taped shut with Arai's red *hanko* and signature over the tape.

"*Doozo*," was all Arai said as he handed Hiroshi the envelope "It's all in here. What I thought would help."

Hiroshi took the large envelope in both hands and waited for an explanation. Would the contents show Takeo Suzuki as the reforming type of bureaucrat? Or as someone who manipulated the system?

"I'm concerned that if his personal reputation is ruined, then all the good work he's done in the ministry will be rescinded."

"Why would—?"

"That's the bureaucratic mindset. Dissension and reversal, if you can accrue enough power. Suzuki-san instituted huge changes that were greatly needed, but he tied too much of it to himself."

"Is there any other reason his reputation might be ruined? He was in a position to profit—"

"I'm not sure."

"There must be some reason he was killed."

Arai looked away. "Even with me, he was able to hide things. He was like a reverse magician. Things permanently disappeared."

"What was he hiding?"

"I put everything I know in there."

Hiroshi started to slide his finger under the sealed tape to open the envelope.

Arai put his hand out. "Do not look at that until you find a quiet place, alone, and decide what to do about it. I have given this to you with the hope you will not let it destroy all the good Suzuki-san accomplished. I know it's impossible to entirely spare all damage to his reputation, but maybe it can be minimized."

Hiroshi nodded and stood up to leave. "I'm not sure how much I can control the media, but I understand."

"That'll have to be good enough," Arai said. "At least he could be given his last rites before the public shame."

"When was the funeral?"

"Yesterday."

"I'm sorry. I didn't know," Hiroshi said.

"It was kept private. I did all the arrangements. He had no close family."

Chapter 33

When the head of the Morning Light nonprofit organization, Junko Ayase, saw Hiroshi come in the door, she called out to the college interns in a loud voice, "Another visit from the police! We must be doing something right!"

The college interns stopped what they were doing and carried laptops over to the meeting table in the center of the room. As before, the photos of young women on the multi-lingual posters stared down at him.

Junko eyed him, too. She pulled her baggy sweater tight around her shoulders as she gestured for everyone to take a seat.

"It was Rin, Yuna, and Nozomi, right?" Hiroshi said, looking at the women in turn.

"You have a good memory," Junko said.

The college students seemed different than his image of most twenty-something women. Hiroshi imagined most spent their free time on shopping, Disneyland, or drinking parties.

"So, what can we do for you today?" Junko asked. "Our coffee machines still broken but we can—"

"I'm fine. I have a photo." He showed her a headshot of the Thai woman pulled out of the canal the night before.

"I heard about this." Junko looked at it carefully and then passed it to the interns, who looked at it and passed it back to Hiroshi.

"Did you hear about this through the media—or before the media?" Junko looked at him. "Why are you asking?"

"Someone let the media know about this before the police briefing."

The interns looked uncomfortable.

Junko said, "We often hear of incidents, yes."

Rin said, "Generally, the media ignore the research reports and statistics we send them. But they pick up on sensational news."

Yuna said, "We're trying to get the government to cooperate with us, but so far we're not even invited to their press conferences."

Nozomi said, "The government and the media react the same—indifferent until it becomes a crisis."

"You haven't seen this girl, or the other one, and have no place to check?"

Junko took the photograph. "Can someone scan this?" Yuna got up to do it.

Junko leaned forward toward Hiroshi. "The girls usually come and go too quickly to even be noticed. They arrive on boats at industrial or private docks, bypassing immigration altogether. And are gone again. A photo doesn't help much. How many were trafficked in last year's study?" Junko asked one of the interns.

"Two hundred," Rin answered without even thinking.

"The Thai embassy has a stack of passports. And it's the same at the Philippine embassy. All fakes," Junko said.

Hiroshi said, "I know. I saw the files."

Nozomi said, "The Vietnamese, Cambodian, and Indonesian embassies cooperate with us more than the Japanese government."

Hiroshi said, "You do get tips and phone calls?"

"Those are confidential," Junko said.

"We're trying to track down a trafficking ring."

"Confidentiality is one of the few weapons we have, along with information." Junko nodded at him, polite but adamant.

"We want to find not just who killed this girl. We want to find the trafficking network and destroy it."

"So do we," Nozomi said. "Every time they get broken up, they regroup, more efficiently. Customers pay secretly. Profits move secretly."

Hiroshi felt like warning them about not cooperating, but he stopped himself. These women were up against corruption, payoffs, and profits that could all be hidden in code-locked accounts and moved anywhere anytime. "The best way to push for change is to work with me. Can you let me know if you hear of anything?" Hiroshi stood up and bowed longer than anyone was expecting before he walked out.

Hiroshi took a taxi to the south side of Shibuya. Aracoin's office was on the sixth floor of a building so new it smelled like the plastic had just been unwrapped. It was just south of Shibuya Station in a long row of office buildings for IT companies and shopping arcades.

Hiroshi stepped into the entryway. One plant and two chairs were backed against the right-hand wall. On the wall, a list of companies and digital currencies gleamed on an acrylic board. Hiroshi took a photo of the names.

A young woman in a business suit stepped from behind an offset wall. She bowed deeply and said, "Detective Hiroshi Shimizu?"

"Yes."

"Could you follow me?" She led him down a hallway lined with frosted glass. The same just-unwrapped plastic odor filled the meeting room. She bowed and left.

Hiroshi sat down and fingered the envelope Arai had given him. He should have read it right away. It was more likely to help than this exchange. He knew what these cryptocurrency people were going to tell him—that they respected the secrecy of their clients.

As soon as she was gone, three young men in business suits with stylish, spiky haircuts entered, as if they'd been waiting nearby. Their two-button collars were open above tight-fitting blazers. Each of them carried a small tablet computer. They were the face of Japan's new economy.

"Thank you for taking the time," Hiroshi said, and handed them all his *meishi*.

Only one of them handed Hiroshi a *meishi*. His name was Goto, and he bowed briefly. Goto said, "How can we help you today?"

Hiroshi looked at each of them carefully. "I need to know about one of your clients, Jack and Jill Studios."

Goto smiled and said, "We would need a court order, or something in writing. Our business model rests on—"

"Secrecy. I know that," Hiroshi interrupted. "Is Jack and Jill one of your clients, yes or no?"

The three young guys leaned back in their chairs.

Goto said, "Even if we confirmed that, it wouldn't tell you much."

Hiroshi leaned forward. "No, it would tell me a lot. It would tell me you're doing business with human traffickers and purveyors of child porn. It would tell me you don't care about who you are involved with as long as you get your mining fees and blockchain maintenance fees."

He hadn't planned on getting angry, but he'd seen Takamatsu do it, and for the first time ever, he wished he had brought Takamatsu along with him. He pulled out a photo of the digital wallet found on the drowned girl and showed it to them.

Goto and the other two leaned forward to look at it.

"It was found on the body of a young woman whose body washed up in Tokyo Bay. The QR code didn't work, but the address and key did, so with a little help from the tech guys at the station, it connected to Aracoin."

Goto looked at him. "We can't be responsible for these paper wallets, especially the old-style ones. That's not what we do. It's not even what we keep track of."

"Your office is connected to a dead girl. That's not going to be good for business. Or for digital currency in Japan."

Goto leaned forward and put his hands together on top of the desk. "We want to cooperate, but it's not like having an account at a bank branch. It's like having parts of the account dispersed through hundreds of small bank branches. That means—"

"I know what it means and how it works," Hiroshi said, raising his voice.

Goto was too young and inexperienced to act unruffled when he was angry. He cleared his throat. "I assure you that we follow the laws for financial transactions, and all policy guidelines."

Hiroshi showed him a photo of Kenta Nakamura. It was grainy, but a reasonably clear shot of his face.

Goto shook his head. "Who is this?"

"He stopped by here, didn't he?"

Goto looked at the other two. They cocked their heads with non-committal gestures.

"You're not sure if he was here? Or you're not sure if you should answer?" Hiroshi asked, scrolling through his photos. "I'll take your silence as a yes. And what about this? I'm sure you know him." He showed them a photo of Takeo Suzuki, one from before his head was smashed in at the porn studio.

Goto cleared his throat again. "He was our contact with the ministries."

"And Suzuki approved your business model, encouraged it even?"

Goto reluctantly nodded yes.

"Who did he talk to here? You?"

Goto leaned back in his chair. "We only talked about setting things up. After that, he talked to our code guy, Harada. I'm not sure what they discussed exactly, but Harada was the one who knew the system inside and out."

The guy to the right spoke up. "He saved us many times when we were just a start-up."

"How did he save you?" Hiroshi asked.

Goto let him talk. "In the early days, there were flaws and bugs that had to be worked out. Harada solved those problems and upgraded security."

"What kind of flaws?"

Goto clasped his hands together and pointed with his two index fingers. "When Bitcoin and others were starting up, someone could send an order to be filled but if the return code was not sent, or got lost, it would appear the transfer didn't take place and the order would be filled from elsewhere."

"It would be sent twice?"

"It could be sent several times without being recorded as received. This all happens extremely quickly. Uncovering the transfer codes could take months. By then, it's been moved again. Several exchanges got hit."

"That's the oldest scam in the books," Hiroshi said. The same trick he uncovered on investment scams had been accelerated for the digital age. "So, this code guy, Harada, protected Aracoin from those kinds of attacks?"

"Yes," Goto said. "And Takeo Suzuki stopped by to check on that, to have it explained to him. Suzuki was a quick learner for an old guy."

"How often did Suzuki come by?"

"Once a week, sometimes more."

"A finance minister was stopping by here once a week? That's a bit—"

"Unusual, yes," Goto said.

"I need to talk with Harada." Hiroshi leaned back in his chair, planning what to ask him.

Goto glanced at the other two, surprised. "We want to talk with him, too."

Hiroshi leaned forward. "Don't tell me. He hasn't come to work."

Goto looked away, his face set in silent anger. "We tried reaching him everywhere."

"Did he take anything with him?"

"He didn't need to. It was all in his head."

Hiroshi stood up. "I'll need a photo of Harada and his address and phone number. That's not encrypted, is it?"

Goto nodded and the other two opened their laptops to find Harada's contact info.

"Why didn't you contact the police?"

"We did. They told us that people disappear all the time and to wait a couple more days. We thought when you called, you'd be bringing us news about him, not a bunch of questions."

Chapter 34

Outside, Hiroshi walked quickly through the crowds in Shibuya. Farther from the station, the old Shibuya hung on. Hiroshi would get lunch at his favorite jazz *kissaten*, where he could recover with coffee, jazz, and curry, and read through whatever was in the thick envelope from Yoshifumi Arai.

He called Akiko and then Sakaguchi to get a local beat cop to stop by the address of Aracoin's security specialist, Harada. He would know how much Suzuki knew, which was, it seemed, what got him, and the others, killed. He might know even more. He would at least know how to find the transaction codes they needed to track down everyone.

On Hiroshi's usual cases, even the most talented investments scammers and money launderers could not hide all their tracks. But with digital currency, money could practically disappear, as if ground to powder and carried away on a cyber-breeze, only to be re-embodied by a magic code someplace far, far away. If the Ministry of Finance was pushing for Japan to become a center for global cryptocurrency, they were either naive or uninformed about how it could be abused.

Hiroshi headed up the hill past the love hotel area and was at his favorite jazz *kissaten* sooner than he imagined. He pulled open the door, and the dark interior and good music soothed him instantly. He flopped into a big easy chair, and the high-end equipment delivered Bill Evans, loud and lucid, each note precisely in place, fluid and felt.

The owner of the *kissaten*, a wizened gentleman with a goatee, wearing a thick indigo apron, came over. Hiroshi asked if it was too late for lunch.

"I can make you something," the *master* said.

"Curry."

"You want *tonkatsu*?"

"Yes. And hot coffee."

"Blend?"

"Yes."

He had owned the place long before Hiroshi started going there in college. A sign on the wall said "No talking." The wall behind the bar was lined with record albums. The vinyl radiated another era when the idea that music, art, and life were all interconnected, not by digitized currency or accessible information, but by values and understanding. It was like Arai's calligraphy, which condensed art, language, history and culture in a way that digital-age workers would never understand.

He closed his eyes to think.

His lunch arrived and Hiroshi looked at the golden curry blanketing slices of *tonkatsu* deep-fried pork and the soft bed of white rice as if for the first time.

Hiroshi pulled out the papers from Arai's envelope and started to read them as he crunched into the deep-fried pork. Bill Evans finished and Charles Mingus' *Mingus Ah Um* came on, rousing memories from long ago, and energy for the day.

As he read the cover page, he put down his fork and spoon and hurried ahead through the pages of elegant handwriting Arai had given him.

Behind the handwritten section were a hundred or so printed documents, which he flipped through. He stopped to think, took another bite of *tonkatsu,* and shuffled ahead to the end of Arai's dozen handwritten pages. He read the last part twice. Arai concluded with the same Chinese saying that was on his wall, as if he knew Hiroshi would ask about it: "*Nande hutu,* it's hard to be confused."

Hiroshi stood up, leaving his curry and coffee, tossed a five thousand yen note on the counter and shot out the door so fast the owner didn't have time to give him change. Hiroshi rushed to the large street down the hill, his hand waving for a taxi.

Hiroshi showed the taxi driver his detective badge and told him to hurry. Inside the taxi, he put in calls to Sakaguchi, Takamatsu, and Akiko. He asked Akiko to call the nearest *koban* police box to Arai's house.

* * *

Hiroshi got there before everyone else and rushed to the door of Arai's house. He should have read what Arai wrote before he went to the NPO and the digital currency exchange. He should have asked more questions.

189

The door was locked. He smashed into it with his shoulder and pulled hard on the handle. Before he could climb over the back wall to the dry garden below, Sakaguchi, Osaki, and Sugamo arrived in an unmarked car.

Sakaguchi beelined for the front door. Two local beat cops rode up on bicycles, one talking into the microphone clipped to his jacket.

Osaki and Sugamo carried large metal tools from the trunk. Osaki held a wedge sleeve over the lock, and Sugamo, with a single swing of a short-handled sledgehammer, knocked the whole mechanism off. Osaki pushed, but the door didn't budge.

Sugamo slammed it with the sledge and the door splintered. Osaki worked in a pry bar and the door crumbled.

Hiroshi was first in with Sakaguchi right behind. Hiroshi looked around desperately. He headed to the windows that looked out on the rock garden and saw the legs dangling from above.

Sakaguchi hurried over and pulled the door open. They both looked up at the body of Arai hanging from a long rope.

"Is this Takeo Suzuki's secretary?" Sakaguchi asked.

Hiroshi nodded yes.

"The contact the chief gave you?" Sakaguchi asked.

Hiroshi kept nodding yes.

Osaki and Sugamo were already calling in the crime scene crew.

Hiroshi stepped out onto the balcony. Arai was swaying gently in the breeze over the unfinished rock garden. Hiroshi looked up to where the rope was tied. He must have leapt from the second floor. With the deep-set garden, it was really the third floor.

Among the papers Arai had given him was his daughter's phone number in London. He should have read the situation better.

More local police arrived on bicycles and Osaki went to talk with them. They were young police officers in uniforms. They busied themselves setting up a perimeter and steering away curious neighbors.

The crime scene crew arrived more quickly than usual. Sakaguchi told them to get him down as soon as they could and told them to be especially careful with fingerprints.

"Isn't it a suicide?" asked a young crew member tucked into protective white clothing.

"Not until you show me it is," Sakaguchi said, waving them back to work.

They hurried to the task.

Hiroshi stood in the garden. Arai had not said that much. Everything that he wanted them to know, he put in the envelope: the explanation, in his elegant Japanese, and the proof-laden documents he must have stolen from the ministry. He should have offered Aria protection, or taken him back to headquarters.

Sakaguchi came over. "I guess you were the last person to see him alive. How was he when you talked with him?"

"I read it too late."

"Read what?" Sakaguchi asked.

Hiroshi held up the stack of papers.

"What's that?"

"Arai gave me this. It's about Takeo Suzuki."

"What about Suzuki?"

"Arai knew that Suzuki was addicted to porn. Arai told him again and again to stay away, but he did what he wanted."

Sakaguchi signed a paper from one of the junior detectives and waved her away. "So, like the chief said, he was a bystander with bad luck?"

Hiroshi shook his head, staring up at the dangling body. "Are they going to get him down?"

"They need to take photos first, check the area up where it's tied."

Hiroshi walked toward the dry hydrangea branches.

Sakaguchi sighed and stepped over to him. "What was in the letter he gave you?"

"When Arai suspected Suzuki was too far gone, he went to the ministry and made copies of documents. Suzuki was getting deeply involved with cryptocurrency. He still had access to one of Suzuki's bank accounts and made copies of Suzuki's cash flow, which was far beyond any official's salary. Maybe he wanted to shock Suzuki."

"Did it work?"

"Apparently not."

Sakaguchi said, "Takamatsu would say he's doing our work for us."

"In a way, he was. But I don't think he was thinking of turning him in. He just wanted to stop him from doing whatever he was doing, to keep him from getting caught. He was protecting the ministry more than Suzuki."

"What was he doing?"

"I'm not sure yet. Arai gave me the dots, but I have to connect them still. There was someone at Aracoin helping him. Arai didn't understand it either, it seems, but he knew enough to know Suzuki was asking for trouble with the cryptocurrency exchange."

"Aracoin is the currency exchange in Shibuya?"

"We better track down Harada, their security programmer, right away. He's the key link now. Maybe the only link."

"We sent someone after you called. We'll hear back after they check it out. So, Suzuki was the target. And we have motive, through a confession from his secretary. That's good."

"No, it's not good," Hiroshi said. "We don't have who did it, and we have one more person dead. Arai took the crucial connections with him, even if he didn't know what they were."

A young detective came out and asked Sakaguchi to sign another form. The photographers arrived and began photographing the hanging body. Sakaguchi and Hiroshi stepped out of their way so they could get shots from all angles.

The crew moved a gurney close and were taking hold of Arai's legs. Two of them called up to the crew members where the rope was tied. To coordinate, they chanted "*Sei, no*," in unison and the top of Arai's body doubled over as the rope slithered to the ground. Two of the crew held him from below and one cradled his head as they moved him onto the gurney.

Hiroshi and Sakaguchi turned to the body and, together with the rest of the crew, bowed their heads and held their hands together in prayer.

They were interrupted by a buzzing from Sakaguchi's phone. He stepped aside, put the phone to his ear and listened as the medical crew bagged Arai's body. He hung up and looked at Hiroshi.

"The computer security guy, Harada, *was* in his apartment," Sakaguchi said.

"I've got to talk to him," Hiroshi said.

"That'll be tough. He was wrapped from head to foot in industrial plastic wrap. Asphyxiated. No sign of a computer, phone, or any other device in his apartment, either."

Chapter 35

The waterproof spy camera was right where Kenta left it stuck to the wall outside Jack and Jill Studios. Both cameras had somehow stopped sending footage. He cut down the camera and opened it up. It seemed fine.

He swapped out the battery and switched the SD card. He checked the angles and stuck the camera back with fresh mounting tape. He wrote the date on the old SD card and dropped it in his pocket. Kenta's shoes crunched on the gravel as he walked across the parking lot to do the same with the other camera.

He felt more and more sure that the cameras would turn up footage of Kirino heading into the studio. Kirino would not let a simple thing stop him from doing whatever he felt needed to be done. He would have to look back through the footage.

Kenta walked out of the parking lot and started down the sidewalk.

He stopped and stared at his car. He couldn't believe it, but of course, he could.

Yoshitaka Kirino was standing by his Nissan GT-R smoothing his long ponytail. In the early dusk, his black clothing glistened.

It dawned on Kenta that Kirino must have put a GPS on his car the last time he got in. He just hadn't noticed. He'd strip the interior down to find it once he dropped Kirino off.

Kirino walked to the door handle and waited.

"Where's your car?" Kenta asked, looking around.

"They dropped me off."

"Who?" Kenta looked around. On the other side of the street, barely hidden between two delivery trucks was the Subaru he'd loaned the three Shibuya *chinpira*. They were supposed to be tracking his computer and iPad, not chauffeuring Kirino around.

"Is that my car?" Kenta took a step toward his dark-blue Subaru.

"Let's go for a drive," Kirino said.

"They're coming, too?" Kenta pointed at the Subaru.

"We've got to drop something off."

"Drop off what? Where?"

Kirino stared at him. "Near Yokohama. Let's go."

Kenta opened the doors with the remote and Kirino got in.

Kenta pulled a U-turn away from the studios and punched it, wondering if the Subaru would be able to keep up.

Kenta drove in silence for a few blocks. "You must have read about the dead girl found in Shinagawa?"

"I don't read the news." Kirino looked out the side window.

Kirino said nothing more so Kenta drove west past the skyscraper hotels and business offices that crowded Nishi-Shinjuku. He pulled onto Central Circular Route and headed south toward Shinagawa with the Subaru not far behind.

Kirino asked, "Tell me what the news said."

Kenta sighed. "It didn't say too much other than her body floated up in front of a restaurant and the police didn't have much."

"They never have much."

"What they say they have and what they really have are not the same." Kenta sped up around a line of late-night truckers. The overhead lights shone into the interior, alternating light and dark over Kirino's black clothing. "They said it was probably a Thai girl, young, and mentioned she might have been trafficked."

"Things don't always go according to plan."

Kenta felt irritated at this kind of vague pronouncement. Vague was a sign of worse to come.

Kirino nodded ahead. "There's space up ahead. Let's feel some speed."

"I thought you didn't like this car?" Kenta sped up.

"I'm rethinking that." Kirino settled back. "I realized boats feel fast, even when they aren't at the highest speed."

"The highway walls are close, so you feel it's faster than on water."

"Maybe."

Kenta's cellphone pinged. He pulled it out as he kept the speed steady. It was the tracking app for the computer. The signal was coming from right behind his car, moving in tandem. Kenta dropped his cellphone back in his pocket. They had his computer, now, too, along with his second car. He wondered if they could break through his passwords. But of course, he'd have someone who could do that, if not in Tokyo, then in Bangkok.

He went over the reasons they might not have told him about the computer, and none of them were good. Tracking a computer with an app was about the limit those three could handle, but they were very good at following orders, especially Kirino's.

Kirino pulled out a small tablet computer and an SD card reader. "Let me see what was on those cards." He held out his hand.

Had he been watching the whole time? Apparently so. Kenta handed over the SD cards he'd just taken from the spy cameras. "The police cut off all the interior cameras. This is only from the outside."

Kirino put the card in the reader and slid the connector into the tablet. The light from the screen lit up his face from below. Kenta kept heading south in the traffic, trying to decide whether to cut toward the Tokyo Bay Aqua-Line or toward Yokohama. The turn might be a good place to lose the three in the Subaru. He'd upped the horsepower on the Subaru so it drove easy at high speed, but on the open road it wouldn't keep up with his turbo-charged Nissan.

But they had a tracker on his car, anyway. And Kirino was beside him. His other plan would work, if he had the chance to get it all set up. The sooner he could drop Kirino off, the sooner he could get to it.

Kirino fast-forwarded through the video. "Why didn't you use color?"

"It's retro," Kenta said, but Kirino didn't get the joke. "It's clearer."

Without looking away from the fast-forwarding video, Kirino asked, "Inside the studio, how was the tablet streaming hooked up?"

Kenta let out an exasperated sigh. "All the video went into a server and was backed up automatically. I could stream through all my devices to make back-up copies."

"So, you're making a copy of *everything* that's filmed in there?"

"Some of the small-time filmmakers tried to skip out on paying for their rental time. A copy of their next bestseller gives me leverage. If it's pirated, they lose almost everything."

"You blackmail them?" Kirino pulled his ponytail with one hand, the other still grinding through the footage.

"That's not how I would describe it."

"And you're sure the video from that day is gone?"

"I told you, and am telling you again, that video is gone."

"Except for the possible copy on the tablet."

"Except for that."

"You didn't keep a copy for yourself?"

Kenta looked over at him. Was Kirino accusing him? That loss of trust, the very need to ask, was not a good sign.

Kirino looked over from scanning the SD card files. He pulled the SD card out of the reader and handed it back to Kenta.

That was not a good sign, either. Kirino usually kept things like that. Unlike at college, when he got caught with all the videos, he wasn't going to be holding the evidence this time.

Kirino said, "So, the girl and the copy of the video she has—"

"*If* she has it."

Kirino looked at him. "Don't interrupt me."

Kenta looked over at Kirino's black clothes lighting up and darkening under the passing streetlights. Kirino's thinking was just as black and white, listening obediently or cheating him, trusted or tossed away. He was shifting and uncertain.

"That's the last link to this?"

"Right. Except for the computer. You weren't going to tell me they found it?" Kenta nodded at the Subaru following behind them.

"What's there to tell? Those three did a good job. Why don't you pick it up a bit, see if those three can keep up?"

Kenta sped up and moved smoothly through the traffic.

"So, as soon as we get that girl, that should be the end. We can't leave a trace."

"The end?" Kenta asked. "It's still a big mess. They'll be following up on that bureaucrat, Suzuki, for a long time."

"Suzuki got what was coming to him."

Kenta tried to process that. "But the director and the girls didn't do anything."

"The director borrowed a bit more than he could pay back."

"He was borrowing from me."

"Not just from you," Kirino said. "That was the problem."

"But that was easily solved. All he needed was one hit film."

"Of course, that's what we were all waiting for."

"He was a great director. He just—"

"He just borrowed too much money."

Kenta had told the director Noguchi to *never* borrow money from anyone but him, certainly not from Kirino. He wasn't even sure how he'd met Kirino, but he had.

"Suzuki was borrowing money, too?" Kenta asked.

Kirino looked over at him. "No, he was skimming money."

Kenta nearly hit the brakes. "He was *what*? From where?"

"In Thailand, if you pay someone, they do what they're paid for, no matter where they are in the hierarchy. Japanese have pride and feel entitled. Suzuki makes me question how I've been doing business here in Japan altogether. It's easier elsewhere."

Kenta sped the car up. Kirino wasn't someone who worked on trust. He ran his business on fear and control, and money. Kirino was cleaning house, his Japanese house, and Kenta would be the last thing to be cleaned. Kirino would do anything to protect his networks.

The profits from trafficking and porn were enough to kill for, but add on the cryptocurrency accounts, drug running, and whatever else Kirino was into, and it was an enterprise—with multiple revenue streams—that was worth protecting.

Kirino said, "And you know, you were right. I think we should just let Shibaura talk."

"I'm sure he's blabbering away. But it will come back on him. Not us."

Kirino nodded in agreement. "That was a good call. Anyway, like I said before, after this blows over, come to Bangkok. You'll learn a lot there."

"That sounds good," Kenta said, knowing he would never set foot in Bangkok now. Even knowing the little he did about Kirino's empire was dangerous. You can't un-know something, delete it like a computer file. You have to get rid of the whole computer.

Kirino looked up at the passing exit signs. "We need to drop off something near here, so find a place to stop and I'll get in with them."

"Let me find an exit."

"We need that girl."

"I'm on it."

"I've got a boat leaving tonight. Bring her where I tell you."

"Just let me know when and where."

At college, he'd been the one to carry the girls from the party to the back room. No more. He might not be able to save the studio, or his Subaru, or the accounts on his computer, but he could save himself.

Kenta drummed the wheel with both hands glancing in the rearview mirror at the dark-blue Subaru before searching ahead down the expressway for an exit.

Chapter 36

Ueno, a former rugby player who barely fit in the squad cars, pushed Takamatsu's leg to wake him up. Takamatsu stirred, yawned, and sat up in the passenger seat. He straightened his tie, reset his cuffs, and smoothed his pant legs.

They'd been following Kenta Nakamura and whoever was in the car with him with little result for a good portion of the day. Ueno brushed the *nori* crumbs from an *onigiri* off his chest and twisted the top back on a bottle of tea.

"The car theft guys might never have picked him up if he hadn't driven around all day," Takamatsu said, still drowsy from his nap.

"It's good you had favors to call in."

"Always help out other sections. You'll need them at some point for one case or another."

"They've got those helicopter cameras."

"Even those don't work half the time. Too many places to hide in Tokyo, tunnels, underpasses, overpasses, parking garages."

"We got lucky."

"You make your own luck. But yeah, the helicopters help. We probably won't use anything but those in the future. Get a license to fly one now."

Osaki bounced his head, thinking about that. "You think the guy in the car with him is our guy?"

"Maybe. Or he'll take us to the guy."

"You think we can keep up if he decides to lose us?" Ueno dropped back several car lengths. "Look at everything he's added to it, wings, splitter, chrome tires, wraparound lights. He must have modified the engine, too."

"He can't do much in traffic," Takamatsu said.

"He can get away from us." Ueno sped up to get around a cluster of delivery trucks, checking behind him in the rearview mirror. "Wonder how he decked out the inside?"

"We might get a chance to find out."

The expressway curved sharply to the right. They could get a better angle into the car's interior, so Takamatsu pulled the long lens of his camera up and squeezed off as many shots as he could.

"Catch anything?" Ueno craned his neck to look.

"That looks like who we're after." Takamatsu checked the camera. "Pale skin. Ponytail. Black clothes."

"He doesn't go together with the first guy."

"They work from opposite directions."

Ueno fell several cars back. The GT-R was easy to see.

"This could be a two-for-one."

"Hope they take us to their drop-off point."

"From Chiba to Shimizu, there's plenty of places to dock a boat."

"You worked down there, didn't you?" Ueno braked suddenly.

Takamatsu rocked forward and put on his seat belt. "I was liaison between the Police Agency and the Japan Coast Guard when I was about your age."

"Sounds impressive." Ueno looked in the rearview mirror for a long time.

"Sounds political. One police chief had it in for me. He didn't like my methods."

"So, he sent you to the coast?"

"He knew I didn't like being near the water."

"What's the problem with water?" Ueno sped around a row of slow-moving cars.

"Never learned to swim. Never saw the ocean until I came to Tokyo."

"Where's your hometown?"

"In Nagano, small village in the Kiso mountains."

"It's beautiful up there."

"I don't like the mountains either." Takamatsu cracked a window and pulled out his cigarettes. "Left there as soon as I could, before I finished high school."

"I grew up on the Shonan coast. Spent every waking minute at the beach."

"Give me the plains around Tokyo. Flat, clear, urban." Takamatsu blew the smoke out the window.

The Nissan GT-R sped ahead and Ueno had to weave in and out of the cars and delivery trucks to keep them in view.

"If the guy gets out and they split up, it'll be hard to follow both of them," Takamatsu said.

"Which will we take?" Ueno looked behind him in the rearview mirror. "Not to mention the guy behind us. There's been a dark blue Subaru following us the whole time."

"You sure?"

"Yeah, very."

Takamatsu looked at his cigarette and threw it out the window half-finished.

* * *

Hiroshi stared at the crime scene crew photographing the last parts of the scene where Arai had died, but it was pointless. "He cleaned up after his boss even in death. A final, loyal duty," Hiroshi murmured.

Sakaguchi put a heavy paw on Hiroshi's shoulder to steer him toward the front door. "Takamatsu called. He's got Kenta, and there's someone else with him."

Outside, Osaki, who was as big as Sakaguchi, and Sugamo, who was young and compact, caught up with them.

Sakaguchi said, "Osaki, you drive, and Sugamo, you head back to the station. They'll have a pistol case with the New Nambu 38s. And there'll be another case that Takamatsu left. Bring both. Keep them secured in the trunk. We don't want to use them if we don't need to."

Sugamo took off for one of the cars parked on the street. A crowd had gathered and the local police were busy herding them back and deflecting their questions.

With Sakaguchi in front and Hiroshi in back, Osaki eased out through the crowd and headed for the nearest entry ramp for the circular expressway heading south. Sakaguchi called Takamatsu to figure out how to triangulate Tokyo's expressways and catch up.

Hiroshi sat brooding in the back seat.

"The car is heading down to Yokohama," Sakaguchi explained. "I mean two cars."

"Two?"

"Seems like they're traveling in tandem."

Hiroshi sat up in the back. "How do they get the girls into Japan?"

"There's a million ways. Each easier than the last," Osaki said, looking in the rearview mirror at Hiroshi.

"Easiest by boat, right?"

Osaki said, "One of the largest coastlines in the world."

"Open, undefended, porous," mused Hiroshi.

"How many drop-off points are there, you think?" Hiroshi asked.

"Around Tokyo Bay down to Yokosuka, it's basically all one big port."

"Suruga Bay alone is huge," Sakaguchi said.

"Only a couple hours' drive to Tokyo," Osaki said.

"So, the girls could come in anywhere," Hiroshi said. "Just like with drugs."

Sakaguchi's phone rang. When he hung up, he said, "That was Takamatsu again. One guy got out and in the other car. They'll follow that car and we'll pick up this Kenta guy coming back this way. We'll go a bit farther and pull a U-turn after we see him. Look for a dark orange Nissan, with some sort of stuff on the outside."

"Stuff?"

"You know, spoilers, whatever. Dark orange should be enough. He's been driving too fast, so must have a laser jammer. Look for him across the expressway."

"An anonymous tip got called in an hour ago," Sakaguchi said. He held up his text screen for Hiroshi to read. "Said there'd be a drop-off at a dock in Shinagawa."

Hiroshi wondered who it could be. Tips were rare. Real tips even rarer. "Was it a man or a woman who called in?"

"A man, the receptionist said, but too quick to trace. Said he'd call back with details."

"Nice of him."

"They'll patch it through to me if he does," Sakaguchi said.

"Are we being set up?"

"Or led away? We won't know until we know. So, let's keep following this guy until the tipster calls in again."

Osaki wove in and out of delivery vans and long-haul truckers.

"I thought you said he'd be heading to one of the ports?" Hiroshi said. "Isn't he going back into the middle of the city?"

"I thought you didn't drive?" Osaki said.

"I don't. Never got a license," Hiroshi said.

Sakaguchi turned around with a look of disbelief. "Not even in America?"

"Maybe the other guy is heading to the port?" Osaki said, speeding up.

Hiroshi said, "There he is!"

The dark orange Nissan shot by in the opposite direction. Osaki stepped on the accelerator and looked at Sakaguchi.

"Yeah, siren and lights until we get back after him on the other side. Let's trust he's staying on the expressway," Sakaguchi said.

Osaki hit the siren, buzzed around the traffic to the next exit, ducked under the highway, pulling cross-wise around construction blocking the underpass intersection, and shot up the on-ramp after the Nissan.

"Just tell me when you want to cut the siren," Osaki said, and leaned forward to see down the expressway.

"That was five minutes," Hiroshi said. "If he's going about a hundred and twenty kilometers an hour—"

"Forty over the limit."

"We can leave the siren on for a bit longer. He won't hear it." Hiroshi leaned forward to look out the front window.

"First time I've ever wanted a traffic jam," Osaki said. He leaned forward and touched the traffic safety *omamori* hanging from a knob on the dashboard. The small protective amulet swung back and forth from its braided silk thread.

"That looks like a jam," Sakaguchi said.

"That was quick. Those *omamori* really work," Hiroshi said.

"I always get the most expensive one," Osaki said.

"Keep the light going and cut the siren. Let's shoot up along the shoulder, catch up with him."

They cruised past the slow-moving line of cars until they got to a tunnel which shrank the highway to two lanes and no shoulder. Osaki cut the light and pulled into the nearest of the two lanes.

"I hate these tunnels," Osaki said.

"Makes it easy to follow," Sakaguchi said.

"Makes it easy to crash," Osaki said.

"Want me to get out and run ahead?" Hiroshi asked. "Faster than this."

"Just be patient. He can't go anywhere," Sakaguchi said.

"Unless he's gone already. Pick me up at the exit." Hiroshi hopped out and jogged down the side of the road. He looked as far ahead as he could and kept moving forward faster than the vehicles.

He wasn't sure what he was going to do if he caught up with him, but from his calculations, he couldn't be too far ahead, unless he had turned off on one of the exits and they had lost him altogether.

When he got to the end of the tunnel, the high walls on either side of the expressway made it feel like a chute, but traffic was starting to move, Hiroshi picked up his pace.

Then, from an angle, he could see a dip below the front of a black van, the kind favored by construction workers and home contractors.

On the other side of the big black van was a dark orange Nissan GT-R.

Hiroshi crouched down and called Sakaguchi. "Got a visual. When you get out of the tunnel, there's a shoulder. I'll be waiting on the right."

Chapter 37

Sukanya and Chiho got up late. When they woke, they shuffled down the hall for another long, hot bath. They soaped and rinsed under the low showers and got into the tub.

Chiho said, "It's not too hot for you?"

"Maybe little hot." Sukanya smiled. "I work bath place before, in Bangkok. Never dry out and smell like soapy perfume always," Sukanya said. "You grow up house like this?"

Chiho laughed. "Far from it. A small apartment, with two rooms, in the countryside. My father died when I was young. I can't really remember him. My mother drank and played pachinko. She always lost. So, she had me do films. In bikinis or wet clothes. Playing with a beachball, rolling in the sand, in and out of a swimming pool. I thought it was fun."

"How old then?"

"Twelve, thirteen. I ran away to Tokyo when I was sixteen."

The room was steaming up and cold drips of water condensed on the ceiling, plopping down on their flushed skin.

Chiho said, "I was surprised Daisuke was researching the internet cafe."

"He smart." Sukanya hummed. "He in *love* with you."

Chiho splashed her. "What about you? In Bangkok?"

"I live with guy, I told you about. He was best one."

"He was nice?"

"Pretty nice. I learn English, kickboxing thing he like, and learn computer."

"What happened?"

"He go back home Germany."

205

"He just left?"

"He gave me some money, but when money run out, I call Ratana and she tell me about this work. We work together many times in clubs, and she always funny, and strong. Come Japan, work work, she say. And get new passport, she say. I can't believe, but I didn't think, just go. Now, I think not so good idea. None of that true."

"I know the feeling of needing to just go."

Sukanya bundled her hair into a ball and twisted the water out. "Where you go now? Can't go back net cafe."

Chiho stepped out and leaned back to wring her hair dry. Her skin glowed red. "I don't know. I've got no job, either."

"Sorry. You help me, then lose everything." Sukanya climbed out of the bath.

Chiho wiggled her finger for Sukanya to turn around. She dried Sukanya's back and wrung more water from her hair from behind. "My sister. Her eyes were like yours. And her shoulders were broad like yours, too. When I ran away to Tokyo, I left her with my mother. I shouldn't have. My mother drank so much she couldn't take care of herself, much less us. I was in India when it happened. I didn't find out until I came back."

When Chiho stopped drying her back, Sukanya turned around.

Chiho was looking down at the floor. "I told my sister never to get in a car with her. I still don't know if my mother crashed on purpose or accidentally, or even where she got the car. Doesn't matter. She couldn't drive well half-sober, much less totally drunk."

On the way back to the room, they stopped to look at the garden outside the glass doors. Daisuke's family's garden ran to wild neglect. A small pond was overgrown with vines. Dry leaves huddled against rocks and bunched on the dragon-beard grass.

Back in their room, two lacquer lunch boxes rested on the low table. Chiho pulled the top off one to reveal breaded fried shrimp atop white rice.

"Ah, my favorite! *Ebi katsu don!* Daisuke must have ordered these."

Sukanya picked up her elephant bag. "Our clothes gone."

Chiho rushed to her bag. All their clothes had disappeared.

The door opened and the old woman from the day before shuffled in. "Your clothes will be done in an hour or so. I thought you could eat something first. Daisuke's grandmother called her doctor, and she'll stop by here in a short while."

Chiho translated and Sukanya looked surprised. "She's coming here?"

"Yes, she's practically retired." The old woman nodded at Sukanya. "She's fine," Chiho said. "Where's Daisuke?"

"He went to the hospital for further checks." The old woman left them to their lunch.

Sukanya said, "I never leave here."

"Me, neither." Chiho chuckled.

When they were done with lunch, Chiho put the lids on the boxes and wiped the table. "We better take a nap. We might be up late."

They put everything into neat order on the table and pulled out *zabuton* to lay down on with their feet up on the *futon* folded at the side of the room, rubbing their full stomachs. Chiho pulled a blanket over Sukanya and snuggled under the other end as they drifted into a deep snooze.

* * *

The old woman slid the door open and Chiho and Sukanya sat up startled.

"This is Hasegawa Sensei," the old woman said.

Hasegawa Sensei set her bag down and knelt on the tatami. She listened as Chiho introduced herself and Sukanya, and explained briefly about Sukanya's bleeding and pain. Hasegawa Sensei observed Sukanya as she listened.

"I'll examine her here, but she will probably need to come to my clinic."

Chiho nodded.

"I want to examine her in private," Hasegawa Sensei said.

Chiho and the old woman got up and went into the hallway. Hasegawa Sensei switched to English. "You speak English?"

Sukanya nodded yes.

"What is the problem?"

"I have lots bleeding."

"How much?"

"More than usual, but less today. It hurt bad, too, so can't sit. But now a little better."

"Just lie back and tell me if anything hurts." She pressed on Sukanya's lower stomach in different places to see if there was pain, and took her vital signs, all the while observing her closely. "No deep pain here?"

Sukanya thought about it. "Little, but better."

"And your heart, no irregular beating?"

"What means?"

"Your heart," Hasegawa Sensei put her hand over Sukanya's heart and tapped a heartbeat.

"I don't notice different."

Hasegawa Sensei gestured for Sukanya to sit up.

"The bleeding and pain, was it from too much activity? Too much sex?"

Sukanya looked away. "I don't call 'sex.' Just shove in."

"And you say you feel better now?"

"Chiho find medicine and these." She showed the doctor the pills, pads, and tampons.

Hasegawa Sensei reached in her bag and took out some pills. "These are a little stronger, so take these for now. This one will slow the bleeding and this one will reduce the pain."

Sukanya took the pills and bowed deeply.

"I think you had a miscarriage. Were you using contraception?"

"Mis-what? What means contracep—"

"Birth control. Condoms."

Sukanya looked away. "I stop. I want Oskar to stay. So, I taking pill many year, but stop. My cycle is change after stop pill. So, I don't know."

"Who is Oskar?"

"Man I living with in Bangkok. But he go back home."

"I think you had a baby but lost it."

Sukanya looked at the mirror, but it only reflected the wall at an angle.

"You must come in to my clinic tomorrow, but until then, you must rest. Under no circumstances—"

"What means, 'circum—'?"

"It means, you cannot leave the house. I'll be at my clinic tomorrow morning and so will you. Until then, I want you to rest. Do not move around too much. Bathe, eat, sleep, that's all. Tomorrow, we'll do more tests, OK?"

"I understand." Sukanya wondered how she was going to go get her passport from Yotaro if she wasn't supposed to move.

Hasegawa Sensei stood up. Chiho came back in and listened to Hasegawa Sensei, nodding at every sentence.

When she was gone, Chiho said, "Resting sounds good to me, too. Let's take another nap." They flopped down on the tatami, put pillows under their heads, and drifted off.

* * *

It was dark when Yotaro's call woke them. Their clean clothes were folded neatly in wicker baskets by the mirror. They hadn't even heard anyone come in. Chiho grabbed her cellphone and nodded at Sukanya.

Sukanya stared at the paneled wood ceiling and listened to Chiho answering in Japanese. Finally, Chiho clicked off. "Yotaro said he has the passports."

"Really? Really? Yotaro is great." Sukanya looked pleased. She got up and started to pull on her clothes. "You say goodbye Daisuke and we go."

"Let's just go. We'll tell him later."

Sukanya stopped dressing and stared at Chiho, then pulled her jeans on and sat down to put her socks on. "You sure?"

Chiho pulled open the in-wall closet, but there were only the *hakama* they had worn to dinner. "I wanted to head out through the garden here, but maybe our coats are by the front door. And our shoes. So front door it is."

Sukanya took her elephant-shaped bag and Chiho took her backpack.

"We'll be back soon," Chiho said.

"If has passport, I leave right away." She dug in her pocket and pulled out the roll of cash. "Is this enough for ticket?"

Chiho looked at it and looked away. "I'll go with you to the airport." They looked at each other.

"Are you ready?" Chiho asked.

"I'm ready. I want thank—"

"Shhh, let's do this first." Chiho put her hand on the door, and a knock came from the hallway side.

"Chiho? Sukanya?"

"Daisuke?" Chiho asked.

The door slid back and Daisuke came in. He hobbled with discomfort, dressed in an old black *hakama* that was big and loose.

"I poked my head in before and you were asleep. I didn't want to wake you."

"How is your arm?"

"It doesn't hurt now, but it feels like it's going to hurt."

"And your leg?"

"Bruised but not broken. It'll heal."

He turned to Sukanya, "Did you get—"

"Everything OK, doctor said," Sukanya said, smiling.

Daisuke spoke slowly. "I have everything set up."

"Set up?"

Daisuke waved his arms for them to be quiet. "When I turned on the computer, I had enough time to download the footage and store it in the cloud."

Chiho said, "So, we have a copy?"

Daisuke said, "We can access it. Once you get the passport, give Yotaro the online address and he can download the videos, or delete them, or whatever he wants to do with them. Then, he can lock us out and we're free. Got it?"

"He'll want to check," Chiho said.

"He can do that, but once you turn on the iPad, the GPS will kick in and whoever found me will find you."

Chiho nodded.

"And if the online address is enough, keep the iPad and take it to the police."

"I don't know what Yotaro will want. He called, but he's hard to read. He was so angry at me still." Chiho looked at Daisuke, confused. "What am I supposed to say to the police?"

"Tell them you found it. Or...it doesn't matter. Just give it to them."

Chiho realized Daisuke had thought it through. She'd had no plan herself, other than to hand the iPad over for the passport.

Sukanya put the iPad in her elephant bag. "I carry. I am cause all this."

Chiho and Daisuke looked at her for a minute.

"You've got to text me at each step," Daisuke said.

Chiho nodded, yes.

"You sure you trust this guy Yotaro?"

"I used to trust him."

Daisuke looked at her closely.

Chiho said, "We need our coats and shoes."

Chapter 38

"See, I told you," Osaki said, and pounded the steering wheel. "We caught up with him, but the smaller the streets get, the harder it is to tail anyone, and impossible without them noticing."

The Nissan had pulled off the national highway near Jiyugaoka and followed city streets, which narrowed as they pulled east and north through the neighborhoods west of the Yamanote Line. Four-lane roads turned to two-lane roads, and then one-lane roads so narrow that two cars could pass only by waiting at cross streets.

Now, they had lost the GT-R altogether.

"He was good," Osaki said. "I was on car theft for a couple years and those guys were amazing, but this guy driving the GT-R is above their league."

"So, what do we do now?" Hiroshi asked.

Sakaguchi said, "We saw him last turn down this street, so just keep going. We're almost in Shimokitazawa now. I don't want to call the local cops or he might get suspicious."

"Call in helicopters," Osaki said. "That always works with car thieves."

"Let's get in as close as we can and then Hiroshi and I will jump out and walk it," Sakaguchi said. "Everyone's cellphones charged?"

"Just be sure he didn't turn down one of these side streets," Hiroshi said.

"We should have brought two cars for this," Sakaguchi said.

"A motorcycle," Hiroshi said.

"You have a motorcycle license?" Osaki asked.

"I don't have that either," Hiroshi said.

Osaki jammed on the brakes to avoid a bicyclist and Hiroshi, riding in the back, shot forward into the back of the front seat.

Sakaguchi twisted around and said, "Seat belt?"

"I was stretching to look down the streets."

"Are you sure he didn't notice us along the way?" Sakaguchi asked.

Osaki hummed and drove more slowly. "He might have noticed, but anyone going that way *could* take this route, so it might seem we're just stuck behind him. I don't know."

Hiroshi said, "I can only see a little way in each direction."

Osaki said, "I think he's heading back and forth from big roads where he can speed ahead, to small side streets, where it's hard to follow. Sewing, we used to call it."

They turned west onto a wider road and cut back to small side streets.

Hiroshi leaned back on the seat. "This is Shimokitazawa. What's he doing here?"

Sakaguchi said, "Picking something up? Or just trying to shake us?"

Hiroshi leaned back and looked down the passing streets on his side.

Sakaguchi looked down the others. Osaki kept his eyes on the mirrors mounted at every cross street. He had to keep braking for cars, bicycles, and pedestrians, all swerving and jockeying for space to get where they were going.

As they got to Shimokitazawa, the residential streets became more commercial and the streets were more crowded and moved more slowly.

Sakaguchi finally said, "Let's get out on foot."

Osaki stopped to let Sakaguchi and Hiroshi out. They worked their way down the small lanes, moving toward the train station. Pedestrians streamed down the middle of the lanes until a car passed and they split to flow around it.

Hiroshi kept a steady pace through the crowd. He saw Sakaguchi on the parallel street when intersections lined up.

At the top of a small rise, Hiroshi looked back and saw Osaki far behind, the car at a crawl, barely moving through the people. At the next cross street, Hiroshi looked back again and couldn't see him at all. Osaki must have turned right to drive parallel on a bigger street.

Hiroshi stopped to check the map on his phone. The streets seemed to have a will of their own, curving, dead-ending, or veering how they wanted. The whole area was laid out for foot traffic long before automobiles ever arrived in Tokyo.

The street he was on went straight for only a short while before veering away from Shimokitazawa altogether. Hiroshi hurried ahead to the corner. When he looked up again, he caught a glimpse of the GT-R heading away from where Sakaguchi was. He wondered if Sakaguchi had seen him.

Hiroshi called Sakaguchi. "Did you see him?"

Sakaguchi said, "I saw him pass. Where are you?"

"I'm in front of a tall building with lots of shops inside, new, concrete."

"I think I see it. Keep going, I'll catch up."

The GT-R pulled left up a steep street. There were no people, so he sped up and Hiroshi had to run to catch up. The car turned right and Hiroshi hustled to keep eyes on it all the way to where it turned downhill again. There were no other cars on the street, but it was lined with young people waiting to get into a club.

The GT-R made a quick turn down a small blind alley between two buildings. Hiroshi waited until the GT-R was out of sight and then hurried down and peered around the corner into a back-alley parking lot. He looked for another exit but couldn't see one. The brake lights of the GT-R went off and he ducked back against the wall of the building.

Hiroshi walked back up to the front, pretending to check his cellphone, waiting for Kenta to come up the gravel slope from the parking lot. From where he was, he could see anyone coming up or down the steep slope to the lot. He could see some people lining up in front of the music club, and pedestrians milling around on the big street.

He called Sakaguchi. "I'm on the street that runs from the south exit of the station. There's a crowd of people. The club is called Lost Melody. I'm across the street."

Sakaguchi said. "Wait until we get there. Osaki picked me up. The streets are crowded." He clicked off.

It would be better to have him in hand, though Hiroshi wasn't sure he could take him alone. He walked down the street, the only guy in a suit jacket amid the casually dressed young people wandering or waiting to get inside the club. A bouncer at the door was taking their money and putting plastic bracelet entrance tickets around their wrists.

Hiroshi walked back down toward the parking lot, but saw nothing other than the GT-R and the back entrance to clubs and restaurants.

There was a large shed for trash. He took a photo of the car and the license plate and sent it to Akiko to run through the database, and then to Sakaguchi. There was no way out of the lot except into one of the three buildings adjoining it, so which one did Kenta go in?

The line in front of the club was long. As soon as some people went in, more lined up. How big could the club be? Sakaguchi sent a text message that they were parked on the next street over.

Hiroshi walked to the door and stood idly scanning the schedule of bands playing that month. The names of the bands meant nothing to him, but the photos and designs carried all the promise of youth—the drive and passion of rock, punk, hardcore, hip-hop, heavy metal, the blast of exuberance.

A new bouncer came up the stairs to take over the door from the bald, leather-clad guy, who ambled down the stairs into the club.

The outside of the building was covered in signs for the interior. There was the big music club in the basement, and small clubs on the upper floors. The building was large, but it still seemed like a lot of people going in. He took a photo of the signs and sent it to Akiko to check out the owner, registration, and taxes of all the places.

He wandered back across the street, where he had a clear view of the door and the blind driveway that dropped down to the lot behind the club.

He called Sakaguchi, "Did you call for backup?"

"Not yet."

"Do you want to go in?"

"Are you sure he went in that club?"

"Not completely. And it's got to be amazingly crowded inside."

"Then let's wait. Grab him outside. I just got a call from the tip line. Same guy. They couldn't patch him through, but he left the name of a dock near Shinagawa. Said there'd be a trafficker there tonight."

"Did he ask for a reward?"

"No, he didn't. That makes me suspicious. Maybe we're getting pulled away."

"Still, someone has to check out the tip. Should we give up here?"

"He mentioned Jack and Jill."

"Our good luck? Or a set-up?"

"Takamatsu and Ueno will go to the dock instead. Sugamo will meet them there as soon as he can."

"Aren't they following the guy who got out of Kenta's Nissan?"

"They'll follow him until the time the trafficker is supposed to show up. If they find nothing, or lose him, they'll go then. And if that doesn't happen, we'll have to choose one or the other."

"Is two people enough, just Ueno and Takamatsu?"

"It'll have to be," Sakaguchi said. "Takamatsu can handle himself."

"Not always."

"We'll wait here. If this is our guy, let's get him before he gets back in his car."

"You want me to wait in the parking lot?"

"That might surprise him. Wait at the top of the drive. We'll be close. There are too many people out in front now. Don't let him get out the front door."

Hiroshi settled in at the front of the club, staring down the drive into the parking lot, waiting patiently.

Chapter 39

When they got off at Shimokitazawa Station, Sukanya took Chiho's arm. Temporary mats were taped to the floor for the remodeling of the station and tarps clipped to scaffolds formed a tunnel to the exits. Outside, they headed toward Yotaro's club, flowing along with the tide of club goers, partiers, and shoppers in the cool of the night.

"He has the passport?" Sukanya asked.

"He said he did. But Yotaro is a hard person to read."

"Maybe he forgive. You don't cause trouble. Is your boyfriend."

"When you get it, are you really going to leave?"

"I cause enough problem."

"You didn't cause it." Chiho patted her arm.

Sukanya put her hand on top of Chiho's and walked slowly, calmed by the small streets. Sukanya wondered how many shoppers there could be in Tokyo. Maybe everyone went out, shopped, ate, and walked around every day.

From small eateries, exhaust fans sent the smell of cooking into the night air. Somewhere in the meandering smells was the whiff of Thai spices. There would be Thai restaurants in America, she was sure. She would find work, new people, a new life. It didn't matter about whatever else Ratana was trying to get. Even a little would be enough now.

"Is this way we came before?" Sukanya asked.

"Yes, you remember." Chiho smiled at her.

"I remember, in case needing to find the station again," Sukanya said.

Weathered, hand-lettered signs hung casually above shop doors and blackboard menus rested on chair backs. Along the walls, there was just enough room to stack potted plants, carved signs, and display shelves with flyers, menus, and maps. Chiho stopped to pick up a free magazine about bands.

"That's my old band-mate," Chiho said, pointing out a photo on the cover. "We were in a band together before the last one I toured with."

"You are famous." Sukanya looked at Chiho and pulled her tight against her. "You left guitar at net cafe? You want go back?"

"It was an old one. I'll get another."

Sukanya pulled Chiho close. "You have good life here. Tokyo young people."

"I don't have enough money to move out of the net cafe."

"But it nice there."

"Until Daisuke got hurt."

"You find another."

"Another guy?"

"No!" Sukanya hit Chiho's arm. "Another place for living. Keep Daisuke."

Outside Yotaro's club, a long line of people waited to get in. The same bouncer in a stud-covered leather jacket stood barking orders for the concert-goers to form a line.

Across the street, people without tickets squatted checking their cellphones with exaggerated poses. Most layered themselves in T-shirts, leather jackets, make-up, piercings, and tattoos. Everyone waited patiently, feigning indifference. The line to get in stretched half a block.

"The band must be popular," Chiho said.

Sukanya felt good in her bouncy, pink and white tennis shoes. If the passport was OK, she would get out of Japan on the first plane. She wanted to celebrate with Chiho somehow, but getting away came first. She would leave her clothes to Chiho and just go.

"You want call Yotaro?" Sukanya asked.

"It's better to just go in," Chiho said.

"Daisuke's plan is OK?"

"It's the plan we have."

They walked to the head of the line. The bouncer saw them and nodded his fireplug head for them to come over. He took two plastic bracelets from a cardboard box and fastened them around their wrists.

Inside the club, bartenders in tight black shirts were getting the bar set up and the sound crew ran around with fanny packs, taping cords in place and checking the soundboard mix. Small spotlights lit

217

the stage and the speakers hummed.

Sukanya followed Chiho down the dark hallway to Yotaro's office. The posters and graffiti glowed in the dim light. Yotaro's office door was halfway open, letting the underwater colors flicker into the hallway. They could hear the bubbling of the aquarium and low voices.

Chiho pushed open the door. Yotaro sat behind the desk and smiled. On either side of the desk stood two tall women in black and red maid outfits with maroon hair. They had the same painted white face with wide black circles around their eyes. One had an oversized, lace bow behind her head. They turned toward Chiho and Sukanya with the same slow motion, as if in a dance routine.

"Meeting's over, girls," Yotaro said, clapping his hands. "I've got business."

Yotaro gestured at the two women. "This is Miko and Chari. They need a guitarist. You'd be perfect, Chiho." Yotaro had on thick, red designer glasses about the same color as the women's hair.

Chiho looked at them and their outfits. "Thanks, but I'm out of practice."

Miko and Chari said at the same time, "Weren't you in the band Maids on Fire? I remember you."

"I used to be," Chiho said. "And in Grapple."

"I loved that band."

"You know them?"

"Of course. Why don't we jam sometime?" Miko said.

"We need a guitarist." Chari looked at Chiho more closely.

Chiho fidgeted her head noncommittally. "You play here every month?"

"Every two weeks. Catch our show. We're on in a few minutes." They hurried into the hall.

"It doesn't hurt to be polite," Yotaro said.

"I was polite," Chiho said.

Sukanya stared at the aquarium, feeling underwater with the bright fish squirming and swimming around in front of her.

Yotaro stood up, leaning and favoring his right leg, bending as he took a step.

"I got a Thai ID. But I couldn't get a passport." Yotaro held up his hand to stop Chiho from complaining. "And I got something else. A police report."

Chiho rolled her eyes. "How is a police report going to help us?"

Yotaro reached into his desk and pulled out a piece of paper and a small Thai ID card. He handed the paper to Chiho and the ID card to Sukanya.

"Pop a photo into the Thai ID and laminate it." Yotaro handed Chiho a *meishi* shop card. "This guy will do it. He's just around the corner. We're old friends."

Chiho squinted down at the cards and the paper. "I'm not so sure about your friends."

"You're right. Some of my friends have left me with big debts," Yotaro said.

Chiho showed the card to Sukanya. "Will it work?"

Sukanya turned it over and nodded it was OK. "No passport?"

Yotaro said, "Passports are not so easy as they once were. This is better. Take this ID and this police theft report to the embassy."

Chiho took the paper and read it, then looked at Yotaro. "How did you get this?"

Yotaro shrugged. "Your boyfriend's running out on me, nearly having my spine broken." He pointed at his leg. "And my leg broken, well, those experiences pushed me to make a lot of new friends."

"What kind of friends?"

"The helpful kind."

"What is?" Sukanya asked, leaning to look at the official-looking paper.

Chiho held it out for her to read, but it was all in Japanese. "It's a police form. It says that your passport was stolen and that the police called immigration to confirm you had a transit visa for Japan through to America."

"What mean?" Sukanya asked.

Chiho looked at Yotaro.

Yotaro limped around the side of his desk, dragging his leg. "It means, if you take this to the Thai embassy, they will give you a new passport, a real one, and then, if you go to immigration, they'll give you a transit visa. And then if you go to the American Embassy, and prove what happened, they'll give you a new visa."

Chiho made a face. "They'll never believe this."

Yotaro shrugged. "Japan would never give a transit visa to a Thai passport holder unless there was a visa on to another country."

"That's not what we agreed on."

"I don't remember we agreed on anything at all," he said, so loud the fish changed direction. "This is a favor. And you know how those go. They're returned. Now, what do you have for me?"

Chiho looked at Sukanya. Sukanya reached into her bag and took out the iPad and handed it to Yotaro.

"That's it?" Yotaro said, chuckling and taking the iPad. "What could be so shocking? Or so valuable?"

"You'll have to get into it first," Chiho said. "You can sell everything that's on there, or hand it back to the people who are looking for it."

"Who's looking for it?" Yotaro handed it back.

"I don't know, but they beat up a friend of ours trying to get this."

"I don't want this. It's toxic."

"There's an online address we made where you can download everything from another computer, too."

"That's probably more toxic."

"It's more valuable."

"An online address?" He dipped his head and looked at her.

"Someone wants this back. And the rest can be sold. Favor returned."

Yotaro closed his eyes and sighed.

Chiho said, "Look, they want this badly. They'll pay for the address to get the information."

"Or they'll throw me off another balcony. I can't fight back as well as I used to." Yotaro pushed himself up on his desk.

"You can send them the link from a distance and keep the movies to sell. It's just a few minutes of downloading and restoring the files."

Yotaro looked at Chiho.

Chiho said, "You know who to contact. We just want out."

Sukanya held the ID and police report, staring at the fish bending and curving, carving S's in the water in fierce, bright colors.

Chiho took her arm, but Sukanya kept staring at the fish swimming in loops and circles.

Yotaro scratched his head and frowned, and then rubbed his head. "I'll see what I can do. But I need the link."

"I'll send you the link when we're out of here."

"I thought this was just some frisky videos. But now you hand me a project, tell me there's more. If this is evidence of a crime, it makes things much more difficult."

Yotaro's phone rang and everyone jumped.

The office door opened slowly.

When Sukanya turned around from the fish, she grabbed Chiho's arm so hard Chiho cried out.

At the door was a well-dressed, handsome young man dangling a car key remote in one hand with a cellphone to his ear.

Sukanya knew exactly who it was.

Chapter 40

Sukanya backed against the cool, moist glass of the aquarium and pulled Chiho close. This guy was the one who kept coming in and out of the studio, checking on the old fat guy taking photos. He was the one who checked the recording equipment and the computers. He was the one who brought in the drugs, barely glancing at what was happening on the set.

Now, here he was, pushing the door shut with his foot.

He unzipped his bag and dug around inside, looking like he knew everything, surveying the office, keeping an eye on the two women and pulling something out of his bag.

Chiho started yelling at Yotaro. Sukanya could grasp the feeling but none of the words.

Kenta stepped toward Sukanya and she started backing away along the cold, smooth surface of the glass, pulling Chiho, who kept yelling at Yotaro.

Yotaro started yelling at Kenta but didn't move.

In a flash, Kenta lunged toward Sukanya and jabbed a needle into her thigh. Sukanya, ready for him, yanked her leg back, twisted, and kicked. The needle clattered to the floor, but before she could stamp on it, Kenta lunged at Chiho. Distracted by yelling at Yotaro, Chiho didn't move away. The second needle caught her full in the thigh, hanging there, until she pulled it out and threw it at Kenta.

Sukanya lunged at Kenta and started punching at his face with both hands. She swung a kick, but Kenta stepped back nimbly, his bag in front of him like a shield, watching closely.

Sukanya rubbed her thigh. She didn't want the hot flash of energy that swept through and clouded her vision during the film shoots. It scattered her mind and made her body feel like it was no longer hers. It had kept her walking until she was drained of energy.

She felt her thigh, checked herself, but there was no rush of intensity like there'd been in the warehouse. This was something different. She backed against Chiho, trying to shield her from anything more.

Chiho leapt at Yotaro, swinging at his head.

Yotaro knocked her hands aside as he hobbled behind his desk.

Chiho kept swinging until her knees buckled and her body swayed. Her shoulder hit the aquarium on the way down, but Sukanya caught her before her head hit the floor. She held Chiho's head against her chest as Chiho slipped into unconsciousness, her body deflated, heavy against her.

Kenta stood watching from the door.

Feeling drowsy, the opposite of the drugs at the film shoot, Sukanya closed her eyes. She could make a run for it. Maybe a couple of Muay Thai kicks would be enough to get past, but then where would she go? She couldn't leave Chiho. It was better to wait for the right moment, when she could reverse this.

She felt for the ID and paper in her pocket and fingered the iPad in her elephant bag. She let herself fall back against the aquarium and her eyes flutter shut. At one club she worked at in Bangkok, men paid to lie down next to sleeping girls. It was hard not to fidget, but the job was to act asleep, and it paid well for doing nothing more than ignoring being touched.

She felt Kenta touch her shoulder, but she kept herself loose, pretending to be asleep. Chiho really was knocked out, her body slack. It would be hard to keep up for long.

She heard Yotaro and Kenta talking back and forth. If she knew what they were saying, she could decide what to do. But she could wait.

* * *

Yotaro said, "It's too dangerous. I can't let you take them."

Kenta pointed at them. "They're already drugged."

"You don't know what you're doing."

"I've got it all figured out. There's no other way but to use these two."

"There has to be."

"It's too late for that now. It's all in place."

"You need to protect these two," Yotaro said. "You have to—"

"Promise? I told you before. No promises." Kenta stopped and looked at Yotaro. "I have to get out from under Kirino. You want to get out from under the loans. Once this is over that's what will happen."

"How do you know this is going to work?"

"I don't, but it's our best shot. You going to help me?"

Yotaro said, "I got a bad leg. Remember?"

"You ever try carrying two girls around? It's not so easy." Kenta looked at the girls, deciding how best to pick them up.

"Get them out of here. Now." Yotaro stayed by his desk.

"Just give me a hand."

Yotaro stared at Kenta. "No. That's all I owe you. We're even now. Debt paid."

"I can't carry both of these girls," Kenta said.

"Leave them here then."

"I still have the last step. Like I explained."

"You didn't explain much."

"It's better if they're sleeping."

"Where are you taking them?"

"It's better you don't know." Kenta pulled the door open and checked the hallway. "I parked out back. Through that hallway, right?"

Yotaro called on the phone intercom. In a minute, the bald bouncer arrived in his studded leather jacket. He looked at the two girls collapsed on top of each other and then at Yotaro.

Yotaro said, "Make sure he gets them out of here. And come back inside right after."

The bouncer held the door open.

Kenta pushed the Thai girl to the side and pulled the plumper, heavier Japanese girl to a sitting position. He squatted down, took her wrists, and hoisted her onto his back. He carried her down the hallway, legs dangling, and raised his foot to kick the latch bar on the exit door.

On the outside landing, he pushed a rock with his foot to keep the door from closing. He scanned the parking lot and headed straight for his Nissan GT-R.

Kenta pulled out his remote to pop open the trunk. He propped her against the side of his car, careful not to scratch the finish, maneuvered her inside, and then slammed the trunk shut.

Back in the office, he gave Yotaro an exasperated look, and pulled the thin, light Thai girl around, twisting and pulling her up until her arms were over his shoulders. Black hair dangling behind her, she was as light as a backpack.

Yotaro and the bouncer did nothing to help. Once again, Kenta found himself doing the worst part of the job. This time, though, it would be to free himself.

"Don't leave their bags," Yotaro shouted after him.

He could hear the bouncer following after him, bringing the bags.

After popping open the trunk, he settled the Thai girl in together with the Japanese girl. They both were sleeping, so that was enough to get them to the drop-off point.

Kenta turned and wiped his forehead. "Put their bags in," he told the bouncer, who stood still holding their bags in the middle of the gravel lot.

Kenta said, "The trunk is designed to fit two golf bags. Plus, they're sleeping. They're fine."

The bouncer shook his head.

"I don't have all night." Kenta walked over and took the bags from him. When he did, the Thai girl hopped out of the trunk.

Kenta snatched at her, but she grabbed the elephant bag and took off running toward the narrow driveway up to the street. He sprinted after her, caught a handful of hair and yanked.

She fell backward and started to kick, landing a strong one on his thigh. Kenta twisted her and wrapped his arm around her neck. He lifted her off the ground, cutting off her air, wondering why the drugs weren't working.

She kept kicking at his knees, even as she coughed.

He set her back down and she stomped on his foot—his accelerator foot. When he stepped away, she grabbed two of his fingers and pulled them in opposite directions. He screamed and lost his grip. Did she break his fingers?

He shook that off as she faced off with him.

"Bring her from car," the girl shouted, swinging her bag in a circle.

This was exactly why he was never going to do this again. Enough with Jack and Jill, enough with this whole business. He'd take these two girls to the spot and make sure what happened, happened, but never again.

225

He dodged as she swung the bag at him with both hands. He tried to catch her English. "I give this iPad, you bring her here."

He looked up the last of the slope to the line of young people ambling in to the club. If she screamed, there would be witnesses.

"I give you code for file. Chiho is free and I give you."

Kenta shook his head. "Code? What code?"

"Bring her now and you can have."

Kenta looked toward the parking lot, at his car, and back at her, sighing. There was always this kind of problem, but this was the last time.

Kenta looked up at the driveway, and took a step to see about the crowd on the street. Before he could decide what to do, he felt a crack on the back of his head. She had beaned him with her bag.

What was inside? Was it the iPad? It was enough to make his head sting. He'd had enough of this little bitch. He should have brought another needle full. What was he thinking?

When she drew her arm back to smack him again, he caught the bag mid-arc, yanked down and pulled her off balance. He grabbed her around the waist, careful of his feet this time, and reeled her in close.

He spoke directly into her ear. "If you don't get in the car, I'll kill your friend. You understand? I'll kill her."

Chapter 41

Sukanya let him push her to the side door of the GT-R. He was handsome, but horrible, and there didn't seem to be anything else she could do to help Chiho except go along. She wanted to tear his eyes out. "No, I see my friend," she shouted at him. "If no, I start yell. Other people is close." She gestured toward the front of the club.

He pulled open the door.

Sukanya reached in her elephant bag and pulled out the iPad. "Here. You take. I take her."

"It doesn't work like that."

She let him push her inside. He slammed the door, locked it, slammed the trunk, and came around to the driver's side.

Before she could react, he reached inside the storage compartment and pulled out a pair of handcuffs, and started to put them on her.

Sukanya twisted her hands away.

He drew his hand back to hit her.

She put her hands up. "I do myself." Sukanya knew it was better to cuff herself. She had learned that the hard way in Bangkok. She slipped one over her left wrist and clicked it.

"Put the other around the handle grip there," he said.

Sukanya slid the other cuff through the handle and clicked it. "All locked. You like? Woman can't fight? Can't move. So strong man." Sukanya held both hands in the air, one cuffed, one free.

He snatched her elephant bag and took the iPad, put it in the storage compartment between the bucket seats and closed the lid. "This is mine."

Sukanya took back her bag, empty now in her shaking hands.

He said, "Here's how it works. You shut up for the ride and I'll let your friend go. Got it?"

227

"How I trust you?"

"You don't have a choice."

Sukanya looked at him, deciding if she did or not, deciding what choices she did have.

"Where you take me?"

"Keep your eyes ahead and don't act suspicious."

"What means 'suspicious'?"

"What? Just act normal."

"I am normal."

"Keep your head down as we pull out of here. And put your seat belt on."

"Like this?" Sukanya put her belt on and scrunched down below the dashboard level. "You not even brave bad man."

He pulled the car onto the main street and quickly punched through an opening in the crowd and headed away.

Sukanya felt afraid of the speed. The streets were so narrow she could reach out and touch the walls. When he slowed down, people brushed the side of the car.

She thought about trying to signal them, show them the cuffs holding her to the door. Or maybe she could slip the cuffs, get the door open, and slip out. But where would she find help? Tokyo was too big and Chiho would still be in the trunk.

She looked at him leaning forward and moving the rearview mirror back and forth and pounded the steering wheel.

They wove through streets wide enough for only one car at a time. They backed up a couple of times to let a car pass, and sped up on larger streets. She could hear Chiho's body rolling in the trunk when he braked or sped up. The sound of her body hitting the walls of the trunk was horrible.

* * *

When the Nissan wheeled out of the lot and took off, Hiroshi raced to where Osaki was waiting with Sakaguchi, and jumped in the car.

"He was too fast," Hiroshi said.

"It's OK," Sakaguchi said. "If the girls are in there now, we've got him."

"If we can catch him," Osaki said.

"Let's make sure we do," Sakaguchi said.

"Where are they going?" Hiroshi asked. He leaned forward from the back seat to see ahead.

"No idea," Osaki said.

"Just keep following them," Sakaguchi said.

"Call in the helicopters," Osaki said. "When they hear that sound, they start to run and make mistakes."

"That's what we don't want," Sakaguchi said. "The streets are too crowded for mistakes."

Hiroshi said, "Looks like it's going to get even more crowded. He just turned toward Shibuya."

"Let's just keep following," Sakaguchi said. "You didn't see anyone in there?"

Hiroshi said, "Someone was in the passenger seat, but he whizzed by too quickly."

"It's good you made it to the car. I was about to leave you," Osaki said.

"When you told me to let him drive off, I thought—"

"If we grabbed him then, we'd have a kidnapper," Sakaguchi said. "But if we follow him to the end, we might have the whole operation."

"We'll have nothing if he gets away," Osaki said, pressing the accelerator.

Sakaguchi growled. "If we find the right time, stuck in a corner or stopped at a light, we'll yank him out of the car."

Osaki pressed the accelerator. "Car like that, you'll have to break the windows."

"That works for me," Sakaguchi said.

Hiroshi said, "If we can get him on a big street, there'll be enough room to take him."

Osaki said, "We'll have to get lucky for that to happen."

"I'll call ahead to the local Shibuya cops. If they're ready and waiting on the big streets, that'll help our chances."

* * *

Sukanya tried to remember landmarks, a glass building there, a wooden temple there, but they blurred together after so many turns. On small streets, he turned again and again. On big streets, he went faster and checked the rearview mirror. The zig-zag stop-start was making her nauseous.

At a long stoplight, Sukanya looked out and recognized the street where she had walked that first morning in Tokyo. The stores open then were closed now, but the streets were still busy. They passed the store with the aquariums where she met Chiho. She could hear the sound of Chiho rolling around in back each time he braked or restarted.

She had to figure out what to do. She caught sight of policemen standing in front of their police boxes, hands on their hips, guns in their holsters.

The car climbed a sharp incline, turned and headed downhill. If this was the way to lose whoever was following, it was going to be over soon, and then she and Chiho would be driven somewhere without other people around, maybe even back to that studio. She had to do something before then.

It was better to do it here with all the people. At least someone would see. Sukanya watched people passing in front of her and tried to think how to get out of the car and tell someone.

When the car stopped at a traffic light, she saw a tall man outside her window gesturing at her. What was he doing? She stared at him for a moment and realized he was motioning for her to get out of the car. She searched for the door lock release, but a crash came from the driver's side and pieces of glass hit her face.

A giant of a man had smashed the window with a baton. Another bash from the baton splintered the front glass into a fine spiderweb of cracks. The giant hit the side glass again, caving it in. He rimmed out the glass and reached in for the throat of her kidnapper.

Sukanya pulled again and again on the handle, pressed a button, but nothing happened. Her hand was held by the cuffs and she waved to the tall man on her side that she couldn't get out. The tall man tugged on the handle from outside, uselessly.

Then, the car shot forward.

* * *

Sakaguchi and Hiroshi stood on either side of the empty spot where the car had just been. Two local beat cops stood there with batons watching the Nissan take off down the street.

"He's heading straight for Hachiko Square," Hiroshi yelled and started running down the middle of Dogenzaka toward Shibuya Station. Crowds of people swarmed the sidewalks and crossed at every stoplight. Cars veered out of the way and braked hard.

Sakaguchi and Hiroshi raced frantically down the street, the two local cops right beside them. Sakaguchi waved for the cars to get out of the way and Hiroshi raced forward.

At the next stoplight, the car braked for people crossing. As the car nudged forward, people scattered, cringing. The Nissan slowed just enough for Hiroshi to grab the back spoiler from one side and Sakaguchi from the other.

When the car punched forward, Hiroshi lost his grip, but he watched Sakaguchi hang on for a minute and then go spinning along the pavement.

Hiroshi paused to see if Sakaguchi was all right, but after a quick roll, he pulled his huge body back to his feet. The Nissan plowed forward.

Hiroshi raced after the car, sweat pouring down his face as his vision blurred. He looked ahead to Hachiko Square, where thousands of pedestrians were strolling across the crossing from all directions at once.

From huge overhead screens, bobbing images of dancing celebrities and smiling faces shone down from above and showered the most crowded square in Tokyo with color.

In a few seconds, the Nissan would have to turn right or turn left, or sail forward into the waiting throngs of people.

* * *

Inside the car, Sukanya snatched glimpses of the people staring at them rocketing downhill. She looked at him trying to drive and brush the glass from his lap. His hand was badly cut and the car swerved when he put his hand to his mouth to lick off the blood.

Sukanya did the only thing she could think of—she unzipped her elephant bag, stretched it taut and dropped it over his head.

He swung at her with his bleeding hand, but she twisted the opening around his neck with one hand as his head bounced and squirmed like a bagged animal.

His fist flung out and caught her in the chest. She gasped at the pain but tightened her grip on the bag by twisting the corner and jamming her feet against the bucket seat to pull as hard as she could.

He hit her again, and this one made her loosen her hold. He thrust one hand under the bag and ripped it off. He snatched at the wheel with both hands.

Sukanya leaned back with her legs high and kicked him for all she was worth.

The car careened sideways and rose on two wheels, skidding into the hip-high granite bollards protecting the vast square from traffic.

The momentum flipped the car into the air.

It landed upside down, the metal screeching until the car slammed into an old train exhibit in the middle of the square.

Dizzy, bleeding, and upside down, Sukanya could see people scurrying out of the way, picking themselves up. She could hear screams and shouts from all directions.

It was enough that someone was yelling. She didn't have the energy left to do it herself.

Chapter 42

When the car came to a halt, the perpetual tide of humans outside the station scattered. A few people took photos, some stood in shock, and everyone gawked at the car rocking on its hood.

Hiroshi raced to the spot, out of breath, Sakaguchi a few steps behind. They knelt down and looked inside at the two bodies swaying upside down from their seat belts.

Hiroshi noticed gasoline leaking from the car. "Everyone back!" he shouted.

Sakaguchi spread his arms and started pushing back the crowd encircling the scene. "Clear everyone out now," he shouted, and people, unused to anything but jams of people in the square, started to back out, looking stunned.

Here and there over the square, people sat injured, with friends or strangers helping or screaming for help. A young man in a hoodie lay cramped on the pavement, not moving. A young girl stood supported by friends, bleeding from her head. Others hobbled away, clutching their arms or legs, holding a hand on themselves in shock.

Local police arrived on bicycles and on foot. Some attended to the injured and others started to drive everyone away down the wide sidewalks away from Shibuya Station. The crowd moved, confused but obedient, stepping back, staring.

The Shibuya police night shift chief arrived. "Is that gasoline?" He ordered someone to try to put some blankets around so it wouldn't spread.

Sakaguchi explained to the chief who they were as Hiroshi knelt down and looked into the interior. He stood back as one of the policemen cleared what was left of the glass with his flashlight and a slim policeman slid inside and under the girl dangling in her seat belt.

He took a knife and cut the seat belt holding her. Her thin, motionless body slid into his arms and another policeman pulled both of them out. He tried to set her on the pavement, but her arm was still handcuffed to the door.

The short, slim policeman stood up covered in blood. The girl's hair fell every which way, covering her face. One of the police covered her with a blanket and checked for vital signs, her arm still stuck in the car.

The Shibuya police chief said, "Where's Sato? Get him over here."

Another young officer came over, kneeled down and pulled a ring of small tools from inside his shirt. The young officer flipped through the choices of picks and shims, trying one, then another on the cuff around her thin wrist. The third one popped the cuffs, and he helped set her down gently on the pavement.

The chief, who had been watching Sato work, said to Hiroshi, "Working the love hotel area, this happens all the time. Lovers get stuck in handcuffs."

Sato said, "Five last week."

An ambulance pulled up at the curb and the crowd parted for them to get through. They hoisted the girl onto a gurney and set to work checking her vital signs and the cuts from the glass. More ambulances arrived and the crew worked on the most seriously injured. Other people waited their turn, checking their injuries and wounds with their hands, gauging the amount of blood.

The slim policeman wriggled back inside the car and turned off the engine. With his knife, he cut the seat belt holding Kenta, who dropped heavily down on the roof of the car. With the help of another policeman, they pulled his limp body out through the window.

Hiroshi eyed the gasoline which, despite the blankets, was spreading over the pavement. The chief started yelling to get everyone away from the station as far as possible out of the square.

Hiroshi went over to the gurney as the girl—the missing Thai girl at last—looked bewildered.

Hiroshi leaned over her and said, "Can you hear me?"

"Back," she managed.

"Back? Is that your name?"

"What? No. *In* back."

"Do you speak Japanese?"

"No," she said and let her eyes close.

Hiroshi peered into the back seat of the Nissan, but there was nothing there. "Back of what?"

"Back of car. What you call? Trunk."

The ambulance crew stabilized her head and checked for wounds.

"Inside trunk. Look." She tugged Hiroshi's sleeve and pointed.

Hiroshi couldn't make out what she was trying to tell him. Sakaguchi came over and frowned.

Hiroshi leaned over to hear. "Inside the trunk?"

"Yes. Inside. Open. My friend. Her name Chiho. Please."

Hiroshi ran to the trunk and waved a couple of policemen over. "We better check the trunk."

The short, slim policeman slid back inside the car and felt around for the trunk release button. He pressed it several times but nothing happened.

Another policeman came over with a large screwdriver, wiggled it into the opening and another cop slid an air wedge into the crack. He pumped until the trunk sprang open.

Chiho spilled out and hit the paving stones with a thump. Everyone leaned down trying to catch her, but too late.

"Over here," Hiroshi yelled to the ambulance crew. Sakaguchi went over to Kenta and put plastic handcuffs around his wrists and the bar of the gurney. Then, he smacked Kenta's face a solid blow with his open hand that would have dizzied any sumo wrestler. Kenta's head snapped to the other side. The ambulance workers stepped back, their eyes shocked above their masks.

Kenta's eyes blinked open and started to move, glassy and reddened.

Hiroshi hurried over and pushed in front of Sakaguchi.

Hiroshi leaned down to talk to Kenta. "Where were you taking them?"

Kenta groaned.

Sakaguchi reached around Hiroshi and caught Kenta another blow on the top of his head.

"Detective, please," one of the ambulance workers, a woman, said.

Kenta shook his head, looked down at his body on the gurney and pulled at the plastic cuffs.

"Where were you taking them?" Hiroshi asked again.

Kenta groaned and struggled to answer. "To Yoshitaka Kirino."

"Was he the one in the car with you earlier? You dropped him near Yokohama? Is that where you're going?"

"He's the one. But he's going to a different place. Shinagawa."

"Where in Shinagawa?"

"Nittsukai Transport, bay fifteen."

"Where's bay fifteen?"

"There are docks there," Kenta said, coughing and tugging again at the plastic cuffs.

"Which docks?" Hiroshi asked, putting up a hand to keep Sakaguchi back.

Blood dribbled from Kenta's mouth, and he worked his mouth to spit, and then swallowed it. He closed and opened his eyes. "He'll be there. At eleven." He exhaled and looked up again and then his head fell to the side.

Sakaguchi shouted, "Take him to the police hospital in Nakano and get security on him. Handcuff him to one of those fixed beds they have. All four limbs."

The Shibuya police chief pointed at three men. "Is three enough?" he asked Sakaguchi.

"I hope so," Sakaguchi said. "And be sure to not leave him alone for even a second."

The ambulance crew hurried over with a third gurney for Chiho. They checked her and got her rolling toward the ambulances. Hiroshi walked alongside her, speaking to get a response. There was none. She looked pale and breathed slowly.

Hiroshi went back to the Thai girl and nodded to the EMTs. "You're going to be OK. Your friend is OK, too. Can you tell me what happened?"

"Are you policeman?"

"Yes. You're safe now. You don't need to worry."

Sukanya looked up. "That man take us."

"We know."

"You look his iPad. In car."

Hiroshi asked the slim policeman to slide in and look for an iPad. "What's your name?"

"My document, he take." Her eyes closed, and the ambulance crew looked at Hiroshi to see if they could take her.

"Just one more minute?" he asked, and turned back to her. "Can you tell me how you got here?"

She looked up at him. "My name Sukanya. That girl Chiho. I don't know man's name. He connect to other bad man. Tall, black clothes."

"Anything else?"

"Daisuke. He help. He explain."

"Where is he?"

"My friend Chiho has phone." Sukanya tried to sit up. "Is Chiho OK?" She strained to see her and the ambulance technicians eased her back down.

"She's going to be OK. What are your friends' last names?"

Sukanya shook her head. She didn't know.

"Where do they live?"

Sukanya shook her head, no, again.

The policeman came with the iPad.

Hiroshi said, "Bag this and send it to the homicide division." The policeman nodded and hurried off.

Hiroshi leaned down to Sukanya. "You're going to be all right. I'll come talk with you in the hospital, OK? You can tell me then."

Sakaguchi pulled Hiroshi away and the ambulances started for the hospitals. "Take these women somewhere close, but not to the police hospital." Sakaguchi asked the Shibuya chief, "Can you send your men with them? I want them guarded and the hospital entrances watched. I'll send some of our people as soon as I can."

Sakaguchi pulled Hiroshi through the crowd to the car.

Osaki had parked in the only empty space, the middle of the crossing. It was open, but in all directions radiating from the center, traffic, human and vehicular, reached as far up each street and walkway as Hiroshi could see.

They got in the car and Osaki put the siren on and headed in the least crowded direction.

Sakaguchi called on the phone, got no answer, and thrust it into his pocket.

"Don't tell me," Hiroshi said. "Takamatsu called."

"Just the opposite. He's not calling, and not answering either."

Chapter 43

As they sped toward the docks, Sakaguchi called Takamatsu every few minutes, to no answer. He called Ueno, but there was no answer from him, either.

Osaki gunned the car through the city side of Shinagawa, past office buildings connected by flyover sidewalks—the nexus for another side of Japan's new economy.

Nearer the bay, the roads widened and fenced-off lots held rusting shipping containers stacked like half-finished towers. Along the water, ship-to-shore cranes jutted into the dark sky like giant spiders waiting motionless for the next arrival.

Sakaguchi checked his cellphone. "Kenta said Nittsukai Transport, bay fifteen, right?"

Hiroshi nodded yes.

"But here's the strange thing, that's the same thing the phoned-in tip said, also. And that's the last place Takamatsu texted from."

Osaki said. "There's probably a dozen Nittsukai storehouses and storage facilities along the coast. Everything goes through those docks."

"People included," Hiroshi said.

Sakaguchi said, "Ueno has his GPS on, so we head for that, bay fifteen or not."

Closer to the bay, Osaki turned in at an empty sentry booth with its boom gate in the up position. A few overhead LEDs spilled pale light from the tops of buildings across the open expanse of concrete and onto the water beyond.

A long row of loading bays ran parallel to the water line. Behind it was a rusted fence topped by barbed wire and tangled with kudzu.

Sakaguchi looked at the loading bays. "Do you see fifteen?"

"I can't see much of anything."

"Where's Takamatsu and Ueno's car?"

"Maybe they parked outside and walked in."

Osaki squinted into the distance. "Look there, a different car. Can you see it?"

"In the shadows?" Hiroshi asked. "Anyone inside?"

"Too dark to tell," Osaki said. "Looks like a Subaru maybe?"

"Osaki, keep an eye on the car." Sakaguchi peered through the window. "Hiroshi, do you see fifteen?"

"Must be on the other side." Hiroshi rolled his window down. Cold, sea air poured in.

Sakaguchi started to get out of the car, but before he could, they heard a gunshot, muffled, from the other side of the building.

Sakaguchi got back in and Osaki pulled around to face the long row of loading bays.

"I'll take the walkway in front of the doors," Hiroshi said.

"I'll circle wide toward the water," Sakaguchi said.

"You can't go in there unarmed," Osaki said.

"Sugamo will be here in a minute with the pistol cases," Sakaguchi said.

Hiroshi hoisted himself up on the shoulder-high ledge running along the front of the loading bays. If Takamatsu wanted him out of his office, he had succeeded. He was as far from a computer now as he was ever likely to be.

This was what he couldn't tell Ayana, his sense of walking into it, how he felt walking toward a gun shot, looking for his colleague, frightened but proceeding. It was like kendo—ready to hit, ready to be hit.

Hiroshi looked at Sakaguchi's sumo bulk moving parallel. He looked small, for once, in the vast expanse of the empty lot and the watery horizon.

The loading area seemed abandoned. Door seals were torn, dock bumpers shredded, and wheel chocks scattered. Hiroshi stepped over the rusting forklift barriers. The bays he passed were shuttered.

Hiroshi poked his head around the corner for a quick glance and pulled back, but then rushed around the corner.

Ueno's big, fit rugby player's body was crumpled on the concrete.

Hiroshi rushed over. Ueno had been shot in the leg. He had lost a lot of blood, which pooled below. Hiroshi tried to put his handkerchief around his leg as a tourniquet, but his thigh was too big, so he jammed the handkerchief into the wound. Ueno stirred at the pain, his eyes fluttering open, breathing hard. 2518]The wound looked deep. Hiroshi checked to be sure there were no others. The back of his head was scraped, but not bleeding. Pressing hard on the wound, he called Osaki, "Bring the emergency kit, and a tourniquet."

"He's got a gun," Ueno said, his usual booming voice a scratchy whisper. "And good aim."

Sakaguchi hoisted himself onto the loading dock with a quick jump and leg-over, as if he weighed no more than a gymnast. He pushed Hiroshi's hand aside and dropped all his weight onto the handkerchief to staunch the bleeding.

"He's got Takamatsu," Ueno gasped. "He was looking for bay fifteen when I got shot."

"Who's *he*?" Hiroshi asked.

"Same guy we followed," Ueno said. "We lost him, came here like you said, and surprised him."

Osaki arrived with the medical kit and pulled out a tourniquet, but Ueno's thigh was thick from years of rugby, so Osaki had to loosen the band before it would fit around. He buckled the strap and twisted the windlass. Ueno shivered. Osaki checked for a pulse lower on Ueno's leg, but the tourniquet seemed to be working, so he piled on clean pads.

"Where's Sugamo?" Sakaguchi asked.

Osaki said, "He had trouble with the pistol cases, but he's on his way."

Hiroshi looked down the line of large square doors. On this side, the doors were painted and the bumpers new.

Hiroshi crept toward the last bay door. It looked open, but no light came from inside. Sakaguchi hopped down to the pavement and walked a wider perimeter.

Hiroshi got to the bay door, poked his head around and pulled it back. In the dark interior, plastic-wrapped boxes on palettes covered the floor. At the back, metal stairs led to the tall overhang of an office.

A siren wailed from far off and Hiroshi turned to hear where it was coming from.

When he looked back, a forklift spun out of the darkness and wheeled to the right.

Hiroshi leapt aside.

A tall man in black drove the forklift with one hand on the wheel. The other hand held a gun on Takamatsu, who was tied on the front lift, his midsection circled with plastic. The man waved the gun in the air, for show, sending his ponytail swaying, and set the barrel back against Takamatsu's skull as he drove toward the water.

Hiroshi ran after it and Sakaguchi ran parallel, but the gun at Takamatsu's head kept them back. Hanging across the tall man's shoulders was an automatic gun, an Uzi maybe. His clothes and the night made it hard to tell.

The forklift came to a quick stop at the edge and spun to face them. The smell of saltwater and dead fish wafted up with the smack of waves against the wall below.

Around them, the open expanse of dockyard extended in all directions. Large metal bollards dotted the edge like stumpy guardians. They wouldn't be much to hide behind if he started firing.

The trafficker held the pistol to the back of Takamatsu's head. Takamatsu kicked his feet, subtly, but clearly. He wasn't that out of it maybe, but it was hard to tell. His arms were free, but there was clear plastic clinging to his Italian suit.

"We know who you are," Sakaguchi shouted. "Yoshitaka Kirino."

Hiroshi stepped a little closer.

From somewhere far over the water came the sound of a speedboat engine.

Hiroshi shouted, "Your name is already with Interpol. They'll be waiting for you no matter where you go, no matter what transport you use."

Sakaguchi shouted, "Let him go. Don't make things worse for yourself."

Kirino pointed the gun back and forth alternately at Sakaguchi and Hiroshi. From the darkness, the speedboat engine revved closer, the bow smacking the water.

"Let him go," Hiroshi repeated.

Sirens grew louder and he caught the flash of lights from the other side of the loading dock. Hiroshi took a step closer. From the water, the speedboat closed in.

From the other direction, the sound of a car blasted through the night air. Hiroshi turned to see the Subaru speeding through the lot.

When the Subaru got to the gate, it swerved, stopped, and backed up. Police cars were arriving, blocking their exit. Hiroshi hoped Sugamo was in one of the cars, along with the pistols. The Subaru spun backward and shot off for the open space of the parking lot in the distance.

Hiroshi turned his attention back to Kirino and Takamatsu. Sakaguchi edged slowly to the side. Hiroshi did the same on the other side, but they weren't close enough to make a lunge for him.

"That's close enough. You're easy to hit even in the dark," Kirino said. He switched hands, pulling the Uzi up to his right and keeping the pistol on Takamatsu with his left. The speedboat sounded louder from the darkness, its rhythmic bouncing and sloshing coming closer.

Hiroshi said, "Let him go and we can talk."

"Always such great deals," Kirino said.

"We know what you've done," Hiroshi said.

The long, thin racing boat, dark black, pulled close, dropped speed, and leveled out in the water. The driver picked up an automatic rifle and slung it forward, ready to shoot.

On either side, Hiroshi saw Osaki and Sugamo spreading out along the dock with their guns ready.

Kirino wrapped an arm around Takamatsu's neck and eased backwards off the forklift toward the edge of the dock with the barrel in Takamatsu's ear. Kirino shouted down to the driver, in a language Hiroshi didn't recognize, and walked backward down the steps to the boat.

Nambu pistols in hand, Osaki and Sugamo hurried to the dock edge and pointed down at the boat, aiming but holding fire.

Kirino propped Takamatsu in front of him on the flat platform at the stern of the boat with his gun against Takamatsu's head. Hiroshi watched helplessly as the driver pumped the engine to circle toward open water, the boat rocking wildly in the waves.

Osaki and Sugamo held position on one knee. Sugamo set down his pistol on the concrete and reached into his waistband to pull out a much larger pistol than the Nambu. Osaki did the same. Sugamo and Osaki aimed the long black barrels at the boat. They could take out the driver, but Kirino would be hard to hit before he got a shot off into Takamatsu's head.

Osaki fired a warning shot into the air. Hiroshi could hear cars zipping around in the distance, and then two or three cars driving closer. Their doors opened and policemen took up positions.

"We're going to shoot unless you put down your weapons," Sakaguchi yelled.

The boat engine roared to life with an angry ripping that churned the water into a plume of spray. The driver pulled the throttle and the boat leapt into the dark expanse of the bay.

Takamatsu and Kirino wobbled for a moment at the back of the boat as the boat bucked, struggling side to side with each other before Takamatsu went sprawling backward into the water.

Sakaguchi shouted, "Fire," and Osaki and Sugamo unloaded the clips at the boat. When they emptied, they both reached for new clips, loaded, and kept shooting.

Sakaguchi ran for the Nambu pistol Osaki had set on the ground and started firing at the boat for all he was worth.

When the distant dark engulfed the boat, the engine cut out, and after a silent moment, a fiery ball exploded over the bay.

Hiroshi kicked off his shoes and dove into the water.

"Call the boats and tell them to hurry!" Sakaguchi yelled. "Takamatsu can't swim."

Chapter 44

Hiroshi swam toward the bobbing lump he hoped was Takamatsu. Hiroshi had tried to gauge the distance before he dove in, but the water was icy cold and a longer drop from the dock than he imagined.

The water smacked him with cold force and he swallowed a mouthful of saltwater. He spit it out and started chopping through the waves toward Takamatsu.

His clothes pulled on him, but he relaxed into his stroke and plunged forward, keeping his eyes on the floating body he'd glimpsed from shore. He saw Takamatsu's head flailing above the surface, unable to tell how far, and doubled his pace.

He sped up for as long as he could before pulling up and treading water to look again, but in the dark he could see nothing but water. He wasn't even sure he was heading in the right direction. He looked back to the dock to see where he was, but it was small and distant.

The boat had carried Takamatsu out farther than he realized. On shore, he hadn't been able to tell if Takamatsu was hurt or not, but he had to get him before he sank under the waves.

Helicopters circled above with lights scouring the bay. Every other wave, Hiroshi could see Takamatsu's head bobbing on the surface, but he seemed to be moving farther away. The fire from the explosion let off a horrible oily stink as he swam forward. The cold started creeping in.

* * *

From shore, Sakaguchi, Osaki, and Sugamo stood watching the eerie fireworks-like afterglow of the burning speedboat, but no one cheered. They stood staring out into the cold black of the bay, looking for Hiroshi and Takamatsu.

Sakaguchi looked behind at the policemen and cars that had pulled in behind them, their lights brightening the dock area and out over the water to where the dark took over. Sakaguchi nodded to Osaki, who quickly tossed the long-barreled pistol into the water and re-holstered the regulation Nambu pistol. Sugamo did the same, and the kicked the pistol magazines into the bay.

Sugamo whispered, "You can't help but hit something with those Desert Eagles."

Osaki shook his head. "Would have been nice to keep those."

Sugamo said, "It's just good Takamatsu hadn't finished the paper-work on them."

Sakaguchi said, "Get the boat captain patched through to your phone."

More police cars screeched to a stop near the edge of the dock, their headlights spilling across the water. Sakaguchi waved for them to pull the cars close and shine their headlights and spotlights into the dark of the bay.

Farther out in the water, search lights from the helicopters lit up the waves in roving patches. One helicopter hovered over the detritus of the speedboat bobbing on the waves. But there was no sign of Hiroshi or Takamatsu between there and shore where they should have been.

Coast guard boats gunned in from both sides and moved toward the remains. More lights skittered across the surface of the water, but the wind had picked up and the surface turned rougher, making it even harder to see. Someone shot off a flare pistol, then another, and the surface of the water seemed to come alive.

"Got get some binoculars," Sakaguchi said. Sugamo started to go get them, but the shore patrol police were already carrying over several pairs. Sakaguchi took a pair and a young cop helped him get them focused.

Another boat sped in and slowed to circle. Sakaguchi kept looking in a straight line from where Hiroshi dove in to where the speedboat exploded. That was the direction Hiroshi must have swum, but with the strong tides in the bay, they could have been carried far away.

One helicopter hovered in place and they could see someone cling-ing to a bobbing chunk of hull from the exploded boat. Coast guard officers dropped a fast rescue craft into the water and steered to him.

As they approached, they threw a harness to him, but he shoved it away.

"Doesn't want to be saved," Sugamo said.

Looking through his binoculars, Sakaguchi said, "He's not going to want a lot of things once we get him to the station."

Another officer leapt into the water with two bright yellow harnesses and slipped one around him. The floating man struggled until the officer punched him, slid the harness around him and the boat's winch yanked him into the air with his head angled down, his arm pinned and his legs wiggling behind him. From the rail, they hooked him and tugged the thin, black-clad figure on board.

On deck, they scuffled in a pile, until the officers stepped back and let him squirm on the wet deck—hands and feet cuffed—like a giant black eel. The coast guard officers circled around him.

"Is that Kirino?" Sugamo asked.

Sakaguchi said, "Looks like our man."

Osaki handed Sakaguchi his cellphone. "This links to the coast guard."

"Is that Kirino?" Sakaguchi asked the officer on the other end.

The voice of one of the crew members said, "He's tall, pale, and dressed in black, and won't stop moving."

"Show him how to be still."

"We tried to, but he's not the talking kind. We asked him plenty, but he's not saying a word."

"He will, once we get him into the station," Sakaguchi said.

"You don't want to interrogate him out here? Salt water's pretty effective."

"Better bring him in."

"We'll do that right now."

"And there's two more detectives out there, one can't swim. Do you see anything?"

"The other boats are still looking. We'll hurry. The water's cold."

Sakaguchi hung up and strained to see what he could in the streams of light dancing around the water's surface. Sugamo and Osaki handed another pair of binoculars back and forth.

The boats started circling the area. Two helicopters started flying a grid, at different altitudes over the area, and the coast guard boats circled wider.

Behind them, the dark blue Subaru sports car raced back toward them and did a series of donuts, spinning to find a way out.

One police car stayed on its tail, pestering and pushing the Subaru in directions the driver didn't want to go. Police cars circled in, tightening the space in which the Subaru could work.

More cars pulled around to block exit routes, forming a cordon through which the Subaru could no longer slip. A few police got out of their cars, positioned their spotlights on the scene, and drew their pistols.

The Subaru whipped in circles, each pass more futile than the last, corralled into a small circle. The low, lean sports car shifted gears, but there was nowhere to go. It pulled to a stop and the doors flew open.

Out popped three young guys, one tall with a ponytail, another tough and solid, and the third squat and fat. They scurried in opposite directions.

A few of the policemen laughed as they reholstered their pistols and stepped from behind the cars to chase the three young punks.

The fat guy was the first to go down, tripped onto his face by a sliding tackle from one of the policemen, who leapt on him and held his face in the concrete while another cop kicked his legs apart and cuffed him.

The stocky guy pulled up and squared off with one officer, holding his hands in a boxing stance, but the officer kept his distance until more officers could arrive and surround him from all sides. He ran forward and swung for one of the officers. The officer parried, trapped his arm, and flipped him hard to ground. Two officers dropped their knees onto him and one gave him the same spread-and-cuff treatment.

The ponytail guy ran faster than the other two, but in every direction, the parking lot was rimmed by tall chain-link fences. Seeing there was no escape route, he slowed to a stop with his hands on his knees, catching his breath before letting himself be cuffed without a struggle.

The police pushed the three guys toward a squat, windowless police truck.

From the backseat of the Subaru came a young woman. She shivered in her tight skirt and held her thin arms into the air, turning away from the brightness of the police lights. She pointed at the trunk, and the police went over to open it.

Inside the trunk were two more women, knocked out or drugged, and wrapped tightly from neck to knee in plastic. The police and ambulance crew hurried over to take care of them.

The coast guard boat pulled up to the dock and the crew hoisted Kirino into the air by winch and then lowered him into the waiting arms of police officers on the dock. Sugamo and Osaki took him from both sides and walked him along the open dock to a waiting car.

Kirino's tall figure, restrained by rope and plastic handcuffs looked thin as a digit in the vast expanse of the dock. Dripping wet, without a jacket and his black shirt torn, he seemed to be almost shivering in the cold night air before he was pushed into the backseat of a police car.

Sakaguchi turned back to the water with the binoculars. "We'll be seeing enough of him in the coming days."

Sakaguchi looked up at two helicopters hovering in place, their searchlights focusing on a section of the water far from where the boat had exploded. He followed their lights down into the water and Sugamo and Osaki pointed to one of the boats which had slowed to a stop. Officers scurried along the opposite side.

The boat's central winch dropped down with a diver and two harnesses into the water. The winch pulled up a dripping mass that hung in the air before it could be set down onto the deck.

A spotlight beam caught Hiroshi slumped over with Takamatsu cradled in his arms before the coast guard officers covered them in thick blankets.

Chapter 45

Hiroshi found his way through the hospital hallways, irritated at having lost his cellphone in the bay. He'd have to borrow a phone to call Ayana. Someone brought clothes from the station for Hiroshi to wear, and they fit, in places.

Sakaguchi was waiting outside the room. An officer was sleeping in a chair across the hallway. Another uniformed cop was standing at the end of the hall.

"You OK?" Sakaguchi asked.

"I'm warmer. Another ten minutes and it would have been hypothermia. How's our Olympic swimmer?" Hiroshi said.

"Chief stopped by. Said you and Takamatsu would be commended," Sakaguchi said.

"He'll forget about that by next week," Hiroshi said. "How's Ueno?"

"He might not play rugby again, but the bullet just hit meat."

"Lucky for him he's got a lot of that."

"Sugamo and Osaki might be suspended for taking the pistols and, um, losing them. Sugamo told the chief he picked up the wrong pistol case and the chief didn't ask too much more."

"They can start catching up with Takamatsu. Being suspended is a badge of honor for him."

"He has the record. He might get commended, but then suspended for the pistols."

"Where did he get those pistols?"

"Confiscated them from some yakuza, but he forgot to enter them as evidence."

"They're at the bottom of the bay now." Hiroshi frowned. "I don't remember anything after getting pulled onto the boat."

"So, you don't know that Takamatsu palmed the cellphone of the trafficker?"

"The cellphone data—"

"The lab guys called and said the data was accessible."

"We'll have his entire network then," Hiroshi said.

Sakaguchi's mouth pulled into a smile.

Hiroshi looked in the room.

"The Thai girl doesn't speak Japanese, but they both speak English, so can you do the honors?"

Hiroshi nodded walked into the room. He looked at Chiho. "You must be Chiho?"

Chiho nodded.

"And you are?"

"I'm Daisuke. I'm planning on having a lawyer here—"

"No need for that," Hiroshi said.

Hiroshi stepped over to the bed. Sukanya's deep brown eyes looked into his and she tried to put her hands together into a *wai*, but the IV drips and taped splints kept her palms from coming together.

Hiroshi spoke to her in English. "Are you OK?"

"Yes, OK," Sukanya said, sitting up a little.

"You were very brave. You made him crash, right?"

Sukanya said, "I plan on kill him. But crash was OK."

Hiroshi translated that for Sakaguchi. His eyes squinted in amused appreciation.

Chiho pressed the button to raise the head of her bed.

"Can you tell me what you saw? That night. It's important," Hiroshi asked. "In the studio that night."

Sukanya readjusted herself as the angle of the bed changed. Chiho took her hand and Daisuke at the foot of her bed, his arm in a sling.

Sakaguchi handed Hiroshi his cellphone to record what she said, and showed him where the photos were saved.

Hiroshi nodded for her to go ahead. "What is your name?"

"My name is Sukanya."

"What is your family name?"

"I leave village when very young. I put some name when need fill form, but not real name."

Hiroshi nodded. "How did you get to Japan?"

Sukanya continued. "I come Japan for work with two other girls. We promise passport for America."

Hiroshi showed her a photo of the girl at the studio. "Do you know her name?"

"Celeste. I don't know real name. Other girl taken away. I don't see again. I want to know she have our passport."

"Is this the girl?" Hiroshi showed her a photo of the girl who had washed up in the canal in Shinagawa.

Sukanya looked away and started to cry. "She—?"

Hiroshi said, "I'm sorry. Do you know her name?"

"Name is Ratana. No family, she say. Leave home young, too. She my friend in Bangkok. We come together to Tokyo." Sukanya took a big breath. "Where she die?"

"She drowned. We're still investigating."

"So, only me left."

"Was he there, too?" Hiroshi showed her a photo of Kenta.

"Yes. At studio, he know all people. But you want know who kill, right?"

Hiroshi nodded.

"I tell you who is worst man. Is tall, thin man, pale, mean, speak Thai and Japanese. He drive us from boat to warehouse."

"Is it this man?" Hiroshi showed her a photo of Yoshitaka Kirino, the one Takamatsu took from a distance, and then a close-up mug shot.

Sukanya looked away. "That man. He talk Ratana and me in Bangkok. He arrange all."

Hiroshi moved on and showed her a photo of the Ministry of Finance minister, Takeo Suzuki.

"Yes, him and director is there. And Celeste. Three is dead."

"So, who did it?"

Sukanya shook her head. "I didn't see."

"You didn't see?"

"I heard."

"You must have seen something," Hiroshi prodded.

"I run and hide."

"Before you hid, what did you see?"

Sukanya looked up at the ceiling, frowning. "The studio have just few people left. Two guys is go home and assist girl is going for dinner."

"And then?"

Sukanya breathed in and out. Chiho held her hand tighter.

"Four men come in studio. They have mask over faces."

"Masks?"

"Yes. But tall thin one. I know him. His eyes same, moving is same. The three other men, maybe same chase me. They speak Japanese. I can't understand."

"Who was speaking?"

"There is four men who talk fat man, but he won't get out of chair. They start to pick him up, but director is yell them, and they hit director. He is down. They go back fat man and he not answer, so they hit and he is on floor, they kick and kick. Director comes over and they do same him. Kick, kick, but not real kick like Muay Thai, just on ground."

"You saw this?"

"Celeste is watching and whispering me. Then, Celeste pull away from me. She grab a stand you put light on and run out. I don't know why. Maybe drug. Celeste, she have bad reaction to drug. I see in Bangkok people crazy with this, jump off balcony, run into traffic. She like that."

"So, Celeste ran out?"

"I grab for her and call her back, but she go hit one guy hard with that thing."

"A tripod?"

"Yes, and she land on his head. I am happy to see, but then other guy grab her and hit, hit, hit. I move behind the wall and see nothing else. I am hiding behind the sand bags holding the wall, and some curtain pull over me."

"So, what else did you hear?"

"They fight. I listening, but listening mostly if they come for me."

"Did they?"

"Yes, but I pull curtain around me and don't move. I know how to not move, just breathe, like sleep."

"You didn't hear anything else?"

"I hear scream...and hitting. For long time. Then, silence." Sukanya looked at all of them one by one, Hiroshi, Sakaguchi, Chiho, and Daisuke. "I wait long time. I think they take everyone away, so come

252

out. Three is still there, dead. I take clothes, iPad, computer, and coat. Money, too. Then I run," Sukanya said, and looked up at Chiho.

Chiho patted her hand and held it tight.

"It's OK," Hiroshi said. "You did the right thing. And you didn't see the four men after they beat up the old man, Celeste, and the director?"

Sukanya said, "I didn't even hear four men is leaving. They walk quiet, very quick."

Listening to her story, they hadn't noticed a man limp in the door.

"Yotaro!" Chiho shouted and started towards him. Daisuke held her back with his good arm. "I called him," Daisuke whispered to her.

"Who is this?" Hiroshi asked.

"I'm Sukanya's employer," Yotaro said, with a smile.

"What?" Chiho shouted. "Yotaro, I'm going to—"

Yotaro held up a hand. He rested his cane against his waist and reached in his pocket, flipped through several papers and handed official documents to Hiroshi. "As you can see, Sukanya is part of my staff since we have a high number of Thai customers. She's an excellent cook."

Hiroshi and Sakaguchi stared at him.

Yotaro returned their look with a steady face.

Hiroshi said, "Go on."

"So, the other night, unfortunately, Sukanya, while at work, had her purse stolen. Inside my club, I am ashamed to admit. Fortunately, I had a copy of her passport with her visa for Japan. I didn't make a copy of all the pages, but I do have this front part with her work visa for Japan. Perhaps you officers could help facilitate this by writing a stolen property report? I've already told my local *koban* about this—"

"Where's your local *koban*?" Hiroshi asked.

"In Shimokitazawa. My club is called The Lost Melody. I asked the local police to beef up security. Stealing is bad for business."

Hiroshi held the paper up. It looked official enough, but somehow not quite right.

Chiho glared at Yotaro. Daisuke held her back, pushing her arm with his hand.

Sakaguchi took the papers and folded them into his pocket.

"I'll need those back," Yotaro said, reaching for it.

"I'll need to check on these." Sakaguchi handed his *meishi* to Yotaro. "Why don't you stop by the station tomorrow?" Sakaguchi dropped his huge hand on Yotaro's shoulder. "And if anything happens to these two women, I'm going to be sure you get years of prison time. At minimum. Are you clear?"

Yotaro reeled back as if offended. "I assure you I will stop by the station, since I need Sukanya back to work. Japan is internationalizing, you know. We need workers of all kinds."

Daisuke reached in his pocket and took out a notebook. He wrote down something on a piece of paper, tore it out and handed it to Hiroshi.

"What's this?"

Daisuke shrugged. "It's the address to download the footage from the cameras at the studio."

"How did you get this?" Hiroshi asked, looking at the address and password in his hand.

Daisuke nodded at Sukanya. "She wouldn't try to make up a story like that if it didn't fit the video evidence, would she?"

"Why was she working there at the studio?" Hiroshi asked Yotaro.

"Well, my employees sometimes take part-time jobs without telling me. Not my place to judge. Times are hard. Maybe I should pay them more?" Yotaro said with a straight face.

Sakaguchi hummed from deep in his huge chest.

Hiroshi took Daisuke's notebook and wrote down a number. "Contact Junko Ayase at the Morning Light NPO. She'll find you a better immigration lawyer than the one who forged these."

Chapter 46

When the detectives were out of earshot, Chiho twisted away from Daisuke. Yotaro leaned away from her with his cane in both hands, but before he could take a step back, Chiho reeled back and cracked him across his face. His designer glasses went flying.

Sukanya yelled, "Chiho. Don't hit. Please. He help us. A little."

Chiho ignored her. "How could you drug us?" Chiho scream-whispered in Yotaro's face.

"I didn't drug you—"

"You let us be drugged. What were you doing? Selling us to be killed?"

Daisuke took her arm with his one good arm and held her back.

"He could have killed us," Chiho raised her voice to a yell.

"Chiho, the detectives will hear you," Daisuke said.

Yotaro said, "That wasn't going to happen. Once you were in the car—"

"The car *crashed.*" Chiho took a step toward him.

Yotaro nodded in agreement. "That was not in the plan."

"None of this was in *our* plan."

"Kenta was going to take you someplace, but we couldn't have you running around, arguing, hitting him. Kenta had to show Kirino something believable."

"Who's Kirino?"

"He's the guy that's been chasing Sukanya. The guy who killed the people in the studio."

"Kenta wanted to show him what? Drugged girls being tortured to death?"

"Yes, for example. On a video feed. I don't know exactly how or where Kenta was going to do all this, but—"

"But you handed us over anyway." Chiho raised her hand to smack him again, but Daisuke held her back.

Yotaro hobbled over to pick up his glasses. The thick red frames were broken. He turned them around, irritated, and stuffed them in his shirt pocket. "I didn't know all the details. I didn't want to know, but I have to believe Kenta had all that worked out. He was not going to go back to jail again. He wanted Kirino gone. And he wanted to keep the details to himself."

Chiho folded her arms over her chest.

Sukanya watched from her bed.

Yotaro said, "Let me explain. It's not as bad as it seems."

"How could it be worse?"

Daisuke went over and shut the door. When he stopped holding her back, Chiho lunged and cracked Yotaro another good one.

Yotaro held up his arm. "Would you stop that!"

Daisuke pulled her away. "Calm down and listen, Chiho."

Yotaro resettled himself on his cane and looked exasperated at Chiho. "You're acting like you used to in the band. You won't let anyone else talk. And you only think from your point of view."

Chiho wouldn't look at him, so Yotaro talked to Daisuke.

"The plan did not go as expected," Yotaro said.

Chiho groaned.

Yotaro said, "The plan was Kenta's side of things. I didn't trust him completely, but I trusted him enough not to hand you over to get you killed. Kirino would not be easily fooled. Anything with him had to look real."

Chiho went over and took Sukanya's hand. Sukanya smiled at her and nodded for her to calm down and listen.

Chiho turned back, her eyes down, listening at last.

Yotaro said, "The plan was to drug you, put you in the back of the car..."

"Who said you could drug us? Who?" Chiho started toward him again, but Sukanya held her hand tight and Daisuke stepped to block her.

"It wasn't something I could ask." Yotaro pounded his cane on the floor. "I thought you'd be OK with it, since you did it before."

"That was a long time ago when I needed money. And it was in a safe place. I trusted...well...I trusted people back then."

"The drugs were to protect you. All Kenta was going to do was put you in the trunk, take you somewhere, negotiate by video with Kirino..."

"That's *all*?" Chiho stopped looking at him.

"All you got were a few bruises," Yotaro said, raising his voice. "Look what *you* did to *me*? You trusted that idiot boyfriend, but you won't listen to me? I'll be using a cane the rest of my life. I need more surgery because my leg hurts every day. Every single day."

"We could have been killed." Chiho looked at the floor.

"What do you think they were trying to do to me when they dropped me from the balcony?" Yotaro shouted.

Daisuke said, "Let's all calm down. Chiho, just listen. OK?"

Chiho took a breath and looked at Yotaro with a proud, angry, half-sorry face.

Yotaro spoke in a softer voice. "Let me go back a bit. When you and your addict boyfriend left me with debt, these guys came around, politely at first, then not so politely. I had to get cash to pay them off, but I had loaned money to another club owner who couldn't pay *me* back. I met Kenta through some of the bands, and he was willing to loan me money, but he wanted part of the club. To make matters worse, the landlord in Shibuya said he was selling the building, so I had to move the club with little notice. That cost a fortune. Most club owners gave up rather than move. Where did I get money to keep going? Kenta."

Chiho turned to Sukanya, "I'll explain it to you later, OK? Aren't you getting tired? Don't you want to sleep?"

"I'm OK. You listen him." Sukanya smiled.

"Why are you smiling?"

Sukanya laughed. "Thai people have one smile for every feeling. My smile now is we're OK."

Chiho rubbed Sukanya's arm.

Yotaro said, "So, when Kenta came to ask for a favor, saying he'd write off the rest of my debt, so I could get back to owning my own business, I had to say yes. He was the one who got the fake police report for Sukanya, and he's the one who got the fake ID. When it was over, you two could do what you wanted. You'd have a little hangover from the drugs."

"A little hangover. That's what you call this?" Chiho pointed at Sukanya.

"You are both all right," Yotaro said. "Kenta is the one who's in trouble now. The police must be interrogating him. He'll probably go to prison again. He trusted me enough to give me his passwords in case he got caught. I promised to take what I needed and give the rest to his girlfriend. He trusted me more than I trusted him."

"And what about Kirino?" Chiho said.

"From what I can tell from the video feeds Kenta put all over the docks, Kirino is now in police custody. That's not as good as dead, but it's second best. I'll find out for sure tomorrow morning at ten when I go to the police station. Until then, there's not much to do."

"They could let him go and it's back to—"

"But they won't," Yotaro said. "Kirino was caught with something worse than Kenta had in mind. And I guess they'll find more on him."

Daisuke said, "Kirino will never see light outside a prison again."

Yotaro held up his hand to calm Chiho and continued, "If he didn't turn in the trafficker, you two would have been chased forever, or worse. Look what he did to Daisuke."

Chiho said, "You could have just called the police and told them what was happening."

Yotaro shrugged. "People like me and Kenta are not exactly trusted by the cops. I don't even want to speak with the cops now that it's over. Kenta will have to take care of himself. He said he could."

Chiho said, "This all sounds like you made it up afterwards."

"Granted, business is a lot about controlling the narrative, but everything I've told you is what happened. Kenta had to scare you to make any video look real. And frankly, you deserved *something* for what you did to me." Yotaro pointed with his cane at his broken leg.

"I didn't deserve that. And Sukanya didn't deserve anything."

Yotaro looked away. "Kenta was set on getting this guy caught. Obsessed with it. And willing to risk everything to make that happen."

"Kenta's no hero." Chiho snorted.

"No, he's not. He's just a businessman, like me, trying to make things work."

Chiho said, "You could have just told me."

"Acting cute and sexy while you're playing guitar on stage is one thing, but this needed another level of reality altogether. I couldn't have told you."

Daisuke sighed. "You're both here now. And OK. And if that document is enough to get Sukanya a new passport and visa—"

"It will be," Yotaro said.

The calm white noise of the hospital filled the room.

Yotaro looked at Chiho. "That band you met in my office really does need a guitarist." Yotaro looked at Sukanya and changed to English. "And Sukanya, I really do need a cook."

Sukanya rubbed Chiho's hand. "I like cooking, but never have own kitchen before."

"Make a list of what you need," Yotaro said.

Chapter 47

Sakaguchi and Hiroshi drove to the police hospital where most police went for serious medical issues, and where prisoners needing treatment could be watched.

On the way, Hiroshi called Ayana on Sakaguchi's phone, but got no reply. She had been understanding when he'd stayed out all night before, but this was the longest ever he hadn't even checked in. He left a message: "This is Sakaguchi's phone. I lost mine swimming." Her match in the kendo competition would start in the afternoon. Maybe she was getting ready.

Sakaguchi parked in the lot near Nakano Station and they signed in at the hospital entrance.

Hiroshi said, "I could use something to eat first."

"Me, too," Sakaguchi said. "There's got to be a convenience store somewhere in the hospital."

"I've got no money," Hiroshi said. His wallet was with his cellphone at the bottom of Tokyo Bay. They followed the corridors to a convenience store that serviced the hospital. It sold supplies like underwear, bottled water, snacks, and fruit and flowers for *o-mimai* visiting gifts.

Sakaguchi picked out a handful of *onigiri* rice balls and hot tea. Hiroshi took two metal bottles of hot espresso and a handful of *wakan* nine-ingredient chocolate bars, whatever those were.

Hiroshi held up the last one and read the back. "This chocolate bar helps anxiety, insomnia, nasal congestion, menstrual flow, cholesterol, constipation, coughing, pain, vertigo, gallstones, diarrhea, gastroenteritis, eczema, bladder infection, depression, and circulation."

"Circulation?" Sakaguchi got them a shopping basket.

" 'Nature's Viagra,' it says."

"Oh, circulation *there*," Sakaguchi said.

"It contains jujube, bitter orange, safflower, ginger, Japanese peppermint, Chinese licorice root, cannabis seed, gardenia, evergreen wisteria. You can't even fit all the ingredients on the back of the box."

Hiroshi put in a couple extra of the bars and Sakaguchi paid.

They found a row of low chairs in the hallway down from the convenience store with a window looking out on the parking lot. The sun came in at an angle, and they put the bag between them, watching cars and taxis coming in and out as they ate.

"I'm going to take a few days off," Hiroshi said, unwrapping an *onigiri*.

"I'll put it in as medical leave. The report can wait."

"Akiko will get started on it."

"Let her do the whole thing."

"Akiko isn't getting paid half of what she should be."

Sakaguchi nodded. "All I can do is put in for a bonus."

"I'm going to call her." Hiroshi borrowed Sakaguchi's phone again. "Akiko? Can you get started on the report?"

"I already did," Akiko said. "You jumped into the bay? Are you all right?"

"Now, I'm eating chocolate. Can you order an espresso machine?"

"Ours is working fine."

"Send it to Junko Ayase at Morning Light and put a copy of all the documents from Arai into the box. Send it anonymously."

Akiko said, "Will those documents be helpful?"

Hiroshi said, "They'll be embarrassing."

"Are you coming in today?"

"I'm taking three days off. Call if you need anything. Or, actually, you can't call, since I don't have a phone."

"What happened to it?"

"It drowned."

Sakaguchi's phone rang as soon as Hiroshi hung up. He handed it back, and opened another *onigiri* while Sakaguchi spoke on the phone.

"That was Sugamo and Osaki. Kirino won't talk, but those three *chinpira* are talking their heads off. They told them almost everything."

"You'll go help with the interrogation?"

261

"Sugamo and Osaki are doing fine." Sakaguchi took one of the candy bars, unwrapped it and chomped it down in two big bites.

When they finished eating, Hiroshi and Sakaguchi got up from the sunny, quiet spot on the chairs with a lot of sighing and stretching, groaning and checking what hurt. They divided their trash into burnable, non-burnable, plastic bottles, and cans, stuffing everything into the right slots in the divided trash containers outside the convenience store.

* * *

They walked into Kenta's room without knocking. One arm and one leg were handcuffed to the railing of the bed and he was covered with bandages across the far side of his body. He had a patch over one eye on the far side, as if only one side had been injured.

Hiroshi went over and shook him awake.

Kenta's eyes opened. "Oh, the detectives are here at last. Welcome. Glad you could make it."

Hiroshi said, "Don't get too comfortable here. The prison hospital doesn't have these luxuries."

"Did the doctor allow two of your limbs to be unshackled?" Sakaguchi asked. "I told them all four handcuffed. Since you like cuffs so much."

"It was hard to use the bedpan." Kenta shut his eyes and used one elbow to work his body upward enough to move his head higher on the pillow. "All right, I'm ready."

"For a start, we have you for murder, trafficking, drugs, blackmail, and illegal monetary instruments," Hiroshi said, smiling down at him.

"What you don't have is an arrest warrant, or a video camera. And I don't have my lawyer."

Sakaguchi stepped over to take a look at his injuries, leaning over the bed to scrutinize the bandages.

Kenta pulled his leg away and stretched his un-cuffed hand. "What happened to Kirino?"

"He's in custody," Sakaguchi said.

Kenta's eyes opened wide. "He survived?"

Hiroshi said, "He's not talking, so now's your chance. If you're going to tell us something worthwhile, it'll reduce your prison time. You know how it is in there."

"Cooperation should keep me *out* of prison."

"Reducing your time is the best you're going to get at this point."

Kenta shrugged. "When I was a student, I couldn't afford a good lawyer. But now I can. That makes a world of difference."

"Your association with Yoshitaka Kirino alone is enough to get you a life sentence."

"Apparently you're not interested in hearing what I know about Kirino."

Hiroshi tapped the railing and Sakaguchi let his hand drop onto the other end of the railing. "The other members of the trafficking ring—"

"Those Shibuya punks? They couldn't form a ring. Kirino did all that."

"Seems like you know how it runs."

"I do. From a distance." Kenta closed his eyes. "You should be thanking me."

"Thanking you?" Hiroshi said, "That kind of comment always makes our day. Gives us something to regale other detectives with back at the station."

"How did you know where Kirino would be?" Kenta asked, his eyes wide open. "Someone called in a tip. Do you know who that was?"

Hiroshi looked at Kenta.

Kenta returned a defiant glare. "Me."

"Kenta!"

All three of them turned to see a well-dressed woman run in the door and over to Kenta. She leaned over and kissed him. Her hair flowed over Kenta's head and they nuzzled each other.

Sakaguchi and Hiroshi were left to stare at her tight-fitting business suit from behind.

She stood up and faced the detectives. Her eyes were red and a single tear had dropped onto her chest right above her gold necklace and chic blouse. Her hair was cut simply and parted on the side. She dug inside her business bag.

"How did you get a phone call out?" Hiroshi asked. "No one is supposed to—"

"This is Mina Kuroki," Kenta said.

"Your girlfriend?" Hiroshi said.

Mina handed her *meishi* to Hiroshi and Sakaguchi. "*And* his lawyer."

They took her name card and read the details of her law office, Kuroki and Associates, LLP, one of the older firms in Japan, located in Akasaka. They both knew the name.

Hiroshi sighed. "Well, we're going to keep him for a long time, until he tells us something useful."

"We'll be filing for bail this afternoon, with the full weight of my firm." Mina shut her bag with a sharp click and brushed her hair back. She was handsome with lush lips and round cheeks brushed lightly with cosmetics.

Hiroshi said, "We'll see if he can keep his story straight before then."

Mina moved her low heels to a wider stance. "Don't worry. One thing Kenta can do is keep stories straight. My father, head of the law firm, will be handling this case. With the slight conflict of interest, I must recuse myself. If you want to interrogate him, you need to follow procedures. Coming to the hospital isn't the right one. That'll be all for now."

Sakaguchi chuckled and stepped back to let Hiroshi handle this.

Hiroshi said, "He had two girls in his car, one drugged and one handcuffed. He's known to associate with a human trafficker and he hasn't answered yet where he was on the night of the murders at Jack and Jill."

Mina smiled. "As you might guess, that night, he was with me."

"And the girls in his car?"

Mina looked at Kenta. "High sex drive. The girls were past the age of consent."

"You sure about that?"

Mina nodded confidently.

"None of that is going to fly. He's doing time."

"We'll see."

Kenta said, "I was taking those girls out of harm's way, away from Kirino, not to him. I called in the tip where Kirino would be. Nittsukai Transport in Shinagawa, bay fifteen, right?"

Hiroshi kept his face impassive and thought that through. "So, you'll give us everything on Kirino's network, routes, associates, financing and—"

"And video proof," Mina said. "But we're going to need assurances."

Hiroshi stared at her. "Video?"

Mina stared back. "Do you want to know what Kenta has or not?"

"And Takeo Suzuki?"

Kenta squirmed on the bed.

Mina looked at him.

Kenta nodded OK. "Suzuki was secretive, and clever, but I'll tell you what I know. He's dead anyway."

Hiroshi tapped the bed railing by the handcuffs and looked at them both again. "We're taking the trafficking ring down with or without your help. Keep that in mind."

Hiroshi walked out and followed Sakaguchi down the hall.

Chapter 48

When Hiroshi and Sakaguchi entered Takamatsu's room, he was sleeping under a thick blanket with three IVs snaking out of his arm and machines bleeping by the side of the bed.

Hiroshi walked over and peered down at Takamatsu. His face, usually so full of energy, seemed to have collapsed, as if all the muscles and fat had been removed, leaving skin on bone. He had never looked so old.

Takamatsu opened his eyes.

"How's our Olympic swimmer?"

Takamatsu groaned and started to stir.

"New Olympic event, cold water floating. It's just for you."

Takamatsu coughed and swallowed. "That was the coldest I've ever been in my life."

Hiroshi said, "We brought you something."

"A new body? This one is wearing out." He coughed from deep inside.

"Japanese-Chinese herbal chocolate." Sakaguchi handed the chocolate to Takamatsu.

"I don't have my glasses," Takamatsu said.

"It cures everything. Bad eyesight, too, probably."

Takamatsu held the chocolate out, trying to read the label.

A nurse came in, looking at them with a busy frown. "He needs to rest," she said.

Sakaguchi asked, "How is he?"

She jotted down readings from the machines. "He swallowed a lot of salt water. Together with a low body temperature, that could have been bad. He was very disoriented when he came in."

That was the first time Hiroshi had known Takamatsu to be anything but fully present in any situation.

"I was a little sleepy was all," Takamatsu said.

The nurse fussed with the IV drips. "He remembered his name, but not much else. He fell into a temporary coma, but seems to have woken from it."

Takamatsu said, "They're monitoring my kidneys and blood pressure, two things I didn't even know still worked."

The nurse shook her head. "He's still not hydrated yet. Every river in Tokyo flows into the bay, so we pumped him full of antibiotics as a precaution."

Takamatsu raised a hand, waving it at the nurse.

She turned to him and leaned over clutching his chart to her chest. "And no, you cannot have a cigarette." She turned to Hiroshi and Sakaguchi. "After he woke up, he kept asking for a cigarette, said he had some in his pocket. He came in here wrapped in a thermal blanket."

Takamatsu coughed. "They took my favorite Italian jacket."

Sakaguchi handed the nurse his *meishi*. "Can you call directly if anything changes?"

She nodded yes and bustled out. She seemed used to police, and probably to prisoners, too.

Takamatsu waved Hiroshi over. "Can you bring me some nicotine gum? I'm going crazy."

Hiroshi pointed at the *wakan* nine-ingredient chocolate bar. "Try this for now. It probably cures nicotine addiction, too."

"I don't want to cure it. I want to satisfy it."

"Just eat the chocolate."

"What's in it?"

"Everything."

"That's exactly what I'm missing at this point—everything."

Sakaguchi said, "Tell us what happened. You didn't say a thing when we pulled you out of the water."

"How's Ueno?"

"Shot in the leg. Not surface, but not deep."

"He's all muscle, that guy," Takamatsu said. "Did you find those girls in the trunk?"

"They're all right," Sakaguchi said.

"Those three punks? I wanted to work them over, but after Ueno got shot, it was just me."

"They didn't need any working over in the station. They started telling us everything to save themselves."

"And you caught that tall, thin one? He was a bad one."

"He clammed up, but he won't step outside four prison walls ever again," Hiroshi said. "So, what happened at the dock?"

Takamatsu eased himself up a bit and Hiroshi adjusted his pillow.

"They jumped me, those three, and I barely had time to pull out my expandable baton. I got a few cracks in, but the thin guy, what was his name?"

"Kirino."

"He had a gun, several guns, and shot Ueno right away. He didn't hesitate."

"We heard a gunshot."

"That was later, maybe a signal to the boat. Ueno was bleeding for a long time."

"They said he'd lost a lot of blood," Sakaguchi said. "What were they doing inside the loading dock?"

"They had a big machine that stretch-wraps boxes on a palette. They put one of the girls on there and wrapped her until she couldn't move. They had finished two of the girls, but the third ran when I came in. I guess they caught her?"

"Two girls were in the trunk, and one was in the back seat. But they're all OK. We're getting a translator to get the details."

"I fought as best I could, but they put me on the machine, too, started it turning. I managed to get my hand in my pocket for my knife, and started slicing away before it could get my arms. Otherwise, I would've been done for."

Hiroshi nodded.

"See, Hiroshi? You have to have a baton and a knife with you always."

"I got it," Hiroshi said. "Then what?"

"You arrived." Takamatsu looked up at Hiroshi.

Sakaguchi said, "Did you track him all the way there?"

Takamatsu said, "That was a bit strange. It was like he didn't care if we followed. Ueno and I were doubly cautious because it was too easy, like he wanted us to follow, but not follow too easily. We lost

268

him, and went to where you told us, and he was there."

"You think he was waiting for you?" Hiroshi asked.

"That's why we parked far away and snuck in by foot."

"We found the car."

"In hindsight, if we'd driven in maybe Ueno wouldn't have gotten shot. We'd have had something to hide behind at least."

"He'll be all right."

Takamatsu chewed more of the chocolate bar and Hiroshi handed him a glass of water.

"I think he set us up. He wouldn't have hesitated to kill us."

"He's a vicious one."

"When I heard the girls screaming, I had to do something. I didn't know how far away backup was."

"Why didn't you call in to speed us up?" Hiroshi asked.

Takamatsu looked at him and then at Sakaguchi. "It happened too quick. There wasn't a chance."

"What happened on the boat?" Sakaguchi asked.

"I grabbed his cellphone. He was on the thing constantly. I figured I could float for a while, and maybe someone would find me." Takamatsu ate more chocolate.

"So, you jumped into the bay so we'd start firing?" Hiroshi was trying to fit the sequence of events together.

"If I'd known it was so cold, I would have stayed on board."

"If you'd ridden farther from shore, you'd have never been found."

"Did he know you'd taken his cellphone?" Sakaguchi asked.

"He must have realized it. But the explosion came pretty soon after," Takamatsu said. "Those Desert Eagle pistols pack a punch, don't they?"

Sakaguchi said, "Don't mention those again."

Takamatsu nodded OK. "But aren't you glad you had them?"

"Someone's got to be put on suspension for the missing pistols—Sugamo and Osaki, probably."

"They'll survive. I always did," Takamatsu said, crumpling the chocolate wrapper.

"You might be suspended again, too, unless the chief goes through with the commendation."

"I'll take both. No sense being stuck in the middle."

"There's little chance of that. It'll be one or the other, or both," Hiroshi said.

"Let Sugamo and Osaki finish the interrogation of Kirino first, though. They deserve that," Takamatsu said.

"So far, it's been all questions and no answers from him. But we have enough without any confessions from him," Sakaguchi said.

"And you can get the whole operation?"

Hiroshi nodded. "With the cryptocurrency at the center of it all."

Takamatsu looked at him and blinked. "No, the victims are at the center. Everything else is secondary."

Hiroshi let out a grudging grunt of agreement.

Sakaguchi stretched his neck in a slow circle and reset his feet, ignoring an incoming phone call.

"That chocolate has warmed me up. What's in there?" Takamatsu smiled at last, his typical suggestive grin.

Sakaguchi reached in his pocket. "And by the way, I brought this from the station." He handed Takamatsu an official-looking printout.

"I don't have my glasses," Takamatsu said, holding up the form for Hiroshi to read to him.

"Everyone in the office kicked in. Even the chief. It starts next week," Sakaguchi said, deadpan.

"What starts next week?"

"We signed you up for adult swimming lessons." Sakaguchi's big body shook with amusement.

Takamatsu let out a dry chuckle. "I don't need to learn. I've got Hiroshi."

Hiroshi turned toward the door. "We better let you rest. You're getting sentimental."

"Thank everyone for me, can you?" Takamatsu said, patting the paper against his chest. "I can picture my swimming instructor already."

Chapter 49

With Shibaura out of the way, Haruka had a lot of errands to do for Jack and Jill Studios. Without him messing up the studio, she could see how to merge her experience in accountancy and in adult films with a desire to do something more.

She spent the morning going from city office to tax office to lawyer's office dressed in a gray business jacket over formal pants and a loose lemon-yellow top that disguised her full figure and grab-you smile just enough to get business done.

At each place, Shibaura's *hanko*, the seal that allowed the bearer to conduct any legal, banking, or official activity, opened things up. She went to three different banks, transferring funds.

While she waited at the last bank, she called Jun, a former actor turned contractor and told him to meet her at Jack and Jill Studios.

Jun and two other young men met her in front of Jack and Jill Studios. She looked them over and wondered if they were more than just buffed gym rats.

"Jun, so great to see you!" They hugged. "It's been ages."

"You're doing all right," he said. "I'm happy to help. For old time's sake."

Jun was a tall, handsome man, who had been a stand-in for tall samurai leads in old films, Ken Takakura even. He was tanned and his hair buzz cut, with a crisp turtleneck and camel hair jacket.

She led them inside to the office. Jun sat on the sofa and the gym rats stood around indifferently.

She opened the wall safe and took out the fake passports she'd brought from Shibaura's home safe. She put them into an envelope, which she addressed to Hiroshi Shimizu. Halfway done, she changed

271

her mind. She held Hiroshi's *meishi* up with her long fingernails, orange and yellow with small cherries glued on, and called his office number and left a message that she had important things to give him, from Jack and Jill Studios.

She put several SD digital video storage cards in another envelope and wrote Hiroshi's name on that one, too.

"Could you help me with these, you two? Bring a box." The two gym rats came over and she directed them to take certain DVDs off the shelves and put them in the box, and other DVDs into separate shopping bags. "We're getting rid of all these, so just set them by the office door."

Haruka put a big duffle bag up on the desk. "This is my down payment," Haruka said, handing it to Jun.

Jun looked inside. It was filled with wrapped stacks of foreign cash— Thai baht, Philippine pesos, Vietnamese dong, and Chinese yuan. The police had confiscated everything from the studio, but had not stopped by Shibaura's home, where he kept more than in the studio.

Jun looked amused. "You always were a funny one."

"Look, I'm too busy to change all this money, and you probably know the best place to do it. So, tell me how much the total was, and I'll consider that as your first payment."

"Payment? For what?"

"Remodeling and painting contractors"

"Tell me what you need," Jun said.

"I want to paint the whole building purple and pink."

Jun pulled out a notepad from his inside pocket and started making a list.

"I want all the sets taken down and thrown out."

Jun wrote everything down and nodded to the younger guys. "You want them to stay? You said you needed security."

"Actually, I think I'm fine. The next person stopping by is a detective, but I'll need them tomorrow."

One of them picked up the duffel bag with the foreign currency and the other one the last box of DVDs, and they headed for the front door.

"And do you know a good locksmith?" she shouted after him down the stairs.

Jun shouted back. "Sure. How soon?"

"Right now," Haruka said.

"You'll be here?"

"Waiting on the detective."

Haruka sat down to the account books. The painters called to make an appointment, and a set builder who remembered her from the old days called to say he could stop by tomorrow.

Before she could redo all the accounts, the locksmith, an old man in a khaki uniform with a young assistant dressed the same, arrived.

"You want them all changed?" the old man said, setting down his bag of tools. His young assistant dropped his heavy canvas tool bag on the floor and started writing down what Haruka dictated.

Haruka took them around and pointed out every door she could think of. "There may be more doors on the roof or something, can you check?"

The younger locksmith could not stop staring at Haruka.

"If your assistant can focus on his work?" Haruka said, smiling.

The old man said, "Do you want an estimate first?"

"No, but I need the important doors done today."

"You want alarms, too?"

"An alarm system."

"This place is big and there's a lot of entry points. I'll have to call for extra help."

"Then do it," Haruka said, her voice stern but pleasant.

The older man nodded politely and he and his assistant went off to work.

Haruka went back to her office and waited for Hiroshi.

When Sakaguchi and Hiroshi stepped into the office, Haruka stood up and offered them her hand. "I have something to give you." She pointed at the bags of DVDs. "Those are for you."

Sakaguchi walked over and looked. "We have enough already."

Haruka smiled. "You want to make the case about child pornography and human trafficking, don't you?"

Hiroshi and Sakaguchi looked at her.

"The ones you want are in those bags," Haruka said. "And here's this." Haruka handed Hiroshi the envelope with the SD cards.

He held it up. "What are these?"

"Women can use cameras, too, you know."

"What's on them?"

"Yoshitaka Kirino."

Hiroshi and Sakaguchi looked at her.

Hiroshi tucked the SD cards into his pocket. "What about Kenta Nakamura?"

"Draw a line between loan shark and entrepreneur and Kenta lies somewhere along that continuum, depending on the day."

"So, you're going to testify on his behalf?" Hiroshi said.

"He's not a bad sort." Haruka leaned forward, her cleavage cushioning a thick gold necklace.

Hiroshi said, "Anything else you want to tell me?"

Haruka nodded. "I would really like to get back to work."

"Here?" Hiroshi looked surprised.

"Yes, here. Jo Shibaura signed everything over to me."

"You have to get a judge's order to release the site." Hiroshi looked at Sakaguchi, who shrugged. "I can't even figure out how you got in here."

"I can go through other channels. I just thought I'd ask you first," Haruka said, smiling.

The three of them stood looking at each other.

"Well, we've been up all night, if that's all?" Hiroshi said.

"I'll walk you out," Haruka said.

Hiroshi picked up one of the bags of DVDs and Sakaguchi the other two, and they followed Haruka down the stairs. She led them through a back corridor below the large room with the sets.

Sakaguchi walked ahead.

Hiroshi said, "So, you're going to be making pornography?"

"Pornography is what men make. *Passion-ography* is what women make. Sex inside a story is more erotic. Several women I used to work with are now writers and directors. We start creative meetings next week, but we need meeting space. And space for a nursery."

"A nursery?"

"It's *womenomics*. The prime minister's policy," Haruka said. "I've got great films lined up from people like Yoko Kawase."

"Isn't that the assistant to the murdered director?"

"Yes. She was stuck as an assistant, but she's made wonderful short films on her own. She'll be coming back to Tokyo to do a feature."

"So, the future of erotic movies is women?"

"The female demographic is robust. Research shows women like living rooms, clean sheets on big, soft beds, lots of foreplay, and threesomes. Lesbian scenes, of course."

Hiroshi was not sure what to say.

"Women will be the subjects of their own lives and make their own decisions."

"About sex?"

"About everything. My female writers are already working on screenplays that break norms. And, I hope, establish new ones."

"That's ambitious," Hiroshi said.

"We'll change the economics of it, too. Better contracts and royalties, seminars on investing, all the things a real employer should provide." Haruka looked at Hiroshi. "If our films can put more women in control, that's good, right?"

Hiroshi nodded. "It sounds like you've been planning this for a long time."

"Shibaura owned this studio, but he would never listen to me. He just wanted more of the same old, same old, and then not even that."

"Erotic movies never really did much for me. I like doing more than watching."

"Very old school. Nice. Listen I'll send you a subscription."

"Subscription?"

"Yes, I'll be streaming them online." Haruka pulled back the large sliding door and stepped out into the parking lot. "I need to pave this parking lot, too. I can't even walk in from my car."

Hiroshi looked at her. "I've got to run. I've got a kendo competition."

"Oh, really? Watching or doing?"

Hiroshi cleared his throat. "Watching. My girlfriend."

"Now, *that's* erotic!" Haruka said. "I could use that in a film."

Chapter 50

Hiroshi got out of the taxi in front of the Tayasumon Gate and hurried across the bridge over the moat and under the old wood gate toward the Nippon Budokan. Inside the old, octagonal building, he took the steps two at a time.

At the top, he had to stop to catch his breath, feeling exhausted. He looked for a vending machine, but it seemed to be the only place in Tokyo without one. Apparently, canned espresso was not allowed to be sold inside the sacred space dedicated to martial arts.

Inside the Budokan, a large banner hanging across the high ceiling read: "All-Japan Inter-Prefecture Women's Kendo Competition." The audience ranged from children to students, parents and grandparents, everyone coming together to watch and honor the practice and spirit of kendo.

On the floor, eight rectangles were marked out by white lines. Three judges moved back and forth, closely watching the paired opponents inside each rectangle. The kendo contestants set their wooden swords in place and leapt toward their opponents with loud *kiai* shouts that echoed through the arena.

Hiroshi settled in and checked the schedule, searching the floor for Ayana.

At the end of the first match, the contestants bowed to their opponents, to the judges, to the audience, and to the *dojo*. Hiroshi looked at the program and up at the sign board announcing the names in each of the rectangles.

And there she was! He was just in time. He could have picked her out even with her helmet on, but it was a relief to see her face as she strode out and took her place. It was her first all-Japan championship.

Hiroshi watched as she squared off against her opponent. He hoped her anger, or frustration, or whatever it was that made her not answer her phone, would propel her forward and not throw her off.

Seeing her move gave him a second wind. Ayana twisted to find an opening, moving her arms lightning-quick to land strike after strike, to attack and defend. Each time, she stepped back, poised. Her timing had always been excellent, far better than his, and her stance was balanced. He watched her land a strong, fast blow on the side of the other contestant's helmet and move past without being touched. To watch her, as if for the first time again, was an utter delight. It was erotic, he had to admit.

The drum echoed time and the opponents took off their helmets, bowed and waited for the results. Hiroshi stood up, hoping she might see him, but she stayed focused, patiently waiting for the scoring.

As he'd known she would, Ayana won.

Hiroshi snatched up his program and hurried down the stairs through the crowd to the lower level of the Budokan. He was directed by a guard to the exit where the contestants came out.

He finally saw her talking with sensei. The distinguished teacher spoke to her intently, his gray hair flying around his wrinkled head. It was the moment to press the teaching, to be sure she took away the right lesson, and Ayana listened closely and humbly.

When he finished, Ayana bowed to him, pirouetted, and bowed again to the hall. Hiroshi caught her eye and then the sensei's eye, which held a glimmer of congratulation. He bowed to sensei, before he was quickly taken up with other pupils.

As she walked out to him, Ayana didn't meet his eye again, but maybe she was thinking over the match and whatever sensei had just told her.

Hiroshi followed Ayana into the corridor. She rolled her bag up to a spot by a large concrete arch.

"Congratulations."

"That's the wrong thing to say."

"Then I don't know the right thing."

"You're supposed to have a bit more kendo inside you."

Hiroshi nodded. She was right. This was a victory, not of her own, but of the right form, of directed practice. It was contribution, not conquest, universal not personal.

"Well, at least I can pull this for you," Hiroshi said, pulling on her bag.

She relinquished it to him. She handed him her *shinai* sword and *men* face mask, wiped the sweat from her head, and took a long drink from her water bottle.

"When did you get here?"

"Right before your match."

"Where have you been?"

"I can explain."

"You need to."

"I lost my cellphone."

"Schoolboy excuse."

"No, really, I lost it in Tokyo Bay."

Ayana stared at him as she undid her *do* chest armor. "Well, you're going to have some interesting voice messages waiting for you."

"I'm sure I will. Can we just head home? I'll explain on the way."

Her T-shirt was dripping with sweat and she dried herself with a fresh towel.

"You looked great in the match."

"Not the right comment."

Hiroshi sighed. "I'm doing the best I can here. I've been up all night, frozen, exhausted..."

Ayana reached behind herself to untie her *tare* stomach guard from around her waist.

Hiroshi couldn't stop staring at her as she let her hair down and retied it into a high, tight ponytail. He was grateful she didn't yell at him there, but it was going to be a long walk home.

"Your form looked good from the stands."

"That far away, it might have looked OK, but I was a little off in my timing. I need to get my footwork down."

"Doesn't everyone?" Hiroshi asked.

Ayana leaned down to put the *kote* fencing gloves in her bag and Hiroshi helped fit them into the bag.

Hiroshi watched her slip off her *kendogi* jacket, and put on a thick sweatshirt, making her look less martial, though her *hakama* below were still thick and protective. She put on tennis shoes and pulled on a fleece warmer that covered her neck and stretched over the top of her head. She said goodbye to some of the other women who passed by. When all was packed, she looked at Hiroshi.

"Are we walking back?" Hiroshi asked.

"If you're not too tired from staying out all night," Ayana said.

They walked out of the Budokan and headed through the park to the big gate and over the moat. They skirted the Yasukuni Jinja shrine and headed up Waseda-dori. They walked in silence past several high school and university campuses. She kept the thick warmer over her head. Hiroshi couldn't even see the side of her face.

At the bridge by Iidabashi Station, she stopped and looked over the Kanda River and the Sobu and Chuo Line train tracks running parallel to the water. The four-lane Sotobori-dori followed the river opposite the train lines. Tall buildings lined up outside the parallel paths of train, river, and road on both sides.

Ayana turned to him. "So, really, where were you? I haven't heard from you for nearly twenty-four hours."

"It was an intense twenty-four hours." Hiroshi looked serious. "I don't want to tell you everything because you will just worry more. Is that OK?"

Ayana nodded yes.

"So many things happened. But after a long chase, halfway across Tokyo, we cornered the men we were after."

"The traffickers?"

"I ended up in Tokyo bay, rescuing Takamatsu."

"In the water? It's freezing."

"Takamatsu can't swim."

Ayana turned away and looked down at a cafe that extended over the water, pressing against the round, smooth railing. "Go on," she said without turning around.

"I lost my cellphone when I was swimming. And my wallet, too. I had to go to the hospital—"

"But you're all right?"

"I got checked out and then had to get the last couple pieces in place, at the hospital and at, um, a film studio."

"Film studio?" Ayana shook her head.

"Can I explain all this to you over the next three days?"

"Three days?"

"I've got three days off. Medical leave."

"Three days?"

"Can you get time off?"

"I already have tomorrow off. It's Sunday."

"Can you get more time?"

"I don't want to spend three days just listening to you talk about your work."

"I don't want to do that either."

Hiroshi turned her toward him, pulled back her scarf, and pulled her close. She took a step back and leaned against the railing as he leaned down to kiss her.

Her lips stayed taut at first, but he persisted, and she finally loosened them and Hiroshi felt them moisten against his.

Her arms wrapped around his back, and as they kissed more deeply, both of their bodies relaxed into each other against the railing of the bridge, and the world felt very far away.

If you enjoyed this book, please consider taking a minute to write a review on your favorite book-related site. Reviews really help indie writers like myself.

About the author

Michael Pronko is the author of three mystery novels and three collections of writings about Tokyo. He has written about Japanese culture, art, jazz, and politics for Newsweek Japan, The Japan Times, Artscape Japan, and other publications for over twenty years. He has appeared on NHK Public TV, Tokyo MXTV and Nippon Television. He also runs a website, Jazz in Japan, about the vibrant jazz scene in Japan. His award-winning collections of essays about life in Tokyo are available at online retailers and from his website, as are the Japanese language versions. His first two novels in the Detective Hiroshi series won numerous awards. Michael is a professor of American Literature and Culture at Meiji Gakuin University in Tokyo, teaching courses in contemporary American novels, film adaptations, and American art and music. When not teaching, writing or listening to jazz, he wanders Tokyo contemplating its intensity and figuring out the stories to come.

* * *

For more on the Hiroshi series: www.michaelpronko.com
Follow Michael on Twitter: @pronkomichael
Michael's Facebook page: www.facebook.com/pronkoauthor

ALSO AVAILABLE BY MICHAEL PRONKO:

Memoirs on Tokyo Life:
Beauty and Chaos: Slices and Morsels of Tokyo Life (2014)
Tokyo's Mystery Deepens: Essays on Tokyo (2014)
Motions and Moments: More Essays on Tokyo (2015)

The Detective Hiroshi Series:
The Last Train (2017)
The Moving Blade (2018)
Tokyo Traffic (2020)

A book is a group project, and a large group helped me with this one. Japanese culture is big on thanks and on apologies, so immense thanks and apologies to the following:

My students for teaching me about literature and language.

My editors, BLR, AB, RS and NLF, for setting the words and the story on a better path.

AA for romping through drafts and slinging killer emails.

MM for cover design, talk, humor, and more design.

And my wife for everything else. I couldn't do it without you and wouldn't even try.